P
AWARD-WI
STEFANI
CHARLOTTE C

MURDER ON THE CLIFF

"Sly . . . an ironic background for murder!"
—Margaret Maron,
author of *Corpus Christmas*

"Delightful."
—Audrey Peterson,
author of *Elegy in a Country Graveyard*

"Thoroughly enjoyable, richly detailed."
—Annette Meyers,
author of *The Deadliest Option*

MURDER AT TEATIME

"A gripping mystery, with a splendidly authentic background of the magical Maine coast."
—Janwillem van de Wetering,
author of *Inspector Saito's Small Satori*

MURDER AT THE SPA

"Clever, original, suspenseful!"
—David Stout, Edgar Award-winning
author of *Carolina Skeletons*

"Engaging . . . The solution Charlotte finds is ingenious and believable."
—Tower Books Mystery Newsletter

"This vicarious . . . spa experience is a delight, as is Graham."
—Criminal Record

Charlotte Graham Mysteries
by Stefanie Matteson

MURDER AT THE SPA
MURDER AT TEATIME
MURDER ON THE CLIFF
MURDER ON THE SILK ROAD

MURDER ON THE SILK ROAD

Stefanie Matteson

DIAMOND BOOKS, NEW YORK

This book is a Diamond original edition, and has never been previously published.

MURDER ON THE SILK ROAD

A Diamond Book / published by arrangement with the author

PRINTING HISTORY
Diamond edition / November 1992

ISBN: 1-55773-814-9

Diamond Books are published by The Berkley Publishing Group,
200 Madison Avenue, New York, New York 10016.
The name "DIAMOND" and its logo are trademarks belonging to Charter Communications, Inc.

PRINTED IN THE UNITED STATES OF AMERICA

10 9 8 7 6 5 4 3 2 1

In memory of
Char Lappan
1946–1986

AUTHOR'S NOTE

FOR TRANSLATIONS OF the Chinese classic the *I Ching* or *Book of Changes*, the author is indebted to the Richard Wilhelm translation, rendered into English by Cary F. Baynes, copyright © 1950 by the Bollingen Foundation, New York, N.Y. New material copyright © 1967 by the Bollingen Foundation. Copyright © renewed 1977 by Princeton University Press. Excerpts reprinted by permission of Princeton University Press, Princeton, New Jersey. In some cases, the author has altered the Wilhelm/Baynes text slightly.

For the words of the song "John Chinaman, My Jo," the author is indebted to the book *Songs of the American West*, compiled and edited by Richard E. Lingenfelter, Richard A. Dwyer & David Cohen; University of California Press; Berkeley and Los Angeles, 1968.

The poem "I'm nobody! Who are you?" by Emily Dickinson is from her *Collected Poems*, originally published in *Poems, Second Series*, 1891.

• I •

GRASPING THE COINS in her perfectly manicured fingers, Kitty Saunders threw them down on the surface of her long pine kitchen table. They were antique bronze Chinese coins with a square hole in the center, and with Chinese characters inscribed on both sides.

After spinning like tops on the hard surface for a few seconds, the coins finally came to rest, and Kitty leaned over to study them, her brow furrowed in concentration. "Yang, yang, yin," she said. Picking up her pencil, she drew a broken line on a notepad. "Eight," she said. "Young yin."

Charlotte was mystified. Kitty was telling her fortune using the *I Ching*, the ancient Chinese book of oracles. The *I Ching* had replaced the tarot cards as Kitty's latest fortune-telling enthusiasm. Before tarot cards, it had been the crystal ball, and before the crystal ball, it had been astrology. At one point, it had even been palmistry, but that was more than forty years ago now, when they were both starting out in summer stock on Cape Cod. Palmistry wasn't in fashion anymore. A social historian could have charted the fortune-telling fads of the late twentieth century from the history of Kitty's enthusiasms.

Kitty was about to throw the coins again. She was shaking them with all the intensity of a craps player on a roll in Las Vegas.

Charlotte remembered the first time Kitty had told her fortune. She had said that the three horizontal lines on the side of her hand underneath her pinkie meant that she would have three husbands. With only one husband on hand at the time, three had seemed like an unlikely number, but in fact the total had turned out to be four. So far, that is. Though she had no intention of marching down the aisle again, the powers that determined the circumstances of her life had always conspired to take her by surprise, and there was no telling what might happen in the years she had left. Actually, Charlotte had always considered the tally of her marriages to be anomalous. She had never intended to be the kind of woman who accumulates a string of surnames. She had always wanted the security that comes with mating for life, but everything about her life had turned out to be dramatic instead.

"Yin, yin, yin," said Kitty as the coins spun slowly to a stop for a second time. "Six. Old yin." Again, she made a notation on the notepad. This time it was a broken line with an *x* through the middle, which she drew above the first broken line. "The *x* shows that it's a changing line," she explained.

Her explanation meant nothing to Charlotte. "Don't I have to ask a question?" she asked as she peered over the tops of her reading glasses at the notepad on the other side of the table.

"Not with the *I Ching*. Although you can if you want to. But the *I Ching* will give you the answer to whatever's on your mind at the moment, whether or not that's the subject of your question."

"In other words, it intuits the question."

"Exactly," said Kitty as she shook the coins again.

"I guess the question on my mind is, 'What I am going to be doing next?' " After more than forty years in front of the cameras and on the stage (it was now 1984, and she had made her first movie in 1939), Charlotte might have been expected to have more job security than she had had when she was just starting out. But it didn't work that way: the actor's job lasted only as long as it took to shoot the movie or for the run of the show. After that, it was invariably a matter of twiddling your thumbs and waiting for a call from your agent. At least she didn't have to comb the columns of *Variety* anymore: her face was as familiar to three generations of moviegoers as a member of their own family. But the anxiety of those early years had never left her. In spite of her fame, there was still a fearful place in her heart that believed there would never be another job. She even had nightmares about it, the way other people had nightmares about failing final exams.

"If that's the question on your mind at the moment, that's the question the Sage will answer," said Kitty knowingly as she drew a solid line above the two broken lines of the reading.

"The Sage?" Charlotte raised a dark, winged eyebrow in an expression of haughty skepticism that was one of her screen trademarks, along with her clipped Yankee accent, her broad-shouldered jackets, and her long, leggy stride, as forthright as a man's.

"Now don't you go raising an eyebrow at me, Charlotte Graham," chided Kitty. "Remember the tarot cards? The easiest reading I've ever done. On the eve of the Academy Awards, I turn up the Wheel of Fortune card. It didn't exactly strain my powers of prediction to foretell that you would win an Oscar."

"It didn't strain your powers or anyone else's," added Charlotte. "Everybody and his brother was predicting I would win. I was odds-on favorite with Jimmy the Greek. I deserved to win."

"So? Sometimes everybody says someone is going to win, but they don't," said Kitty. "Which might very well have been the case for someone who had already won three Oscars. They might have thought you were hogging the awards, and they'd have had a point."

"So who's the Sage?" asked Charlotte, ignoring the comment. She had long ago learned that she was skating on thin ice when it came to discussing her career with Kitty, who had sacrificed her own career to marriage and motherhood, and was jealous of Charlotte's success.

"That's how the *I Ching* is referred to," said Kitty as she picked up the coins for the fourth time.

"My, my. Aren't we taking all of this very seriously?"

Kitty smiled as she threw the coins down on the table.

Actually, it wasn't that Charlotte had too little work. She had too much work. She'd just made four movies back to back, and now had offers for several more. They had kept her busy, they had brought home the bacon, and they had been competently—if not brilliantly—directed. But none of them had given her any satisfaction. They had been froth, light and easy. She wanted something she could sink her intellectual teeth into. In the past, she had always turned to Broadway when she got bored with Hollywood, but Broadway was just as boring as Hollywood these days. Musicals, mostly. Not that she had anything against musicals. She'd even done a couple, though her voice was nothing to rave about, as the critics had duly noted. But the plethora of musicals denied space to serious plays, especially those that put an audience in the uncomfortable position of having to think. Gone were the days when Miller was playing on one corner and O'Neill on the next.

Again, Kitty made a notation: another straight line.

Should she go for more of the same thing she'd been doing? A halfway decent script had recently come her way, with a role for a lively grandmother who is forced to curtail her glamorous lifestyle when she assumes the care of her grandchildren after her daughter dies. Or should she hold out for something more meaty? Maybe the *I Ching* would help her decide. God knows, she wasn't doing very well at it on her own. She'd read a dozen scripts since she'd been in Maine, but apart from the glamorous grandmother, nothing even remotely interested her, and a lot of it she found downright repugnant.

As Kitty picked up the coins once again, Charlotte gazed out at the rose-bordered cove that lay at the foot of Kitty and Stan's lawn. Though her roses at home had bloomed before she'd left, it would be another week or two before these came out; spring came late to the coast of Maine. The morning sun sparkled on the sea, and the sea gulls wheeled and dived above the surface of the water with raucous cries. She had fallen in love with this corner of Maine on her first visit to the Saunders, who had moved here after Stan had retired from his job in public relations. So much so that she had ended up buying a cottage of her own—not on the offshore island where Kitty and Stan lived, but perched on a pine-studded mountainside overlooking the harbor. It was her retreat from the craziness of Hollywood and the congestion of New York. In its peaceful solitude she could gather up her fractured self, like a Chinese monk in a misty landscape painting.

But that wasn't to say there couldn't be too much peace and quiet. She didn't know how Kitty and Stan could stand living here year-round. A few blessedly serene weeks was enough for her, and she had been here two already.

After two more throws, Kitty had finally finished. On the notepad was a stack of six lines: two broken lines, two straight lines, a broken line, and a straight line. Two of the broken lines had *x*'s through the middle.

Kitty was now leafing through the gray-jacketed volume of the *I Ching*. Sitting next to her teacup on the table were a couple of books of interpretation.

"The verdict?" asked Charlotte.

"Just a minute," said Kitty, raising a pink-lacquered fingernail. "I'm reading." She read for a few minutes, a smile creeping across her lovely face. She had lost none of her good looks with age. Finally, she set the book down. "You're going on a trip," she said.

"Kitty, really!" protested Charlotte. "Couldn't you have been more original? How about, 'You're going to meet a tall stranger with dark hair who can't be trusted'?"

Kitty pursed her lips. She didn't appreciate it when Charlotte made light of her prognostications. "That's what it says!" She slid the notepad across the table to Charlotte. "This is Hexagram Fifty-six: The Wanderer."

"I'm going back to New York on Monday," said Charlotte glibly.

"Not to New York. To a foreign country, an unusual foreign country. Not Europe, but somewhere more exotic. According to the *I Ching*, you're a nomad, someone who's always on the move. In your professional life you're always searching for new challenges; in your spiritual life you're always searching for answers; and in your sexual life . . ." Kitty looked up.

Charlotte considered. "A sexual nomad," she said, and then shook her head with amusement. "True enough, I suppose."

"The image is of a grass fire on a mountainside in pursuit of fresh fuel," Kitty continued as she read. "The position you are now in is of a fire that's lingered too long in one spot. Unless it finds fresh fuel, it will burn out. That's where the trip comes in: you have to keep moving to keep your creative fires burning."

Charlotte leaned back in the Windsor chair, and sipped her tea thoughtfully.

"I'd say it's pretty close to the mark," observed Kitty.

"Right on the mark is more like it," said Charlotte. Her opinion of the *I Ching* had suddenly gone from good-natured skepticism to serious respect. As a metaphor for her life in general and her current situation in particular, a fire on the mountain couldn't have come any closer to the truth. "What else?" she asked, her interest piqued. "Does it say where I'm going to go?"

The corners of Kitty's mouth turned up in a smile of triumph. "Actually, this reading is very interesting. Sometimes the readings can be pretty cryptic, but this one's as clear as glass." She pointed to one of the books that lay open on the table. "This book advises you to be adaptable; it says the country will be one in which the manners and customs will be very exotic."

"Does it say when I'm going to leave?" asked Charlotte. She hoped it would be soon. The idea of a trip was beginning to sound like the perfect antidote to her professional ennui. Although she had traveled widely, it was almost always work-related, and she'd never had the time to see the sights. She remembered a shoot in Capri on which she'd never gotten around to seeing the Blue Grotto.

"No," said Kitty, who had turned back to the *I Ching*. "But it does say that you should take along plenty of money. Also that you'll be traveling with a 'faithful and trustworthy friend' "—she emphasized the direct quotation—"who will be of much value to you on the trip."

"What else?" Charlotte prompted eagerly. By now, she was mentally spinning the globe in search of all the faraway places she had always wanted to see: the upper Amazon, the steppes of Central Asia, the source of the Nile, the roof of the world, the Taj Mahal, the rain forests of Papua New Guinea, the palm-fringed islands of the Pacific, the Pyramids of Egypt—the list went on and on.

"I'm not sure exactly," replied Kitty. "It says that you're going to find a home in foreign parts, but it always speaks metaphorically. I would interpret it as saying that as a result of your travels, you are going to establish a more permanent connection with this foreign country."

"More permanent connection?"

Kitty shrugged. "I can't be any more specific. It talks about a 'circle of friends' and a 'sphere of activity.' " She consulted one of the books of interpretation again. "This book talks about being honored by strangers, but only if you act appropriately; it says that you have to observe protocol."

"Phew!" said Charlotte, who was trying to take it all in.

"Wait, we're not finished yet," said Kitty. Taking up her pencil, she drew another hexagram on the notepad. "The *I Ching* is the Book of Changes. The two broken lines with the *x*'s through them change into straight lines, which gives us another hexagram. The second hexagram sheds further light on the first."

Charlotte hadn't followed her, but it didn't matter. She sat back, and awaited the rest of her fortune.

"Here it is: 'Coming to Meet,' " Kitty announced, after consulting the index. Turning to the text, she studied it for a minute, and then said, "It's one of those cryptic ones, but I'll do the best I can."

"Shoot," said Charlotte.

"Your encounter with this circle of friends is predestined by fate and promises to be of some historical importance. But in order for the encounter to succeed, you will have to meet one another halfway. Both parties will have to be fully equal both to one another and to the situation."

Charlotte waited for her to go on, but she didn't. "That's all?"

"Sorry," said Kitty with a shrug. "That's the best I can do."

• 2 •

CHARLOTTE LEFT KITTY'S right after lunch. Because the Saunders lived on an island, coming and going from their house depended on the tides. The island was joined to the mainland by a sand bar that was exposed when the tide was out. If you didn't cross over to the mainland during the two hours before or after low tide, you had to either wait eight hours until the bar was exposed again, or take a boat. After crossing the bar, Charlotte picked up her car and drove back to her cottage. In her lifetime on the move—sexual nomad, indeed!—Kitty and Stan had been her rock of stability. Other friends and acquaintances had come and gone, but Kitty and Stan and a handful of others had been the constants in her life. They had met on Cape Cod when they were starting out: Charlotte and Kitty as actresses, Stan as a painter. Kitty and Stan had gone onto other things—Kitty to being a wife and mother, Stan to a career in public relations—but they had remained friends. And although it astonished Charlotte when she thought about how little they had in common—Kitty and Stan belonged to a certain suburban type, as easily categorized as any common bird species (plumage: slacks of lime green or brick red; habitat: elegant country clubs on the outskirts of major Eastern cities; behavior: friendly, courteous, and as unconscious of the world-at-large as a horse wearing blinders)—it was a great relief to have friends to whom she was not Charlotte Graham, the movie star. Their presence in the summer community of Bridge Harbor was one reason she had bought her cottage there. She was a nomad, true; but even a nomad finds it hard to move into a strange community without knowing anyone. And they appreciated her company as well. Although they claimed not to mind their isolation—they had moved here so that Stan could pursue his dream of being a marine painter—Charlotte suspected that they sometimes got lonely in their secluded little offshore world.

Actually, it was Kitty and Stan who were responsible for her buying the cottage. Knowing that Charlotte had been thinking about getting a summer place for some time, they'd called her as soon as it had come on the market. They'd suspected that she wouldn't be able to resist it, and they had been right. From the moment she'd seen the cottage clinging like a limpet to the rocky mountainside, she had fallen in love with it. It had been built in the late nineteenth century by an artist, one of the area's first "rusticators," as they were called—the painters, writers, and intellectuals who first cultivated the area as a summer resort. Every evening, after dining at the hotel at the base of the mountain, the cottage's previous owner had made his way on foot back up the rocky mountain path by lantern light. And although there was now a road for cars, Charlotte often did the same. It gave her great pleasure to hike up the mountain after a pleasant meal at the big old hotel. She ate at the hotel most nights. Not only because she wasn't much of a cook, but also because her tiny kitchen wasn't equipped for cooking. It was the lack of an adequate kitchen that had soured many prospective buyers on the place. But not Charlotte: she had fallen in love with the kitchen window. The view from the sink was like looking into an elegant terrarium. A few feet away from the window was a wall of pink granite studded with mosses and lichens in shades of green and gray and gold. Tiny jewel-like ferns and flowers grew in its crevices. A fascinating still life that changed with each season, it was in direct contrast to the view from her veranda, whose peekaboo vistas looked out over the spires of pines and firs to the sails and masts of the boats in the harbor, and beyond the harbor, to the rocky green hills of the Saunders' island.

Taking a seat in one of the green-painted Adirondack chairs on her veranda, Charlotte looked out at the view. Though it was early June, the leaves still weren't fully out, and she could see much farther than she'd be able to later on in the season. The heat of the sun had warned the sap of the balsam firs, and the air was fragrant with its resiny scent. Putting her feet up on the railing, she pondered her immediate future. She had come to Bridge Harbor two weeks ago for the annual ritual of opening up the house, a euphemism for repairing the damage done over the winter. This done, she had followed her usual prescription for relaxation, which included hiking, sailing, and lying around and reading, mostly for pleasure. She had also scanned dozens of the books and scripts that flowed in steadily from her agent. It was time to go home, and to come to a decision about which of the scripts to accept: the glamorous grandmother, the wife of the man with Alzheimer's disease, the domineering mother-in-law? What had happened to the movies? she often asked herself. They weren't fun anymore. Everything had to make a social statement, and the more banal, the better. She was willing to take the bad with the good. After all, it was work. But there was a limit to how much dreck she could put up with. Reluctantly, she picked up another script from the pile she had carried out with her. A rich dowager who founds a shelter for bag ladies? Ugh. Maybe it *was* time for a trip to Papua New Guinea.

It was precisely at this moment that the phone rang. The caller was her stepdaughter, Marsha Lundstrom. Marsha was the daughter of her fourth husband, from whom she'd only recently been separated. She'd always imagined that the ideal man for her would be one who had achieved something in his own right, someone who wouldn't be threatened by being Mr. Charlotte Graham. When Jack Lundstrom had come along, she thought she had finally met her match. A businessman who had built his family-owned manufacturing company into an international conglomerate, he was handsome, successful, cultured—and a widower. But it hadn't worked out. After forty years of marriage to a traditional wife, he had found it difficult living with a woman whose priorities did not include giving dinner parties for his business associates and redecorating the house (or rather, houses). But they remained good friends and frequent companions. What *had* worked out was her relationship with his grown children. They had answered her need for a family, something she had never had. She was especially close to Marsha, who also lived in New York. They shared a love of art, and often went together to museum and gallery exhibits.

The low, fluty voice that met her ear over the telephone was tremulous with excitement. "Charlotte. I'm *so* glad I found you. I thought you might be off on location somewhere."

"What is it?" asked Charlotte. From Marsha's tone, it was clear that her news wasn't anything bad, but what good news would merit such a glowing delivery? Charlotte wondered.

"Are you sitting down?"

Charlotte sat back on the old sofa covered with worn and faded chintz which faced the massive pink granite fireplace that dominated her rustic, cedar-paneled living room: "Yes," she replied.

"What are you doing for the next six weeks?"

"A few appointments. Nothing in particular, really." She was almost afraid to ask the next question: "Why do you ask?"

"How would you like to go on a trip?"

Charlotte leaned back and took a deep breath. She looked down at her forearms: the hairs were standing up stiffly. "To where?" she asked.

"China," Marsha replied. "The People's Republic of. Specifically, to the northwestern frontier, on the ancient Silk Road. We leave on June sixteenth. We'll be gone about a month."

"That's only two weeks away!"

"Yes," said Marsha. "Can you be ready?"

She waited for a reply, but Charlotte was still swallowing air.

"Before you answer that question, let me fill you in a little."

It was one of those serendipitous opportunities that come along once in a lifetime. The Oriental Institute, a New York institution devoted to East Asian culture, was sponsoring a study tour of China for several of its staff members. Marsha, who was an authority on Chinese poetry, was among them. Although the tour would visit several sites, their main destination was to be the oasis of Dunhuang, a center of Buddhist worship on the ancient Silk Road that had only recently been opened up to Western scholars.

"Two other staff members were scheduled to go," Marsha continued. "One of them was Averill Boardmann. Are you familiar with the name?"

"No," replied Charlotte.

"He was murdered by a vagrant during a robbery attempt in April. It was a tragic thing. I don't even want to talk about it. But his death leaves a vacancy that the Institute is anxious to fill. Actually, although the director *says* he wants to make it possible for someone else to take advantage of the trip, what he really wants is to recoup some of the Institute's expenses. They're offering the trip at a discount, but it's still expensive. The Institute has contacted other scholars, but the ones who have the time don't have the money and vice versa. Now they're turning to friends and relatives of staff members. I would love for you to come along. What do you say?"

Charlotte's head was spinning. Since she had no professional commitments for the next few weeks she'd planned to take care of personal business, and had made appointments with her accountant, her doctor, her car mechanic, and so on. But those could all be rescheduled. She also had an appointment with her agent on the West Coast to talk about projects. But that could be rescheduled too. In fact, there had been few times in her life when she had been as free to take advantage of such an opportunity as she was now. Or as eager. "Yes," she replied. And then: "Yes, yes!" But then she was beset by doubts. What would she do while Marsha was busy working? Oh, well. She was bound to find something in this exotic country to occupy her time.

"I'm *so* pleased," said Marsha. "Daddy said he didn't think you had anything doing at the moment. Somehow I had the feeling that you'd be able to go. There's a lot we have to take care of," she added, turning to business. "Will it be possible for you to be back in New York by Monday?"

"Yes," Charlotte replied. "I was planning to leave here on Monday anyway. A day earlier won't make any difference." But it would mean that she would have to start packing right away, she thought.

After making arrangements to meet Marsha, she went into the kitchen and fixed herself a drink. The real estate agent who had sold her the cottage had pointed out that a big kitchen wasn't a necessity as long as you had a refrigerator for ice and mixers, a sink to rinse out glasses, and enough counter space for a cocktail shaker and a bottle or two. Charlotte had laughed—he was an agent who knew his customers. As she returned to the living room, she was shaking her head. *You are going on a trip to an exotic foreign country with a faithful and trustworthy friend*, Kitty had said. Taking a seat on the sofa, she propped her legs up on the coffee table and took a sip of her drink: a Manhattan, straight up. She needed it. The phone had rung, and her life had changed. That's how things happened in her business: a phone call or a letter. The changes were always sudden, and they always left her reeling. A trip to China. She didn't believe in supernatural explanations. Marsha's call must just have been an eerie coincidence. A very eerie coincidence.

Dismissing the subject of coincidences from her mind, she turned instead to the subject of China. Like so many others, her knowledge of China was sketchy—so sketchy, in fact, that it could be summed up in fifteen hundred words or less. Culture: the Chinese had invented paper, gunpowder, and pasta; geography: the capital was Beijing (being from another generation, she still called it Peking); politics: the People's Republic was established in 1949 following the Communists' defeat of the Nationalists. Add a little bit about the Cultural Revolution and the subsequent downfall of the Gang of Four, and that was about it. There was little else *to* know: it was a country that had been cut off from the rest of the world for thirty-five years. It had been only five years ago, in 1979, that full diplomatic relations between the United States and China had been restored, opening the door to tours such as this one.

Setting down her drink, she got up and fetched the big old atlas from one of the bookshelves that flanked the massive fireplace. Like most of the other books, it had come with the house. And like most of the other books, its pages were spotted with mildew from the dampness. After a considerable bit of searching, she finally found Dunhuang: it was a tiny dot on the border of Mongolia. To the south were the peaks of the Himalayan massif; to the north, the vast open spaces of the Gobi Desert.

It was very, very far away. In fact, it was about as far away as you could get. Setting down the atlas, she picked up the phone and dialed Kitty.

The second call came just an hour later as Charlotte was packing up to leave. It was from Bunny Oglethorpe, a summer resident whom she had met at various local functions. The Oglethorpes were the most prominent family in an area of prominent families. Bridge Harbor was typical of other Eastern summer resorts in that the original summer rusticators had been succeeded by tycoons who built enormous summer "cottages" with dozens of rooms and dozens of servants in which they spent the few frenzied weeks of "the season" trying to outdo one another with lavish parties. Though the advent of the income tax and the elimination of the servant class had done away with that lifestyle, Bridge Harbor was still inhabited by descendants of these well-known families who carried on the tradition of spending the season on the coast of Maine. Bunny was the daughter-in-law of the richest of the original tycoons, and the reigning matriarch of Bridge Harbor society.

What on earth did Bunny Oglethorpe want with her? Charlotte wondered. The old rich were one of the few elements of American society that refused to be impressed by movie stars. It was an attitude that Charlotte found refreshing, and another reason she felt comfortable in Bridge Harbor.

"I was just talking with Kitty Saunders," Bunny said, her strangulated vowels reeking of wealth and privilege. "As you may know, we work together on the Bridge Harbor library committee."

"Yes," Charlotte replied. The library was a favorite charity of the summer residents. It was part of the summer ritual that energies otherwise devoted to raising money for the New York Public Library were here turned to a library in a former one-room schoolhouse.

"She tells me that you're about to set off on a trip to China."

"Yes, I am." Word traveled fast around Bridge Harbor, especially if it was the loquacious Kitty who was the messenger. "I'm leaving in two weeks."

"Was Kitty correct in saying that you're going to Dunhuang?"

"Yes, that's right. Do you know it?"

"I've never been there, no. But I'm very familiar with it." She hesitated for a second, as if considering how to phrase the next sentence, and then went on. "I'd like to ask a favor of you. Related to your trip. Have you ever been to visit the Oglethorpe Gardens?"

Charlotte was taken aback by the non sequitur. What could the Oglethorpe Gardens possibly have to do with her trip to China? "Yes," she replied once again. This time it was her voice that carried the note of hesitation.

Oglethorpe Gardens was one of the most magnificent private gardens in the country, created during the twenties by Bunny's mother-in-law as a showcase for her collection of Oriental sculpture. It was open to the public on Wednesday afternoons. Charlotte knew it well.

"Good," Bunny replied. "Then you know the moon gate?"

"Yes," said Charlotte.

"Can you meet me there at three-thirty this afternoon?"

Charlotte checked her watch. It was two-thirty. "Yes. I think so."

"I'll see you then."

The Oglethorpe Gardens were located on the grounds of the former Oglethorpe estate. The hundred-room summer "cottage" had long ago been razed, but the grounds were still in the hands of the family, and the garden was maintained as it had been for sixty years. It was one of Charlotte's favorite places. She had visited often, not only on the afternoons that it was open to the public, but at other times as well. It was one of those places you could never have found unless you knew where it was. Charlotte had come upon it quite by accident one day while hiking one of the trails in what she had thought was the state park. From a distance, she had seen the sun glinting off the head of what appeared to be a golden Buddha nestled among the pines on the slope of the mountainside below her. Her curiosity aroused, she had bushwhacked a trail down the hill, and found that it was a golden Buddha indeed. From that moment, her first visit to this secret garden in the woods had taken on the unreal atmosphere of a dream. From the gilded Buddha, she had been drawn to a high wall of rose-washed stucco crowned by glazed Chinese tiles. Following the wall, she had come to a round wooden door with a giant wrought-iron ring for a door pull. This was the moon gate to which Bunny had referred. She hadn't expected the door to open when she tugged on the door pull, but it had—revealing a spectacular sunken flower garden whose rainbow of colors dazzled the eye. It had been an unforgettable thrill, not knowing what was behind that door and discovering one of the world's most beautiful gardens. She now knew that the glazed, "imperial yellow" coping tiles had once capped the wall surrounding the Forbidden City in Beijing. They weren't reproductions of the tiles, but the actual tiles themselves, shipped over piece by piece from China after the Chinese dismantled the wall. That's how the robber barons had done things: if you coveted a castle from the Rhineland, the ballroom of a French chateau, or the wall of a medieval city, you simply paid someone to disassemble it and rebuild it for you in Bridge Harbor or Newport. As for the statuary, the gilt-bronze Buddha was one of dozens of exquisite pieces purchased on collecting trips to the Far East, which were scattered throughout the woods surrounding the garden proper, as well as within the garden walls themselves.

Since her discovery on that magical afternoon, Charlotte had figured out her own route to the garden through the woods of the state park (which had originally been Oglethorpe land), and was a frequent visitor. The gardeners never objected to her presence, probably because there were so few people who managed to find their way to the garden on foot. The entrance road was patrolled by a security guard, and visitors were usually transported to the garden from a parking lot on the main road by minibus. Rather than driving to her mysterious rendezvous with Bunny, however, Charlotte chose to walk, and arrived shortly before the appointed hour.

To her surprise, the person awaiting her at the moon gate wasn't Bunny, but Howard Tracey, the police chief of Bridge Harbor.

"Fancy meeting you here," she said as she approached.

Tracey smiled, his round cheeks bulging like a chipmunk's under the brim of the baseball cap that he always wore—the Boston Red Sox, of course. No self-respecting New Englander would have been caught dead wearing the hat of any other baseball team.

"What's up?" she asked as she joined him at the moon gate.

"I'd better leave it up to Mrs. Oglethorpe to tell you," he replied, removing his cap in the presence of a lady, an old-fashioned gesture that Charlotte always found charming. "Suffice it to say that she has a problem that might require a bit of detective work."

"In China?" asked Charlotte.

"Could be," said Tracey, with the Yankee talent for avoiding a direct answer.

She had first met Howard Tracey two years ago when a neighbor of Stan and Kitty's was poisoned. At the time, Charlotte had already earned a minor reputation as an amateur sleuth—the result of having solved a case in which her co-star in a Broadway play was murdered on stage. The reporter who had covered the case for a New York magazine later wrote a book chronicling her role in cracking it. A best seller, it was called *Murder at the Morosco*, after the lovely old theatre in which the murder had taken place. When the Saunders' neighbor became the victim of some malicious mischief, Tracey had asked Charlotte to investigate. When, subsequently, the neighbor was murdered, she had helped solve the case. The bonds forged in that encounter had since been welded into a solid friendship. Though Tracey liked to play the role of the simple country police chief, his unassuming manner concealed a brain that was as sharp as that of the savviest New York homicide detective.

As Charlotte and Tracey chatted about the weather—the perennial topic of conversation in Maine, where it could change dramatically from one moment to the next—Bunny Oglethorpe pulled up in her car, a vintage Oldsmobile. The descendants of Bridge Harbor's tycoons weren't pretentious folk. Driving a fancy make of automobile was considered ostentatious, and among the bluebloods of Bridge Harbor being nouveau riche was almost as bad as being . . . well, poor.

"Hello," said Bunny as she emerged from the car.

She was a tall, thin, stately woman, whose long, patrician face—which must once have been pretty, but not inordinately so—was framed by a thick fringe of white bangs. The rest of her hair was pulled back into a bun. Today she wore a big hat of pink straw.

"I'm sorry if I've kept you waiting," she said as she joined them at the moon gate.

"You haven't kept us waiting at all, Mrs. Oglethorpe," said Tracey, with just the right note of deference toward the matriarch of the family whose generous donations supported not only the library, but the church, the fire department, the summer repertory theatre, the Friends of the State Park, and probably dozens of other worthy causes that Charlotte wasn't aware of.

Bunny greeted both of them with a handshake, and then said to Charlotte, "I'm so glad you could make it, Charlotte. You must be very busy getting ready for your trip." She gestured toward the moon gate. "Shall we?" she said.

As Tracey held the heavy wooden door open, Charlotte followed Bunny through the gate. Entering the garden, she found herself pausing to blink. One of the most intriguing things about the garden was its sunny brilliance, which was all the more striking by contrast with the piny darkness of the woods outside.

Turning left, Bunny led them down a gravel path lined with recently set out annuals to the shade garden, which was at the north end of the walled enclosure. "Have you told Miss Graham about our mission?" she asked Tracey as they walked along, the gardeners nodding deferentially as they passed.

"No, I was saving that for you," Tracey replied.

"Good," she said approvingly.

The focal point of the shade garden was a three-sided shrine with a roof of imperial yellow tiles that sheltered a sculpture of a Buddhist monk in meditation. The sculpture presided over a smooth green oval lawn surrounded by an informal planting of low, green plants and shrubs. By contrast with the bright sunken flower garden, the mood here was serene and meditative.

But, Charlotte noticed as they drew near, the pedestal on which the sculpture usually rested was empty. The more fragile sculptures in the collection, the Buddhist monk among them, were taken indoors for the winter, and set out again in the spring. But the sculptures were usually returned to the garden in April, and this was already June.

Leading them past a small moss-edged reflecting pool in which a big green frog sat picturesquely on a lily pad (he was usually there, and Charlotte had often wondered if the gardeners who kept everything else in such perfect order had arranged for his residency as well), Bunny paused on the terrace at the foot of the shrine, and waved a long arm dramatically at the empty pedestal.

"Where's the sculpture?" asked Charlotte.

The Buddhist monk was Charlotte's favorite, and the collection's showpiece, as indicated by its place of honor. It was small—only three feet or so high—but exquisite. It was also very old: Charlotte couldn't remember the date exactly, but believed it was eighth century. She especially loved the way the corners of the monk's mouth turned up in an enigmatic smile that reminded her of the archaic smiles of the ancient Greek kouroi.

"Gone," said Bunny. "It disappeared eight weeks ago." She turned to the police chief. "What was the date, Chief Tracey? We should tell Miss Graham."

"April fourth," said Tracey. "Three days after it was set out for the season. The robber or robbers deactivated the burglar alarm system, loaded the sculpture into a van—we could tell the type of vehicle from the tire tracks—and drove away. Simple as that."

"Chief Tracey has been telling us for years that the sculptures were vulnerable to theft," said Bunny. "We should have listened."

"*Some* of them are vulnerable," the chief corrected. He nodded at the Spirit Path to the east of the sunken garden. The path was lined by a double row of weathered stone tomb figures that must have been ten feet tall, and weighed a couple of tons apiece. "I don't think anyone's about to haul those away."

"Do you have any leads?" asked Charlotte.

"One," said Bunny as she fished around in her big straw handbag. "Which is why we asked you to come here today." Pulling out an airmail letter with a Chinese postmark, she handed it to Charlotte.

The letter was from the Bureau of Cultural Properties of the People's Republic of China, and specifically from a Mr. George Chu, who was identified as the director of the Dunhuang Research Academy at the Caves of the Thousand Buddhas in Dunhuang, Gansu Province.

Charlotte looked up. "Did the sculpture come from Dunhuang?"

Bunny shrugged her wide shoulders, from which hung a white cable-stitch cashmere sweater. "All I know is that my in-laws bought the sculptures on their collecting trips to the Far East. It's very probable that it's from Dunhuang. I don't think the Chinese government would go to all this trouble if it wasn't."

Charlotte turned back to the letter, which identified the sculpture as coming from Cave 206, and having been removed in the earlier part of this century. It went on to say that scholars working at the Dunhuang Research Academy had traced the statue to an art dealer in Hong Kong, and from there to the Oglethorpe collection. Apart from restoring the paintings and sculptures in the caves, the letter said, one of the Academy's major goals was to seek the return of artworks "stolen" by Western museums and art collectors.

"Therefore, we beg you to restore this precious sculpture to its rightful owner, the People's Republic of China," the letter concluded. "What we hope is that Dunhuang can eventually be reconstituted as a single unit with everything intact as it was at the turn of the century and as it should be. The artworks that have been stolen from Dunhuang are China's national treasures and I feel very strongly in my heart that they should be in China."

"I don't understand," said Charlotte as she finished reading the letter. "What does this have to do with the fact that the sculpture is missing? Do you think the Chinese stole it back?"

"I'll defer that question to Chief Tracey," said Bunny.

"Not exactly, but pretty close," he replied. "There have been a series of international thefts of artworks that originally came from Dunhuang. Some manuscripts were stolen from the British Museum; some temple paintings were stolen from the Louvre; another piece of sculpture was stolen from the Fogg Museum at Harvard. That one's on Interpol's list of the twelve most wanted stolen art objects. And there have been others as well. Interpol has succeeded in tracing some of these items back to Dunhuang. The Academy has refused to return them. They claim they were stolen in the first place."

"Did they steal them, then?"

"This fellow Chu denies it," said Tracey, "and Interpol tends to believe him. A more likely scenario is that they were stolen by an individual or a group of individuals who were using the letters sent out by Chu as guides as to what artworks to target next. Every institution or individual"—he nodded at Bunny—"that has had an artwork stolen has received one of these letters."

"What would their motivation be?" asked Charlotte. "Patriotism?"

"Ayuh," said Tracey, using the Maine substitute for the affirmative. "There have been a number of cases where the theft of artworks has been motivated by patriotism. For example, a Mexican journalist stole—or liberated, depending on your point of view—an Aztec codex from the French National Library; a group of Scottish nationalists stole the Stone of Scone from Westminster Abbey; and an Italian nationalist stole the Mona Lisa from the Louvre."

"We never would have known about any of this if it wasn't for Chief Tracey's research," interjected Bunny. "The state police never even thought of looking into the international situation."

Charlotte wasn't surprised. It was Tracey's dogged legwork that had resulted in the recovery of some valuable stolen herbals in the previous case on which she had worked with him.

"But why resort to theft?" asked Charlotte. "If indeed the artworks were stolen originally, couldn't the Chinese have gotten them back through legal channels?" She ignored a disapproving glare from Bunny.

"Not likely," said Tracey, shaking his head. "A few museums have voluntarily returned artworks to their countries of origin. A Danish museum returned some ancient manuscripts to Iceland, for instance. But most don't want to set any precedents that they might have to live up to later on. If the British Museum, to use the best-known example, were to return its holdings to their countries of origin, it wouldn't have anything left. The Elgin marbles, of course, are the best-known example."

Charlotte had read about the Greek government's efforts to persuade the British Museum to return the Elgin marbles, which had been removed from the Acropolis by Lord Elgin in the nineteenth century.

"In fact, the term Elginism has come to refer to the plunder of cultural treasures in general," Tracey continued.

Bunny snorted in contempt. "Plunder! I'd like to know what would have happened to these sculptures during the Cultural Revolution if they hadn't been removed from China. If these countries had cared about their artworks in the first place, they wouldn't be facing these problems now."

"I expect you're right, Mrs. Oglethorpe," said Tracey, ever deferential. "Anyway, to get back to the case at hand . . . We suspect that this theft is part of the greater pattern of thefts of artworks that originally came from Dunhuang. But we also might be dealing with a common thief, or even a very knowledgeable thief who wanted to make it *look* like this theft was part of the greater pattern of thefts. That's where you come in, Miss Graham."

"Charlotte, please," she said. After two years, Tracey still insisted on calling her Miss Graham. "What do you want me to do?"

"Yes, Charlotte," said Tracey with a smile. "We want you to see if you can locate Mrs. Oglethorpe's missing sculpture. In the other cases, the artworks were returned to their original sites. If indeed the theft of this sculpture is related to the other thefts, it should have been returned to Cave 206 at Dunhuang. Mrs. Oglethorpe will provide you with a photo for identification purposes. I know you're familiar with the sculpture—"

"It's my favorite," said Charlotte.

"Mine too," added Bunny.

"But there are hundreds of caves at Dunhuang, and probably thousands of sculptures, a good many of them of Buddhist monks," Tracey continued. "They might all begin to look alike. If you do find that the sculpture is there, we can then try working through international channels to get it back."

Bunny shook her head in disgust. "Try, is right," she said.

"If it's not, we can continue looking elsewhere. We've been trying to find out through Interpol if the statue's in Dunhuang, but so far we haven't had any success. When Mrs. Oglethorpe heard from Kitty Saunders that you were going to Dunhuang, she couldn't believe our luck."

"It's as if fate had interceded on our behalf," said Bunny.

"Yes," Charlotte agreed. "It is."

·3·

THREE WEEKS AND two days later, Charlotte found herself in the ancient Chinese capital of Xian, the setting-off point for the ancient Silk Road. Their group of three—Charlotte, Marsha, and Victor Danowski, another Sinologist from the Oriental Institute—had already been in China for a week. They had toured the Forbidden City in Beijing, viewed the treasures of the Shanghai Museum of Art, and, most recently, visited Xian's fabulous terra-cotta army: thousands of life-sized clay warriors, each with its own individual characteristics. The warriors had been buried with an ancient emperor to protect his tomb. But all of this was a preliminary to the highlight of the tour, the Caves of the Thousand Buddhas, which were reached via a forty-three-hour train ride that followed the route of the ancient Silk Road. By now, Charlotte had learned a little about Dunhuang: at the juncture of the two major caravan routes—one leading west to the Middle East, the other south across the high passes of the Himalayas to India—it had been a center of Buddhist worship for over a thousand years. The Caves of the Thousand Buddhas was a complex of nearly five hundred caves that had been carved out of a sandstone cliff face, many of them commissioned by traders and dedicated to the success of their expeditions. Each was a treasure trove of Buddhist art, containing richly detailed statues of the Buddha and other religious figures and elaborate wall- and ceiling-paintings. Although the sites they had seen so far had gone far to quench Charlotte's thirst for the exotic, she was looking forward to visiting Dunhuang, which was considered one of the world's least-known wonders.

After a farewell lunch, their guide escorted them to Xian's modern railroad station. They would be taking the Shanghai Express, one of five trains that left each day from Xian for China's remote West. It was Charlotte's introduction to train travel in China, and, from the moment she entered their four-berth compartment, she was captivated. Their compartment in soft-sleeper—the equivalent of first class in a classless society—was charming. From the fold-down table with its starched white tablecloth to the lace curtains at the window and the miniature reading lamp with the silk shade, it was the epitome of cozy, genteel travel. There was even a vase of flowers on the windowsill. They were plastic chrysanthemums, but it was the attempt that mattered.

Charlotte had noticed that the Chinese, despite their poverty, always made this effort to make things beautiful: the incense burning in the ladies room, the old woman in the market who arranged her leeks in the shape of a fan, the plastic flowers in the little vase.

"I love it," she said as they entered. "It's like traveling in the nineteenth century must have been."

"It's exactly like traveling in the nineteenth century must have been," said Marsha as she stowed her hand baggage away on the upper berth. "China is the only country in the world that is still making steam locomotives. Modern antiques, fresh off the assembly line."

After getting them settled in, their guide moved down the corridor to do the same for Victor, who, due to an error on the part of the travel service, had been assigned to a compartment in another car. Charlotte and Marsha had already said goodbye to the guide at the station and given him a generous tip. Until they arrived in Dunhuang, they and Victor were on their own.

"Well, here we are," said Marsha with a wide smile as she flopped herself down on the lower berth opposite Charlotte.

A tall, raw-boned, fresh-faced beauty, Marsha looked more like a downhill skier than the Sinologist she was. But appearances could be deceiving: her passion was for the kind of ancient Chinese poetry that extolled the pleasures of drinking tea, growing flowers, or gazing at the moon.

"Yes," said Charlotte. "Here we are."

The trip had come about so fast that being here still seemed unreal to her. It seemed as if she hadn't had a second to call her own since that bright Maine morning on which Kitty had thrown the Chinese coins down on her kitchen table. She was looking forward to the long train ride; it would give her a chance to catch her breath. Leaning her head against the crocheted antimacassar on the back of the seat, she noticed a duffel bag in the luggage compartment above the door. "Looks like we've got a third," she said, nodding at the duffel.

Marsha turned around to look. "So it does," she agreed, as the ringing of a loud bell signaled their imminent departure. "I think that's the all-aboard signal. He or she had better get here pretty soon."

The train had just started to roll out of the station when the door of their compartment slid open and a man entered. He was about forty, with a babyish face, thinning sandy-blond hair, and tortoise-shell glasses. Handsome, in an intellectual sort of way.

"Hello, Marsha," he said.

"Peter!" exclaimed Marsha with a radiant smile. "What are you doing here? I thought you were in Dunhuang already. Averill told me that you'd be arriving in Dunhuang at the beginning of June."

"I was shocked to hear about Averill. That's the kind of thing that happens only in New York, unfortunately." He shook his head in disgust at the city's woes. "I was in Dunhuang until last week. I'm going back; I had some business to attend to in Xian."

"Well, it's very nice to see you," said Marsha, getting up to give him a friendly kiss on the cheek.

"I knew you were going to Dunhuang, but I didn't expect we'd be on the same train, much less in the same compartment."

"How did you know?"

"I have my sources," he said with a mysterious smile.

He had a pretentious accent that Charlotte figured to be either that of an Englishman living in the United States or vice versa. She suspected vice versa: Englishmen usually held onto their accents for dear life, while Americans generally dropped theirs as quickly as possible.

"How long will you be staying in Dunhuang?" he asked.

"Only about ten days," Marsha said.

"Not long."

"No," said Marsha. "But long enough to examine the manuscripts that were discovered last year, and see if they include anything interesting. Maybe translate a few poems. I hope to come back again next summer."

He turned to Charlotte. "It's very nice to see you here too, Miss Graham."

"Oh, I'm sorry," said Marsha. "Peter Hamilton, my stepmother, Charlotte Graham." She turned to Charlotte. "Peter is an old friend."

Charlotte recognized the name. He was the author of several critically acclaimed travel books. Charlotte had started to read one of them once, but had never finished it. She had found the tone too pompous for her taste.

"I know," he said, extending his hand to Charlotte.

"The same sources?" she said.

"Yes," said Peter. "The same sources who also told me about Averill. But I would have recognized you in any case. What red-blooded American man wouldn't have? We are all your devoted fans, and you still look the same as you did when I was a child; for that matter, when my father was a child."

"If you say the same of your grandfather, I'll get upset," said Charlotte with a smile. "But . . ." she added, "thank you."

In fact, it was one of her life's little benisons that her looks had withstood the test of time. Although her skin was now marred by a few crow's-feet and her jet-black hair (which was dyed) was now worn in a chignon instead of in her famous pageboy, she still looked much the same as she had forty years ago.

"Peter is a travel writer," said Marsha. She mentioned the titles of several of his books. "He's working on a book now about foreign explorers on the Silk Road. What's the title to be, Peter? *Ancient Cities of Desert Cathay*?"

"Close. It's *Sand-Buried Treasures of Desert Cathay*. Or at least, that's the working title. My publisher will probably change it. They usually do. It's due out a year from January."

"Is that your luggage?" asked Marsha, nodding at the bag on the floor.

"Yes," he replied. "In fact, I'd better put it away," he added, as he lifted it up into the luggage rack.

"Then it looks as if we have a fourth still to come," said Marsha, pointing overhead to the duffel bag. "If he or she didn't miss the train, that is."

"Oh, yes," said Peter. "Well, the more the merrier."

The train had passed through the north gate in the crenellated medieval wall that had once surrounded the ancient city, and was heading out into the wheat fields of the countryside.

"How do you two know one another?" asked Charlotte once Peter had taken a seat. "Do you live in New York as well, Peter?"

"Cleveland, originally. I live in London now, but I'm in New York a lot; my publisher's American."

Charlotte wondered how long it had taken for the broad vowels of the Midwest to be transformed into phony old Etonian.

"I know Marsha through the British Library. We've both done a lot of research there, in the Stein Collection." He turned to Marsha. "Fiona and I are moving. I'll have to give you our new address."

"Oh," said Marsha. "You're not going to be in Putney anymore?"

"No," he said. "Hampstead. A little house overlooking the heath." His voice carried more than a hint of pride.

Charlotte knew enough about London to recognize that moving from Putney to even a little house overlooking the heath in Hampstead was *not* a step down. The former home of D. H. Lawrence and John Keats, Hampstead was a kind of Valhalla for ambitious literary types.

Taking a couple of business cards out of his wallet, Peter passed one to Marsha and another to Charlotte. "You'll have to visit us at our new digs next time you're in London, Marsha," he said. "On the weekends, though, we go to Kent—to the country estate of Fiona's parents, Lord and Lady Waverley-Smythe."

He said the names as if he expected Charlotte and Marsha to know who they were, forgetting that he was talking to Americans. Charlotte's only association with the name Waverley was an apartment house on Central Park West where an acquaintance had once had a duplex.

"Of course, we'd love to have you visit us in Kent as well," he added. "Sometimes it's nice to get out of the city. They have plenty of room; it's quite a good-sized place."

Of course it was; otherwise he wouldn't have mentioned it.

"Thank you, I'd love to," said Marsha, taking the card.

"That goes for you as well, Miss Graham," he said.

"Thank you. Would anyone like some tea?" she asked, tempted by the lidded teacups and thermos of hot water on the fold-down table.

"I have something better," said Marsha. After fumbling around in her carry-on bag on the upper berth, she produced a couple of bars of Swiss chocolate, a can of salted cashews, and—miracle of miracles—a nice bottle of white wine and three wineglasses—glass, not plastic.

"Marsha, you're amazing," said Charlotte, leaning over to hug her stepdaughter. "What a wonderful idea!"

Marsha bent down to look out the window. "Have we crossed the Wei yet?"

"It's coming up," said Peter.

"The Wei?" asked Charlotte.

"The River Wei," Marsha explained. "In ancient times, it was the setting-off point for the Silk Road. It was customary when starting out on the Silk Road to have a party. The departing travelers would be feted at the inns on the river banks by friends and relatives, but I think this will do instead."

"It will do very well indeed," said Charlotte.

"I've dreamed of this moment for years," Marsha said as she removed the cork with a corkscrew that she also produced from her carry-on bag. Leave it to Marsha to think of everything, Charlotte thought.

"Haven't you been out here before, then?" asked Peter.

Marsha shook her head. "To China several times, but never beyond Xian. The Silk Road has always been closed to foreign travel."

Peter nodded.

"I gather you've been to China many times before as well, Mr. Hamilton?" Charlotte inquired.

"Peter, please. This is my fourth trip. Second trip to Dunhuang. I was here last year for three months."

"Peter recouped the entire cost of his first trip to China from the sale of antiques he bought here," said Marsha.

"Really?" said Charlotte.

"Actually, I could have financed a dozen trips to China with what I made on that first one. The government has since cracked down, but until a few years ago you could still buy Chinese antiques for a song. I made fifty thousand pounds—that's pounds, not dollars—alone on a pair of porcelain soup tureens that I sold to a Madison Avenue gallery. Now you can't take anything older than a hundred and twenty years out of the country."

"Do they check?" asked Charlotte.

"Very closely. You can only buy items that are marked with a special seal, and you need a special customs declaration form.

You can buy things on the black market of course, but I wouldn't risk it. Unfortunately, the easy money in antiques is a thing of the past. Now I have to pay for these trips out of what I make on royalties, which, if you know anything about publishing, isn't much." He looked out the window. "Here's the Wei," he said.

Turning toward the window, Charlotte saw a shallow, muddy stream winding through the wheat fields on the outskirts of the city.

"I have something else for us too," said Marsha, getting up again to reach into her carry-on bag. From the bag, she removed two circles of willow that had been made by bending a leafy twig into a round shape and fastening it. She handed one across the table to Charlotte.

"What is it?" Charlotte asked, turning it over in her hands.

"It was customary for friends and relatives of travelers departing on the Silk Road to break off a twig from the willows growing on the banks of the Wei and bend it into a circle as a prayer for their safe return," Marsha explained. "And, since we have no relatives or friends to see us off . . ."

"You made the willow circles!" said Charlotte.

"That's very nice. I can use that in my book," said Peter. Removing a little notebook from his breast pocket, he made a notation. "When in China," he said, "it always helps to travel with an authority on Chinese history." He smiled at Marsha. "Preferably one who's a romantic."

"The willow token is the subject of a poem from the Tang dynasty," said Marsha. She recited the poem: 'The traveler's willow tokens are fresh and green. Could I offer you a toast? For you're departing toward the setting sun, and soon you'll be a part of the past.' It's by my favorite poet, Wang Wei."

Charlotte looked out at the swaying willows lining the banks of the yellow river, the edges of their gray-green leaves tinted gold by the afternoon sun. She raised her glass. "I'll drink to our departure toward the setting sun. But not to our being a part of the past."

Reaching across the table, Marsha and Charlotte exchanged toasts first with one another, and then with Peter.

"Also to a faithful and trustworthy friend," said Charlotte, who had told Marsha about the reading from the *I Ching*.

"Who will be of much value to you on the trip," added Marsha.

"*Gan bei,*" said Peter, using the Chinese expression for "Bottoms up."

* * *

They went to the dining car shortly afterward for an early dinner. On the way, they looked in on Victor. He was sleeping soundly, and they decided not to disturb him. Charlotte had already learned not to expect great cuisine in China. Meals they'd eaten in the big cities had been all right, but she'd been told that the farther out you got, the worse the food became, and the meal on the train confirmed that observation. The main dish was a stew consisting mostly of mutton fat, which was served over watery rice. Unappealing to begin with, it was served on grease-coated plates by waiters whose aprons were black with soot. The only thing that kept dining in China from being a complete disaster was the wide array of dishes that were served at each meal. By virtue of the sheer variety, you could usually manage to find something halfway decent to eat. Charlotte usually ended up with rice and green beans in garlic sauce, with fruit, usually an apple, for dessert. It was a diet that must have agreed with her: in the absence of liquor, cookies, potato chips, and the other dietary unpardonables that she was accustomed to, she was feeling better than she had in some time.

They had just been served when they were joined by their missing fourth, a young American named Lisa Gorman. Although she wasn't pretty, her features were intriguing: a dark, elongated face that seemed to have been pieced together out of planes that intersected at various angles, with a long neck that was accentuated by dangling earrings. In the course of introductions, she apologized for not making herself known to them sooner, and explained that she had been sitting with her two traveling companions. She had a strong New Jersey accent whose tough overtones seemed to match her angular face and lanky, muscular build.

"And what brings you to this part of China?" asked Peter, as he helped himself to another serving of the mutton stew, his digestive system obviously being in better shape than Charlotte's. "Sightseeing?"

"Not exactly," said Lisa. "I'm the gofer for a tri-national paleontological expedition that's traveling to Dunhuang."

Peter looked up in surprise. "I knew that Dunhuang is known for its Buddhist art, but I wasn't aware that it's known for its dinosaur fossils."

"Actually, the two go together, as incongruous as it may sound. The same kind of sandstone that's ideal for building cave temples also makes good fossil hunting grounds. Dinosaur fossils have been found in conjunction with cave temples at several sites in China."

"Have you found dinosaur fossils at Dunhuang, then?" asked Peter.

"Not yet. But we hope to find some there, enough to justify a full-scale expedition later on. We'd better find some fossils; otherwise we're apt to run into trouble getting financial backing. It doesn't have to be the world's greatest discovery, but it should be something."

"Then you're an advance team of sorts," said Peter.

"Exactly. The purpose of our trip is to negotiate a formal agreement with the Chinese—specifically, the Institute of Vertebrate Paleontology in Beijing, who are our Chinese hosts; to scope out the lay of the land; and to work out the logistics for next year's expedition."

Peter chewed his stew thoughtfully. "Wasn't there an American explorer who made a paleontological expedition to China in the twenties?" he asked.

"Roy Chapman Andrews," nodded Lisa, earrings bobbing. "He's mostly known for his discovery of nests of dinosaur eggs, but he made a lot of other important discoveries too. We consider our expedition a successor to his. Ours will be the first American team to visit China since his last expedition in 1925."

Though Andrews' exploits had taken place when Charlotte was still a child, she remembered them well. Until he'd come along, no one had known how dinosaurs reproduced. His discovery of their eggs, some with unhatched baby dinosaurs inside, launched a mania for prehistoric reptiles that continued down to this day.

"Have you seen the nests of dinosaur eggs on display at the American Museum of Natural History?" Lisa asked.

Peter nodded.

"Those are Roy Chapman Andrews'—or RCA, as he's fondly known in paleontological circles—eggs," said Lisa. She stopped to take her first bite of the stew. "Yuck," she said, setting down her chopsticks.

"I agree," said Charlotte. "Here, try the green beans," she suggested, passing her the serving platter. "They're not bad."

"Thanks. RCA made his discoveries in Inner Mongolia, several hundred miles to the north," Lisa continued as she helped herself to the beans. "But that area's been picked over pretty well: Mongolian expeditions, Soviet expeditions, Polish expeditions. We thought we might do better in virgin territory."

"What makes you think you'll find fossils in Dunhuang?" asked Peter. He gestured with his chopsticks at the platter of mutton stew. "Would anyone else like more of this?" he asked.

They declined, and he polished it off.

"Several things," Lisa replied. "First, Central Asia is rich in fossil deposits in general; it was never covered by the ocean as were Europe and America. Second, the rock formations there are similar to the Barun Goyot Formation in Inner Mongolia, where RCA made his discoveries."

"Where is your group from?" asked Peter.

"Well, the sponsor is the Museum of the Rockies in Bozeman, Montana. That's where I work. I'm the assistant to Bert Rogers, the field leader. You may have heard of him; he's a well-known paleontologist. But the team is multi-institutional; we also have people from Yale and the Carnegie Museum."

"Will you be staying in the town of Dunhuang?" asked Marsha.

"No," she replied, as she nibbled on the beans. "We'll be staying at a guest house at the Dunhuang Research Academy. I understand it's about fifteen miles south of the town, which is farther out into the desert and therefore closer to the fossil beds. If there are fossil beds," she added.

"That's where we're staying too," said Marsha. "I hear that it's, quote, primitive but charming. Peter's already been there for a few weeks. Do you agree with that assessment, Peter?"

"It's very nice, actually," he said. "I think you'll like it. The food is very good too. A lot better than this." He smiled mischievously. "You'll have to try the local specialties."

"What are they?" asked Lisa.

"Camel palm, donkey penis, and stuffed sheep entrails."

Charlotte arched an eyebrow.

"Yuck," said Lisa again.

After dinner, Charlotte, Marsha, and Peter returned to their compartment, while Lisa went in search of her companions. As the day wore on, the temperature had climbed, and their compartment was now stifling hot. Though they had switched on their compartment's little electric fan, it wasn't providing much relief. Opening the windows helped some, however, and, after opening those in their own compartment, they went out into the corridor to open the windows there for cross ventilation. Afterward, Charlotte understood why the waiters' aprons had been black: the corridor was swirling with dusty, sooty air. Traveling by modern antique had its drawbacks as well as its charms.

With their compartment aired out, they settled in for the evening. Soothed by the rocking of the train and the monotonous scenery, Charlotte was just beginning to fall asleep when she was awakened by Lisa's appearance at the door. Behind her stood a man holding a tray on which stood a pitcher of beer and several glasses. In his cowboy boots, Stetson hat, and Western-style shirt, he looked like an extra for a Hollywood Western, of the good guy variety. Short, paunchy, and bandy-legged, he had a grin that stretched from here to Texas, and the dimples to go along with it. His appearance was so incongruous that a service worker (as any Chinese with a menial job was called) who had been mopping the floor stopped in mid-motion to gape in fascination.

"What's the matter with him?" said their visitor. "Ain't he ever seen a pissant walkin' around with a potato chip on its head before?" With that, he laughed heartily and held the tray out to Lisa. "Lisa told us there might be a party goin' on in this here compartment, so we thought we'd bring along a little *pijiu*," he said. "We hope you don't mind our joinin' you."

Pijiu was Chinese for beer, the beverage of choice in a country where the only other widely available beverages were a sickly sweet orange soda and hot water for tea. Fortunately it was a very low-alcohol beer—what people in the Midwest call near beer—which meant that you could drink a lot of it before you felt its effects.

"Not at all," said Marsha, sliding over to make room on the seat.

"I'd like you to meet Dogie O'Dea," said Lisa. "Dogie's a member of my team. He's considered one of the world's greatest dinosaur hunters. Dogie knows fossil-bearing rock the way other people know horses or dogs."

"I'm pretty damn good at horses too," he said.

"What constitutes being considered a great dinosaur hunter?" asked Peter as Lisa set the tray down on the fold-down table.

"It's a certain knack," she replied. "Some people will have a terrific fossil right under their noses and they won't even see it. Others—like Dogie—seem to be able to sniff 'em out. I kid him that that's why he's nicknamed Dogie—because of his ability to sniff out old bones."

"It isn't?" asked Charlotte.

"It's a nickname from my cowpunchin' days," he explained. "I guess I got it 'cause I'm as stubborn as one. To say nothin' of bein' as ugly as one." He laughed again, a jolly, good-natured laugh.

"As stubborn as a dog?" said Marsha.

"Dogie, I think you'll have to explain," said the tall, dark man who had appeared at the door behind him. Like Dogie, he was dressed in jeans and a Western shirt. "These are cultured ladies from back East, who aren't familiar with our quaint frontier ways."

"As in 'Git Along, Little Dogies,' " Charlotte explained.

"Whoopee, ti yi yo, git along, little dogies," yelped Dogie in the refrain from the old cowboy song.

"How colorful," teased Marsha. "Are you going to jingle your spurs?"

Dogie lifted up a boot-shod foot and checked the heel. "No spurs today, ma'am. But if you wait until we get to Dunhuang, howsoever, I might be able to rustle you up a camel patty or two."

"And this is my boss, Bert Rogers," said Lisa, nodding at the other man.

He was tall and broad-shouldered, with dark, wavy hair, a thick beard, and warm blue eyes. He reminded Charlotte of one of her favorite leading men, whose most appealing quality had been his aura of security. Leaning up against his chest had been like leaning up against a hundred-year-old oak.

Charlotte noticed Marsha's quick glance at the conspicuous white circle on his ring finger. Like Charlotte, Marsha had recently been separated, but unlike Charlotte, she wasn't too old to have given up on romance quite yet.

Within a few minutes, they were all drinking beer and munching on salted cashews from Marsha's stash: Marsha, Lisa, and Dogie on one side, and Charlotte, Peter, and Bert on the other. Except for Dogie, it was a compartment full of long-legged people, and their knees butted together cozily.

"Ugh, I hate this warm beer," drawled Dogie as he took a swig. "The only thing that's worse than warm beer is kissin' your sister."

"How long have you been hunting fossils, Dogie?" asked Charlotte.

"Fifteen years," he replied. "Do you folks mind if we turn on a little music? After all, we are having a party."

"I'll do it," said Marsha, reaching for the knob under the fold-down table that controlled the loudspeaker system. Her interest in their impromptu gathering had suddenly picked up with Bert's arrival.

In a minute, the compartment was filled with accordion music, a selection from the system's bizarre assortment of American show tunes, folk music, and jazz, punctuated by the occasional polka or waltz. But at least it was better than "The East is Red," Marsha had said.

Cupping his hand behind his ear, Dogie smiled broadly as he recognized the tune. "Hot damn," he said, chuckling as he slapped his knee. "It's the 'Beer Barrel Polka.' Ain't this Chinese music a howl." Removing his hand from his ear, he looked back at Charlotte. "Now, where were we?" he said.

"Hunting fossils," she told him.

"Oh, right!" he said. "I was foreman on the ranch where Bert made his first big find. From the moment I saw that huge ischium stickin' out the wall of that dry gulch, I was hooked. Before long, I was workin' for Bert full time. I was too bunged up to ride anymore, anyways," he added.

In the winters, Bert explained, Dogie supervised the preparators, the people who reassembled the bones that were collected on their summer digs. Lisa was one of the preparators on Bert's staff. "The best one," he added.

"Lisa's told us about your expedition," said Charlotte. "We wish you luck in finding fossils at Dunhuang."

"Oh, we know we'll find fossils," said Bert. "The question is whether or not we can bring off the expedition."

"Why's that?" asked Charlotte. "Are the Chinese difficult to work with?"

"No, the Chinese are fine. It's the other Americans who are the problem."

"Case in point," said Dogie, directing his gaze at the corridor, where an immaculately dressed man (How did he manage to look so unrumpled? Charlotte wondered) was closing the windows which they had just opened.

"He'd rather roast to death than get his clothes dirty," said Dogie.

"Who's that?" asked Charlotte.

"Eugene Orecchio," said Dogie. "A rock jock—also known as a geologist—from the Carnegie Museum. Another member of our team, I'm sorry to say."

"Why a geologist, and why sorry to say?" asked Marsha.

"It's a long story, and a far cry from Chinese poetry," said Bert. Lisa must have told him about Marsha after dinner.

Charlotte checked her watch. "We have another thirty-nine hours."

"Yes, I guess we do," said Bert with a warm smile. "Well, Gene is a proponent of the catastrophe theory of dinosaur extinction. He believes that the dinosaurs died out in a catastrophic event caused by an extraterrestrial object—death star is the popular catchword, though it was actually a comet or an asteroid—that struck the earth sixty-four million years ago."

"And you aren't?" said Marsha.

"No self-respecting paleontologist is: the evidence proves that the dinosaurs didn't all turn feet up in a day, whatever Gene might think to the contrary. But he's not a paleontologist, which is the problem. In fact, he's very contemptuous of paleontologists. He has been known to accuse paleontologists of being stamp collectors, not scientists."

"Those sound like fighting words," said Charlotte.

"You bet they are," Bert agreed.

"What makes him think the dinosaurs died out in a catastrophic event?" asked Marsha as she munched on cashew nuts.

Charlotte couldn't help but notice the deep interest that she was suddenly taking in paleontology.

"The K/T boundary. It's the boundary between the sediments of the Cretaceous—K is for Cretaceous, to distinguish it from Carboniferous—and the Tertiary Periods at about the time the dinosaurs died out. The soil from the boundary layer contains soot that the catastrophists say is from fires that blanketed the earth at the time of the catastrophic event."

"And you say what—that a death star didn't strike the earth?"

"No. Only that the dinosaurs weren't wiped out by it. The dinosaurs had been dying out for a long time before. Not that the catastrophic event didn't contribute, but it wasn't the deciding factor. There were lots of factors involved. Not only does the catastrophe theory go against all the evidence, it's much too simplistic an explanation."

Without the cross breeze from the open windows in the corridor, the tiny compartment was becoming uncomfortably hot again. There was also a strong odor emanating from the toilet at the end of the car.

Pulling a red bandanna out of the pocket of his blue jeans, Dogie wiped his cherubic brow. "Speakin' of soot," he said, "I think it's about time that we introduce some soot into this car. What do you say, boss?"

"I think that's a very good idea," Bert replied.

Excusing themselves, the two men went out into the corridor and lowered all the windows which their colleague had just closed. The hot air hit them like a blast from a coal furnace, but at least it was moving.

When Bert and Dogie returned, they poured another round of beers and continued their conversation about dinosaur extinction.

"If all the evidence goes to the contrary, why is the catastrophe theory taken so seriously?" asked Charlotte as she sipped her beer. She had read a lot about the catastrophe theory in the newspapers.

"Two reasons," said Bert. "The main one is that there have never been any significant dinosaur fossils found above the K/T boundary layer. That's not to say there will never be, only that there haven't been so far."

"That would seem to be pretty strong evidence," Charlotte observed.

"Not really. We estimate that the dinosaurs lived on in reduced numbers for hundreds of thousands of years after the catastrophe. To us, that seems like a lot of time, but geologically speaking it's an instant. Finding a fossil from that period would be the equivalent of finding the needle in the haystack."

"But when and if a significant fossil is found, it will blow the impact theory to kingdom come," added Dogie.

"What's the other reason?" asked Charlotte.

"The second reason is political," Bert replied.

"Political?"

"If you believe that a catastrophic event caused a disruption in the earth's climate significant enough to wipe out life on earth, then you must also believe that a nuclear war would lead to a nuclear winter that would wipe out life on earth, and therefore you are a pacifist."

"With God on your side," said Dogie.

"If, however, you believe that the dinosaurs died out gradually, then you must also believe that life could survive a nuclear war, and therefore you are undermining the nuclear-winter hypothesis. Which means that you are a militarist, at best; a right-wing warmonger, at worst."

"I've been called a helluva lot worse," said Dogie.

"By me, for one," said Bert.

"But that's ridiculous," said Charlotte.

"Ridiculous, but true," said Bert. "Grant proposals and research papers have been rejected because their authors—myself among them—contradicted the politically acceptable attitude toward dinosaur extinction."

"I know the mentality," said Marsha. "Someone recently told me that the word Oriental had imperialist overtones. What are we supposed to do, change our name to the Japanese, Chinese, Korean, Vietnamese, etcetera, Institute?"

Bert smiled at her with his navy-blue eyes. In the tiny compartment, the attraction between him and Marsha was almost palpable.

"It sounds horrible," said Charlotte. "Like the McCarthy era all over again, but in ideological reverse."

"Exactly," Marsha agreed. "It's like being called a Communist in the fifties was. Whatever explanation you offered, you were always suspect."

From where Charlotte was sitting she could see Orecchio making his way back down the corridor from the washroom. This was going to be interesting.

"Speak of the devil," said Dogie, who sat next to her.

As he caught sight of the open windows, a frown crossed Orecchio's beetled brow, and he began closing them all again.

"I'm beginning to feel like I'm trapped in a sardine can on the floor of Death Valley," said Dogie, wiping his brow again with the red bandanna. He stood up. "If you'll excuse me, ladies, I have work to do."

Taking up a position to Orecchio's left, he started methodically opening the windows which the geologist had just shut.

By now, their duel over the windows had attracted the attention of the other passengers, most of whom appeared to be on Dogie's side.

His coordination hampered by his temper, Orecchio angrily fumbled with the latches. The more swiftly Dogie opened the windows, the more infuriated Orecchio became. Finally, he turned on Dogie. His teeth were bared, and his hand was pulled back in a fist. Sweat was pouring down his brow.

The temperature in the car must have been a hundred and ten.

For a moment Orecchio just stood there. Then he spoke, his voice a low growl. "If you open up one more of those windows, I'll cold-cock you," he said. Then he added: "Got that, you cowboy asshole?"

Dogie stood his ground, a faint smile playing around the corners of his lips. "You wouldn't dare. If you do, I'll rope, hogtie, and brand you, and throw you so far it'll take the Chinese a week to find you. I'm a pretty good fighter for a stamp collector. Wanna try me?"

Neither of them were big men. Charlotte would have put Dogie's height at five eight and Orecchio's at an inch or so shorter. But Dogie had a powerful, muscular build, while Orecchio was thin and slight.

"Excuse me," said Bert. "Looks like I've got to help out a friend." Standing up to his full height (which must have been six foot four in stocking feet and six foot six with his cowboy boots on), he sauntered out into the corridor. Crossing his arms casually across his chest and leaning his massive shoulder against the window frame, he proceeded to stare quietly at Orecchio.

Orecchio seemed to wither before their eyes. Charlotte thought of the saloon patrons cowering in the old Westerns as the hero bursts through the saloon doors, and had to suppress a giggle.

The moment was defused by the sudden arrival of the conductor, but Charlotte had no doubt that Orecchio would have backed down. Seldom had she seen a man use his size to intimidate so effectively.

After the conductor had stamped their tickets, the moment was over. But it had nearly come to a fist fight.

"I think this calls for some *pijiu*," said Dogie as the two men returned to their seats in the compartment.

"Let me get the beer," said Peter, gesturing for Dogie to sit back down. "I think you've done your work for the evening." Picking up his carry-on bag, he left them to the analysis of Dogie's dispute with Orecchio.

Peter returned a few minutes later with another pitcher of beer.

"How did you manage this?" asked Charlotte in amazement as she picked up the pitcher to refill their glasses. It was ice cold.

Peter spoke a word in Chinese. "It means 'the squeeze,' " he explained. In the Middle East, it's 'baksheesh'; in South America, it's 'the bite.' The terms may be different, but the concept's the same the world over."

"I thought the Revolution had purged the People's Republic of corruption," said Charlotte facetiously.

Peter rolled his eyes. "There isn't anybody in China who can't be bought with cigarettes"—he pointed at his carry-on bag, which was stuffed with cigarette cartons—"or with yuan and there's nothing that can't be accomplished through the back door."

"The back door?"

"Knowing somebody. It's the only way that anything ever gets done in China." He looked over at Bert. "As I'm sure you'll find out when you start to go about organizing your expedition."

The expedition hadn't had an auspicious beginning, thought Charlotte as "My Old Kentucky Home" blared out of the loudspeaker. Over the years she had been on a number of movie shoots that had started out the same way.

They usually turned out to be total disasters.

· 4 ·

THEY ARRIVED AT the railhead at the depressing little town of Liuyan on the afternoon of the second day. Including their sightseeing stopover at Jiayuguan, the fortress at the western terminus of the Great Wall, they had been traveling for forty-one hours. And they hadn't yet reached their destination. Dunhuang still lay another sixty miles to the south. Charlotte had long ago concluded that there was good reason for its being considered one of the least-known wonders of the world.

A Japanese-made minibus was waiting at the curb—if that's what you could call the edge of the dusty beaten-earth road—to take them to Dunhuang. They were a party of eight: Charlotte, Marsha, Victor, and Peter; and the four members of the paleontology team. If the train had been hot, the minibus was even hotter. Although it must have been equipped with air conditioning—the bus appeared to be brand new—it wasn't working. Nor did the landscape offer any diversion from the heat. The pitted band of asphalt that had replaced the ancient camel track skirted the edge of the Black Gobi, so-named for its expanses of coal-black gravel. It reminded Charlotte of the most barren sections of West Texas, but at least West Texas had sagebrush and tumbleweed. This landscape didn't even have a blade of grass. She had read that the top-secret test site for China's nuclear weapons program was located nearby. It didn't surprise her that they had chosen this barren wasteland; there was nothing here that could have been destroyed in a nuclear blast.

After a little over an hour the soil started turning pinkish-red, and struggling patches of vegetation began to appear—tufts of grass, thickets of bush, and even a tree or two. Herds of camels grazing on the thorny bush placidly watched the traffic go by.

Another half an hour, and the appearance of poplar trees in the distance indicated that they were drawing near Dunhuang. Although it had a population of thirty-five thousand, the town turned out to be barely more interesting than the desert around it. A collection of dreary concrete-slab buildings intersected by dusty streets filled with bicycles and donkey carts, it hardly seemed like the Silk Road city of legend. But then it wasn't—the ancient city had long ago been buried by the sands. After passing through town, they continued south on an arrow-straight road colonnaded with poplars that ran through irrigated fields of corn, wheat, millet, cotton, and vegetables. Then, suddenly, they were in the desert. The desert began precisely where the irrigation left off—not the black *gobi*, or gravel and rock debris, that they had seen so much of, but a storybook desert of golden, wind-sculpted dunes stretching away to the horizon. "Like the topping on a lemon meringue pie," said Marsha.

A couple of miles later the road emerged onto a barren gravel plain, and followed the wide, shallow, boulder-strewn channel of a stream for another eight or ten miles. Then it turned into the mouth of the narrow valley that was the site of the caves.

As the member of their group most familiar with Dunhuang (this was his third trip), Victor Danowski was asked to give an impromptu lecture. Like Marsha, he had been invited to Dunhuang to translate the recently discovered manuscripts, but his area of expertise was religious texts rather than poetry.

Assenting to the group's request, Victor made his way up to the front of the minibus. He was a thin, balding, wiry man—a runner, Charlotte had learned when she encountered him on an early morning walk in Shanghai—with a pale complexion, heavy black-rimmed eyeglasses, and a graying Vandyke-style goatee.

"If you'll look to your left," he said, pointing out the window, "you'll see a mountain ridge. That's the Mountain of the Three Dangers, where the wandering monk Lo-tsun had his vision of a thousand Buddhas in a shining cloud of brilliant golden light. He called the phenomenon Buddha's Halo."

"Looks like pretty good fossil huntin' territory to me," said Dogie, as they gazed out at the reddish-purple mountain range that rose from the barren plain, its rugged foothills a glowing pink in the late afternoon light.

"Lo-tsun was traveling in the area in 366 when he had his vision," Victor continued. "Of course, we now know that it was an illusion caused by minerals in the rocks caught in the glow of the setting sun."

"I preferred the shining cloud," whispered Marsha.

"Lo-tsun believed that it was a holy place, and decided to build a cave in the opposite mountain, the Mountain of the Howling Sands"—he pointed to their right—"in which to live and to worship. Over the next thousand years, hundreds of other caves were built by Buddhist worshipers."

"Here are some caves," said Bert, looking out the window.

The cliff face to the west was honeycombed with black holes. To Charlotte, it looked a little like an Indian cliff dwelling.

"Yes," said Victor. "We're now at the beginning of the cave complex. These are the dormitory caves, where the monks and artisans lived."

"What are the structures on the left?" asked Bert, indicating a row of domed structures that lined the road at the top of a series of terraces leading upward from the streambed.

"They're stupas," Victor replied. "Reliquary chambers of famous monks who have died. Mementos of the monks were deposited inside—papers and sutras and things like that." He leaned over to look out the windshield. "Here's the main section of the cave complex coming up now."

Here the cliff was taller, and there were four or five levels of caves. Stucco fronts had been added to protect the entrances, and balconies and staircases built to improve access. If the dormitory caves had reminded Charlotte of a cliff dwelling, these caves reminded her of a retirement condo.

"If you'll look behind the trees, you'll see what looks like a nine-story pagoda," Victor continued. "Actually, it's the façade of the Cave of Unequaled Height, which is the centerpiece of the cave complex. It's believed to be Lo-tsun's original cave, although it's since been greatly enlarged."

Charlotte could just make out the ornate orange-tiled roofs of the many-tiered pagoda through the verdant fringe of green lining the cliff base.

"The Cave of Unequaled Height houses a colossal Buddha that is one and a half times the size of the Great Sphinx of Egypt. And," Victor continued, "if you'll look to the other side, you will see two tall stupas."

The passengers' heads all swiveled to the left.

"If you look directly between those stupas, you'll see another stupa near the top of the ridge of the Mountain of the Three Dangers. That stupa is dedicated to Lo-tsun. Legend has it that it's located on the exact spot where he saw his vision." Victor leaned over again to look out the windshield. "Well, here we are."

Near the end of the fringe of green they crossed a concrete bridge and passed under a gaily painted archway consisting of a series of rooflets capped with green tiles and supported by red pillars. A few minutes later they pulled into the guest house courtyard. Charlotte checked her watch: they had been traveling for precisely forty-three hours and forty minutes.

They emerged from the stifling bus into a courtyard that was shielded from the sun by gnarled old apricot trees thick with fruit; in their refreshing shade, it was cool and quiet. Wind chimes tinkled in the breeze, and birds twittered. The gurgle of water came from somewhere nearby. After the heat and desolation of the desert, the lushness of this little oasis was startling.

They were greeted by a stout, middle-aged man with only one arm. The right sleeve of his rumpled blue Mao suit was pinned to his shoulder to keep it from swinging free. He introduced himself as George Chu, director of the Dunhuang Research Academy. Charlotte recognized the name as that of the man who had written the letter to Bunny Oglethorpe. After a short, formal welcoming speech, he introduced their guide, a fresh-faced young Chinese woman named Emily Lin. Like Chu, she welcomed them in perfect English. Her speech was followed by the appearance of half-a-dozen pretty young service workers carrying washcloths soaked in cool water to sponge off the dust of the desert.

"All *right*," said Dogie with a devilish grin as the girls appeared with their baskets. "Bring on the dancing girls."

After the travelers had washed their faces, they were offered dripping slices of luscious melon to quench their thirst. The combination of the pretty girls and the exotic setting created the most romantic of atmospheres, as if they had just arrived at the oasis by camel caravan instead of by minibus. Charlotte thought of the *I Ching*'s prediction that she would be traveling to "an exotic foreign country." It didn't get any more exotic than this.

Following the melon break, the service workers showed them to the guest house complex, which Charlotte thought delightful, at least by contrast with the drab, Stalinist-era, concrete-block hotels which they were used to. It consisted of half-a-dozen single-story, tile-roofed buildings made of mud brick that had been plastered and whitewashed. The buildings were set amid a network of courtyards shaded by grape arbors and fruit trees, and linked by paths lined with zinnias and dahlias, which were, like most of the flowers planted in China, red. Charlotte's room was simple: plain stucco walls, a tile floor, twin beds covered with pink chenille bedspreads. It reminded her of a roadside motel, but without the bathrooms. For washing up, there was a white-enameled basin painted with gaudy flowers, and a kettle of hot water. After Charlotte had seen her room, a service worker showed her to the toilet facilities. Each of the buildings had a w.c. at one end, of the typical Chinese hole-in-the-ground variety. But there was only one bathhouse for the complex. A sign on the door said that the water was turned on only between the hours of eight and ten in the evening. Charlotte turned on a tap in one of the sinks. Nothing came out. "Primitive but charming" was exactly right.

She was doing her best to wash up in her wash basin a few minutes later when there was a knock on her door. It was Victor, letting her know that dinner would be served in twenty minutes in the dining hall.

Charlotte and Marsha arrived a few minutes early, and took seats at one of the tables, which, in typical Chinese style, was set for eight. They were joined a few minutes later by Bert and Dogie, who explained that Lisa was taking a nap. Bert took the chair next to Marsha. After forty-odd hours on the train, the attraction between them appeared to be blossoming into a full-fledged romance. With them was a Professor Peng, whom Bert introduced as the director of the Institute of Vertebrate Paleontology. He and Bert were old friends, having worked together on several digs in other parts of the world. Peng (the Chinese rarely used their given names) had also just arrived, but by airplane rather than by train. He would be representing the Chinese in their negotiations, and would also be heading up the Chinese delegation to the expedition. He was a genial-looking man in his forties, with walnut-brown skin that was stretched tightly across his face, and smile lines radiating from the corners of his eyes.

They had just completed introductions when they were joined by another man. He was tall and fat, with a ruddy complexion, wire-rimmed glasses, and a picturesque handlebar mustache. Unlike Bert and Dogie, whose idea of sartorial elegance was limited to blue jeans and Western shirts, the newcomer was a men's fashion magazine image of the Western explorer in Central Asia: khaki Bermuda shorts, a fashionably rumpled linen safari shirt, and a red paisley silk scarf tied casually around his neck. But he wore them well. Add a monocle and a bush hat, and he might have been Teddy Roosevelt.

"Larry!" Bert exclaimed, as the new arrival clapped a hand on his shoulder. "I wondered when you were going to turn up." Rising, he shook Larry's hand warmly and then introduced him to the others.

His name was Larry Fiske, and he was another member of Bert's team, a paleontologist from Yale. He had already been in Dunhuang for a week, and was staying at his camp out in the desert.

"We just arrived a little while ago," said Bert. "I was planning to look you up right after dinner. We're chomping at the bit to hear what you've found. What about it?" he asked eagerly. "Is there anything out there?"

Larry's eyes gleamed as he twirled the waxed tips of his mustache. Reaching into his breast pocket, he withdrew a pack of cigarettes and offered it to the others at the table.

Peng took one, as did Charlotte. Though she wasn't a smoker, she enjoyed a cigarette now and then. Then Larry took one for himself, and lit all three with a gold cigarette lighter. Leaning back in his seat, he took a long draw.

"Okay, Fiske," said Dogie. "Let's quit this cigarette shit. We want to know what you've got. Pardon the language, ladies," he added.

Larry smiled, showing large teeth that were stained yellow from nicotine. He leaned forward. "I have found"—he paused for dramatic effect—"the richest fossil grounds that I have ever seen in my entire life."

"No shit?" said Dogie.

Larry raised his right hand in a mock oath. "No shit." He continued, this time speaking more rapidly: "It is absolutely *paved* with fossils out there." He spread out his hands to illustrate. "I've never seen anything like it. It's a veritable paleontologist's El Dorado."

"Damn," said Dogie. His gaze was directed at the open door of the dining hall, where Gene Orecchio was standing with a young Chinese man.

As Dogie spoke, Orecchio spotted them and started for their table, the young Chinese trailing behind. "May we join you?" he asked as he reached the table, indicating the two empty seats.

"Of course," said Bert, trying to be accommodating.

Orecchio's companion wore baggy Chinese trousers with a tie-dyed T-shirt, and a woven friendship bracelet of the type common among American students. He also wore round wire-rimmed glasses that accentuated his high, sharp cheekbones. His shoulder-length black hair was pulled back in a ponytail.

"I'd like to introduce my new acquaintance," said Orecchio. "This is Ned Chee," he said. "Ned is a visiting scholar at the Dunhuang Research Academy. He's from the University of California at Berkeley."

Charlotte reflected that she should have known by his T-shirt, bracelet, and ponytail that he was Chinese-American rather than Chinese. The Chinese government still frowned on any "unseemly" displays of individualism in style.

"Ned has been here for eight weeks," said Orecchio as they sat down, the geologist taking care to sit in the seat farthest away from Dogie. "This is his second trip to Dunhuang."

He spoke grudgingly; it was clear to Charlotte that Ned had attached himself to an unwilling host. If Ned had been here for eight weeks, however, he was probably desperate for fresh company.

"What are you working on here?" asked Marsha.

"My doctoral dissertation in art history," he replied. "It's on sculpture from the Northern Wei Dynasty."

"Then you must have known Averill Boardmann," said Marsha. "He was supposed to be here with us, but . . ."

Charlotte made a mental note that Ned might be useful in tracking down the Oglethorpe sculpture. If he'd been at the Academy for eight weeks, he would know if the sculpture had been returned.

"Yes, I worked closely with him when I was here last year," Ned replied. "I was very sorry to hear about his death."

After introductions were completed, the conversation turned back to dinosaurs, with Bert recapping Larry's story for Orecchio.

"It's just as we had expected," said Peng, explaining that satellite navigation photos had helped them pinpoint the Dunhuang area as having the type of rock formations that could be expected to yield bone.

"Better," exclaimed Larry. "It's better than we ever could have expected. In our wildest *dreams*," he added, flinging out his arms expansively. "Best of all, it's practically a stone's throw from our doorstep."

Charlotte wondered if he was on drugs, so overwrought were his gestures and rapid-fire his delivery.

"Just where is the site?" asked Peng.

"In the foothills of the Mountain of the Three Dangers," he replied, flinging an arm toward the east wall of the dining hall. "About a mile and a half due east of the Cave of Unequaled Height."

"Isn't that where the monk Lo-tsun saw his vision of the thousand Buddhas?" asked Marsha.

"Yes. I was thinking about calling it the Thousand Buddhas Site, but I decided on the Dragon's Tomb Site instead. The Chinese call dinosaur fossils dragon's bones." He turned to Bert, and continued: "It's not at all like Montana, Bert, old man—a bone here, a bone there. It's literally *paved* with bones, and they're not all broken up. I've been finding fully articulated skeletons, as neatly laid out as a skeleton in a coffin."

"What exactly *have* you been finding, Larry?" asked Orecchio. He tried to phrase the question casually, but the tremor in his voice revealed his eagerness to find out what the site held in store.

"Yeah, Lar," said Dogie. "Let's get our chips out on the table. Have you just got some more duckbills or have you got somethin' really excitin'?"

"For the uninitiated among us, duckbills are duckbilled dinosaurs, not platypi," explained Bert as a waiter arrived with a plate of thin-skinned mutton dumplings, and the usual tray of beer and orange soda.

"I've found duckbills all right. Try a nest of baby duckbills with skeletons intact for starters. But that's just the icing on the cake. Yours truly, Lawrence Alexander Fiske, the third"—he puffed out his barrel-shaped chest and thumped it with one fat fist—"has made the greatest dinosaur fossil find of the century. Or maybe the second greatest. Far be it for me to be the one to deny the great Roy Chapman Andrews his due."

The faces of the other paleontologists were incredulous.

"And what is that, pray tell?" said Bert as he passed the plateful of dumplings around. He was clearly skeptical.

"I'm not going to tell you, I'm going to show you." He nodded deferentially to the group. "You are all cordially invited to my camp tomorrow for Show and Tell time. A luncheon buffet and champagne will be served afterwards. Shall we say around ten?" He turned to Charlotte and Marsha. "I would be delighted if you ladies would join us."

"Not even a hint?" pleaded Dogie.

"Okay, a hint," said Larry. "It's not only what I've found, though what I've found is extraordinary enough in and of itself." He paused to cast a sidelong look at Orecchio. "It's *where* I found it."

"Where he found it," Dogie repeated, rolling his eyes to the heavens as he nibbled on a dumpling that wobbled precariously between the tips of his chopsticks. "Don't tell me that you've found the skeleton of the mythical duckbill who survived the cosmic zap."

"You'll just have to wait until tomorrow to find out, won't you?"

The conversation was interrupted by the return of the waiter, this time with a big platter of noodles and another of sauteed mutton, onions, and tomatoes. He also carried a plateful of the unleavened bread, similar to pita bread, that was a specialty of the area.

"How did you become interested in dinosaurs, Mr. Fiske?" asked Charlotte after they had all served themselves. As Peter had told them, the food here was a lot better than the food on the train.

Dogie snorted. "Tell Miss Graham, Larry," he prompted.

"*All About Dinosaurs*, by Roy Chapman Andrews," Larry replied. "I read it in fifth grade, and decided then and there that I wanted to be a paleontologist when I grew up. Some people may snicker"—he glowered in mock anger at Dogie—"but a lot of other paleontologists have come to the profession in the same way. In addition to being a great explorer, RCA was also a great writer."

"The difference between Larry and the others is that he never got over his Roy Chapman Andrews fixation," said Dogie. "RCA collected Oriental art, Larry collects Oriental art; RCA lived high on the hog, Larry lives high on the hog. Wait till you see Larry's camp—I guarantee you, it's a sight to behold. Have you ever been to one of Larry's camps, Peng?"

"Yes, in Argentina," the Chinese paleontologist replied. "I think it is of great benefit to a paleontological expedition to have Mr. Fiske as a member of the team," he added, with a twinkle in his eye.

"Larry always makes camp on the site," Bert explained. "Even when it's not entirely necessary, like here. And his camps are . . . Well, let's just say that when Larry goes into the field, he doesn't skimp on the amenities."

"When Bert and I go into the field, what do we take, Bert?" asked Dogie as he slurped up some noodles.

"A two-man tent, maybe. Usually just a bedroll and an air mattress. A tent for our equipment, which consists of a couple of folding tables and a couple of folding chairs, a Coleman lantern or two, a camp stove . . . "

"Don't forget to mention the most important piece of equipment—a cooler for the beer," volunteered Dogie.

"A cooler for the beer," repeated Bert. "When Larry travels, he travels like a British lord on safari. China plates, silver knives and forks . . . A cook, of course. He always has a cook, and a couple of retainers. What else, Dogie?"

"The silver tea service," Dogie replied. "Larry always serves tea on the dot of four." He pretended to drink from a teacup, genteelly raising a pinkie on which he wore a turquoise-and-silver ring.

"I like the crystal decanter of brandy myself," said Bert. "There's nothing like a brandy and a cigar under the desert stars."

"I try to live up to the standards set by my hero, the great Roy Chapman Andrews," Larry explained. "And I quote: 'I don't believe in hardships. They're a great nuisance. Eat well, dress well, and sleep well, whenever possible.' "

"Sounds good to me," said Charlotte.

"Speaking of eating well, this is delicious," said Bert. He waved his chopsticks at the main dish of noodles and sauteed mutton with vegetables. "Don't you want some, Larry?" he asked, nodding at Larry's empty plate.

Larry raised a hand in demurral. "No, thanks. I already ate—

a couple of sand grouse that I shot this afternoon. Prepared to perfection by my cook. *Tétras au vin à la Dijonnaise*. With *tarte aux abricots* for dessert."

"I haven't the faintest idea what it is he ate, but I can tell you one thing: it had to taste a damned sight better than the chuck we've been gettin' for the past couple of days," said Dogie. "What're we havin' for lunch tomorrow?"

"A surprise," Larry replied mysteriously.

After the usual fruit for dessert—not apples this time, but the luscious local melon and plump green seedless grapes—Victor came over to their table to announce that the staff of the guest house would be putting on a show, and directed them to a terrace outside the dining hall. As they filed out, Charlotte found herself walking next to Orecchio. The two of them were right behind Dogie and Larry. Dogie was grilling Larry, trying to get him to reveal the nature of his find. "Have patience, my friend," Larry was admonishing him. "I'm sure you can wait until tomorrow to find out." Leaning closer to Dogie, he added: "I can tell you one thing, though—it's a find that's not going to make the rock jock very happy. In fact, it's going to blow his precious catastrophe theory right out of the water." From her position behind Dogie and to his right, Charlotte could see the twinkle in the corner of his eye as Larry imparted this confidence. She wasn't sure if Orecchio had heard it or not.

On the terrace, which was covered by a grape trellis, Charlotte ended up sitting next to Ned, and decided to use the opportunity to find out what she could about the Oglethorpe sculpture. Deciding on the direct approach, she explained that she was a friend of the sculpture's owner, and had been asked to look into its disappearance.

"It's not here," said Ned, cutting her off in mid-sentence.

Charlotte hadn't even gotten around to suggesting that it was. "You're one step ahead of me," she said, surprised at his familiarity with the situation.

"It wasn't difficult to figure out what you were leading up to. You've found out about the other thefts of Dunhuang artworks, and you suspect that the Oglethorpe sculpture may have been stolen by the same party. Having learned that some of the stolen material has been returned to Dunhuang, you thought the same might be true for . . ."

"Exactly," said Charlotte. "But how did you know?"

"Did Mrs. Oglethorpe show you a letter she had received from the director of the Academy asking for the sculpture's return?"

"Yes," said Charlotte.

"I wrote it. One of my assignments here has been to track down the owners of Dunhuang artworks and write them letters. It hasn't been as difficult as I thought it would be. A lot of the artworks were sold to Westerners in the twenties and thirties through a Hong Kong dealer who kept very good records, and in many cases they're still in the same hands."

"Have many been returned?"

"Voluntarily, you mean?"

Charlotte nodded.

"Only one: the head of a Buddha I traced to an Englishman who's been living in Beijing since the Revolution. One of those Party sympathizers who refuses to acknowledge that the dream has failed. He still keeps a portrait of Chairman Mao hanging in his living room. He said he would be more than happy to restore the head to its rightful owner."

He said the words "rightful owner" scornfully; apparently, he didn't approve of the job to which he had been assigned.

"Any prospects that the others will be returned?"

Ned shook his ponytail. "None that I can see, though Chu has his hopes. He keeps thinking about the Icelandic manuscripts."

"The ones that were returned to Iceland?" she asked, remembering Tracey's mention of them.

"Yes. By a Danish museum. It was a cause for national celebration in Iceland. It was also the first time that a national treasure had been returned to its country of origin. It's what put the bee in Chu's bonnet about repatriating Dunhuang's artworks. But it's not going to happen. Legally, anyway."

"Why not?"

"Well . . . The Oglethorpe sculpture is unusual in that it's in private hands. The majority of the artworks are in museums—the Louvre, the Hermitage, the British Museum. The museums aren't about to establish a precedent by returning the artworks to Dunhuang. If they did, they'd have the whole world down on their backs demanding the return of this and that."

It was just what Tracey had said, Charlotte thought.

A small orchestra dressed in exotic costumes was setting up at the front of the two rows of benches that comprised the informal auditorium.

"Besides," he went on. "It's too complicated. Who's to say to what culture an art treasure belongs, anyway? Though I wouldn't say this in front of Chu, a case could be made that the Dunhuang artworks aren't Chinese treasures, but Buddhist treasures, and, if they are returned at all, should be returned to a country in which the Buddhist faith is still widely practiced."

He had a point. "What about illegally?" she asked. "How many of the artworks that were stolen from western museums have been returned to Dunhuang?"

"All except three: the Oglethorpe sculpture, a temple banner from the Cleveland Museum of Art, and a Bodhisattva from the Fogg Museum. But the last two were stolen within the last four weeks. The Oglethorpe sculpture was stolen ten weeks ago. The Oglethorpe sculpture baffles me. All of the other stolen artworks reappeared here within three or four weeks of the theft."

"In the places that they were originally located?" asked Charlotte.

"Yes. I keep checking Cave 206 to see if the Oglethorpe sculpture has turned up, but it hasn't. Not in the past two days, anyway. That was the last time I checked. I'll tell you, it's really something to go into one of these caves and find that something which was removed seventy-odd years ago has mysteriously been returned."

"But how do the person or persons who stole the artworks get into the caves to put them back? Aren't the caves locked?"

"Yes. There's a chance that someone could have replaced the manuscripts, anyway—some of the repatriated material has been manuscripts—during a tour. Some stolen manuscripts reappeared in Cave 17 a couple of weeks ago."

"We're going there tomorrow," said Charlotte. Cave 17 was the cave where a British explorer named Sir Aurel Stein had discovered a cache of tens of thousands of ancient manuscripts during the early part of the century. Stein's discovery was considered one of the archaeological high points of the century, comparable to the discovery of the Dead Sea Scrolls.

"It's the chief tourist attraction," said Ned. He continued: "But although the manuscripts could have been returned during a tour, that certainly isn't true of the sculptures. And some of the artworks were returned to caves that aren't on the tours. Only about forty caves are open to the public, out of a total of four hundred and ninety-two."

"Which means that the person or persons who stole the artworks has to have access to the keys," said Charlotte.

"Or is collaborating with someone who has access to the keys."

"Is anyone here looking into the thefts?"

"Are you kidding? If their national art treasures suddenly start reappearing, the powers that be certainly aren't going to question it. And you can bet Chu is going to be the first one to turn a blind eye to whatever's going on. If he knew what I've been up to, he'd probably have me shipped out on the next camel caravan to Afghanistan."

"What *have* you been up to?"

"Nothing much, really. Keeping my eyes and ears open, mostly. I can't help it. Every time I send out one of these letters, I start wondering when the object in question is going to be reported stolen. Then, when it is, I start wondering when it's going to reappear in Dunhuang."

"Any ideas?"

He shook his head. "Some zealot who wants to prove himself to his country. But beyond that . . ." He shrugged.

The orchestra was stringing a backdrop between two apricot trees; it was a crudely-drawn rendering of a camel caravan on the Silk Road.

"The irony is that ten years ago, during the height of the Cultural Revolution, ideologues earned points for destroying ancient artworks," Ned continued. "They were considered relics of a feudalistic past, symbols of bourgeois decadence. Now the Party extols ancient artworks as products created through the efforts of the laboring peoples of the past."

"Were many artworks here destroyed?"

"Not too many, fortunately," he replied. "Some sculptures were tipped over, but that's about it. One reason that the art here has survived for nine centuries is that it's so far off the beaten track. But other places around here got it. Have you been to Crescent Lake yet?"

"Not yet," said Charlotte. "We're scheduled to go there on Saturday."

"There used to be a cluster of exquisite little temples and pavilions there, also centuries old. But they were burned down by the Red Guards."

Their conversation was interrupted by the appearance at Ned's side of Emily, the pretty young Chinese guide who had delivered the welcoming speech that afternoon. As she passed him by on her way up the aisle, she gave him a discreet little squeeze on the shoulder.

At the front, Victor introduced her to the audience. "During her working hours," Victor said, "Emily is a guide at the caves, but this evening she will be serving as mistress of ceremonies for the show that the service workers are putting on in honor of the new arrivals."

By now, the benches were filled. In addition to their group, there was a party of Germans who were advising the Chinese on the conservation of the cave paintings, and a group of Japanese Buddhist monks. The staff stood around at the edges, or leaned up against the columns supporting the trellis.

Ned explained that the staff had dreamed up the little show mostly as a diversion for themselves. "It can get pretty boring out here in the desert after a while," he said.

At the front, Emily whispered in Victor's ear.

"Emily asks me to remind everyone that the staff is putting on this show in their spare time, as a tribute to their guests."

Ned translated in a whisper: "In other words, tips please."

Emily went on to explain that there would be three acts: dancing, acrobatics, and guitar music. Then their "honored guests" would be invited to participate in the entertainment.

Charlotte commented on her beautiful English.

"Educated at Beijing University," Ned explained. "Plus a year at London University. She got this job because of her English, but she really deserves a much better one. But"—he sighed—"this is Communist China. The Party decides where one can best serve the people."

"Was it in London that she acquired the name Emily?"

"Yes. She took the name in honor of her two favorite authors—Emily Brontë and Emily Dickinson. I think she's memorized every poem that Emily Dickinson ever wrote. Her favorite lines are 'I'm nobody! Who are you?' Which is not surprising in a country where nobody has a chance to be anybody."

Charlotte returned her attention to Emily. Even in pigtails and the ubiquitous blue drill Mao suit, she was lovely, with a grace and dignity that was lacking in most Chinese women.

The homeliness of the Chinese women was a mystery to Charlotte. The Taiwanese women she'd seen had been beautiful, so it wasn't a racial thing. Nor did she think it had to do with diet, clothing, or makeup. It was as if the constrictions on their freedom had somehow been imprinted on their features.

The fact that Emily was an exception to the rule was obviously not lost on Ned. Or rather, she thought with a smile, Heathcliff.

Emily proceeded to introduce the first act. It was a traditional dance set to rousing music played on folk instruments: a snakeskin drum, a bamboo flute, and an assortment of oddly shaped stringed instruments made out of gourds. The music had a strong Middle Eastern flavor, the heritage of Dunhuang's location on the Silk Road. The performance met with enthusiastic applause, and was followed by several other dances performed by young women wearing brightly colored embroidered gowns. They danced with restrained dignity, arms swaying and wrists twirling like the figures in an ancient Chinese painting.

The dancers were followed by an acrobatic act put on by a young man whom Charlotte recognized as their waiter from dinner. He was quite good, turning handsprings, walking on his hands, and executing flying somersaults with apparent ease. He even managed to juggle some plates.

Ned explained that he was a failed candidate for the People's Acrobatic Academy who'd been shipped out to Gansu Province.

"You seem to know a lot about what's going on here," said Charlotte.

"After eight weeks you get to know this place pretty well. Every time a new group of guests arrives, I get to see this show. It's pretty boring after you've seen it half-a-dozen times, but it's the only show in town."

"Now I would like to introduce one of our foreign guests, Ned Chee," said Emily. "Mr. Chee is a visiting scholar at the Dunhuang Academy."

"Sometimes it gets so boring that you have to take part yourself in order to keep from falling asleep," he added with a self-deprecating smile as he stood up to take his place in front of the audience.

When he reached the front, Emily handed him a guitar.

"I'm going to play a piece from Carl Orff's *Carmina Burana*, which I adapted for the classical guitar," he announced as he took a seat on a bamboo stool. He proceeded to play the rapid, complex music with stunning virtuosity.

When he had finished, Emily again stood up before the audience. "Now we would like to hear from our foreign guests," she said.

The first to perform was a Japanese monk, who played Mozart on a bamboo flute borrowed from one of the local musicians. Next came a German who sang a Schubert *lied*. Finally, Dogie took the stage. He sang cowboy songs, accompanying himself on the harmonica: "Git Along, Little Dogies," "Home on the Range," and "The Cowboy's Lament."

For a finale, he explained, he had chosen a song called "John Chinaman, My Jo." With Emily translating, he explained that the song was about the problems encountered by Chinese immigrants to California in the mid-nineteenth century.

"My ancestors," commented Ned.

After Dogie had sung the first stanza, Emily translated the words for the Chinese. They were: "John Chinaman, my jo, John,/You're coming precious fast;/Each ship that sails from Shanghai brings/An increase on the last;/And when you'll stop invading us, I'm blest, now, if I know./You'll outnumber us poor Yankees,/John Chinaman, my jo."

He continued with other stanzas, about pigtails, about washee shops, about an almond-eyed wife. Charlotte suspected that the original tone had probably been derogatory, but if it had been, Dogie was choosing only the most innocuous stanzas. Each stanza was translated by Emily for the Chinese, who were obviously amused at seeing their culture portrayed from such a different angle.

Between the stanzas came a chorus of Chinese-sounding gibberish, in which Dogie invited everyone to participate: It went, "Ching ching chow, chingee ringee roo,/Chingeeroo was a Chineeman,/Ring chingee choo."

The Chinese held back at first, but by the fourth go-round, they were belting out the words. It was a rousing finale to a pleasant evening, and a fitting celebration of their arrival in Dunhuang.

•5•

AFTER BREAKFAST THE next day Charlotte and Marsha met Bert, Dogie, Lisa, and the others in the lobby for the hike out to Larry's camp. Charlotte had covered her exposed skin with SPF 30 suntan lotion, and was wearing big sunglasses and a coolie hat she had bought at the No. 1 Department Store in Shanghai. If there was a reason she still looked much as she had when she was younger, it was the care she had taken over the years to protect her delicate complexion. Marsha also wore a hat, a big floppy sunbonnet. In fact, as a group, they represented quite a variety of headgear, and must have looked odd indeed to the clerk behind the desk. Bert wore an Australian bush hat, Peng a pith helmet, Lisa a flowered baseball cap, and Orecchio, looking as neatly pressed as he had on the train, a porkpie hat right out of the L. L. Bean catalogue. In addition to his usual Stetson, Dogie wore a T-shirt that bore the legend "So many dinosaurs, so little time." They all wore substantial shoes: Bert had warned them that sandals weren't sufficient protection in the desert, where midday temperatures could reach a hundred and twenty in the shade.

Although Larry had offered to pick them up, Bert and Dogie had declined his offer, preferring their introduction to the terrain to be on foot, and the rest of the party had gone along with them. The camp was only a mile and a half away. After crossing over the bridge spanning the stream, which was only a trickle at this time of year, and passing through the poplar grove lining the banks, they joined the main road, which they followed north for about a hundred feet before turning off on the rutted track leading out to Larry's camp. The turnoff was marked by the twisted corpse of a dead donkey, a lesson on the hardship of the desert. Its skin had mummified in the dry desert air.

Though it was hot, the going was easy and it took them only about ten minutes to climb the series of terraces that led upward from the road to the spot where the pair of tall stupas framed the Cave of Unequaled Height. Though they looked small from the road, the stupas were actually twelve or fifteen feet high—multistoried pagodas in miniature. Unlike the stupas lining the stream bed, these weren't reliquary stupas, but rather a kind of good luck monument for travelers, Marsha explained. From the stupas, it was another seven- or eight-minute walk across fairly level ground to the base of the foothills.

Unlike the deserts of the Southwest with which Charlotte was familiar from the mercifully few Westerns in which she had appeared, this one was devoid of vegetation: no saguaro, no barrel cactus, no sagebrush—only the occasional patch of a scrubby bush called camel thorn. Nor was the ground dusty, but rather a gravel that crunched beneath your feet. It was a little like walking across a huge sheet of coarse sandpaper. The only signs of wildlife were the big black birds that hung in the air over the foothills, and the terns that skittered across the sand like sandpipers on a New England beach. Bert and Dogie took the lead, followed by Orecchio, Peng, and Lisa. Charlotte and Marsha brought up the rear. The paleontologists all walked the same way—slowly, with their torsos bent over, their eyes glued to the ground, and their heads swiveling from side to side, as if they were looking for a lost wallet. Occasionally they would squat down to look at something on the ground, and then get up and move on again. "The paleontology stoop," Lisa called it.

At the foothills, the terrain abruptly became steeper and rockier, and the color of the ground changed from gray-yellow to the rusty red flecked with glittering minerals that produced the illusion in the last rays of the setting sun that the mountain ridge was bathed in flames.

It was here that Dogie made his first find. He had wandered off the track to investigate a little knoll off to one side.

"*Pijiu!*" he yelled as he bent over one side of the knoll, the word "beer" being the agreed-upon signal for a fossil find.

"Looks like Dogie's sniffed out a bone again," said Bert as they rushed over to see what he had discovered.

Dogie was squatting at the side of the knoll, brushing the dust off a hollow-eyed skull, about a foot long, with a parrotlike beak.

It was resting on a little pinnacle of sandstone, as if nature had neatly presented it to them as a gift.

"Now ain't that a purty sight," said Dogie, tilting back his Stetson to wipe his temple with his forearm. "An intact *Protoceratops* skull." With a flourish, he gave the skull a loving caress with his camel's-hair brush. "Just a settin' there, as plain as can be."

"I assume *Protoceratops* is a dinosaur," said Marsha.

"Yep," said Dogie. "*Protoceratops andrewsi.* Named after Roy Chapman Andrews, who found dozens of 'em in Mongolia. A horned dinosaur from the late Cretaceous. Not a big deal, but it's a good sign." He looked up at Orecchio. "How's that for a postage stamp, Gino?"

Orecchio scowled, his heavy black brows drawing together in annoyance.

Squatting down next to Dogie, Bert removed a knife from the holster on his belt, and scraped some encrusted sand from the jaw. "Flag it, Dogie, and we'll look for the rest later on," he said.

"Aye, aye, boss," said Dogie, with a salute.

Once Dogie had marked the site, they continued on. Another hundred feet or so up the mountain, the jeep track turned to the north. Ahead, the faint tracing of a footpath that must once have been used by pilgrims wound upward toward the reliquary stupa near the top of the ridge.

They paused here to rest. Bert removed a leather canteen from his pack and passed it around. As they drank, they looked out at Larry's camp, which was situated on a small plateau at the edge of a ravine. Though it was probably a hundred yards away, the clear morning air made it look much closer.

"My, my," said Dogie, who was studying the camp through a pair of binoculars. "Look who we've got here." He handed the binoculars to Bert, and pointed toward the camp. "Beyond Larry's camp. On the other side of the ridge and a little ways up. It looks like he's by himself."

Bert raised the binoculars to his eyes. "Bouchard!" he muttered. "Damn! I wonder how long he's been here."

"What is it?" asked Marsha, who sat on a rock next to Bert.

"There's a second camp," said Bert, handing her the glasses. "On the other side of the ravine." He pointed. "Hidden behind the ridge."

Marsha took a look and passed the binoculars to Charlotte, who could just make out the blue top of a small domed tent. Above the tent flew the red, white, and blue flag of France.

"It belongs to Jean-Jacques Bouchard. A French paleontologist."

"Larry must be madder than a wet hen," said Dogie.

"Why?" asked Charlotte.

"Bouchard's a parasite," Bert explained. "If this were the Gold Rush—which it is in a way, it's just a different kind of gold—you'd call him a claim jumper. He waits for another prospector to strike it rich, and then he moves in and starts picking out the choicest nuggets."

It was like lobstering, thought Charlotte. Woe betide the lobsterman who ventured to trespass on another's lobstering territory.

"That's the way the guy *has* to operate," said Dogie. "He couldn't find a fossil himself if he tripped over it. Now, scorpions are another story."

"Scorpions?" said Charlotte.

"Yeah, he's one of the world's reigning experts. A little interest that he picked up in the field. It just so happens that scorpions and dinosaur fossils occupy the same kind of territory."

"I wouldn't even mind him poaching on our territory," said Bert. "I feel a little sorry for the guy—there's something pretty pathetic about a fossil hunter who can't find fossil—except that he's such a bad scientist."

"In what way?" asked Charlotte. She was getting a small lesson in the sociology of dinosaur fossil hunting.

"A hundred years of progress in field technique, and he still behaves like a nineteenth-century fossil hunter out picking up specimens on a Sunday afternoon excursion," Bert explained. "In my mind, his most egregious sin—and he has many of them—is that he doesn't mark the place that he finds a bone."

"Meaning that you can't go back and find the rest of the skeleton?"

"Exactly. Or that you can't study the ground the fossil came from. He's a chronic violator of the first law of fossil collecting, which is 'If you're not going to mark the location, don't collect the fossil.' A fossil without a location is useless; you might as well throw it away."

"That is not his most egree—whatever—sin," said Dogie.

"What is?" asked Marsha.

"Destroyin' fossils. Rumor has it that he smashed the remainin' fossils at a site in Tanzania after he had picked out the best ones for himself," he said. "So a rival paleontologist wouldn't find them."

"We don't know for sure that he did that," said Bert.

Dogie made a face at Bert, mocking his goody-goody attitude.

"But aren't you all part of the same expedition?" asked Marsha.

"Yes. But we each have our territories, just like you and Victor divide up the manuscripts between the religious texts and the secular ones."

"I see," said Marsha. "And that ridge is the DMZ."

"You've got it. Larry tried to get Bouchard excluded from this expedition," he continued, with a sidelong glance at Peng, who stood a short distance away, out of earshot. "He wrote a letter to Peng describing some of Bouchard's more memorable stunts, and suggesting that he was an incompetent scientist."

"Needless to say, Bouchard wasn't too happy about it," added Dogie.

"But he's here," observed Marsha.

"Politics," said Dogie disgustedly.

Charlotte sat on a rock, sipping from Bert's canteen and studying Larry's camp. It looked more like a movie set. She had seen similar camps erected for indulgent directors in locations which, if they weren't quite as remote as this, were close to it. But that was the power of the studio, not a university.

"Yale must have a lot of money," she said, nodding at the camp as she passed the canteen over to Lisa.

"Not Yale," said Lisa. "Larry's family. He's one of *the* Fiskes. He uses his trust fund to fulfill his fantasies of the explorer's life. Hey, I'd do the same if I had the dough. Bert told you how Bouchard finds fossils; now let me tell you how Larry finds fossils. Or rather, *procures* fossils."

"How does he procure fossils?" prompted Charlotte.

"Not like Dogie—with his head swiveling from side to side like a mechanical doll and his body bent over in the paleontology stoop," Lisa said.

Dogie stuck his tongue out at her.

"Larry's technique involves the liberal distribution of cold, hard cash. His typical M.O. is to go to the market in whatever area it is in which he's looking for fossils, and put out the word that he's looking for old bones and that he'll pay cash for them. Then, he sits around and drinks tea for a couple of days and waits." She paused to take a long swig of water from the canteen. "Then, when somebody brings him some interesting-looking bones—which somebody invariably does—he asks them to lead him to the spot where they found them, and bingo, he's made a find. No sweat, no aching back, no sore feet."

"I think it's dishonest," said Dogie, with a good-natured grin.

"You're just jealous," teased Lisa.

"But he didn't do that here, did he?" asked Charlotte. "From what Peng said, you expected to find fossils here."

"Yes," replied Lisa. "But we didn't know exactly where." She waved an arm at the tortured landscape surrounding them. "He managed to find the fossil-bearing rock pretty fast. I'll bet you twenty to one that a week ago you could have found him in the Dunhuang bazaar passing out the yuan."

"Judging from what he said last night, his technique must have paid off," said Charlotte.

"We'll soon see," said Orecchio with a hint of skepticism.

A few minutes later they had reached the camp. The working area was a large tent whose sides had been rolled up to let in the breeze. There were three large tables and a mahogany camp desk, of the type from which Napolean might have commanded the troops at Waterloo. Behind the desk was a leather swivel chair. A bar tray held an assortment of fine liquors.

"How did he get all of this stuff out here?" asked Charlotte.

"Has it shipped," replied Lisa, flopping down in the swivel chair. "There's nothing that you can't accomplish if you have enough dough," she said as she spun herself around in the chair. "He had this same stuff in Tanzania, in Chile, in India. All the comforts of Abercrombie and Fitch."

Bert and Dogie wandered over to investigate some dinosaur bones that were spread out on the tables. There weren't many, but Larry had only been here a short time. Orecchio and Peng took seats in a pair of burgundy leather armchairs that were placed on an Oriental carpet in one corner of the tent.

"I wonder where everybody is?" asked Lisa.

"We're early," said Orecchio, checking his watch. "It's still only ten of. He'll probably be here any minute."

Standing at the side of the tent, Charlotte looked out at the campsite. In the middle was an old well sheltered by a stone hut. Arrayed around the well were other tents that served as kitchen, sleeping quarters, storeroom, and so on. A white Toyota Land Cruiser was parked at the center near the well.

As she was standing there, Charlotte suddenly became aware of a faint noise coming from the vicinity of a small tent set some distance away from the others, which from its position overlooking the valley she assumed to be Larry's. It sounded like the high-pitched beep of a household smoke alarm. Nearby was a tiny tent whose size and shape identified it as the latrine.

Using nature's call as an excuse, she set off down the hill to investigate where the noise was coming from.

As she approached the tent that she thought was Larry's, the beeping grew louder. On the other side, she suddenly came upon an elegant little tableau. A small table covered with a linen tablecloth held a silver tray with a crystal decanter of brandy and a brandy snifter. Next to the table were a canvas chair and a camp stove on which stood a pot of espresso. Finally, there was a telescope mounted on a stand for gazing at the desert sky. *There's nothing like a brandy and a cigar under the desert stars*, Bert had said as he reminisced about past digs with Larry.

But, it suddenly struck her, it was now almost ten o'clock. The tableau should have included coffee and croissants, not brandy and a telescope. All at once, she had a sense that something was very wrong. Bert had said that Larry had a cook and several retainers. Where were they? Then she noticed that some papers which must have come from one of the tables in the work tent had blown away and were scattered all over the campsite. If the retainers had been here, they should have picked them up. Also, an animal of some kind had gotten into the garbage.

The camp looked deserted, not just empty.

And why were the flaps of Larry's tent drawn? In this heat, it must have been stifling inside. The flaps of the other tents were all rolled up.

"Hello," she said, drawing closer. The beeping was coming from inside. No one answered. After a minute, she repeated herself. "Hello," she said again, this time a little louder. "Mr. Fiske?" Still no answer. Hesitantly, she opened the tent flap a crack. But it was too dark inside to see. Finally she drew it all the way back. The first thing she noticed was the white veil of a mosquito net draped over the cot. A necessity, she thought, as she waved away the mosquitoes that whined annoyingly around her head. As her eyes adjusted to the dimness, she realized that she wasn't alone: a man was lying face-up on the cot under the mosquito netting. Moving closer, she took in his elegant silk paisley pajamas, like those the movie stars of her era used to wear for lounging around their elegant on-screen apartments. Then her horrified eyes unwillingly registered the rest: the man was Larry, and he was dead. His mouth was open and his face was contorted in a gruesome expression, like those of the gargoyles that adorned the roof ridges of Chinese temples. He must have been stabbed in the chest. The gold silk of his pajama top had a dark red bloodstain in the center. The smell of the fresh blood was metallic, like the end of a freshly sheared copper pipe.

Suddenly, the air in the tent felt unbearably close and hot. She recognized the feeling: it was the same one that still sometimes overcame her on stage, the feeling that turned her legs into mush and her voice into a feeble croak. There it was called stage fright; here it was just plain panic. *Time to get out of here*. A second later, she was standing outside the tent, hanging onto the tent pole and gasping for breath.

Beep, beep, beep, beep.

It was the travel alarm clock on Larry's bedside table. Taking a deep breath, she went back into the tent, and pushed the alarm button down. The beeping stopped. *There, that was better. Much better*. Next to the clock on the bedside table lay a wallet made of alligator hide. Only the finest: "eat well, dress well, sleep well" was his motto. Sticking out of the wallet was a thick wad of Chinese money. The motive wasn't robbery, then.

Outside again. *Breathe deeply*. Inhale: *one, two, three four, five*. Exhale: *one, two, three, four, five*. Again. Gradually, her breathing returned to normal, and her heart stopped fluttering like a caged bird in her chest.

Overhead, one of the big black birds she had seen circling over the foothills soared on an updraft from the valley floor. Though it had looked small from a distance, she now realized that it was enormous; its wingspread must have been well over six feet. She also realized from its great hooked beak what kind of bird it was.

A vulture.

It was Orecchio who notified public security, which was the Chinese equivalent of the police. He'd offered to jog back to the guest house, and called from there. A young police officer named Ho wearing a dirty white-jacketed uniform met them in the guest house reception room shortly after their return. He had a thin black mustache which Charlotte assumed was supposed to look William Powell-ish, but actually looked more like a pair of tadpoles having a tête-à-tête under his nose. The reception room was identical to all the others they had visited in China— at the art museum in Shanghai, at the cloisonné factory in Guangzhou, at the embroidery shop in Beijing: brass spittoons in the corners; photographs of a smiling Zhou Enlai and a stone-faced Hua Guofeng on the walls; and overstuffed chairs clad in ill-fitting slipcovers, the back and arms protected by crocheted doilies, spaced with geometric precision around the perimeter of the room. A large floor fan in one corner whirred, creating the illusion of coolness. They each took a chair: their party of six; Ho, looking appropriately officious; and his earnest young assistant, who had slightly crossed eyes that blinked every few seconds, like those of a turtle basking in the sunshine. After a few minutes, they were joined by Chu, who wore a dark gray Mao suit that matched the frames of his heavy, thick-lensed eyeglasses as well as his hair, which stood up stiffly in the severe style favored by the cadres, as Party officials were called. He held a cigarette between the thumb and forefinger of his one remaining hand, like a gangster in a Grade B gangster movie. Occasionally, he leaned back to spit into a cuspidor in the corner behind him. As they all drank steaming cups of bitter green tea from lidded cups, Ho asked a few questions: the name of the victim, the location of the camp, the purpose of their visit. Then, after notifying them that he would probably want to talk with them again, he got into a police jeep and sped off into the desert toward the Mountain of the Three Dangers.

The interview was disappointing. Charlotte had the feeling that something more should have happened. The police didn't seem to care. To them, Larry was just another foreign national who had had the temerity to inconvenience them by being murdered on Chinese soil. Never mind that he was a Fiske, that he was a paleontologist from Yale, that he was a man of vigor and imagination. That didn't mean anything to them. After the interview, there was little else to do but carry on. They adjourned to the dining hall for lunch, but Larry's murder had robbed them of their appetites. And the few bites they were able to get down were interrupted every few minutes by the other guests. The word was out that an American paleontologist had been murdered in the desert, and foreigners and Chinese alike were curious. The waiters stood around in little knots at the edges of the room, looking on as the other guests came forward with their questions. When did it happen? What's going to happen next? Who will conduct the investigation? The only person who was able to reply to any of them was Peter, whose years of foreign travel had left him with a good knowledge of official procedure in such situations. The investigation would be conducted by the Chinese police, he told them. The State Department had no authority to interfere, but they would probably send out an official to handle other arrangements, such as notifying Larry's family of the death and transporting the body back to the States. As for the most frequently asked question—Who do you think did it?—nobody had the slightest idea.

After lunch, Marsha went off to study her manuscripts, and Charlotte retired to her room. She felt as if she was coming down with the flu. Her throat was scratchy and her lungs were congested. She was upset about Larry's death: it had been horrible, seeing him lying dead like that on his cot, the bloody stab wound in his enormous chest. But her sickness was more than a reaction to that. It was also a reaction to the desert dust. Marsha had warned her that "China catarrh" was common among tourists, as well as among the Chinese themselves, many of whom routinely wore face masks. Everyone in China always seemed to be coughing up phlegm, and cuspidors could be found in every hallway and corner. Her guidebook had suggested that tourists take along antihistamines, and she took one now. She wanted to feel better for her first cave tour, which was in a half hour. Though it seemed disrespectful somehow to take part in an art tour on the afternoon of the day she had found Larry's body, she had nothing else to do but sit around in her stifling room, and a tour might help get her mind off his death. It was to be a tour of Cave 17, the cave in which Sir Aurel Stein had found the secret library. The lecture was to be given by Victor Danowski. In return for the invitation to study at Dunhuang, the Chinese authorities had asked that the scholars from the Oriental Institute aid them in promoting tourism by giving lectures to the tourists who arrived daily by the busload from the hotels in "Dunhuang town," as it was called to distinguish it from the location of the caves.

Three minibuses were pulling up outside the guest house just as Charlotte was setting out for the caves a short while later. The first two held tourists who were arriving for the trip to the cave; and the third was the shuttle bus that the guest house provided for the convenience of guests and staff. Emily was just getting off the shuttle bus as Charlotte emerged from the compound gate. Though Emily had disembarked right behind Ned, they gave no sign of knowing each other. If they were an item, Charlotte imagined that they would have to be very discreet. She had just been reading in the English language edition of the *People's Daily*, the Communist Party organ, about a Chinese woman who was jailed for "incitement to debauchery" as a result of her relations with a French diplomat.

Emily fell easily into step next to Charlotte on the road that led to the foot of the cliff. "Are you taking the tour of the secret library?" she asked.

"Yes," said Charlotte.

"Oh, good," she said sweetly. "I am going to be your guide."

"You speak excellent English," said Charlotte. "Ned told me last night that you studied at London University."

At the mention of Ned's name, a blush crept up the girl's lovely throat. "Thank you," she said. "I would like very much to study in the United States some day. In New England, preferably. I am a great admirer of the Massachusetts poet Emily Dickinson. Are you familiar with her poetry?" she asked.

"Yes," said Charlotte. "In fact, I have a volume of her poems with me." Charlotte always brought poetry to read on trips. She had long ago learned that she would never finish a novel, and poems had the virtue of being conducive to the kind of pleasant thoughts that brought sleep to the jet-lagged.

"You do!" said Emily, her brown eyes opening wide in excitement at coming across another fan of her favorite poet.

She wore a demure embroidered blouse of white silk with a black bow at the throat, and black cloth shoes with white anklets. If she had been wearing a long black skirt instead of the standard-issue baggy black pants, her outfit could have come from the closet of the reclusive poet from Amherst.

"I would like very much to talk with you about her sometime," she continued as they joined the tourists who had gathered at the gate in the fence at the foot of the cliff: German conservators, Japanese monks, Chinese from Hong Kong, and a couple of groups of American and Australian visitors.

"I would like that very much as well," Charlotte replied.

Excusing herself, Emily went in search of Victor, leaving Charlotte to browse at the souvenir stand, whose odd assortment of merchandise included painted silk fans, plaster casts of the Venus de Milo, reproductions of the terra-cotta warriors form Xian, and Santa Clauses playing electric guitars.

She was about to buy a rice-paper rubbing of a Tang horse for her step-granddaughter, Marsha's brother's daughter, when she was accosted by one of the Australian tourists—a plump woman with gray bangs and a sun visor.

"Pardon me," the woman said. "Has anyone ever told you that you look just like the movie star—what's her name?—the one who was married to Gary Corbett."

Charlotte had been married four times, but people only seemed to remember Gary. He was the only one of her husbands who had been a movie star. The fact that he had also been a drunkard and a womanizer was forgotten—even, sometimes, by her. "Do you mean Charlotte Graham?" she asked.

"Yes," the woman said. "That's the one."

"Not only do I look like Charlotte Graham," she said with a smile, "I *am* Charlotte Graham." She was accustomed to being mistaken for herself by fans who couldn't quite believe that they were face to face with the real article.

The woman stared at her, her large gray eyes opening wide in amazement. "No!" she said. "You're having me on."

"Here it is, right here," she said, pointing at the name on the traveler's check she was using to pay for the rubbing.

"Oh, my God," the woman hooted, peering over Charlotte's shoulder at the check. "I have to tell my friend. I'll be right back." She stuck out her hand. "Vivian Gormley. Nice to meet you." Then she turned to find her friend.

Mercifully, Victor arrived before Vivian could return. Charlotte was tolerant of her fans. More than tolerant: she loved them; they had brought her great happiness and success. But in a situation like this one, where she couldn't easily get away, she preferred anonymity.

"Hello, everyone," said Victor, taking a position at the head of the group. "My name is Victor Danowski, and I'll be your lecturer this afternoon. This is Emily Lin, our guide. We're going to visit the secret library, which is located at the other end of the cave complex." He pointed to the north. "Follow me, please."

With Victor setting a brisk pace, the group took off down the avenue that ran along the foot of the cliff. Every so often there was a sign with an arrow which directed them to the "Secret Library."

After perhaps half a mile, Victor paused at the foot of a staircase leading up to the caves.

"Here we are," he said. "Before we go up, I want to tell you a bit about the caves we are about to see: Cave 16 and the secret library, Cave 17. Cave 17 opens off of Cave 16, which is much larger. It was discovered in 1899 by a monk named Wang Yuan-lu who had taken refuge in the caves after fleeing a famine in his native province. Impressed by the artworks and saddened by their neglect, Wang made it his personal mission to restore the caves to their former glory. He was setting up some newly made statues in the cave now known as Cave 16 when he noticed a crack in one of the frescoed walls. Seeing that the space behind the crack was hollow, he opened up the wall and discovered a small room filled with ancient manuscripts and paintings that had been hidden away sometime during the eleventh century, for reasons that are still unclear. The most popular theory is that they were hidden to protect them from an imminent invasion by a barbarian tribe of Tibetan origin."

Charlotte tried to concentrate on the lecture, but her mind kept returning to Larry's murder. It seemed to her that he must have been killed early that morning. He hadn't been dead for long—that much was clear from the fresh smell of the blood. She also doubted that he had awakened: there were no signs of struggle, and there wasn't even much blood, a sign that he had died quickly. "Dead men don't bleed," a detective had once told her. It appeared to have been a simple death. She guessed that the murderer had simply stolen into the sleeping man's tent and stabbed him in the chest. With a knife, she presumed, though the murder weapon was missing. She hadn't noticed it in the tent, and, though she had kept an eye out on her way back to the work tent, she hadn't seen it. She had been reluctant to look around too much for fear of disturbing the scene. She had learned that much from her experience with police work. Don't walk around, and don't touch anything. She had made the mistake of tampering with the weapon in the first murder case she had been involved in. She had rotated the barrel of the revolver to see if there were bullets left in any of the chambers, and gotten her fingerprints all over the murder weapon. But she could be forgiven in that case: she was the person who had fired the bullet, killing her co-star on stage in the murder scene in a Broadway play. The killer had substituted a real bullet for the blank in the stage prop. Once she had realized that it was real blood oozing from the wound in Geoffrey's chest, her first impulse had been to check the barrel. She couldn't quite believe that the bullet that had killed him had come from her gun.

Now she was party to another murder. In Geoffrey's case, it had been clear to her from the outset that the murderer was his lover, whom he had recently jilted for someone else. It had simply been a matter of gathering the evidence to put him behind bars. This was a different matter.

"Okay," said Victor after he had answered some questions from the audience. "Onward to Cave 16. I'll tell you about Sir Aurel Stein when we get to the top." Turning, he led the way up the rock-cut staircase.

The cave was the lowest in a group of three, one on top of the other. It was sheltered by an entrance façade that was similar to that of the Cave of Unequaled Height but not as grand: a glazed tile roof with upturned eaves supported by red-painted columns. After climbing the stairs, the group assembled in the cave, which Emily had unlocked with a key from a big iron key ring. The cave was quite large and was elaborately painted with figures of Bodhisattvas, which Victor defined as Buddhist deities who had postponed Nirvana in order to help others on the path to enlightenment. A group of garishly painted statues—Buddhas, Bodhisattvas, and guardian warriors—occupied a horseshoe-shaped dais at the back of the cave. These must have been the statues that Wang had been setting up when he had accidentally discovered the secret library. An opening in the wall on their right appeared to be the entrance to the secret library.

Victor stood in front of the dais, the light from the entrance illuminating his pale face. Flanking him were Emily and Chu, who had also joined the tour. "Now we come to Stein," he said, picking up the thread of the story. "Sir Aurel Stein was a British explorer of Hungarian descent who had already made several expeditions to Central Asia when he visited the caves in 1907. Upon his arrival, he heard a rumor about a hidden deposit of ancient manuscripts. He was eager to question Wang about this, but Wang was away on a begging trip. Returning to the caves a few months later, after the monk had returned, Stein decided on a two-pronged strategy to gain Wang's confidence. The first was to express admiration for his efforts at restoring the caves." Victor turned to point at the statues. "If you'll take a look at the statues behind me, which Wang commissioned as part of his restoration, you'll see that this must have required more than a bit of dissimulation. The second strategy was to draw parallels between his own explorations and those of the Chinese monk Hsuan-tsang, who had made a pilgrimage to India in the seventh century. It was the second strategy that bore fruit. As it turned out, Hsuan-tsang was Wang's patron saint, and Stein's reference to the beloved monk convinced Wang that he should show Stein a sample manuscript from the secret library. By fortuitous coincidence—"

"Fortuitous for the British, disastrous for the Chinese," interjected Chu. He went on: "I would also like at this point to correct any mistaken impressions that it was the British so-called explorer Aurel Stein who discovered the library. As Comrade Danowski's lecture has made very clear, the library's discoverer was the Chinese monk Wang Yuan-lu."

Victor continued with a look of patient forbearance. He had no choice but to be placatory; he was there only on the sufferance of the Chinese. "By a coincidence that was fortuitous for the British and disastrous for the Chinese, the manuscript that Wang picked at random from the thousands in the cave turned out to be a sutra that Hsuan-tsang had translated himself from originals that he had brought back from India. Impressed by this auspicious omen, the priest proceeded to open the secret library to Stein."

"Now I'll read you the pertinent section from Stein's journal," Victor continued. Removing a sheet of paper from a folder, he proceeded to read from the entry in Stein's diary: " 'The sight the small room disclosed was one to make my eyes open. Heaped up in layers, but without any order, there appeared in the dim light of the priest's little lamp a solid mass of manuscript bundles rising to a height of nearly ten feet, and filling, as subsequent measurement showed, close to five hundred cubic feet.' It was," Victor interjected, "one of the most fabulous archaeological discoveries"—he looked over at Chu—"correction: *finds*, of the twentieth century. Each night," Victor continued, "Wang would remove a bundle of manuscripts and take them to Stein for further study. Meanwhile, Stein and his group were discussing—"

"They weren't discussing, they were plotting," interrupted Chu.

Victor gave his goatee a nervous little tug, and went on. "They . . . plotted . . . how to convince Wang to sell them the manuscripts."

Charlotte could see that this was going to be a very tedious lecture if Chu was going to keep translating it into ideologically pure language. But Victor, who seemed to be accustomed to the interruptions, kept on, somehow managing to ignore Chu without appearing to challenge his authority.

"Finally," Victor continued, "Stein managed to convince Wang to allow him to remove some of the manuscripts to a 'certain temple of learning in the distant West,' which was, of course, the British Museum. In exchange, he offered Wang a donation of silver for the restoration of the caves."

"In other words, he bribed Wang," said Chu.

Victor ignored him. "In all, Stein carried off twenty-four cases of manuscripts—thirteen thousand in all—and five cases of paintings, embroideries, and other art objects to the British Museum."

"The monk sold the cultural heritage of China to the foreign imperialists for a hundred and thirty pounds," said Chu calmly.

Charlotte was getting tired of Chu's interruptions. He had made his point. Why not let Victor get on with it? Chu himself must have been getting tired, for, after this last comment, he turned and left, much to their relief. Victor diplomatically refrained from saying anything, but it was clear that Emily was glad that her boss had decided to give them a break.

The lecture now proceeded uninterrupted.

"As you may know, the prize of Stein's haul was the oldest printed book known to mankind: the *Diamond Sutra*, which was printed in 868 A.D. It is now on display in the British Museum." Victor went on to relate the rest of the story: "The next year, another Western explorer, the French Sinologist Paul Pelliot, also persuaded Wang to sell him several cases of artworks and manuscripts; these are now in the collections of the Louvre and the Bibliothèque National in Paris. Pelliot was followed by explorers from Russia, Japan, and the United States. When the Chinese government heard about the foreigners' purchases, they demanded that Wang ship the remainder of the contents of the secret library to Beijing. But Wang distrusted the government, and justifiably so. Only a few of those manuscripts ever made it to the capital; the rest were lost or pilfered by corrupt officials along the way. In fact, they still turn up from time to time at rare book dealers."

"Imagine that," said Vivian Gormley in a loud voice.

"I saw one in Finland just last year," Victor commented. "But the story doesn't end there. As it turned out, Wang hadn't turned all of the remaining manuscripts over to the government. He had shrewdly held back a nest egg of manuscripts that he considered of special value, and when Stein returned several years later, he was able to buy another six hundred manuscripts. After that, the door was closed to Western explorers, but that wasn't the end of the discovery of ancient manuscripts at Dunhuang. Last year, a Chinese art student who had been restoring a sculpture of an earth god accidentally discovered a cache of manuscripts that had been sealed inside the sculpture's belly. It appears that these manuscripts had been hidden there by Wang prior to his discovery of the secret library. It was to translate some of these recently discovered manuscripts that the Chinese authorities invited me and my colleague, Marsha Lundstrom, to Dunhuang."

Victor replaced the sheet with the entry from Stein's diary in his folder. "Are there any questions?" he asked.

"Yes," said the inquisitive Vivian. "Are there any other manuscripts still hidden away?" She waved an arm at the statues of Buddhas and Bodhisattvas on the dais. "Inside these statues, for instance?"

"No one knows," he replied. "There are twenty-four hundred statues at Dunhuang." Flicking on his flashlight, he aimed the beam at the hole in the right-hand wall of the cave. "Now we'll take a look at the secret library."

·6·

"WE'LL GO INTO the secret library one at a time," Victor announced. "Then I'll tell you some more about the scholarly significance of the contents. And then we'll talk about the frescoes of Dunhuang in general"—he waved an arm at the murals on the walls—"and of this cave in particular."

One by one, the members of the group stepped up to the hole in the cave wall. "It's only a hole" and "there's nothing there" was the theme of their reactions. They were right, Charlotte discovered when her turn came. It was indeed an empty cubicle about ten feet square by ten feet high with some Buddhist frescoes on the walls. But to call it only a hole was a bit like calling the Parthenon only a pile of marble, she thought, as she tried to imagine what it must have been like for Stein to look upon the enormous cache of ancient manuscripts. Instead, the image that floated to the surface of her mind was that of Larry's body. The still, dusty air inside the cave reminded her of the still, dusty air inside the tent, and she found herself overcome by the urge to bolt. She felt as if she would faint if she stayed in the cave a second longer. It was the same feeling that sometimes overcame her when traffic was backed up in the Lincoln Tunnel.

Lowering her head, she climbed back through the hole and made her way through the group to Victor and Emily. After mumbling an apology, she excused herself and left the cave. Outside, she descended the rock staircase and took a seat on the nearest bench, which was already occupied by Chu. Lowering her head between her knees, she took a couple of deep, slow breaths, and felt the wave of faintness slowly recede.

"Are you feeling better?" asked Chu after she had raised her head back up.

"Yes, thank you," she replied.

"The caves sometimes have the effect of making people feel faint. I have felt faint on a number of occasions in the caves myself. Especially when I am not feeling well anyway."

He had the rattly breathing of the heavy smoker, and Charlotte suspected that he probably had emphysema. She nodded. "I think it was seeing Mr. Fiske's body this morning." She tried to explain: "Being inside the cave was like being inside his tent. The air in the tent . . ."

Chu raised his hand as if to say, *Don't trouble yourself.* Then he cleared his throat and spat on the pavement.

Charlotte found the spitting habits of the Chinese disgusting. But they weren't surprising. In addition to being constantly subjected to the dusty air, the Chinese all smoked like chimneys.

The broad-faced Chu stared silently out at the cliff wall, his sandal-clad feet planted squarely on the ground and his Mao jacket tightly buttoned up to his neck. "Where are you from in the United States?" he asked after a while.

"I live in New York now, but I'm originally from New England—the state of Connecticut. Have you heard of it?"

Chu nodded his head. "I have a son who's studying at Boston University. He's a mathematics major there. He'll be returning to Dunhuang for the summer tomorrow night. He'll be working as a guide at the caves."

"How very nice. Do you have connections in the United States, then?" She added: "I thought you might because of your name." Western names were becoming popular in China as a result of liberalization—Emily was a typical example—but George Chu belonged to another generation.

"No. No connections. George is the homonym for my Chinese name. I prefer to use it in the company of Westerners. I was educated at an American missionary school," he explained. "It was there that I picked up the nickname. That was before Liberation, of course."

Charlotte said nothing. She had already discovered that it was futile to press the Chinese when it came to details about their pasts.

But Chu went on to answer her unspoken question: "I come from a bad class background," he said.

He said it matter-of-factly, as if saying "I come from the Midwest."

"My family were supporters of the reactionary Kuomintang regime," he continued. "My father was one of the officers responsible for overseeing the transfer of China's national art treasures from Szechuan, where they were stored during the Sino-Japanese War, to the National Palace Museum."

The irony of Chu's confidence wasn't lost on Charlotte: the man who had been railing against Stein for removing artworks from the caves at Dunhuang was the son of the man who had been at least partly responsible for removing China's greatest art treasures to Taipei.

"We visited there on our way to the People's Republic," said Charlotte. She had marveled at the fabulous embroideries, paintings, bronzes, and jades that had once belonged to the collection of the imperial court at Beijing.

"Then you can understand the magnitude of my father's crime against his country. For this crime I spent eleven years in a reform-through-labor camp. I assembled radios in a factory—ten hours a day, six days a week. In my spare time I studied the works of Chairman Mao."

"I'm very sorry," said Charlotte.

"There is nothing to be sorry about." He removed a pack of cigarettes from his pocket and shook one loose. "As a result of my reeducation, I was able to develop my socialist awareness. By learning from the workers, I gradually came to understand the crimes of my class, and was able to shake off the shackles of my bourgeois reactionary upbringing."

As he raised the pack of cigarettes to his lips, Charlotte noticed that his wrist bore deep, ugly scars, the kind that, in a man who had spent so many years in prison, could only have come from the chafing of manacles, and she realized with a shiver of horror that his other arm had probably been lost to some sort of festering wound.

"I expected the Communists to execute me," Chu continued as he lit his cigarette, "but they treated me very well. After I was rehabilitated, the Party gave me a good education. I am very lucky to have the opportunity to make up for the past errors of my family in my current position. I owe a boundless debt of gratitude to the Party."

Charlotte was astonished at how lightly he wrote off the eleven years he had lost to political upheaval, to say nothing of the loss of his arm. She supposed he was better off than some, better off than many, in fact: he was alive, and he had come out of his ordeal with an enviable career. But she suspected that his soul bore scars that ran much deeper than the angry purple brands on his wrist.

There were a dozen questions she wanted to ask him. Why hadn't he fled to Taiwan with the Kuomintang? What had been the fate of his family? What had it been like to be imprisoned in a reform-through-labor camp for eleven years? But she knew there was no point in pursuing this subject. By now, she had been in China long enough to know that once the ideological lingo started to flow, the door of communication had been shut. He reminded her of the fierce-visaged warriors in the cave. It was as if a chink of his armor had momentarily fallen out, revealing a soft yellow spot of tender flesh.

She searched her mind for a safe topic of conversation. She wanted to maintain her rapport with this man. Though now wasn't the time, she wanted at some point to talk with him about the Oglethorpe sculpture, and specifically, to ask him to return it if it should reappear at Dunhuang. She finally settled on artworks. "I would like very much to see the artworks from Dunhuang in the British Museum some day," she said.

"You can't," he replied, removing the cigarette from between his lips with his thumb and forefinger. He smoked mechanically, without pleasure.

Charlotte looked over at him in surprise. "What do you mean?"

"There is only one artwork on display: an embroidered temple banner. And of course the frontispiece of their most precious piece of booty, the *Diamond Sutra*. The rest is in storage. In 1914, they had an exhibit. If you want to see these things, you have to buy the catalogue from the exhibit." His voice was deeply bitter. "Two volumes. Two hundred pounds a volume."

"But there must be hundreds of artworks from Dunhuang in their collection," said Charlotte.

Chu nodded. "There are. In fact, the British Museum is in possession of so many art treasures that it cannot possibly display them all. So they are stored in the basement." He shrugged. "It is ironic, is it not? They were unearthed by Stein in Dunhuang only to be buried again in Bloomsbury."

In a way, Charlotte wasn't surprised. The nineteenth-century explorers, especially the British ones, had been acquisitive. Their goal had been to bring back as much plunder as possible from foreign lands for the greater glory of the Crown. Never mind actually appreciating it.

"For this, Stein was knighted," Chu added bitterly. For a moment, he smoked silently. "I myself am only familiar with the treasures of Dunhuang from the British Museum's catalogue," he added.

For a moment, Charlotte thought she saw a flicker of—what was it: yearning, hope, anticipation?—in the impassive eyes behind the thick lenses.

"It is my dream to see these treasures some day for myself."

The diplomatic representative from the United States embassy in Beijing, whose name was Bill Reynolds, arrived the next morning. Though he was really a cultural attaché, he had been drafted to attend to the details of Larry's death because he had happened to be in Ürümqi, the capital of the neighboring province of Xinjiang, on business, and was therefore able to get to Dunhuang in only twenty-four hours instead of the usual two or three days. Upon his arrival, he convened a meeting of American nationals in the reception room, at which he reassured them that the State Department was at their service to protect their interests and to handle any problems that might arise in connection with Larry's death. In other words, the State Department would stand behind them if they ran into any problems with the police. He also informed them that he would be making arrangements for the transportation of Larry's body back to the States (it was now at the People's Mortuary in Dunhuang), and for the disposition of the contents of his camp and his room at the guest house, as soon as the body and belongings were released by the police. He also filled them in on the police investigation. He had just come from the Public Security Bureau where a local man was being held in connection with the murder. Apparently, a portable high-tech shortwave radio that had been stolen from Larry's campsite had been found in his possession. Though the local man claimed a foreigner had given it to him, the police were holding him for the murder.

"If anyone has any further information regarding Larry's death, I'll be happy to convey it to the proper authorities," Reynolds concluded.

* * *

"How did he lose his arm?" Marsha asked.

They were eating lunch: Charlotte, Marsha, Peter, Lisa, and Victor. The discussion was about Chu, who had sat in on the meeting with Reynolds, chain-smoking as usual. The only time he had stopped was to spit into the cuspidor.

"In prison, as a result of being manacled," Peter replied. "It was a common form of torture to keep people manacled with their hands behind their backs for months on end. Their wrists would become infected from the chafing, which sometimes resulted in the amputation of the lower arm."

"How horrible," said Lisa with a shudder.

"What was he imprisoned for?" asked Marsha.

"For being a class enemy. Translation: for being rich."

"Is being rich a crime worthy of imprisonment?"

"In Communist China, it is. Or rather, was. Even being a poor relation of a class enemy was considered a crime."

Marsha was disbelieving. "There must have been something more than that."

"There was," said Charlotte. "I talked with him about it yesterday."

The table's attention turned to her.

"His father was an officer in the Kuomintang, or rather, the reactionary Kuomintang regime, as he put it. He was the officer who was responsible for making the arrangements to transfer China's national art treasures from the Palace Museum collection to Taipei."

"Oh, I see," said Marsha. "But he must not be considered a class enemy any longer if he has this job."

"No," said Charlotte. "He's been rehabilitated." She spoke facetiously: "He's very grateful to the Party for his present job, in which he feels he can make amends for the past errors of his family."

"I wouldn't be surprised if he were a radish," said Peter in his supercilious voice.

Charlotte was damned if she would ask what a radish was.

"What's a radish?" asked Lisa.

"Someone who's red on the outside and white on the inside."

They smiled at the aptness of the expression. But Charlotte was convinced that however white Chu might once have been, he was now red to the core.

Reynolds arrived at the same time as the first course: the long noodles—literally, "dough strings"—that were the local staple. If ever the appearance of a State Department official could be counted upon to be reassuring, it would be his. He was a tall, thin man with smiling blue eyes and a gracious smile.

"I recognized you in the reception room," he said to Charlotte. "I've always wanted to meet you. Ever since I saw you in *Dark Journey* when I was about eleven. I fell in love with you then, and I've been in love with you ever since. But I'd appreciate it if you didn't let on to my wife of thirty-five years."

"I won't," she said, returning his handshake. In his khaki chinos and green- and white-checked short-sleeved shirt, he looked about as out of place on the southern fringe of the Gobi as a Chinese nomad would have looked sipping a gin and tonic on a Connecticut patio.

"May I join you?" he asked. "There's something I'd like to speak with you about. In addition to Fiske's death, that is."

"By all means," Charlotte responded, indicating a vacant seat. "This is my stepdaughter, Marsha Lundstrom," she said, as Reynolds extended his hand. "And the travel writer, Peter Hamilton."

"Oh, yes," said Reynolds, shaking Peter's hand as well. "I've read some of your books. Enjoyed them enormously. Are you working on a book here?"

"Yes," Peter replied. "It's to be called *Sand-Buried Treasures of Desert Cathay*. About the role of Western explorers on the Silk Road."

"For or against?" asked Reynolds as he took a seat.

"For, of course. If Stein and the others hadn't hauled off the artworks from Dunhuang, they'd probably have been lost. I'm leaving tomorrow to visit the caves at Bezeklik, which are very similar to those at Dunhuang, except that hardly a statue was left standing after the Red Guards got through with them."

"The stories of the destruction are horrifying," said Reynolds.

"And not only by the Red Guards," added Victor. "The Moslem iconoclasts were just as bad, if not worse. I visited a series of cave temples where every fresco that hadn't been removed by the Germans had been horribly defaced by the Moslems; there wasn't a single face of the Buddha that hadn't been slashed."

Peter nodded. "At Bezeklik the peasants scraped the pigment of the frescoes off the walls to use as fertilizer. In my eyes," he went on, "the Westerners who rescued the art from these caves are heroes."

"Don't let Chu hear you say that," said Victor. "He'd kick you out of here before you could say 'The East is Red.' "

After being formally introduced to Lisa and Victor, Reynolds helped himself to food from some of the dishes which had been served, and which included, in addition to the noodles, fried rice and a couple of vegetable dishes.

"Meat seems to be in short supply here," said Charlotte as she passed him a dish of her favorite green beans in garlic sauce.

"It's not that it's in short supply; it's the lack of refrigeration. Slaughtering a sheep or a pig in the summer is a chancy undertaking. Have you tried the local melon, yet?" he asked.

Charlotte described how they had been greeted with juicy slices of the local muskmelon. "I've been told their sweetness is due to the properties of the local soil and water," she said.

Reynolds nodded. "Dunhuang is famous for its melons, and for its grapes. During the Tang Dynasty the melons were shipped by camel caravan to the imperial court at Xian, where they were prized as a delicacy. In fact, this area used to be known as the 'sand and melon county.' "

"What is it that you wanted to talk with me about?" asked Charlotte, who'd had enough polite talk about melons.

"Two matters, actually," he said, nibbling on the green beans, which he held expertly between the tips of his chopsticks. "The first is *The Crucible*."

For a moment, Charlotte was stumped. "You mean Arthur Miller's play?"

Reynolds nodded. "I saw you in the original Broadway production. In 1954, I think it was."

"It was 1953. From January to June. I thought everyone had forgotten that fiasco." Charlotte had played Elizabeth Proctor, the Salem wife who is jailed and finally hanged as a witch. The play had closed after only six months. The critics had dismissed it as an anti-McCarthy polemic.

"I could never understand why it closed so fast."

"Spineless critics. Nobody wanted to go out on a limb to praise a play that they interpreted as a political diatribe against McCarthyism. They were afraid they might end up in front of the House Un-American Activities Committee, or worse."

"Pretty sad commentary," said Reynolds.

"Pretty sad time," said Charlotte. She had never been directly affected, thank God. Though she had always appeared in a wide variety of roles, her public image was inextricably linked to the elegant, sophisticated women she had played in her most famous ones. The idea that she could ever have been a Communist would have struck even the most zealous red-baiter as ridiculous. Others she knew hadn't been so lucky. They had been forced to take the stand to answer what the House interrogators had nicknamed the Sixty-four Dollar Question, after the radio quiz program that was popular at the time: "Are you now, or have you ever been, a member of the Communist party?"

Reynolds nodded in agreement.

"What about *The Crucible*?" she asked. Though the original production hadn't been successful, the play had gone on to a long and critically acclaimed off-Broadway run several years later, after the McCarthy issue had subsided, and had since come to be considered an American classic.

"The Chinese Academy of Dramatic Arts wants to mount a production. They're looking for an American actor or director to serve as their adviser. The director of the Academy called me last week to ask if there was anyone I could recommend, and today I run into you; it seems like fate."

"You are fated to make friends in China," said Marsha.

Marsha was right. Kitty's reading from the *I Ching* was coming true again. She explained to Reynolds about the reading, and how it had predicted that she was fated to make friends in a certain "sphere of activity" that would lead to a more permanent connection with the foreign country she was about to visit.

"Well, here's your chance," said Reynolds. "It will be a first—the first time a play by an American playwright will be staged in the People's Republic of China with a Chinese cast. What do you say?"

Here was the intellectual challenge she was looking for, Charlotte thought. The idea of putting on *The Crucible* before a Chinese audience was thrilling to her. "I don't speak a word of Chinese," she said. Actually she spoke three phrases: "Hello," "Thank you," and "How much?" Along with "Where is the toilet?" they were all one needed to know in any language.

"Doesn't matter. There will be translators."

"Tell me more," Charlotte demanded eagerly. "Beginning to end. Everything you know. I would absolutely *love* to do this."

"The idea is the brainchild of Nan-sung Kong, the director of the Chinese Academy of Dramatic Arts," said Reynolds, slurping up the dough-strings. "He's an avant-garde director, to the extent that China has an avant-garde."

"What's he like?"

"Very enthusiastic, very creative, very emotional. More like an American than a Chinese, I'd say. And certainly not like a native of Beijing, who are known for their reserve."

"Where and when?"

"In Beijing. The production is scheduled for next summer. But the work would have to begin before that—in the late spring."

"Has the project been approved? Somehow I can't imagine the Party endorsing a play about the Salem witch trials."

"So far, so good," said Reynolds. "China has changed a lot in the last few years. It's changed so quickly that I sometimes can't believe it myself," he added. "Who would have thought a few years ago that enterprising peasants would be getting rich, but it's happening."

"I've been amazed at the variety of goods in the free markets," said Marsha, who had often commented in the changes since her last visit.

"There are a lot of things you can buy at the free markets now that you can't buy anywhere else. It's astounding to think that only a few years ago free markets were banned. We could see a new phase coming, but we weren't expecting this. It's a little frightening."

"Why frightening?" Marsha asked.

"Because it's changed so fast in the four years since the new economic policies were introduced in 1980 that it's impossible to predict where it's going to go. None of the new rights that the people are enjoying are guaranteed. They're all bonuses that could be taken away tomorrow."

"You mean, another crackdown is in the offing?" asked Charlotte.

"Probably. The political atmosphere reminds me of that in the fifties during Mao's campaign to encourage intellectuals to suggest ways in which the work of the Party could be improved. His slogan for that campaign was 'Let a hundred flowers bloom, let a hundred schools of thought contend.'"

"What happened?" asked Charlotte.

"It was followed the next year by the Anti-Rightist Campaign in which the intellectuals who had spoken out were all thrown in jail. They had made the mistake of taking Mao at his word."

"Well, if the crackdown does come, let's hope it's not the production of *The Crucible* that sets it off," she said.

For a while, they chatted about the proposed production. That it would take place was by no means a certainty. There were a lot of contingencies: if they could get the space, if the Chinese actors whom the director had in mind would be available, if the American cultural exchange group that had agreed to underwrite part of the expense would come through with the money, and so on. In fact, it seemed so uncertain that Charlotte doubted it would ever come off. But then, the *I Ching* had told her it would, and so far the *I Ching* had been right.

As she chatted with Reynolds, Charlotte savored the challenge. She had a million questions. Would the Chinese audiences draw the parallel between the witch trials in a Massachusetts village three centuries ago, and their own recent history? And, if they did, would the message be too inflammatory for the government to accept? How well would she work with actors with whom she couldn't communicate directly, and who had been trained in an entirely different acting tradition? Then there were the strictly practical matters. How long would she have to stay? Would there be other American advisers? If so, in what capacity would they serve? Would she have any power to influence the actors' performances, or would their direction be mostly in the hands of the Chinese director? Her mind was swirling with these questions and many more as she made her way back to her room, leaving Marsha to confer with Victor about their lecture schedule.

She was just entering the courtyard in front of her building when Reynolds accosted her. "Oh, hi," she said, turning around. "Are you staying here, too?"

"No. I'm staying in Dunhuang town. But there was something else I wanted to talk with you about—in confidence." He nodded toward an old Coca-Cola machine of the type that had disappeared long ago from just about everywhere in the United States except gas stations in the deep South. "Can I buy you a Coke?"

"I'd be delighted," said Charlotte.

He returned a moment later with two Cokes, or "Luoky Colas" as they were called here, and gestured toward a bench at the side of the courtyard, which was shaded by a twisted old pear tree. "Would you like to sit down?"

Charlotte looked at him questioningly as he handed her the Coke.

"I read *Murder at the Morosco*," he said.

"Yes," said Charlotte, wondering what he was getting at.

"I also heard about the murder case in Maine that you helped solve," he continued. "What I wanted to ask you about is this: the State Department has no authority to interfere with the Chinese police in their investigation into Fiske's death. We're completely at their mercy, and, frankly"—he looked over at her with his smiling blue eyes—"after meeting with the local police this morning, I don't have a lot of confidence in their abilities."

"I know what you mean," she said.

He went on. "But even if they were the most competent investigators in the world, I'd be concerned about their ability to conduct an investigation in which at least some of the people involved are English-speaking. I'm going to request that they bring in some higher-ups from the Foreign Affairs Division in Lanzhou, but I'll have to go through official channels, and that will take time. Meanwhile, it would be a great help to us if we had someone on the spot to look after our interests, someone whose abilities we trust." He paused for a moment to watch a mother goose make her way across the uneven concrete blocks that paved the courtyard; she was trailed by a line of little goslings. "Especially someone whose traveling companion is fluent in Chinese."

The mother goose and her offspring disappeared behind the stalks of the sunflowers that lined the opposite wall of the courtyard.

"Like me, for example," said Charlotte with a smile.

Reynolds smiled back. "Like you, for example."

"And what exactly are our interests?"

"To make discreet inquiries among the American guests at the Dunhuang Research Academy as to where they were at the time of the murder, et cetera, with the aim of finding out who killed Larry Fiske. Right now, Ho's chief suspect is some lice-ridden good-for-nothing who, from everything I can gather, gets thrown in the hoosegow for every crime and misdemeanor committed in greater Dunhuang whose solution isn't readily apparent."

"It sounds like the *modus operandi* of the Dunhuang police

doesn't differ much from that of the police anywhere else," Charlotte observed.

"Ho took me over to the local jail to meet this guy this morning," Reynolds continued. "His name is Feng—the town drunk, apparently. And a beggar, to boot. I could smell him long before I saw him. I doubt he could find his way out of a paper bag, much less kill an American for no apparent motive."

"I thought the motive was theft."

"That's the party line, but it doesn't make sense. There were a few things missing: a shortwave radio, a calculator, a wristwatch. The cook helped the police identify the missing items. But they were all things that the servants might have walked off with when they fled. It's my theory that whoever did kill Fiske planted the radio on the poor wretch they have in jail right now. A real thief would have taken the money from Fiske's wallet, but it wasn't touched."

Charlotte had come to the same conclusion.

Reynolds went on. "And to be quite frank, if I don't buy their solution to the murder, the Fiske family isn't going to buy it either, and they're going to be on our backs for more answers."

"From the little I know about them, the Fiske family isn't one that you want to have a run-in with," added Charlotte.

"Exactly. If we don't come up with some satisfactory answers, they'll probably round up a Congressional delegation to investigate."

"Do you have any idea who might have wanted to kill him?"

"I was going to ask you that question."

"Actually, I do have a couple," Charlotte replied. "They're pretty slim ones, but they're places to start."

"Shoot."

"One is Eugene Orecchio."

"The geologist from Pittsburgh?" asked Reynolds.

Charlotte nodded. "On the evening we arrived"—it was only the evening before last, Charlotte thought, but it already seemed like ages ago—"we sat with Larry at dinner. By we, I mean Marsha and I and Bert Rogers and Dogie O'Dea, whom we had met on the train. Bert and Dogie are also paleontologists."

Reynolds nodded. "I met them this morning."

"Larry was very excited. He announced that he'd just made a big discovery—one of the biggest discoveries of the century, he called it. Orecchio was there too. Larry invited us all out to his camp. He said he wanted to show us his find rather than tell us about it."

"That's when you found the body."

Charlotte nodded. "As we were leaving the dining hall, I overheard Larry tell Dogie that Orecchio wasn't going to be very happy about his discovery."

"Then Fiske and Orecchio weren't close colleagues," said Reynolds.

"Professional adversaries, from what I gather. They subscribed to rival theories about the reasons for the extinction of the dinosaurs." She briefly explained the nature of the dispute. "I'm not sure if Orecchio overheard Larry, but I presume that if I could hear him, he could too."

"And you think that Orecchio killed Fiske because he had made some kind of discovery that would have invalidated his catastrophe theory."

"Maybe," said Charlotte. "It's a start."

"Who's number two?"

"The French paleontologist, Jean-Jacques Bouchard. He was also an enemy of Larry's. Apparently his scientific technique is sloppy—he doesn't label what he picks up and that kind of thing—and Larry had tried to have him excluded from the expedition. Without success, obviously."

"Ho told me that Bouchard has a camp near Fiske's."

"Like about a hundred yards away."

"It sounds as if you've given this matter quite a bit of thought already," said Reynolds, taking a long swig from his bottle of Luoky Cola.

"How can you help it when you've just stumbled over a dead body with a stab wound in the chest. Any news on the murder weapon, by the way? Or on the time of death?"

Reynolds shook his head, then looked over at Charlotte. By contrast with his usual genial manner, he was now very serious: "I don't want to get you into anything that you don't want to get into."

"I can only look at so many frescoes," she said. If she had been worried about how she was going to occupy her time while Marsha and Victor were studying their manuscripts, she had no worries on that score now.

He continued. "If the Chinese authorities accuse me of putting you up to looking into the murder for us, I'm going to deny it."

"So this is how Foggy Bottom works," she teased.

"That's how it earned its nickname—for the murkiness of its policies," he said. "In spy jargon, you're out in the cold." He went on: "But I do want you to be careful. I don't want you getting yourself into trouble. The last thing I need is another body on my hands. Besides, I wouldn't want the actors guild on my back. The Fiskes are going to be trouble enough."

"I doubt you'd get anyone from the union to come here to investigate," said Charlotte. "No room service, no hot tubs. For that matter, not even any private bathrooms." She gazed out at the Mountain of the Three Dangers. "Though it does bear a faint resemblance to Palm Springs."

"Without the golf courses and the palm trees," said Reynolds.

"Would you mind if I went out to Larry's camp?" she asked. "I'd like to find out what it was that he discovered. Maybe I'll be able to find some field notes or something."

Reynolds placed his palm on his chest in a gesture of helplessness. "How is a little ole diplomat from Beijing supposed to keep track of everything you crazy tourists do to amuse yourselves in your spare time?" Then he added, "I've posted a round-the-clock guard at the camp to protect Fiske's belongings. But I'll see to it that you're allowed access."

"Is there anything else?" asked Charlotte. "A pledge of secrecy? A manual of covert operations?" She smiled. "I'm only kidding. But seriously, if there's any particular way in which you'd like me to proceed, just tell me."

"Deng Xiaoping is famous for a slogan that he uses in defense of his economic policies," Reynolds replied. "It goes, 'It doesn't matter whether a cat is black or white as long as it catches mice.' There is one thing, though," he added. "I don't want to hear too many of the nitty-gritty details."

"Gritty is right," said Charlotte, wiping the sand from her brow. The wind gusting over the dunes that capped the Mountain of the Howling Sands rained sand down on their heads.

Reynolds smiled. "In fact," he said, "I don't want to hear any details at all, gritty or not. I just want to be presented with the mouse: boxed, wrapped, and neatly tied with a bow."

After the usual postprandial siesta, Charlotte went to see the colossal Buddha in the Cave of Unequaled Height. It was truly an awe-inspiring sight to stand at its gigantic feet and look up at its strong, plain face, which gazed down through half-closed eyes at the petty foibles of humanity from a hundred feet overhead. The giant Buddha's gilded countenance shone in the light from openings in each story of the nine-story pavilion fronting the cave, and from the long tapers that stood in large, sand-filled boxes at its feet. Unlike the other caves, which were dormant relics of an ancient past, the largest of the caves was still used by worshipers who came to pray and to light votive candles in memory of their departed ones or to bring themselves good luck. The atmosphere was otherworldly. The chimes dangling from the upturned eaves jingled in the wind; the joss sticks burning at the Buddha's feet filled the air with a fragrant, mysterious haze; and the flames of the votive candles flickered in the dim light. Charlotte could easily imagine what it must have been like for the Silk Road traders who prayed here for a safe journey before setting out across the infamous Taklimakan Desert to the west, a nine-hundred-mile sea of massive, shifting dunes that was considered the most hostile desert in the world. She had been told that the name meant "Once you get in, you can never get out."

Charlotte was part of a scheduled tour of the Cave of Unequaled Height, which was directed by Emily. Emily was accompanied by her Chinese-American Heathcliff, who had come along not as her boyfriend but in his official capacity as an expert on Chinese sculpture. She had already explained that the giant Buddha—the largest of three colossi at the caves—had been constructed during the Tang Dynasty in the cave that was believed to have been the one built by the monk Lo-Tsun in 366.

"To enable pilgrims standing on the floor of the cave to view the face of the statue from so far below, the head was enlarged out of proportion to the body," Emily explained. "If you'll look closely, you'll also see that the features of the head—the eyelids, nostrils, lips, and hair coils—have been molded in high relief so that they will be clearly visible from below."

For a few minutes, the group, most of whom were with a party of German tourists, studied the statue as Emily explained about the Buddha's ear lobes, which were elongated from years of wearing heavy earrings, and were a symbol of his renunciation of a life of the flesh for one of the spirit. "Now we'll look at the Buddha from above," said Emily.

Flashlights in hand, she and Ned led the group up the stairway. It was a bit like visiting the Statue of Liberty. They climbed and climbed—past the knees, the waist, the chest, the face. At each level there was a platform for viewing the statue. Charlotte was most impressed by the hands: huge gilded slabs that must have been twenty feet long.

Finally they reached the highest platform, from which they looked down on the gilded top of the Buddha's head. It was covered with coins and cigarettes.

"What are the cigarettes doing there?" asked one of the tourists.

"They've been thrown there by people who've made wishes," Emily answered. "If your coin or cigarette stays on the Buddha's head, your wish will come true. But if your coin or cigarette falls, your wish won't come true."

"What happens to the money?" asked one of the Americans. It was a typically American question, Charlotte thought.

"It goes toward the restoration of the caves," Emily replied. She gestured for them to step up to the railing. "Please feel free to try it," she said. "I have extra coins, if you don't have any."

Taking a five-fen coin, which was worth about two and a half cents, out of her purse, Charlotte stepped up to the railing, closed her eyes, and made a wish. It was the same wish she had been making for the last forty-odd years: for a good property. Only in this case, she had something specific in mind.

"Let a hundred flowers bloom," she said to herself as she leaned out over the railing to throw her coin.

It came neatly to rest in one of the Buddha's tightly wound hair coils.

·7·

THE TOUR OF the Cave of Unequaled Height ended with the obligatory melon break, which took place every afternoon at around four, and was as much a part of the daily routine as afternoon tea in London. The ritual was performed by Ned. Squatting on the pavement at the foot of the cliff, he cut open a bunch of melons with the ornate knife that the men of the area wore strapped to their belts especially for this purpose. First he cut the end off of each melon to clean the knife, and then he cut it into slices, which Emily passed around. As Charlotte sat on a bench eating her melon, she pondered how to go about looking into Larry's death. She was eager to go right out to the camp. But if Larry had left field notes, she would need an interpreter—she didn't speak dinosaurese—and Bert, Dogie, and Orecchio had been holed up in the reception room with Peng all afternoon drafting some kind of formal agreement about dinosaur bones, of the if-you-find-it-you-can-keep-it-but-we-get-to-borrow-it-back-if-we-want-to variety. Then it struck her: Lisa. Lisa could help her—she knew as much about dinosaurs as any of the others. She quickly finished her melon, and, after thanking Emily and Ned, went in search of Bert and Dogie's girl Friday.

She found her a few minutes later in the courtyard of her building, which was adjacent to Charlotte's. She was washing out her laundry under a spigot. Each of the courtyards had a spigot, which was where the guests washed their clothes, brushed their teeth, and even washed their hair. It reminded Charlotte of overnight camp. The water from the various spigots drained into a ditch, which ran all around the compound, and which served to irrigate the fruit trees, flower gardens, and trellises.

"Hi!" said Lisa, as Charlotte approached. "Welcome to Foo

Young's laundry. I'm trying the Third-World approach," she added, indicating the wet clothes that she had spread out on nearby bushes to dry.

"Don't they have a laundry here?" asked Charlotte.

"Yes, but it takes three days and I don't have three days worth of clean clothes." She looked down at the pair of cutoffs she was wearing. "I'm down to my last pair of shorts. How's everything in the art world?"

"It's not the art world I'm thinking about at the moment, but the dinosaur world. Specifically, Larry's dinosaur world."

"What about it?" Lisa asked as she rinsed out a T-shirt.

Charlotte explained about her doubts (they were really Reynolds' doubts, but she was abiding by his request for discretion) as to the motive for Larry's murder, and told her about her theory that Larry's death was somehow linked to his claim that he had made the biggest find of the century.

Lisa was skeptical. "I wouldn't believe everything Larry told me," she said. "He had a way of exaggerating things."

Charlotte felt a pang of disappointment. She hadn't even considered the possibility that Larry might have exaggerated. But then she remembered his feverish glow of excitement—so bright that she'd thought he might even be on drugs. No—she was sure he had really found something. "Would you like to go out to Larry's camp with me?"

"To see if we can find what it was that he found?"

Charlotte nodded.

"I would love to," Lisa cried. "I've been *dying* to get a better look at what's out there. We were supposed to go surveying this afternoon, but then the boys [which was how she referred to Bert and Dogie] got tied up with Peng, and we weren't able to. When do we leave?"

"How about right now?" They had more than three hours until dinner, and the light was still good. Since there were no time zones in China—the entire country was on Beijing time—it didn't get dark until eleven o'clock.

"Great," Lisa said as she spread the T-shirt out on a bush. "I've just got to get my sunglasses and a hat."

"Me too," said Charlotte. "Meet you here shortly?"

"Sounds fine."

Twenty minutes later they were turning at the twisted corpse of the mummified donkey onto the rutted track that led across the valley floor to Larry's camp. Lisa was suitably equipped with camera, canteen, and binoculars.

As they walked, Lisa chatted about fossil hunting. "The *Protoceratops* skull that Dogie found yesterday is a good sign," she said. "To have found anything is a good sign, but to have found a nice skull right on your doorstep like that is a very good sign indeed. Sometimes you can spend weeks looking in a promising site and not come back with anything but a sunburn."

"Larry told us at dinner that night that the site was paved with fossils," Charlotte commented as they climbed the series of terraces that led upward from the bed of the wide, shallow stream that paralleled the road.

Lisa threw her a doubting look. "I heard him say that once before, about a site in Peru," she said. "The area *was* paved with fossils: mammal bones—late mammals, too. Not to put down mammal bones—they can tell us a lot about mammalian evolution—but it wasn't exactly the world's greatest discovery."

"Forgive my ignorance," said Charlotte. "But what exactly are you looking for here? I know that you're looking for dinosaur bones, but are you looking for any particular kind of dinosaur bones? I guess what I'm asking is, is there any particular thesis that you're trying to prove or disprove?"

"The answers are yes and yes," Lisa replied. "We are looking for particular kinds of bones, namely those of new species, and we are trying to prove a thesis, namely that Asia and North America were once connected, and therefore gave rise to similar kinds of dinosaurs."

"What about finding fossils above the K/T boundary layer?"

"If you mean are we looking for fossils above the K/T boundary layer, the answer is no. If you mean would we like to find fossils above the K/T layer, the answer is yes. They aren't something you look for; they're something you come across. Teeth, bits and pieces. A fully articulated skeleton has never been found above the K/T boundary layer. That's where the catastrophists get their ammunition. They say that bits and pieces alone aren't enough to prove that the dinosaurs survived the catastrophe. Because they're so small, they could have been washed away from their original sites and redeposited in more recent sediments."

"But the discovery of a fully articulated skeleton above the K/T layer would prove that the dinosaurs survived the catastrophe, wouldn't it?" She went on to repeat what she had overheard Larry saying to Dogie.

"Yes. A fully articulated skeleton would prove that dinosaurs survived the catastrophe, but not only did Larry not discover a fully articulated skeleton, nobody else is likely to either."

"Why not?" asked Charlotte as they passed the pair of towering stupas that framed the Cave of Unequaled Height. They cast long, narrow shadows in the soft, pink, late-afternoon light.

"People have a mistaken notion about dinosaur fossils. They're not easy to find. The fossil record isn't rich. After all, these critters have been out of the picture for sixty-four million years. Take *T. rex*, to use a popular example. Only half-a-dozen skeletons of *T. rex* have ever been found. Combine the fact that a fully articulated skeleton is a rarity with the fact that the dinosaurs were already dying out at the time of the catastrophe, and you see that the chances of finding an intact skeleton above the K/T boundary layer are pretty slim. My guess is that Larry found a few bones. He would have delighted in dangling them in front of Orecchio's nose." A shadow crossed the angled planes of her face. "Too bad he didn't get the chance."

After a few more minutes of hiking, they reached the point a hundred feet up the slope of the mountain where the jeep track turned to the north, and where they had rested the day before.

For a few minutes, they looked out at the camp, which was situated on a plateau on the other side of a nearby butte.

"Quite an establishment for one person," commented Charlotte.

"Yes," said Lisa. "Roy Chapman Andrews all over again. Right down to the table linens and crystal brandy decanter. I'll never forget the time he invited us to his camp for oysters and champagne—that was on a dig in Mexico. He'd had the oysters flown in from Veracruz."

"Tough life," said Charlotte, and immediately regretted her words. It wasn't a very gracious thing to say of someone who'd just been murdered.

"Yes," said Lisa. "It's easy to be envious of somebody who has so much money. But nobody ever begrudged Larry his wealth. It was because of his generosity. Not only with his money, but with his spirit. It sounds corny to say, but his was a life that enriched those of everybody around him."

Charlotte felt even worse about her crass comment.

A few minutes later they had arrived at the camp, which was being guarded by a young Chinese man. Reynolds delivered as promised. Upon seeing them, the man stood up, and ushered them into the work tent.

On her earlier visit Charlotte had failed to notice the artworks that decorated the tent: a couple of Chinese landscape paintings hung from the back wall, and a huge temple jar stood next to a brass-studded trunk. "This place is really something," she said as she looked around.

"The art is a Roy Chapman Andrews affectation too," Lisa explained. "RCA collected Oriental art; Larry collected Oriental art." She walked over to inspect the scroll paintings. "I expect he just bought these recently. Otherwise, he'd have shipped them back already."

For a few minutes, they looked at the paintings, which were exquisite. Charlotte especially liked one of a monk in a hut by a silver lake.

"What is it that we're looking for exactly?" she asked as they turned back to face the work area of the tent.

"A field diary," Lisa replied. She walked over to the big mahogany camp desk. "My guess is that it would be in here." She ran her fingers over the dust-covered surface. "I remember this desk," she said. Tears rose in her hazel eyes, and she blinked them back.

Charlotte joined her at the desk, and started going through the drawers. "What would it look like?" she asked.

"Usually, it's just an ordinary three-ring binder. But in Larry's case, you never know—probably hand-bound in Moroccan calf and stamped with gold."

"Like this?" said Charlotte. She pulled a tan notebook out of the middle drawer. It wasn't hand-bound, but it was covered in leather and stamped with a pattern of dinosaurs in gold.

"That looks like it," Lisa said as Charlotte handed the book to her. Placing it on the desk in front of her, she took a seat in the leather swivel chair. "Did he mention when he made his big discovery?" she asked as she started leafing through the pages.

"I gathered that it was on that day: Thursday, June twenty-eighth," replied Charlotte, who was leaning over her shoulder.

Lisa flipped through the pages to that day, and then looked up at Charlotte. The angled face under the flowered baseball cap was puzzled. "It's not here!" she said. The word "here" came out in Jerseyese: *heah.*

The page for Thursday, June twenty-eighth, had been ripped out. There was an entry for Wednesday, describing the areas in which Larry had been working on that day: location, type of soil, terrain, and so on. But nothing for Thursday except a few shreds of paper clinging to the spiral binding.

"Maybe you're right," Lisa said. "Maybe he really did find something."

"But what?" asked Charlotte.

"I've got an idea." Lisa began rooting around in the drawers. "There should be a master map that's marked off in grids, with each survey locality mapped. Maybe we can figure out something from the master map, if not what he found, then where he found it." She had finished searching. "It's not here," she said.

"What about there?" said Charlotte, who had spotted a cardboard tube leaning up against the back wall of the tent. Retrieving it from its storage place, she brought it over to the desk and slid out the contents: it was a large gridded map entitled "Dragon's Tomb Site, Gansu Province, PRC." Dragon's Tomb was the name that Larry said he had given his site.

"This is it, all right. Paleontologists like to name their sites," Lisa explained. "It's one of the privileges of discovering a site. Just like naming a new species is one of the privileges of discovering it." She picked up a bone from the desk, and used it to hold down the corner.

Charlotte reached out to touch the bone, which looked like a leg bone of some kind. "What's this?" she asked. It was incised with Chinese ideographs that had been filled in with black ink to make them stand out.

Picking it up, Lisa turned it over in her hands. "It's a dragon bone," she said. "They're dinosaur bones—this looks like the femur of a duckbill to me—which were used by ancient soothsayers for divination. Here are the readings." She pointed to the ideographs. "They're from the *I Ching*."

"No kidding!" Charlotte exclaimed.

"The bones were heated, which would cause cracks to appear," Lisa explained. "The fortune was revealed by the pattern of the cracks." Handing it to Charlotte, she added: "Someone probably brought it to Larry. It's amazing what turns up when you put the word out that you'll pay cash for old bones."

"It's beautiful," said Charlotte, running her finger over the polished ivory surface. The patterns created by the ancient calligraphy reminded her of the ornamentation on a fine piece of antique scrimshaw.

Lisa had returned her attention to the map. "Look at all these localities! It looks as if the site really *is* paved with fossils." She began counting the localities, each of which was marked with a red dot and numbered. "Thirty-seven in just a few days' work."

"The problem is, which is the one we're looking for?"

"I think I've got it," Charlotte said. "Presumably Larry numbered the localities consecutively as he went along, which would mean that the highest numbers should correspond to the most recently discovered ones."

"Of course! The one we're looking for would be here," said Lisa, pointing to the grid that included localities thirty-four through thirty-seven. "Unless he hadn't gotten around to marking Thursday's localities on the map."

"We can check that too," said Charlotte. Lifting the map, she pulled the field diary out from underneath. "Look," she said, pointing to the entry for Wednesday. "Here are thirty-one, thirty-two, and thirty-three."

"Which means that he was working on thirty-four, thirty-five, thirty-six, and thirty-seven on Thursday, and that one of those is the one we want," added Lisa. She returned her attention to the map.

"Can you tell where they are?" asked Charlotte.

"They're to the south of here; it looks like about three hundred yards," Lisa replied. "On the north slope of a ravine, about halfway up." She looked up at Charlotte. "Shall we check it out?"

Charlotte smiled. "I don't see why not."

Unlike the walk out from the guest house, the going to the south of the camp was treacherous. The terrain was a wild expanse of badlands eroded by ancient rainfall into ravines and gullies interspersed with bluffs, ridges, and buttes. There was no way to go directly from point A to point B. Their way was blocked at every turn by outcroppings that jutted into the sky, or by huge rounded boulders that cascaded down the slopes. Although the terrain was desolate, it had a stark kind of beauty. At this time of day it was a study in contrasts: the pink and lavender bands of sediment on the walls of the ridges contrasted with the brilliant blue of the sky; the deep shadows cast by the gullies and ravines contrasted with the glowing red of the summits, which had caught the rays of the declining sun; and dark cloud shadows glided effortlessly across rough surfaces of purplish-red sandstone.

Lisa led the way. She had a long, lanky frame, and the easy, swinging stride of someone who was accustomed to walking. Like Bert and Dogie, she walked with her eyes focused on the ground, looking for fossils. But it didn't take a practiced eye to find them. Even for Charlotte, they were easy to spot. The fragments of white bone were everywhere. They seemed to ooze out of the purplish-red earth like bones in a horror-story graveyard. The twenty-foot-square sections represented by the grids on the master map had been marked off with strings and stakes, and each locality had been marked with a number painted in red on a nearby rock. As they walked on, it became clear that Larry had chosen only the best of the localities to mark—the most complete, most readily accessible, and the most well-preserved. Hundreds of unmarked fossil fragments lay scattered around on the ground. Fossils that might have been treasures at a less productive site were worthless here, Lisa observed.

Charlotte was reminded of the legend on Dogie's T-shirt: *So many dinosaurs, so little time*. "Dogie would be calling for a lot of *pijiu* if he were here this afternoon," she observed.

"He'd have to bring in a whole keg," Lisa agreed as she squatted down for the umpteenth time to examine a large skeleton. "Larry was right. It's a fossil-hunter's paradise out here. I've never seen anything like it. Here's a duckbill," she said, "complete except for the skull."

"What happened to the skull?"

"Probably carried off by a carnivore. They liked the skulls; they were the tastiest part. Bert calls it Rogers' Law of Fossil-Hunting: the skull of the best specimens is never preserved. Unfortunately, it's the anatomy of the skull that tells us the most about how dinosaurs are related to one another."

As they went along, Lisa talked about the stratigraphy of the site. The strata were undisturbed, she said, which meant that the ground hadn't been disturbed by seismic activity or by ancient erosion, and therefore that the history of the landscape was clearly revealed by the patterns of the strata.

"Here," said Lisa, handing Charlotte the binoculars and pointing to the flank of a nearby butte that was lined with stripes of pale greenish-gray, soft orange-pink, and glowing golden ochre. "The K/T boundary layer is the dark narrow band that you see sandwiched between the layers of sandstone."

Charlotte studied the dark layer that ran evenly through the rock like a layer of chocolate filling in a vanilla layer cake.

"The dark band is actually a seam of low-grade coal called lignite. It was formed from the soot that blanketed the earth as a result of the devastating wild fires that broke out after the catastrophe," Lisa explained.

"I thought you didn't believe in the catastrophe theory," said Charlotte as she handed back the binoculars.

"I don't. Or rather, we don't. But that's not to say that a catastrophe didn't occur. We just don't think that it was the sole cause of the dinosaurs' extinction. A factor, maybe, along with other factors such as overpopulation, disease, falling sea levels, cooling climate, deforestation, competition from mammals—you name it. There are a million possibilities."

"Which do you subscribe to?"

"All of the above, and a few more. I think the dinosaurs died out gradually from a combination of converging environmental factors, all of them mundane. That's the trouble with the gradualism theory—it lacks the pizazz that the catastrophe theory has."

"In other words, whatever could go wrong, did."

"Yes, and all at the same time," said Lisa. "Well, within a few million years, anyway. Which amounts to the same time, geologically speaking."

They paused at the crest of a ridge overlooking a steep ravine. Taking a seat at the base of a giant boulder, they gazed out over the landscape. Though it had cooled off considerably since midday, the boulder still retained the heat, and leaning against it was like leaning against a warm radiator.

Charlotte removed her coolie hat and let the breeze that had come up as the day had waned play over her burning temples.

Below, a plump mother sand grouse led her brood across a patch of ochre-colored sand that had collected in a low-lying area at the foot of the ridge. She looked like a cross between a pigeon and a partridge, but her walk was more ungainly than either one.

"Their toes are padded like a camel's so that they can walk in the sand," said Lisa, who was also looking at the grouse.

"They remind me of Larry," said Charlotte. "He was telling

us at dinner that night about his last meal; it was sand grouse, or rather, *Tétras au vin à la Dijonnaise.*" As she spoke, she reminded herself that she should track down Larry's cook and ask him some questions.

"Ah, yes," said Lisa. "Eat well, dress well, sleep well. Well, I guess those days are gone." She sat with her long legs stretched out in front of her. Like the sand grouse, she was also shod for the terrain—heavy boots of the type usually worn by lumberjacks or construction workers.

Charlotte coveted them. If she kept up these hikes in the badlands, her sneakers were going to be torn to ribbons.

"As near as I can tell, localities thirty-four to thirty-seven must be on the far side of the next ridge," Lisa said, pointing at the ridge that paralleled the ravine below them on the opposite side.

It took about fifteen minutes for them to clamber down one slope and back up the other, and another ten to climb to the top of the next ridge. Thirty-four was near the top. Exposed to view was the skeleton of a small horned dinosaur with a long name, a relative of *Protoceratops*. Lisa pronounced it a very nice find.

The next locality was partly concealed by an outcropping. But once they had scrambled down the slope to get a better look, even Charlotte could see that this was Larry's "find." It looked as if the hand of God had laid out a box of giant Lincoln logs in a dinosaur pattern on the purplish-red slope.

"Holy shit," said Lisa as she caught site of the skeleton. Grabbing Charlotte's arm, she just stood there, muttering the phrase over and over again. It was an incantation: "Holy shit, holy shit, holy shit."

"What is it?" asked Charlotte. It was clear that it was that rarity that Lisa had spoken of—a fully articulated skeleton—and it was obvious that it was huge, but beyond that Charlotte had no idea what it could be.

With Charlotte in tow, Lisa slowly drew nearer, all the time staring at the enormous mass of bones and muttering "Holy shit."

The skeleton was as long as a city bus. The tail alone must have been twenty feet. It stretched across the hillside, each vertebra the size of a turkey platter. The four-foot thigh bone reminded Charlotte of the line from *Ozymandias* about the "two vast and trunkless legs of stone" in the desert.

Lisa still wasn't talking. Her bulging jaw hinges were moving up and down like a mute trying to utter a word that wouldn't come out.

"What is it?" Charlotte asked again.

"A *T. rex*," she finally replied as she removed her camera from its case. "Virtually complete, except for the skull. Every piece in the right place. *T. rex* on the half shell." Moving closer, she circled the skeleton, taking a series of shots from various angles.

Looking out over the long tail, Charlotte noticed the narrow band of black that marked the K/T boundary layer snaking through the far wall of the ravine. Then she suddenly realized that it was *below* where they were standing. "It's above the K/T boundary layer!"

Lisa nodded. "By about five hundred feet. There's absolutely no doubt that this is Tertiary strata," she said. "Our reptilian friend here might as well be wearing a T-shirt that says 'I Survived the Death Star.' "

For once, Larry hadn't been exaggerating. Not only was it the biggest find of the century, with the possible exception of Andrews' discovery of the dinosaur eggs, it was, according to Lisa, probably the biggest find of all time: a nearly complete *T. rex*. Apart from the skull, only a few foot bones were missing, and they might yet turn up somewhere nearby. Not only that, it was above the K/T boundary layer. The chance that a nearly complete skeleton could have been churned up from older sediments and redeposited above the K/T boundary layer with each bone in its proper place was nil. Larry's discovery of the *T. rex* was irrefutable proof that the gradualists were right. It was also a good bet that it was the reason for his murder. At the moment, Charlotte's chief suspect was Orecchio, who wouldn't have wanted to see the theory on which he had staked his professional reputation invalidated. But there were a number of problems with Orecchio as a suspect.

Theoretically, Orecchio murdered Larry to destroy the evidence that refuted his theory, hence the missing page in the field log. But it seemed to Charlotte that there was a good chance that some other member of the expedition would eventually have discovered the *T. rex* skeleton, if not this year, then next. In which case the murder would have been pointless. But Lisa thought otherwise. She agreed that there was a chance, but it was a slim one. Finding dinosaur fossils wasn't an exact science, she said. It required a practiced eye, a nose for fossils, and a great deal of luck.

"It's easy to miss a fossil," she told Charlotte as they headed back to the guest house. "Sometimes it's just a glint of bone or an outline in the rock. If your mind is on something else, or if the light's wrong, or if you're looking in the other direction, you can miss it."

"But this was more than a glint of bone," said Charlotte.

"Yes, but it was also hidden underneath that outcropping. Someone else might have been five feet away and still not have seen it. As for next year—it might not be there next year. All it takes is one big sandstorm, and it's buried for another couple of million years."

"What about elsewhere?" asked Charlotte. "If Larry found a fully articulated skeleton in Tertiary strata, isn't it likely that another one would turn up somewhere else in the world?"

"Possible, but not likely," Lisa said. "At least, not in Orecchio's lifetime. And he probably doesn't care what happens after he's dead, as long as he's succeeded in preserving his scientific reputation while he's alive."

They arrived back at the guest house at about seven-thirty, dirty and sweaty. As Charlotte was washing up for dinner, she thought about her conversation with Lisa. If Larry's murder was going to be pinned on a member of the expedition, Lisa obviously wanted it to be pinned on Orecchio. But there was another motive for killing Larry that Lisa hadn't brought up, perhaps because the idea was so distasteful to her. Larry might have been murdered by someone who wanted to stake his own claim to the *T. rex* skeleton. The person who discovered the *T. rex* would go down in the annals of paleontology, just as Andrews had for his dinosaur eggs. Was a reputation in the pages of the history books worth the risk of murder? Charlotte thought it was. And for this motive, there were any number of suspects: Bouchard, who had the advantage of proximity; Peng, who may have wanted to claim the find for the Chinese; and even Bert and/or Dogie. She would have to find out what all of them had been doing between the time when Larry had left the compound and the time when she had found him dead. No doubt they would all claim to have spent most of that time in bed, which would leave her exactly nowhere, but she felt as if she should go through the exercise of inquiring anyway.

She was trying to figure out how to go about this, when circumstances decided the question for her. On her way to the dining hall, she stopped at the guest house's souvenir kiosk to pick up a packet of throat lozenges, and found herself standing next to a man whose suntan, knapsack, and dusty clothing made her think he might have been camped out in the desert, and whose inquiry as to the price of a carton of cigarettes—*Duoshao gian?* which was "How much?" in Chinese—came out sounding a lot like *Combien?*

"Excuse me," she said. "Are you Mr. Bouchard?"

He turned around to face her. He was a middle-aged man with a big torso mounted on skinny, sticklike legs. He had a bushy black beard, the hawk nose that was typical of the French, and a stiff mat of black hair combed straight forward in the style of a Roman charioteer.

"*Oui*, yes," he replied. "I am." He looked woefully unhappy. His mouth was turned down at the corners, and his eyebrows drooped at the outer edges, giving his face a sad expression.

Charlotte felt a little sorry for a paleontologist who was so bad at finding fossils that he had to resort to poaching on his colleagues' territory. "My name is Charlotte Graham," she said, extending her hand.

"I recognize you from your films," he said.

"I'm interested in learning more about the circumstances of Mr. Fiske's death. I know that you've been camped nearby. I wonder if I could ask you a few questions about the events of that evening?"

Charlotte could see his confusion. Why on earth was an American movie star asking him questions about the death of a rival paleontologist? Or maybe his confusion was due to the fact that he didn't understand English.

"I'm a friend of the family's," she explained, improvising as she went along. "They're not satisfied with the investigation that's being conducted by the local authorities. Since I happened to be here anyway on an art tour"—she gestured vaguely at the cliff—"they asked me to look into his death."

Her lie sounded believable, even to her. She decided she would use it again if the need arose.

"Ah, *oui*," he said, "I understand."

He did speak English.

After paying for the cigarettes, he put them away in his knapsack. "I understand that it was you who discovered the body," he said. "Therefore, you are probably better able to answer the family's questions than I. But"—he threw up his hands—"what would you like to know?"

"How long have you been camped in the desert?"

"Since last Saturday. I've actually been camped in the desert for nearly two weeks, but my camp was originally farther to the south. Of course, I have a room here as well, where I shower. I eat most of my meals here too, although I sometimes eat out at my camp."

"Why did you move your camp?"

"There weren't any fossils where I first made my camp."

"And Mr. Fiske? How long had he been camped there?"

"A couple of days longer. I'm not sure exactly. I think he set up his camp the Thursday before."

In other words, Charlotte thought, Bouchard had moved his camp as soon as he found out that Larry had discovered fossils at his site. He was a claim jumper, just as Bert had said. "Did you ever talk with him?"

"No. We weren't friends."

"But you were part of the same expedition."

He shrugged.

"Why weren't you friends?"

"Professional conflicts. I'd rather not get into it."

"Of course," said Charlotte, sympathetically. Then she plowed ahead, deciding to get right to the point: "If you weren't friends, then you must not have been aware that he had made a big discovery."

"He was always claiming to have made big discoveries," said Bouchard with a dismissive wave of his hand.

"This time he really did make a big discovery. He found a nearly complete *T. rex* skeleton. On the day before he died."

For a few seconds, Bouchard stared at her, his jaw hanging limp.

Charlotte didn't know how to take his reaction. It could have been the equivalent of Lisa's "holy shit," or it could have been the reaction of someone who has just realized that his plan to claim Larry's discovery as his own has been foiled. "How do you know he found a *T. rex?*" he asked.

If she really had been conducting an investigation for the family, it wouldn't have been out of place for her to be aware of Larry's find: it would have been recorded in his field diary. Bouchard shouldn't have been surprised that she knew about it—

unless *he* was the one who had removed the missing page.

"I saw it," she replied. She explained about the missing page, and how she and Lisa had figured out the location of the find from the master map. As she spoke, a question arose in her mind. If the person who had ripped the page out of the field diary wanted to destroy evidence of the find, why hadn't he taken the master map as well? He might not have known of its existence, but she doubted that would be the case for someone like Bert or Dogie, who had worked closely with Larry in the past. It was far more likely to have been overlooked by someone like Bouchard whose field technique was sloppy to begin with, and who probably didn't go to the trouble to make maps himself.

Bouchard listened, the face behind his bushy black beard a blank.

"Do you have any idea who removed the page from his field log?" She was accusing him, and he knew it. She knew he would answer no, but she wanted to get a sense of whether or not he was lying. As an actor herself, she was pretty good at discerning when people weren't telling the truth.

"No," said Bouchard, his bronzed brow wrinkling in a phony frown. "I don't. Is that all for today?" He turned to walk away. "I have work to do." He was clearly irritated at the accusatory nature of her questions.

"One more question," she said.

He turned back impatiently.

"Were you at your camp on the night Mr. Fiske was murdered?"

"Yes, I was," he said. "But I didn't kill him, if that's what you're implying. And I think I've had enough of your questions," he added sharply.

"I wasn't implying anything," she said. "I just wanted to know if you saw or heard anything unusual that night."

"Nothing. I was asleep. I went to bed early, at around eight. I already went through all of this with the security police. I didn't see anything until you arrived the next morning. Then I saw the police, and I concluded that something had happened. Why don't you speak with Fiske's help? If anyone saw anything, it would be they."

"I intend to," she replied. "How about early the next morning?" she asked, remembering how fresh the blood had smelled.

"I thought he was murdered during the night."

"We don't know for sure. It might have been early the next morning."

"I did see somebody early the next morning."

"Who was that?"

"Dogie O'Dea."

·8·

BOUCHARD SAID HE had seen Dogie heading toward Larry's camp about seven-thirty, which was at dawn here. When Charlotte asked him what he had been doing at that hour, he had replied, "*Je pissais.*" He didn't know if Dogie had actually made it to the camp, he said; he had gone back to bed. Nor had he told the police about seeing Dogie. It had been his impression from what the police had told him that Larry had been murdered during the night. Therefore, he didn't think the fact that he had seen Dogie early that morning was relevant.

Charlotte's chat with him left her confused. She suspected it was he who had ripped the page out of Larry's field diary, which would point to his being the murderer. And if he had already been in the area for almost two weeks, he would have had ample time to dig up a beggar on whom to plant Larry's shortwave radio. But if he was the murderer, why hadn't he told the police about seeing Dogie? It was a stupid murderer indeed who didn't take advantage of every opportunity to pin the crime on somebody else. Maybe he'd figured it wasn't necessary: if he *had* stolen the shortwave radio with the intention of framing Feng, he would have been secure in the knowledge that everything was taken care of—until Charlotte came along with her news that the Fiske family wasn't buying the police's explanation, that is. Maybe he had only cooked up the story about seeing Dogie when he realized that his plot wasn't going to work. She had another question as well. If Bouchard had murdered Larry with the intention of claiming Larry's discovery as his own, how had he known that Larry hadn't already told someone about his find? Larry might have told them all about it at the party that evening. Then again, Bouchard might not even have known that Larry had gone to the party. Larry had arrived at the dining hall at around eight-thirty. If what Bouchard said was true, he was already in bed by then. On the other hand, maybe there was another explanation altogether. Maybe Bouchard had simply taken advantage of the fact that Larry had been murdered to find out what it was that he had discovered.

She tried to picture the scenario in her mind. After a week of fossil hunting, Bouchard isn't finding anything. But he learns—perhaps after a little reconnaissance—that his rival is finding fossils galore at another site. He moves his camp, and is doing very well. But perhaps he's wondering, What's Fiske got that I haven't? Though Bouchard claimed that he and Larry didn't talk, maybe he was lying. Maybe Larry said or did something to tip Bouchard off that he'd made a big find. Then comes the morning of their discovery of the body: from his tent, Bouchard sees their party arrive. Then he sees them go, and the police arrive. He wonders what's up. He wanders across the DMZ, and is told by the police that Larry has been killed. The body's removed, and for a short while, the camp is left unguarded. Or, if it is guarded, the guard is inattentive. Taking advantage of the unexpected opportunity, Bouchard searches Larry's work tent, discovers the field diary, and tears out the previous day's page. Maybe he doesn't intend to claim Larry's discovery as his own, at first. Maybe he just wants to find out what it was that had made Larry so proud of himself. But when he realizes the significance of Larry's find, the thought dawns on him that this is his chance to make it big.

That was one scenario, anyway.

There was also another. As much as she wanted to keep it from doing so, it insisted on taking form in her mind: that of a bandy-legged former cowboy wearing a tan Stetson—a pissant walking around with a potato chip on its head—stealing out into the desert in the pale dawn light to murder his colleague. Bouchard had said he recognized Dogie by his hat. There was a motive too: always the bridesmaid, never the bride. Though it was Dogie who had the nose for fossils, it was Bert who had the credentials, Bert who had the position, Bert who got the credit, Bert who was the boss. But a find like the *T. rex* was too big for its discoverer to be given second billing. Bert and Dogie were like Siamese twins. What had Dogie been doing out in the desert at seven-thirty in the morning without his pardner? Unless it was to murder Larry.

* * *

The opportunity to question Dogie came right after dinner. The guests had been invited on an evening excursion to the Lake of the Crescent Moon. They made up two mini-busloads: a small group of Germans in one, and six Americans—Charlotte, Marsha, Bert, Dogie, Lisa, and Peter—in the other. The Lake of the Crescent Moon was Dunhuang's other major tourist attraction, and, like the caves, it had been so for almost sixteen centuries. The long-ago worshipers at the caves had once stopped at the lake to replenish their water supplies before setting out across the waterless deserts to the west. "The skill of man made the Caves of the Thousand Buddhas," went a local saying, "but the hand of God fashioned the Lake of the Crescent Moon."

The lake was situated amid the Southern Dunes, the immense sand dunes on the outskirts of town. The minibus dropped them off near a crude shelter made out of sticks and poles at the side of the road, where a herd of camels was tethered to a rail. One by one, the camel driver in charge loaded them onto the kneeling beasts, who grumbled, growled, and protested in every possible way, including showering mouthfuls of revolting cud over anyone who tried to be friendly. "And I thought a dogie was a stubborn beast," said Dogie, as a camel driver heaped abuse on a resentful camel who kept trying to stand up while it was being saddled.

At last they were all mounted. At a flick of the camel driver's whip, the animals took off with loose, swinging strides across the shallow sand hills, bells jingling. Charlotte found her perch atop the camel very comfortable. Unlike the one-humped dromedary of the Arabian Desert, the Bactrian camels of the Gobi had two humps, and the space between them made a natural saddle, which was padded by a thick straw mat with a quilt thrown over it. The bridle was a rope made of twisted camel hair that was attached to a wooden peg running through the camel's nostrils. But it was an item of tack that was hardly necessary. The camels had made this trip so many times that they could have done it in their sleep.

The range of enormous sand dunes which was their destination stood before them like a sea of petrified waves. Despite the hour, the sun still burned in a brilliant blue sky, but its low position cast the eastward flanks of the dunes into deep purple shadow, and bathed the westward flanks in a golden glow, leaving a line along the crests as sharp and sinuous as the division between yin and yang on the ancient Chinese symbol of the cosmos. The camel's slow, steady pace was so rhythmic, the heat radiating from the sand so comforting, and the cool breeze so intoxicating that Charlotte felt as if she could almost go to sleep, but when she found herself riding next to Dogie, she realized that here was her chance to ask him some questions.

Dogie was not tranquilized by his surroundings, nor was his camel, which seemed to have a mind of its own. As he jerked the reins to keep it from breaking away, he let out a steady string of expletives of the four-letter variety, ending with one in Chinese. The camel blinked its long eyelashes placidly, unperturbed by Dogie's insults.

"What does the Chinese word mean?" asked Charlotte. "I didn't have any problem understanding any of the others," she added.

"Dog fart," he replied with a grin. "Ain't it great? I picked it up from our guide in Beijing. It's a Chinese favorite, along with turtle's egg. But I prefer dog fart, especially for this pig-headed pile of shit."

Charlotte laughed.

"They say there's nothin' a cowboy fears 'cept a decent woman and bein' set afoot," Dogie continued. "But I'll tell ya—I'd rather be set afoot any day of the week than to be saddled to this hair-covered compost heap."

As Dogie struggled with the temperamental beast, Charlotte pondered how to delicately bring the subject around to Larry's death, and then, deciding that there was no delicate way to go from dog fart to murder, plunged right in. "I spoke with Bouchard this evening," she said. "Right before dinner."

Dogie looked over at her. "About what?"

"Larry's murder. I didn't realize it when I met him, but I'm an old friend of his aunt's. When she heard through a mutual friend that I was here, she called me and asked me to look into his death on behalf of the family." Thank goodness she had dreamed up that excuse, she thought.

"Oh," said Dogie.

"The family's not satisfied with the police's explanation of his murder. She asked me if I had any other ideas, and I told her I did. I told her that I thought Larry might have been killed by someone who wanted to claim his discovery of the *T. rex* for himself."

Lisa had told Bert and Dogie about the *T. rex* skeleton as soon as she got back. They had skipped dinner to go out and take a look, and the conversation on the minibus ride out had been of little else.

Dogie looked over at her questioningly. "Like Bouchard?"

"Someone removed the page for Thursday from Larry's field diary. I don't know why anyone would do that unless they didn't want the discovery attributed to him. Bouchard is the likely choice: he was camped nearby, and, from what you've said, he has a reputation for horning in on other people's discoveries."

"Claim poacher *extraordinaire*."

"The only trouble is, I can't figure out how he would have found out about Larry's discovery of the *T. rex*. He said they didn't speak to one another, which from what you say about their relationship is probably the truth. But he must have known that Larry had made a discovery of some kind. . . ."

"That's easy," Dogie interjected. "Spies."

"Spies!"

"Bouchard pays off the help at his competitors' camps to bring him tips. He was camped somewhere else for almost a week, right? The day after Larry discovers fossils, Bouchard pitches a new camp within a hundred yards. I don't think it was a little birdie who told him, do you?"

"A spy!" said Charlotte, thinking aloud. "Of course. The spy tells Bouchard about Larry's find, and Bouchard either kills Larry to claim his find, or takes advantage of Larry's death—again, it's the spy who tells him that Larry's dead—to go through his field diary and remove the critical page."

"Makes perfect sense to me," said Dogie.

In the latter case, the spy scenario also explained the problem of opportunity. In spite of what she had thought earlier, Charlotte doubted the police would have left the camp unguarded. But if a spy had told Bouchard about the murder, he would have had hours to search the tent before anyone got there.

She looked over at Dogie, who was still jerking his camel's reins. "I asked Bouchard if he saw anyone in the vicinity of the camp that morning."

"And . . . ?"

"He said he saw you."

The face under the Stetson broke out into a smile as wide as the brim of the hat. "He did, did he? I always said that guy was a sonofabitch."

"Were you there?"

"Yes, ma'am. I was," Dogie confessed, hanging his head in mock humility. "Not at the camp, but out in the desert."

"What were you doing there?"

"Ridin' the mornin' circle, as we used to say. I was itchin' to see what it looked like out there. If what Larry said was true, it was a fossil hunter's wonderland. I woke up at six, and couldn't get back to sleep. Besides, the early mornin' is the best time for fossil-huntin' in the desert."

"How long were you gone?" she asked. If she could pinpoint the time of Larry's death—she would have to talk to the Chinese counterpart of the medical examiner—the time that Dogie was in the desert could be important.

"About an hour and a half, I'd say."

For a moment, they rode in silence. There was only the swishing sound of the camels' hooves as they struck the sand, and the sound of Dogie humming an old country-and-western tune.

As he hummed, Charlotte remembered the chorus, which went, "Hang me, hang me, you oughtta take a rope and hang me . . ." She smiled to herself. Dogie certainly didn't seem to be taking her questions as seriously as Bouchard had.

"What was that sonofabitch doin' up and about anyway?" asked Dogie as he jerked the reins again to show the camel who was boss.

"To quote him exactly, taking a piss."

"Just my luck that that frog woulda been takin' a piss."

"Did you find any fossils?"

"Only that *Protoceratops andrewsi* skull. I didn't go that far. Never really got up into the foothills."

"The same one you found when we were with you?"

Dogie nodded.

Charlotte was baffled. "Why did you pretend that you'd just found it when you'd already found it earlier that morning?"

"I didn't want Bert to know that I'd been out already. It woulda been like—I don't know—ownin' up to sneakin' a look at your Christmas presents, or somethin'." He began humming the "Hang Me" tune again.

Or, Charlotte thought, he didn't want to own up to being out in the desert because he didn't want anyone to know that he was the one who had murdered Larry. "Then Bert wasn't with you," she said.

He shook his head.

"Aren't you roommates?"

Dogie nodded. "Yep, we're bunkies all right."

"Which means that Bert was in your room. Which means that he could confirm how long you were gone."

"Negative to Bert's bein' in the room. Negative to Bert's bein' able to confirm how long I was gone."

"If he wasn't in your room, where was he?"

"In someone else's room," Dogie replied, looking over at her with a twinkle in his eye. "Someone you know very well. A relation, in fact."

Charlotte raised a dark, winged eyebrow.

It took another five minutes to reach the lake, which was clear blue and shaped like a crescent. It was completely encircled by enormous sand dunes that looked as if they were going to swallow it up at any moment. But they never did, which was said to be a curious circumstance of the wind patterns. It had stood in the same place for centuries without its outline ever changing.

The camels carried them to a grassy area enclosed by the curve of the shore, where they dismounted. Leaving the surly beasts to graze on the camel thorn and drink from the waters of the lake, they followed their guide to a cluster of carpets that had been spread out at the water's edge. After they were all sitting down, their guide produced a sackful of large ripe peaches, which he passed around. As they ate the juicy peaches, he filled them in on the history of the lake. The area where they were sitting had once been the site of a cluster of ancient temples and pavilions whose steps and terraces had led down to the water's edge. These temples and pavilions, which had been a tourist attraction since the fourth century, had been burned down by Red Guards during the Cultural Revolution.

"There were bad elements in the Red Guards who wanted to turn the campaign against the feudal counterrevolutionary customs of the old society into a campaign for the destruction of cultural relics," he explained. "But now the Party has launched a campaign to care for our cultural relics, which it extols as valuable treasures created by the laboring peoples of the past. The revolutionary committee of Dunhuang has plans to rebuild the temples and pavilions exactly as they were."

After the guide had delivered his spiel, he left with the Germans to climb the enormous dune which loomed over the opposite shore, and which was famous even in Marco Polo's day for making a sound like thunder rumbling when sand slid down its flanks. The ancient traders had made offerings to the singing sands, believing they had supernatural powers. Tired from their busy day, their group elected to stay behind to enjoy the scenic beauty of the spot. Charlotte sat in silence, gazing at the patterns made by the shadows on the rippled surfaces of the dunes and by the cool, crisp wind on the limpid surface of the lake. Lulled by the tinkling of camels' bells and the lapping of wavelets against the sandy shore, she felt like the monk in the hut at the edge of the silver lake in Larry's landscape painting. She was glad they were going to rebuild the temples: it was a magical, almost surreal, spot. Here, more than any other place she had yet been, she had a sense of old China.

She could tell that it was the same for Marsha. She sat looking out, encircled in Bert's protective arms, just as the lake was encircled by the dunes. It was at places like this that the Tang Dynasty poets whom Marsha so loved—drunk on wine and life—had penned their exquisite nature poems.

"Look at the moon," said Marsha.

A crescent moon had risen in the azure sky, echoing the shape of the lake. It was reflected in the surface of the water.

"It reminds me of Li Po," said Peter who had been uncharacteristically quiet. When no one asked who Li Po was, he went on: "He was a High Tang poet who drowned himself one night while he was trying to catch the moon's reflection in the water."

For one who was usually so stylish, he was looking very ordinary—if not downright proletarian—in brown wool slacks and a cheap navy-blue sweatshirt that looked as if he had bought it at the local market.

"He was drunk," he added. "A weakness for wine being his chief vice." As he went on about the poet, he was interrupted by Dogie.

"You know," Dogie said as he deftly picked some peach skin out of his teeth with a toothpick, "where I come from we have a sayin' that's appropriate to situations like this one."

"What's that?" asked Peter.

"The bigger the mouth, the better it looks shut."

At Dogie's words, Peter's face flushed red right up to his balding temples. Then he not only closed his mouth, he clamped his lips angrily together. After a few minutes, he wandered off to join the Germans.

The mood among those remaining was quietly celebratory. They were still talking about Larry's discovery, which had justified their advance expedition and relieved any fears about a larger expedition not coming off. As Bert put it, they weren't going to crash. He had lit a pipe, and the light, sweet fragrance of the tobacco perfumed the evening air.

"The life of a paleontologist is like that of a gold prospector," he said as he drew on the ebony pipestem. "It's a gamble: you live on the hope that you'll hit pay dirt with the next pan. It's that hope—and the occasional little nugget—that keep you going through the heat, the bugs"—he swatted at a mosquito—"the monotony, the claim jumpers, the backbreaking labor, the lack of grant money." He paused, and stared out over the surface of the lake.

His conversation was prone to these lapses. It was as if the big skies and wide open spaces of the plains had insinuated their way into his speech.

"And, like a gambler, you get hooked. When you do hit pay dirt—enough to keep you going, anyway—you raise the stakes. You're not satisfied just to work your claim. You want to find that hundred-pound nugget of solid gold lying in the sand like a giant hen's egg. And some of us *are* lucky enough to find it. We found the *Ultrasaurus*—the biggest dinosaur ever to walk the earth, longer than a football field—"

"Now that was a giant hen's egg," interjected Dogie. "If it craned its neck, it could have peered into a sixth-story window." He shook his head at the memory. "I'll never forget comin' across that femur stickin' outta the rock. It was so big it looked like the trunk of a petrified tree."

"It's a thrill that you never forget as long as you live," Bert continued. "The moment is engraved in your memory. It's impossible to describe: you've been working and working and working, and suddenly . . ."

As she waited for the gap to close, Charlotte realized what the attraction was between Bert and Marsha: he was a fossil hunter with the soul of a poet.

After half a minute, he went on. "At least Larry died having found it—that giant hen's egg lying in the sand."

Charlotte had already told Marsha about Bouchard's seeing Dogie in the desert early that morning, or claiming he had. Now she told her what Dogie had said, namely that Bert had spent the night with her. "He intimated it—he didn't come right out and say it. But he might as well have."

They were sitting on the beds in Marsha's room drinking tea from lidded cups. Identical to those in Charlotte's room, the beds were covered with old-fashioned rose-pink chenille bedspreads. The combination of the bedspreads and sitting face to face reminded Charlotte of the heart-to-hearts she used to have with her sister when they were girls.

Marsha slumped back on the bed, propped up on her elbows. She shook her head in self-disgust. "I vowed I wouldn't get myself into this situation again, and here I am, in it right up to my knees."

"Is he married?"

"No, it's not that. He's separated, soon to be divorced. He says his wife left him because he loved duckbills—that's his specialty, duckbilled dinosaurs—more than he loved her." She rolled her eyes. "Just what I need, a man who loves dinosaurs more than he loves women. He's also younger than me."

"So what. Your father is younger than me."

"Really?"

"Only by a few years." Actually, it was seven, but she didn't remind Marsha of that. Nor did she tell her that she'd had affairs with men who were a lot younger still. To Charlotte, age didn't matter. "I gather you like him."

"A lot. We have a lot in common. We both like old things." She smiled. "It's just that Bert's are older, by about sixty-four million years. He wants me to come out to Bozeman to visit. It's a no-win situation. If it works out, guess what? I get to commute to Bozeman, Montana. Just the place for a scholar of Tang Dynasty poetry."

"I've been there," said Charlotte. "We filmed *Big Sky* in Bozeman. It's beautiful country. Besides, maybe he'll commute to New York."

Marsha considered. "Maybe."

"It might be fun spending your summers in exotic places looking for dinosaur fossils," Charlotte added.

"More like backward, dirty, and roach-infested places." Marsha stuck out her foot to crush a huge cockroach that had just crawled out from under the bed; the carcass smelled like a bus-stop urinal. "That's the one thing I can't stand about Dunhuang, the roaches."

She looked up at Charlotte. "Listen, Stepmom. I don't need you to egg me on."

Charlotte laughed. "As long as you don't—"

"I know," interrupted Marsha. "As long as I don't marry him."

One of the many things Charlotte and Marsha shared was their readiness to march down the aisle. In Marsha's case, it had been twice instead of four times, but she was a lot younger than her stepmother. Charlotte had often counseled her not to marry every man she fell in love with, which had been her own mistake.

"What does the *I Ching* say?" asked Charlotte. The book lay open on the bed, along with the plastic tray that usually held the teacups and thermos bottle, but now held three of the antique Chinese coins that were used for casting a hexagram, and a notepad on which a hexagram had been written down.

Not surprisingly for a Chinese scholar, Marsha was also a fan of the *I Ching*, though she frowned on using it for what she called "parlor game divination." To do so was to trivialize a deeply profound book, she said. She called it "a key that unlocked the unconscious mind."

Marsha passed the book over to her. The hexagram she had cast was Hexagram 31: "Wooing." Charlotte read aloud from the interpretation. " 'This hexagram represents the universal attraction between the sexes.' Sounds like it's to the point," she observed. "What does it advise you to do?"

Marsha sighed. "I haven't gotten to that part yet."

Charlotte laid the book down on the bed. "To get back to the subject at hand: I don't think Dogie killed Larry. . . ."

"Dogie wouldn't kill a flea," protested Marsha, which showed how much she had already come under Bert's influence.

"Granted. I don't think he'd kill a flea, but you never know. Question: What time did Bert leave to go back to his room?"

"A little after four-thirty."

"Four-thirty! Are you sure?"

"I'm positive. I looked at the clock."

"Why so early?"

"I don't know. Maybe he wanted to sleep in his own bed. Maybe he didn't want Dogie to find out about us for some reason."

Or maybe he was with Dogie, Charlotte thought. Maybe Dogie had been covering up for him, figuring that she wouldn't bother to check with Marsha. Maybe Bouchard wasn't the only one who was spying on the competition.

"Why don't you ask him?" said Marsha.

"I will."

Back in her room, Charlotte lay on her bed and studied the patterns on the stucco ceiling. She was exhausted—it had been a long day: the meeting with Reynolds, the tour of the Cave of Unequaled Height, the discovery of the *T. rex* skeleton, and the excursion to the Lake of the Crescent Moon. But she didn't feel sleepy; her mind was spinning with questions. If Bert was with Dogie, why hadn't Bouchard seen him? she wondered. Maybe he just hadn't noticed a second person. He said he had been half-asleep. Or maybe it had been Bert that Bouchard had seen rather than Dogie. He had really only admitted to seeing a light tan Stetson, which could have been worn by either one. And if either Dogie or Bert or both *had* been in the desert, what was their purpose in being there? If they weren't really hunting for fossils, that is. And, if it was to murder Larry, how had they managed to cook up the scheme to frame Feng so fast? Unlike Bouchard, they had arrived in Dunhuang only the day before. Or, if they hadn't murdered Larry, might they have taken advantage of Larry's being dead to steal the critical page from his field diary? Unlike Bouchard, they wouldn't have needed a spy to tell them that Larry had struck pay dirt: he had told them so himself the night before. Dogie had condemned Bouchard for poaching on his rival's territory, but who was to say that poaching wasn't as endemic in the paleontology business as bribing building inspectors was in the construction business? Finally, if what Dogie said was true—if Bert hadn't been with Dogie and he hadn't been with Marsha—where the hell *had* he been? When it came to all-night places of entertainment, Dunhuang was about as meagerly endowed as Bozeman, Montana.

Charlotte's eyes traveled around the room: the towels hanging on the rack, thin as T-shirts, full of holes, and stiff as cardboard from being hung in the desert air to dry; the ever-present thermos of hot water and packet of tea; and the ever-present bugs, namely the huge cockroach that was slowly making its way across the floor, feelers waving. And on her dresser, the gray-jacketed volume of the *I Ching* that Kitty had given her as a going-away present.

What the hell? she said to herself.

She wasn't usually given to this sort of thing, she thought as she sat back down on the bed with the book. In fact, she despised this sort of thing. She had worked with actresses who wouldn't show up if their horoscope wasn't favorable. They were like the Roman senators who wouldn't go to the forum if they tripped on the doorsill on the way out of the house. Unprofessional. And if there was one thing Charlotte despised, it was the lack of professionalism.

But . . . Marsha considered the *I Ching* a profound book of spiritual guidance, the oldest book of spiritual guidance in existence, in fact—over three thousand years old. Her attitude toward it was entirely pragmatic; its function was simply to satisfy specific psychological needs of the user. "Don't ask it a question," Marsha had advised her. "Trust it to give you insight into whatever it is that is troubling you at the moment."

Fetching her purse from her dresser, she pulled out her wallet, opened the change compartment, and fished out the square-holed antique coins that Kitty had given her. She also took out a pencil and a pad of paper. Then, kneeling down on the thin pink rug between the beds, she threw the coins down on the tiled floor. She threw them six times, marking the result down each time on her notepad.

The hexagram she cast was Hexagram 57: "Wind." The interpretation was "Success will be achieved by unceasing effort toward a clearly defined goal, like the wind that bends trees and sculpts mountains." Her reading included lines that expanded on the initial judgment. The first warned her that by drifting "indecisively to and fro," she was dissipating her energy. Instead of deliberating on the problem, she should act with "military decisiveness." The second advised her that by taking "energetic action," she would catch her prey. And the third informed her that although "the beginning has not been good, the moment has come when a new direction should be taken."

As before, the *I Ching* had gone right to the heart of the matter. It had told her in no uncertain terms that it was time to stop fooling around and *do* something. But what? She reviewed the *I Ching*'s advice. While keeping her goal clearly in mind, she should take resolute action. But in a new direction; her current deliberations weren't getting her anywhere. She decided that the question it was answering had to do with Larry's murder. Her object was to find out who had killed him. What could she do to advance that goal? Talk to his servants, but that was hardly a new direction. And then it came to her: she could find out who it was that had planted the shortwave radio on Feng!

And for that, she would need Marsha.

She found her stepdaughter where she had left her a few minutes before, sitting cross-legged on her bed, studying the *I Ching*. Or rather, a book of interpretation. "I'm still on 'Wooing,' " Marsha said. "Listen to this: 'If you are trying to make a decision with regard to a relationship, you should give close scrutiny to the attitudes, surroundings, and friends of the other person. By taking stock of the forces influencing him in such a way, you will gain insight into his character and his life pattern. You will then be able to better judge his effect on your own character and needs, and come to a decision about whether such a relationship will ultimately be of benefit to you.' " She sighed.

"Sounds like excellent advice," said Charlotte. "I guess you have some serious thinking to do."

"Yes. I guess I do," Marsha replied, then smiled at her stepmother. "But so do you."

"What do you mean?"

"Daddy just called. I just came back from talking with him. He's going to call you back in a few days. He wants to know if you'll go with him to a businessman's round-table convention in the Virgin Islands. It will be four days—September fourth through the eighth—at Little Dix Bay on Virgin Gorda."

Charlotte sighed. Jack's expectation that she attend functions of this sort had been one of their main areas of conflict. To put it simply: she hated them. The forced company of the other wives drove her crazy. She had absolutely nothing in common with women whose idea of achievement was finding a bargain at Neiman Marcus. Then again, a few days in the Caribbean didn't sound too bad. And Little Dix was spread out enough that she could get away from the others. There was also Jack: in spite of everything, he was good company.

Marsha was looking up at her, awaiting her answer. She was sympathetic. She too would have hated the life that her father expected of Charlotte, but she also loved him and wanted to see the two of them stay together.

In any case, Charlotte was too tired to think about it right now. "To change the subject . . ."

"Avoiding it is more like it," said Marsha with a smile.

"That's exactly right," said Charlotte. "Or putting it off, anyway. Do you have anything on your schedule tomorrow?"

"I'm supposed to be giving a lecture on the Tang Dynasty murals in the caves in the afternoon, but my morning's free."

"Good. How would you like to take a break from matters of the heart and go into town?" She explained about her consultation with the *I Ching*, and about her decision to look into who had planted the shortwave radio on Feng. "I thought I'd ask around the market, but I'll need an interpreter."

"Sounds fine to me. I was thinking about visiting the bazaar tomorrow morning anyway. There's a market every day, but the big bazaar is on Sunday. It's supposed to be one of the most fascinating on the Silk Road."

"Great. I'll make the arrangements for transportation. Is right after breakfast all right with you?"

"It's a date," said Marsha.

·9·

CHARLOTTE AWOKE WITH one thought: more than anything else, she wanted to be clean. She desperately wanted a hot shower, or even a cold shower. She felt as if she had spent the day on a windy beach. She was coated with a fine layer of grit. There was grit in her hair, grit in her teeth, grit between her toes. Even the creases in her pillowcase were brown with grit. But a shower was an impossibility until this evening, and even then the chances that she would beat out the Germans who had been monopolizing the showers for the last two days were slim. What she really wanted was a long soak in a hot tub, but she wasn't asking for miracles. Instead she settled for a thorough wash-up in her enameled washbowl, and a prayer for enough hot water to go around that evening. She was getting quite adept at washing up in her washbowl, but it wasn't the same. When it came to hardships, she was of the same mind as Roy Chapman Andrews: she didn't believe in them; they were a nuisance. At least she had a good breakfast to look forward to, she thought as she brushed her teeth a few minutes later at the communal spigot. The breakfasts here were wonderful. In fact, the food in general was very good, just as Peter had said on the train.

She met Marsha in the dining hall at eight-thirty. Since dawn didn't come until seven-thirty, everything was behind time here. People went to bed later and got up later. Breakfast was at nine, lunch at one, and dinner at eight, which was fine with her—she was on a New York schedule. Breakfast consisted of a delicious omelet, toast with fresh butter (in contrast to the rancid butter that had been served on the train) and a delicious pear jam, coffee lightened with warm milk, and "orong juice," which was one of the beverage specialties posted on a sign in the dining hall, along with Luoky Cola and Ven Mouth Wine.

Eating in the dining hall was a little like eating in a high-school cafeteria—you never knew who you were going to sit with. Their dining companion that morning was a slight young Chinese man with a thick shock of black hair. He wore tinted aviator-style glasses, blue jeans, and a red-and-white Boston University T-shirt. His name was Chu and he was the director's son, home from college in the United States on summer break. He had Chu's broad face and flaring eyebrows. He had just arrived the night before, and would be working at the caves for the summer.

"My father has spoken of meeting you," said Chu junior, once they had introduced themselves. He smiled, a grudging, toothy grin. "He wouldn't admit it, but I think he was quite thrilled to meet you."

"Why is that?" asked Charlotte.

"He was quite a fan of yours in his youth. He used to see all of the Western pictures in Shanghai."

Charlotte found this to be one of the oddest things about being a star—having fans in these remote corners of the globe. For a time, she could have gotten off a plane almost anywhere in the world and been recognized. "Your father didn't say anything about having seen my films," she said.

"He wouldn't have," said Chu junior. "He doesn't like to talk about his past as a member of a counterrevolutionary bourgeois family. Though I don't see why it matters now that he's been rehabilitated. I saw one of your films myself a couple of years ago, before they were banned."

"My films have been banned?" said Charlotte.

"Not only your films. All forms of Western culture have now been banned as part of the national campaign against spiritual pollution. The party is trying to halt the spread of decadent bourgeois ideologies, which it views as being culturally contaminating."

Charlotte wasn't sure how to take his comments. Was he a reformer who was speaking sarcastically, or a supporter of the Party conservatives?

Marsha assured her later that it was the latter. Only the most ideologically pure students were allowed to study abroad. It was an honor awarded only to Party trustworthies and their sons and daughters.

"Then he was serious about my films being considered spiritual pollution," said Charlotte as they headed out to the minibus.

"I think he was," Marsha replied.

Charlotte laughed. "My movies have been called a lot of things over the years, but this is the first time they've been called spiritual pollution." She wondered again if China was ready for *The Crucible*.

The ride to town took about twenty-five minutes. The first fifteen minutes were through the desert. After they had passed the Southern Dunes, they crossed a river and entered the verdant patchwork of green and gold fields on the outskirts of the town. The Chinese had actually moved giant sand dunes, shovelful by shovelful, to reclaim these fields from the desert, a feat that Charlotte found astounding. A few minutes later, they passed through the southern gate of the town. The driver of the minibus dropped them off at the traffic circle at the center of town, where a loudspeaker mounted on a telephone pole blared "Edelweiss." Why didn't "Edelweiss" blaring out of a loudspeaker qualify as spiritual pollution? Charlotte wondered. If she were a Party cadre, it would have been first on her "banned in Dunhuang" list.

"What are we supposed to be looking for here?" asked Marsha as they headed down a dusty beaten-earth road crowded with donkey carts and bicycles, their bells ringing, toward the bazaar.

"I'm not sure exactly. If Larry wasn't murdered by the local ne'er-do-well—and I don't think he was—that means that Larry's murderer must have planted the shortwave radio on him, probably while he was drunk."

"Which means that we're looking for someone who might have seen a foreigner hanging around this local ne'er-do-well. By the way, do we know the local ne'er-do-well's name?"

"Yes, it's Feng."

By now, a crowd of curiosity seekers was trailing them. For once, it wasn't Charlotte who was drawing the attention, but rather Marsha, whose blond hair and wide blue eyes made her something of a freak among the ethnically homogenous Chinese, for whom anything but black hair was an oddity.

"You'd think the circus had come to town," said Marsha, looking around.

As she spoke, a big-wheeled donkey cart with a gay canopy to shield its passengers from the sun came to their rescue, pulling up to a stop with an ear-piercing squeak. It was driven by a sweet-faced young man wearing a green Mao cap, who said, "You ladies go to market?"

Charlotte and Marsha nodded.

"You ladies want ride to market?"

They nodded again.

Hopping down from his perch, the young man gallantly helped them onto the platform of the cart, which was covered with a dirty piece of old carpeting. Then, with a flick of his whip, the cart was off, weaving its way at high speed in and out among the bicycle and pedestrian traffic. Occasionally, the driver yelled something that sounded like "Hoosh, hoosh," which they concluded from the way pedestrians scattered meant "Get out of the way."

"This reminds me of a ride through Times Square during five o'clock rush hour with one of those devil-may-care cabbies," said Charlotte as she gripped the wooden side of the cart for dear life.

Marsha smiled.

They arrived about seven minutes later. After dropping them off, the driver charged them four dollars for the trip—almost as much as the same ride would have cost in New York.

Charlotte thought about what Reynolds had said about peasants getting rich. "If this is the free market at work, maybe they should go back to Communism," she said, after shelling out the eight yuan.

"I guess we should have bargained first," said Marsha ruefully.

The bazaar was a broad dirt street lined with market kiosks, a chaotic jumble of street hawkers, food vendors, and milling pedestrians—exotic, colorful, and noisy. Wandering around, they marveled at the wide array of goods and produce for sale. It was here that peasants came to sell the produce they grew on the private plots that had been banned until recently by the government. The produce included tomatoes, peppers, cabbages, carrots, eggplants, melons, dried apricots, and greens—parsley, chives, and scallions—tied into artistic little bundles. A garlic vendor stood motionless, his neck and arms hung with strings of threaded garlic, like a hula dancer covered with leis. A woman passed by with her purchases thrown over her shoulder: a bunch of live chickens bound up by the feet. In addition to the produce there were all sorts of goods: inner soles, combs, nuts and bolts, rolls of plastic sheeting, lengths of rope tied into shanks, and canvas bags full of seeds.

There were also clothes, yard goods, and jewelry. Charlotte was especially taken with the silks: bolt after bolt of exquisite brocades interwoven with gold thread. She was tempted to buy some, but what would she do with it? Then there was the food, which reminded her a little of New York City's Ninth Avenue. A vendor of shashlik, the local version of shish kebab, juggled his skewers on a smoky charcoal grill. Noodle sellers in white caps kneaded long, thick ropes of dough. But the most interesting were the vendors of services. It seemed as if almost any everyday need could be accommodated on the sidewalks or in the open-fronted kiosks. One enterprising tailor had set up his sewing machine on the sidewalk. He could mend a shirt or sew on a button on the spot. Another entrepreneur sat behind a workbench repairing watches. Blacksmiths hammered out farm implements and horseshoes; barbers shaved their customers' stiff black hair into bristle cuts; carpenters turned out table legs and dresser knobs; knife grinders sharpened daggers with silver hafts inlaid with polished stones at grindstones turned by bicycle wheels; porcelain menders fixed cracked and chipped plates and cups; bootmakers made boots; dentists even pulled teeth.

Charlotte found it fascinating.

They stopped to window shop at the kiosk of an old herbalist with a mouthful of shiny metal teeth. On his shelves were arrayed an assortment of jars of various sizes which reminded Charlotte of the jars that had lined the shelves in her high-school biology lab, with their slimy-looking contents pickled in formaldehyde. Equally disgusting were the tidy rows of dried snakes and lizards that hung from the ceiling. Dried bats that had been mounted on cardboard with their wings outstretched were tacked to the rough board walls. In addition there were collections of various kinds of antlers, dried birds' heads, and other, unidentifiable, items.

"Not a bottle of aspirin in sight," said Marsha.

Charlotte was rummaging through a cardboard box on the counter. "Look at this!" she said. "A boxful of dragon bones." They were large and small. Some were incised with Chinese ideographs; others were not. "I saw one of these at Larry's camp. Lisa told me they were dinosaur bones."

"Some of them probably are. The powder is sold as an aphrodisiac. I'll have to tell Bert that they're for sale here," she added with a little smile. "I'm sure he'll have a professional interest."

Charlotte laughed, provoking a shiny smile from the herbalist, who was taking a customer's pulse—not a Western pulse, Charlotte knew from friends who'd had acupuncture, but a reading of the body's energy patterns.

"I'm going to ask if he has anything for my rash," said Marsha. Since arriving in China, she had been plagued by a poison-ivy-like rash on her arms and legs. When the health-seeker had left, Marsha explained her problem.

For a minute, they talked. Charlotte presumed that the herbalist was asking Marsha questions about the rash. Then he looked at her tongue and took her pulse. Finally, he gave her his pronouncement.

"He says he has an herb that will cure my rash in three days," said Marsha as the herbalist mixed up a lotion from the jars lining the shelves.

As Marsha waited for her prescription, Charlotte took in the market scene. At the end of the row of stalls which included the herbalist's kiosk was an open, dusty area that appeared to be a parking lot for donkey and ox carts. The animals rested on the ground near their carts, sleeping or nibbling on fodder. Under a row of stunted trees on the far side of the parking lot a group of four beggars squatted on the ground. One of them was a boy with a stringed instrument. It was Dunhuang's equivalent of the Bowery.

She nudged Marsha.

Beggars were few and far between in China. The government viewed them as examples of the failure of Communism, and they were rounded up and stowed away out of sight. But occasionally you did see them. Charlotte had even seen a beggar on a staircase landing in the Beijing Friendship Store.

"I see," said Marsha, as she paid the herbalist, who calculated her bill on an abacus. "What do you think we should do?"

"Ask the herbalist if he knows of a beggar by the name of Feng, and if he associates with that group over there."

Turning back to the herbalist, Marsha asked him the question. After he had responded, she translated for Charlotte. "He says he knows him, and that he usually can be found sitting under those trees with the others. But he's not there now because he's in jail."

"Ask him if he's seen any foreigners associating with him."

Again, Marsha put the question to the herbalist. Even without understanding the language, Charlotte could see that he wasn't going to answer. The wall had come down, and his genial face had frozen into a stiff mask.

"He says he doesn't know."

It was one thing to oblige a customer who has just made a purchase, but it was another to be overly cooperative in a matter that was nobody's business but public security's.

Marsha raised a hand as if to say "That's okay" and thanked him for the lotion. After bowing to her, the herbalist gestured in the direction of the beggars. "Why don't you ask them?" he was clearly saying.

They took his advice. The beggars had nothing to lose by answering a few questions from some nosy foreigners.

As they approached, the boy stood up, revealing a leg that was withered to a spindly stick. He started playing a Chinese melody on his instrument, which looked like a lute. When he had finished, he took off his cap and held it out. Charlotte and Marsha each donated a few fen, and the boy sat down again.

Marsha picked the most alert-looking of the adults to address. In front of him was a dish of dry crumbs, which symbolized his poverty. Despite the heat, he was smothered in layer upon layer of rags. Except for his Chinese features, he might have been a typical New York street person.

In answer to Marsha's question, he shook his head. Then he turned to the others and repeated it for them.

It was the boy who answered.

"He says he saw a foreigner talking with Feng on Friday morning," said Marsha. "But he doesn't know what they were talking about."

Maybe they were on to something here, Charlotte thought. Larry had been killed Thursday night or early Friday morning. Which meant that whoever killed him had to have planted the shortwave radio on Feng sometime later in the day on Friday. "Ask him what the foreigner looked like," she urged.

The boy responded to Marsha's question with a jabber of Chinese. He was a skinny, filthy little thing with an oversized cap and a smile to go with it. He reminded Charlotte of Dickens' Artful Dodger. She was sure he would have picked your pocket in a trice.

When he had finished, Marsha turned to Charlotte with a discouraged expression. "He says he doesn't remember."

"Maybe there was something else. Ask him if there was anything at all about the foreigner that impressed him—his clothing, the way he walked, his tone of voice . . ."

Marsha repeated the question, but the answer was no.

"That was a bust," said Marsha, as they headed back to the place where they were scheduled to meet the minibus.

"Oh, well. Nothing ventured, nothing gained. Not that we gained anything."

They were halfway to the bus stop when Charlotte felt a tug on her leg. She turned around; it was the Artful Dodger. He was chewing a big wad of pink bubble gum, and carrying the lute under one arm. "Hello, lady," he said with an engaging smile. He then proceeded to blow a gigantic bubble.

After the bubble had popped, covering his grimy face with a layer of sticky pink froth, Marsha squatted down to speak with him. After a moment, she stood up and turned to Charlotte: "He says there is something else he remembers about the foreigner."

"What?"

"He was carrying a *pipa*. It's a kind of Chinese lute—a short, pear-shaped lute with four strings. It was popular during the Tang Dynasty."

The boy held up his instrument as if to say "similar to this."

Charlotte gave him a few coins, and he was off.

After lunch and a siesta, Charlotte headed out to the cliff for Marsha's lecture, which was on the influence of the art of Dunhuang on Chinese landscape painting of the Song Dynasty. The idea was that the themes and techniques that brought Chinese landscape painting to its zenith in the twelfth and thirteenth centuries were already apparent centuries earlier in the paintings in the caves at Dunhuang. Though Charlotte should have been doing other things, like finding out where Bert had been on the morning of the murder, or where he claimed to have been, she felt an obligation to put in an appearance. After all the trouble Marsha had taken to arrange the trip for her, the least she could do was attend her lecture.

It was a small group that met at the souvenir kiosk at the foot of the cliff. Maybe it was because the Dunhuang murals didn't have the drawing power of the secret library or the colossal Buddha. Or maybe it was that the hotels in Dunhuang town weren't fully booked. But if others had left, the irrepressible Vivian Gormley was still around, this time with her friend in tow. "I'm so glad we ran into you again," she said. "We're leaving later on this afternoon for the next oasis." She yanked her friend forward. "This is my friend, Beverly Watts. She'd like your autograph too." She turned to her companion: "Give her your notepad, Beverly."

A timid hand reached forward with the pad.

"Sign it 'To my adoring fan, Beverly Watts,' " commanded Vivian.

Charlotte signed the notepad in her round, bold scrawl, and handed it back to Beverly, whose thin skin looked like crepe paper.

"Thank you so much," said Beverly, clasping the notepad to her breast.

If there were any other autograph seekers in the group, Marsha effectively put them off by announcing that they would now set out for Cave 323, which was located at the northern end of the cave complex. As they walked along the paved avenue at the foot of the cliff, Marsha informed her audience that Cave 323 wasn't among the caves that were usually open to the public. She had convinced Chu to allow the group to visit this particular cave because it contained especially fine paintings of the Pure Land of the Western Paradise that illustrated her landscape theme. It would be the first time that she herself would be seeing these paintings outside of the pages of a book, she said, and her excitement at the prospect conveyed itself to her charges.

Midway along the cliff face, they were joined by Emily, who came running up, her ring of iron keys jangling. It was clear that she was upset about something. Her eyes were red and swollen from crying, and tears stained her cheeks. As they walked on, she talked earnestly with Marsha in Chinese. When they reached the northern group of caves, Marsha stopped to tell them more about Cave 323, which dated from the Tang Dynasty. "The Tang caves represent the peak of artistic achievement in Dunhuang," she said. "During this period, the Tang rulers consolidated their rule over China and extended their domain into Central Asia. This period was also the great age of Buddhism. The strength of the empire is reflected in the worldliness and sophistication of the paintings, and the influence of Buddhism is reflected in the proud bearing of the statues of the Bodhisattvas, priests, and saints."

Now that Emily had regained her composure, Marsha interrupted her talk to introduce her, and then went on: "The Tang Dynasty produced several sects of Buddhism, including the Pure Land School, which was centered around the worship of the Amitabha Buddha, or the Buddha of the Future, and his Western Paradise.

Unlike the austere doctrines of early Buddhism, which taught that Nirvana could be reached only through unceasing effort over the course of many incarnations, the Pure Land School taught a doctrine of salvation by faith. Through faith, one could enter directly into the heaven of the Western Paradise. The painting of the Western Paradise that we will see today was meant to inspire the beholders' faith in the paradise that was theirs if they were devout in their practice." Turning, Marsha pointed to the door of an isolated cave high above them on the cliff face. "We're headed to the cave on the uppermost level. It's a climb of about sixty feet." She smiled at the group. "Are we ready?"

The group assented, and they started climbing, with Emily taking the lead. Charlotte brought up the rear with Marsha. The route was like a maze set on end: up irregular rock-cut staircases, across narrow plank verandas, through low-beamed doorways, and up steep access ramps. Fortunately, they were shaded from the sun by the cliff face.

"What's wrong with Emily?" asked Charlotte as they climbed.

"Chu just called her in for a little heart to heart about her relationship with Ned. He reminded her that as a representative of her motherland, she shouldn't be demeaning herself by consorting with foreigners and the like."

"He makes it sound like it's against the law," said Charlotte.

"Until just recently, it was. Chu maintained that it still was, but Ned wrote away to the ministry in Beijing for a copy of the document allowing marriages between Chinese and foreigners."

"Oh, I see. We're talking marriage."

"Yes. When Ned produced the document, Chu was forced to admit that Chinese-foreign marriages were legal, but Emily still needs his permission, as her Party representative, and he says he won't grant it. He told her that capitalists get married and divorced just for the fun of it."

"What are they going to do?"

"The same thing one would do in dealing with any other bureaucracy: go above his head to the next rank of Party cadres."

Charlotte had paused to catch her breath. She had always enjoyed excellent health, a lucky circumstance that was in large measure responsible for all that she had achieved. A big ingredient in the recipe for success, she had learned, was sheer stamina. But she was also showing the wear and tear of her sixty-odd years. "Why don't you go on ahead," she said.

She was joined shortly after Marsha had gone on by Vivian Gormley, who had lagged behind with an another Australian. Under her sun visor Vivian's round face was bright red with the exertion of the climb. For a moment, Charlotte wondered if Ho might have another dead foreigner on his hands.

"I'm glad we're not doing this at high noon," said Vivian as she removed the sun visor to wipe her dripping brow.

After a few minutes, they continued on. The last leg of the climb was a rickety bamboo ladder which led to the porch fronting the cave. Arriving at the top, Charlotte felt a little as if she had already ascended to one of the celestial paradises that Marsha had described.

As they awaited the stragglers, the group took in the view, which hammered home how tiny and vulnerable this oasis was. Beyond the fringe of waving poplars and the stream bed dotted with the stupas honoring forgotten monks, there was only gravel wastes, sand dunes, and badlands.

And Larry's camp.

All Charlotte could see of it was the white Toyota hidden in the shadows of the foothills of the Mountain of the Three Dangers, and the dome of Bouchard's blue tent, but the sight nevertheless brought the problem of Larry's murder to the forefront of her mind.

The Artful Dodger had said that he had seen Feng talking to a foreigner carrying a lute. Recalling a trip to Russia she had taken years ago as part of an international cultural exchange in which everyone had gone home with a balalaika, she guessed that the lute must have been a souvenir. In any case, it shouldn't be hard to track down Dunhuang's equivalent of a music store, and ask the proprietor if a foreigner had recently purchased a stringed instrument. Maybe he could give a better description than the Artful Dodger had.

When the last person had reached the top, Marsha again addressed the group: "I'm very pleased that Mr. George Chu, the director of the Dunhuang Research Academy, has allowed us to see this cave today. It contains a very fine and detailed example of a paradise scene, which is a typical subject of this period. Unfortunately, the pigments are flaking off, which is why this cave is usually closed to the public, so I'll have to ask you to be especially careful not to brush up against the walls."

Then Emily unlocked the door of the cave, and they all entered.

By contrast with the hot glare outside, the inside of the cave was chilly, gloomy, and deathly still. Unlike the caves housing the secret library and the colossal Buddha, which were visited daily, this cave conveyed a sense of having been shut up for ten centuries.

As Charlotte's eyes became accustomed to the dim light, the paintings on the walls of the antechamber gradually emerged from the darkness. There were paintings on either side depicting processions of elegant Bodhisattvas carrying trays of fruits and flowers. They were long, narrow figures wearing jeweled necklaces and armlets, and flowing robes girdled with jeweled belts. They appeared to be walking toward the inner chamber, and their stance suggested that they had halted for a moment to bid the viewer to accompany them.

"I have a stupid question," said one of the tourists. "Are the Bodhisattvas male or female?"

"That's not a stupid question at all," Marsha replied. "In fact, they're both. They took the form of court ladies, but they have tiny mustaches to make them conform to the convention that they could be of either sex."

Their tadpole mustaches reminded Charlotte of Ho's.

After admiring the Budhisattvas, the group passed through a narrow doorway into the inner chapel. Marsha had picked the cave for its frescoes, but it was the statues that interested Charlotte. As in Cave 16, the center was occupied by a Buddha whose rich maroon robes glowed in the light of Marsha's torch. Mounted on a horseshoe-shaped dais, he was surrounded by the figures of half-a-dozen divine attendants, several of which lay scattered around on the floor in pieces, like giant dolls in a doll hospital. The one nearest Charlotte had a hole in its back.

"Why does the statue have a hole in the back?" someone asked. It was the same question that Charlotte had been about to ask.

"It was toppled over by looters centuries ago," Marsha explained. "Most of the statues at Dunhuang are hollow. They're constructed of clay modeled on a wooden armature. The looters were looking for hidden treasure inside them. The monks often hid manuscripts and other valuables in the statues' bellies, believing that the treasures gave them spiritual power."

"Imagine that!" said Vivian as she looked down at the torso of a fierce-visaged guardian spirit, bare-chested and heavily muscled.

Charlotte thought of Chu, the warrior with the chink in his armor.

"Before we talk about the painting," Marsha continued, "I want you to travel back in time for a moment, and imagine this cave as it was during the Tang Dynasty. It would have been hung with silk temple banners, and lit with torches. Candles and incense would have been burning at the feet of the Buddha, and the walls would be resounding with the chanting of the monks. Now, let's look at the mural of the Western Paradise on your left." She shined her torch at the wall, revealing a mural that must have been twenty feet long and ten feet high. As they looked at it, Marsha pointed out the main features. The center of the mural was occupied by Lord Buddha, who sat on his magnificent lotus throne amid a majestic assembly of haloed divinities. Below him was a lotus pool, in which newborn souls in the form of babies emerged from lotus flowers under showers of falling blossoms. In the foreground, peacocks strutted across marble-tiled courtyards, and an orchestra played for dancers turning graceful pirouettes. In the background, a paradise of palaces, pavilions, and gate towers stretched off into the misty distance.

It was a gorgeous painting. Charlotte was especially struck by the colors, almost all of which seemed to have lost nothing with age, despite what Marsha had said about their having deteriorated. Two colors predominated. One—the shade of the lotus pools—was a limpid bluish-green somewhere between teal and turquoise that reminded Charlotte of the translucent glazes of the celadon bowls she had seen at the National Palace Museum. The other was a rich red ochre that reminded her of the desert sandstone. To her, they were the colors of China. The only sign of deterioration was in the pale pink flesh tones, which Marsha explained had oxidized to a dark chocolate brown, making the faces look as if they'd been painted by Rouault rather than a Tang master.

As Marsha explained the technical details of the painting—the nature of the plaster that was laid on the walls, the type of pigments that were used, how the designs were laid out—Charlotte wandered around the chapel, feeling as if she herself were submerged in that delicate, glowing green light. She was especially taken with the graceful *asparas*, the angel-like figures who hovered above the rooftops of the palaces and pavilions or darted swiftly in and out of the spiraling copper-colored clouds of the heavens.

The scenes on either side of the paradise mural were equally fascinating. Framed by a beautiful mosaic of flowers, they depicted the everyday life and concerns of the earth dwellers: women ground wheat, made pottery, or laid fruit out to dry in the sun; men hunted, fished, cut timber, forged iron, or transported their produce to market on the big-wheeled donkey carts that hadn't changed in eleven centuries.

"I think I like these little paintings even more than the big one. They really show you what life was like back then," said Vivian, who had joined Charlotte. "Look at this one!" she said, shining the beam of her flashlight on a painting. "The young couple is getting married!"

Captivated by the images, Charlotte found herself following Vivian along the low, narrow passageway that encircled the central pillar. She'd been told that when the caves were still active centers of worship, the pilgrims has moved clockwise around these pillars in their meditations, in the direction of the sun. In places, the stylized lotus pattern of the square bricks that paved the floor had been worn almost smooth by their feet.

She was studying a battle scene populated by dozens of the elegant, prancing steeds for which the Tang Dynasty was noted, when a piercing scream shattered the stillness.

It was Vivian. She was about ten feet away, in the chamber at the rear of the central pillar. Her arms were flapping around at her sides, causing the beam of her flashlight to zigzag wildly. She looked like a very plump chicken that was trying to fly.

Charlotte rushed toward her. She had just climbed the step up to the chamber behind the central pillar when she tripped over something. Shining the beam of her own flashlight at the floor, she could hardly believe her eyes. It was a leg—a human leg, not the limb of a broken statue. The foot was sticking stiffly out over the step; it was a large foot, and it was clad in a brown and black boat shoe. With the beam of her flashlight, she followed the leg up to the rest of the body, which was that of a man lying on his back in the path that had been worn in the floor by the pilgrims' feet. His face was turned toward the back of the cave, but he was clearly dead. He'd been stabbed in the chest. Like Larry, except that he appeared to have been stabbed several times, and there was much more blood. The blood had left a dark blotch on his navy-blue sweatshirt, and a puddle on the floor which had flowed into the pattern in the molded bricks, throwing the lotus design into clear relief. There were also gashes on his left forearm where he had thrown up his arm to protect himself. Even his hands were bloody: more gashes on his palms and the undersides of his fingers indicated that he had attempted to grab the knife away from his attacker. But despite all the blood, there wasn't the strange coppery smell that had permeated the air inside Larry's tent. The blood was dry. Like the pigment in the pink paint used for the skin tones of the figures in the wall paintings, it had oxidized to a dark chocolate brown.

Though the victim's face was turned away from her, Charlotte knew right away who he was. He was wearing the same clothes he had been wearing the evening before at the Lake of the Crescent Moon—brown wool slacks and a navy-blue sweatshirt. It was Peter Hamilton.

• IO •

THE DISCOVERY OF Peter's body was followed by the arrival of Ho and his entourage. Once again, they all sat in the overstuffed armchairs of the reception room, sipping bitter green tea and answering questions. Chu chain-smoked and spat, Ho wriggled his mustache, and Ho's dim-witted assistant blinked stupidly. The fan whirred, and the photographs of Chou and Hua stared down from the walls. If Charlotte had been confused before, she was all the more so now. For two days, she had been operating under the assumption that Larry's death was linked to his discovery of the *T. rex* skeleton, an assumption that was supported by the missing page in the field diary. But it seemed improbable that Peter's death was also linked to the discovery of a dinosaur fossil. It was possible, of course, that the two men had been killed by different people, for different reasons. But the chances of two murderers being at large in an oasis less than a mile square were highly unlikely. There was also the matter of the mode of death. Both victims had been stabbed, which pointed to a single murderer. True, they had been stabbed in different ways—Larry had been stabbed once and Peter several times—but that could be accounted for by the fact that Larry had been asleep. He didn't have a chance to fight back, hence the single, simple stab wound. As for Feng: since he'd been locked up in jail since Friday, there was no chance that Ho would be able to pin the murder on him this time.

After a subdued dinner and a brief tour of the Academy's museum, whose few sorry relics—plates, jars, water pitchers, and tools used by the Dunhuang artisans—pointed up how few portable objects the Western explorers had left behind, they had all retired to their rooms. Charlotte felt as if she needed a good night's rest. Larry's death had been a shock, but she hadn't lost the feeling of solid ground beneath her feet. Peter's death left her feeling as if she were enveloped in billowy copper-colored clouds, like one of the *asparas* in the paradise painting. But they were roiling, noxious clouds that choked her breath, fogged her vision, and caved in when she tried to put her weight on them. Then there was her throat, which was still scratchy and swollen. Tea would help, she thought, as she straightened up her room. After fixing herself a cup, she got out her *I Ching* coins. Maybe the Sage, as Kitty called it, would help her decide how to proceed. She could still go to the music store, but apart from that she had no ideas. There was no point in questioning Bert now. He might have been a remote suspect in Larry's death, but she couldn't conceive of any way in which he could be connected to Peter's death.

This time the *I Ching* was no help. Or rather, it described her situation with perfect accuracy, which was no help at all. The hexagram that she cast was Hexagram 3: "Difficulty at the Beginning." The situation was still dark and unformed, the *I Ching* said, describing it as "teeming, chaotic profusion." It was up to her to wrest order from the chaos, but to find her way, she had to separate first and unite later, "just as one sorts out silk threads from a knotted tangle and binds them into skeins."

Thanks a lot. But the Sage did offer one ray of hope: it said that the chaos was a result of the conflict among the many elements that were struggling to take form. Therefore, order was implicit in the chaos. As long as she kept her goal in sight and proceeded in an "orderly manner" rather than boldly plunging into the "forest of obstacles," she would succeed in her undertaking. The question was, What was an orderly manner?

Bill Reynolds supplied her first clue the next morning. He had been in Dunhuang since Larry's death, waiting for the police to release Larry's body and effects. There was no point in his making the eleven-hundred-mile journey back to Beijing, only to have to turn around and come back in a few days. He intercepted Charlotte after breakfast in the courtyard where she had spoken with him on Saturday. Once again, they sat under the twisted old pear tree, drinking Luoky Cola. Peter's death had come as a shock to him too; it was a rare occurrence for an American to die in China, let alone be murdered. An elderly tourist occasionally had a heart attack, but that was about it. And for two Americans to be murdered in the same town was virtually unheard of.

Reynolds' narrow forehead was creased with worry. "The Fiske family is bringing up the heavy guns. They've already requested a full-scale Congressional investigation, and there's no telling what kind of shit's going to hit the proverbial fan now that two American nationals are dead."

"I'm afraid you're going to have a problem with Peter's family, too." She told him about Peter's hyphenated in-laws, Lord and Lady Waverley-Smythe, who, if they were as prominent as Peter implied, weren't going to settle for any trumped-up explanations from the police, either.

"Damn," was Reynolds' response.

"Have the police told you anything about Peter's death?"

"Only that the murder took place during the night, and that he was stabbed five times in the chest with a knife with a six-inch blade—the same type that was used in Fiske's murder. They haven't found the knife."

On the cliff, Charlotte could see the white-jacketed security police scurrying like ants over the walkways and verandas, searching for the murder weapon, she assumed, or for any other clues that might turn up. "What about Larry's death?" she asked. "Anything new—from the interviews with the servants, for instance?"

Reynolds shook his head. "The servants insist he was killed by the *kwei*, the devil spirits. And everybody else claims to have been asleep in bed, except for O'Dea, who was out hunting for fossils in the desert."

What about Bert? Charlotte wondered to herself. Had he lied to the police about being asleep? "When was the last time anyone saw Peter?" she asked.

"The evening of the murder, on the way back to his room. When he didn't show up at the library the next day—that's where he had been working—Chu thought he had gone to Bezeklik. He told us he was going there when we were talking about the destruction that took place during the Cultural Revolution, remember?"

Charlotte nodded.

For a moment, they sat there silently, looking up at the cliff.

Then Reynolds spoke. "Speaking of the Cultural Revolution, I finally got Kong, the director of the Chinese Academy of Dramatic Arts, on the horn yesterday. I told him you were interested, and he was thrilled. He wants to meet with you in Beijing. Will you be able to do it?"

"Yes," she said, pleased that the project seemed to be falling into place. "But what about the campaign against spiritual pollution? Chu's son told me about it yesterday. He said that all Western films have been banned. Does the ban extend to plays, as well?"

"It would have, but the campaign against spiritual pollution is history. Chu's son is a little behind the times. The Party bureaucracy abandoned it after it was generally conceded to be a failure."

"I'm glad to hear it," she said.

For a few minutes, they worked out the details of her meeting in Beijing. Then Reynolds checked his watch. "I'm meeting with Ho again in a few minutes. I'll let you know if anything more comes up. Oh, there's something else," he added, pulling out a key from the pocket of his khaki chinos.

"What's this?" she asked as he handed it to her.

"The key to Hamilton's room. He's been staying in the old guest house, as it's called. It's actually a temple with sleeping quarters for pilgrims, which Wang built. With the money he received from Stein for the manuscripts, I might add. It's at the foot of the cliff opposite the secret library."

"And?" said Charlotte.

"And, I thought you might want to look around a little. The police already searched it, but they didn't find anything. You'll find it just as it was when he died. Since his possessions are under our jurisdiction, they didn't remove anything. I didn't notice anything out of the ordinary either, but then I don't have your talent for detection. I'd appreciate it, however, if you were discreet."

Charlotte smiled. "I will be," she said.

"Second room on the left," said Reynolds.

"No gritty details?" said Charlotte.

"No gritty details."

Searching Peter's room was certainly an orderly manner in which to proceed, Charlotte thought as she headed toward the temple. In fact, if she were to pick the most orderly manner, it would be to start there. She could have waited until nighttime to search, but she was curious. And now was a good time, before the daily onslaught of tourists from Dunhuang town. The paved avenue at the foot of the cliff was deserted. There were no groups of Chinese from Hong Kong having their pictures taken in front of the caves, no groups of fat Australian tourists with their shoulder bags and sun visors. There was only the tinkle of wind chimes, the chirrup of birds, the mutter of chickens, and the crying of a baby from the settlement of peasant homes hidden among the poplars and fruit trees. She was halfway along the cave complex when she encountered Victor sitting on a poplar-shaded bench in front of the library, a modern building that adjoined the museum.

She stopped to say hello. "Taking a break?" she asked.

"Sort of," he replied. "Cooling off would be more accurate."

The strain of reading the manuscripts must have been getting to him, Charlotte thought. He looked very pale and tired, and his sharp brown eyes were ringed with deep maroon circles. "Out here?" she asked. It must have been well over ninety degrees.

"I'm cooling off mentally, not physically. I just had a run-in with Chu. He won't let me decide for myself which manuscripts to work on. He brings them out to me one at a time, like a kindergarten teacher passing out cookies, and I have to look each one over and decide whether I want to work on that one or not." He sat with his hands clasped between his knees. As he spoke, he squeezed his fingers tightly together. His voice was bitter. He raised a hand to tug nervously at his goatee, and then continued. "Without being able to look over the whole lot, I have no way of knowing whether the manuscript I've chosen to work on is the most important one or not."

"It sounds like Wang parceling out the manuscripts to Stein," she said. It also sounded as if Chu delighted in using his authority to cause trouble, she thought, remembering Emily's tear-stained face.

"Exactly, except that I'm not likely to win Chu over by professing my belief in his patron saint. Or by lavishly distributing silver for the restoration of the caves. I wish Averill were here," he said. "He was much better at raising hell about these kinds of things than I am."

"Chu's probably getting back at Westerners in general through you," she said. She went on to tell him how bitter Chu had been about the fact that the Stein Collection at the British Museum was inaccessible.

"I'm sure you're right," Victor agreed.

"Is Marsha having the same problems?"

"Not that I know of. But she works on the secular manuscripts, which are much less common than the religious texts. Because there are so few of them, they're all interesting. She's translating some Tang Dynasty ballads now." He looked up at her. "Where are you off to?"

She evaded the question. "Just taking a walk," she replied.

"Well, enjoy," he said with a wave. "I guess I'll get back to work."

As Victor stood up, Charlotte ambled down the avenue. Once he was inside, she increased her pace. Just past the museum there was a small orchard planted with gnarled old fruit trees—apples, apricots, and peaches. Beyond the orchard lay the courtyard of the old temple. As she climbed the steps, she imagined that this was how the temples at the Lake of the Crescent Moon must have looked before the Red Guards had burned them down: quaint tiled roofs with upturned eaves, lattice-covered windows, intricately carved and painted woodwork. No one was around. The only signs of life were the butterflies that hovered over a plot of zinnias, and a couple of brown chickens who seemed to have made a nest under their shade. Crossing the deserted courtyard, she climbed a set of low steps to the loggia, which was supported by red-painted columns. Opening the ornate wooden door, she found herself in the spacious temple hall, which had a shrine at one end with gaudily painted statues of Buddhist deities similar to the ones in Cave 16. More of Wang's bad taste, she gathered. The doors to the sleeping quarters opened off the temple hall.

Going to the second room on the left, Charlotte took out the key—it was even bigger and heavier than the keys to the caves—and unlocked the door. The room was much larger than hers—it had probably been meant to house groups of pilgrims rather than individuals—but it was even more austere. The bed was a brick platform known as a *kanga*, which served as a bed in Central Asian houses, and which was covered with an old mattress and some bedding. The only other furnishings were a chair and a desk. On the desk were a typewriter, a stack of books, including several spiral-bound notebooks, and a large three-ring binder that bore a title card on the cover: *Sand-Buried Treasures of Desert Cathay*. Opening the three-ring binder, Charlotte found that it contained a typed draft of the book, annotated with handwritten notes indicating deletions, additions, and corrections. A table of contents listed the chapter headings: *Let Us Talk of Silk, At the Western Gate, On Ancient Central Asian Roads, The Ruined Cities of the Taklimakan, The Manuscript Race Begins, Of Loot and Treasure*, and so on. Scanning a few pages, Charlotte was struck by the tone, which seemed more lively than that of Peter's other books. She wanted to read it, but it would never be finished, now.

There was also a photograph in a silver frame, of Peter and a beautiful young woman, probably the aristocratic wife, Fiona, of whom he had spoken—or rather, boasted—on the train. They were sitting in a grandstand under a red- and white-striped tent, drinking champagne and eating strawberries. A sign identified the location as the Center Court at Wimbledon. She imagined that notifying Peter's wife was Reynolds' job. She didn't envy him the task.

She looked around the room. She hadn't the slightest idea what she was looking for, and felt a little odd about being there, as if she were a voyeur of some sort. Then she saw Peter's wallet. It was lying on the floor next to the *kanga*, with some papers.

What the hell, she thought. That's why Reynolds had given her the key, wasn't it? She quickly went through it. There was money: U.S., British, and Chinese—both the regular currency and the Foreign Exchange Certificates that were issued to tourists—and there were credit cards, at least a dozen of them. She supposed a travel writer would need a wide selection. There were also membership cards for the Royal Central Asian Society, the Royal Geographic Society, and the Authors' Club. She had once been a guest at the Authors' Club. It was a stodgy old place whose walls were lined with mahogany bookcases filled with books presented by its members, mostly British aristocrats who fancied themselves writers, though its history included some illustrious names—Thomas Hardy and Somerset Maugham among them, if she remembered right. She couldn't imagine why a young American like Peter would want to be a member, unless it was the snob appeal.

His suitcase turned up nothing out of the ordinary, either.

She was about to leave, when a book in the stack on the desk caught her eye. Its title was *An Iconographical Index to the Caves of the Thousand Buddhas*. Opening it up, she discovered that it was an index to the subject matter of the cave paintings. With the help of the index, an art historian would presumably be able to trace the development of painting by studying how a particular subject—a donkey cart, for example—had been depicted in the cave paintings over the course of nine centuries. She was leafing through the book, which was lavishly illustrated with reproductions of the cave paintings, when a sheet of paper caught her eye.

On it was written a list of hexagrams from the *I Ching*. There were at least a dozen of them, listed vertically. Even more intriguing was the fact that a cave number was penciled in alongside each hexagram: Cave 114 next to the first, Cave 264 next to the second, Cave 291 next to the third, and so on.

As a recent initiate into the mysteries of the *I Ching*, Charlotte wondered what it meant. Had Peter also been a follower of the *I Ching?* Could the caves that were indicated by the pencil notations contain paintings of scenes from the *I Ching?* But how, for example, could you depict a scene of "Difficulty at the Beginning," which was the hexagram that she had cast last night? And even if the caves did contain depictions of ideas expressed in the hexagrams, of what relevance was it to Peter's work, which concerned the exploits of Western explorers? Her mind was toying with these questions when she noticed that the cave number next to the fifth hexagram was Cave 323, the cave in which Peter had been murdered. It wasn't likely that it was a coincidence. There were four hundred and ninety-two caves at Dunhuang. Which meant that the chances were pretty good that this list had something to do with Peter's death. But what?

Proceed in an orderly manner, she told herself. First, she had to find out what the hexagrams meant, particularly the fifth one. She now noticed that there was a copy of the *I Ching* on the desk, but looking up all the hexagrams on the list would take a while. She didn't want to risk being discovered at it. Sticking the list of hexagrams in her pocket, she opened the door to look out into the temple hall. The coast was clear. After grabbing the iconographic index for good measure, she quietly left.

Back in her room, she studied the list. Now that she had time to look at it more closely, she noticed that it was a photocopy. The original must have been quite old: there were fox marks and water stains and dark spots that looked like mildew. She could also see that the original had split along the creases where it had been folded. And that the hexagrams had been written down with a brush, rather than a pen.

Picking up her copy of the *I Ching*, she looked up the fifth hexagram. It was Hexagram 29: "Deliverance." The judgment didn't tell her anything that she could form into a clear picture. But the reading for the changing line was different. It was:

Six in the fourth place means:
A jug of wine, a bowl of rice with it;
Earthen vessels
Simply handed in through the window.
There is certainly no blame in this.

The interpretation said that in times of difficulty, ceremonious forms should be dropped. Never mind that the gifts are simple and are presented without formality, it is sincerity that is important. In other words, don't clutter your life with pretense.

But it wasn't the interpretation that interested her; it was the image. Picking up the iconographical index, she discovered that it was cross-referenced. In addition to looking up the subject matter and finding out what cave it could be found in, you could also look up a cave and find out what subjects were depicted in it. She quickly turned to Cave 323, and scanned the list, which included descriptions of the processions of Bodhisattvas, the figures in the paradise scene, and the scenes from daily life in the side panels. Near the bottom, she found what she was looking for: a listing for a "woman passing a jug of wine and a bowl of rice through a window." Voila!

Now the question was, Who had written down this list of hexagrams, and to what purpose? Followed by: What had Peter been doing with it? and what did it have to do with his murder? Looking at the list again, she noticed something else about it: there were check marks next to the first four hexagrams, but not next to the fifth or any of the succeeding hexagrams. She also noticed that all the hexagrams had one changing line, which seemed a curious coincidence when the possibilities ranged from zero to six. If ever there had been any question of her becoming bored at Dunhuang—and she suspected that after a while one Bodhisattva would begin to look just like the next—there was little possibility of that now. When it came to puzzles, Peter's list of hexagrams made the *Times* of London crossword look like child's play.

Leaning back on her bed, Charlotte pondered Peter's murder. One question that baffled her was, How had he gained access to the cave? She doubted he would have had keys. His purpose in being at Dunhuang was to study the role that Western explorers had played in the history of the caves, not to study the art. He could have stolen the keys, she supposed. Or, he could have been meeting someone—someone who did have access to the keys: a member of the Academy's staff, for instance. As she lay there, the thought struck her that it might have been Peter who was returning Dunhuang's stolen cultural relics to their original sites, but she immediately dismissed the idea as absurd. If there was anyone who was convinced of the right of Western institutions to the artworks that Western explorers had taken from Dunhuang, it was Peter. But then she had another thought. Maybe Peter had been on the other side of the issue: maybe he was a looter himself. The looting of Dunhuang's treasures had been going on for centuries. Who was to say that it wasn't still going on? Especially when Asian art was in greater demand than ever.

She remembered Marsha talking about the lively business in the heads and hands of the sculptures. She had often seen these on display in the galleries on Madison Avenue, elegantly mounted on pedestals of marble or semiprecious stone. Who would miss another head or a hand from among the twenty-four hundred statues in the caves? Peter had admitted to making fifty thousand pounds on a pair of antique soup tureens that he'd sold to a Madison Avenue gallery. That was before the government had cracked down on the exportation of antiquities. But she imagined that someone as sophisticated about foreign countries as Peter was would know how to get contraband artworks out of the country. The Chinese claimed that the revolution had purged their society of the corrupting evils of the profit motive—many Chinese still considered a tip a form of subornation—but Charlotte suspected that somewhere in the Celestial Kingdom there was a grasping Chinese "facilitator" who was as eager to accept cold, hard cash in exchange for performing an illegal service as any South American petty bureaucrat. "The squeeze," Peter had called it, when he had produced the cold beer on the train. And if a facilitator was out there, Peter could find him. She thought of his mysterious business trips—to Xian, when they had run into him on the train—and the trip he was supposed to have taken to Bezeklik, and wondered what kind of business it was he was referring to.

The unformed darkness was beginning to take shape, and a little light was beginning to trickle in. Thank you, *I Ching*. She now had a working hypothesis: Peter had been stealing artworks from the caves. Her little tour of his room had even offered a motive: the Cleveland native with the Bertie Wooster accent had a beautiful wife who was a member of the British aristocracy. From her friendship with Tom Plummer, the journalist who had written *Murder at the Morosco*, Charlotte had a pretty good idea of how much money could be made in the writing business. And it wasn't enough to support a lifestyle that included a house overlooking the heath in Hampstead and all the trimmings. Peter's books had been applauded by the critics, but that didn't mean they had been best sellers. She guessed they had probably sold ten or twenty thousand copies apiece, which was hardly enough to have brought in the kind of income necessary to keep up with the Waverley-Smythe set. Peter had admitted as much on the train. A rich wife would help, but he struck Charlotte as the type who would feel as if he had to keep up the pretense, at least, of supporting himself. She would bet that the income from the sale of a head here, a hand there, would come in very handy. But her working hypothesis still didn't explain the list of hexagrams, and the list of caves that went along with it. Nor did it tell her who had killed Peter Hamilton.

Proceed in an orderly manner. Her next step should be to take another look at Cave 323, she decided. Maybe the painting of the woman passing the jug of wine and bowl of rice through the window would offer some clue. She also wanted to look at the other caves on the list. And for that, she needed Marsha. The caves were ordinarily kept locked, but Emily had entrusted Marsha with her ring of keys. Marsha was scheduled to repeat her lecture on the Tang Dynasty early the next morning—at daybreak, in fact, which was the only time of day that the caves were illuminated by natural light—and Emily had allowed her to keep the keys until then. She checked her watch: it was just after eleven. The best time to look at the caves would be after two, when everyone was asleep. Marsha had gone out to the dinosaur dig with Bert and Dogie early that morning, and she didn't know if they were planning to come back for lunch or not. She supposed she could wait until this evening, but she didn't want to.

Grabbing her big straw coolie hat and her tube of SPF 30 sunblock, she headed out to the dinosaur quarry.

She had been a bit worried about finding the Dragon's Tomb Site again on her own, but she needn't have been. As she drew near the mountain, she noticed that the desert floor was marked with a new track, which led off to a spot at the base of the foothills a few hundred yards to the south of Larry's camp where half a dozen vehicles were parked. The parking lot turned out to be the debouchure of the ravine in which the dinosaur quarry was located. It took her only a few minutes to climb up the ravine to the quarry, around which a camp had already sprung up. The quarry itself was shaded by a large awning made of reed mats supported on bamboo poles, and a work tent had been erected on a flat shelf on the opposite slope of the ravine. Nor did the dinosaur skeleton look the same: all that had been visible when she and Lisa had found it were the giant legs, part of the backbone, and a section of the forty-foot tail, which had curved back into the hillside like a giant, serpentine garden hose. Now, the top surface of most of the skeleton lay exposed, and the long tail was fully uncovered. "All there," said Dogie, "except for a few pieces at the very tip." As was most of the neck, its individual vertebra looking like slices from a small tree trunk.

Near the quarry, a tape player had been set up on a rock for the entertainment of the crew, which included nearly a dozen people. In addition to Bert, Dogie, and Lisa, there were the pith-helmeted Peng and the four members of his team, and Orecchio, who worked nearby, measuring the distances between the various strata and recording his findings in a notebook. Finally, there was Marsha, who was crouched over the skeleton with an awl, scraping the rock from a bone that appeared to be part of the large rear foot. The tape deck was playing a Beatles song, "Rocky Raccoon."

Charlotte squatted down next to Marsha, who had adopted Lisa's working garb of cutoff jeans and a halter top, and headgear straight out of Lawrence of Arabia, in which the back of her neck and her upper back were shielded by a bandanna tucked under the back of a baseball cap, in this case one that bore the legend "Society of Vertebrate Paleontology" and a picture of a dinosaur. Love had brought her a long way from court poetry of the Tang Dynasty. "What are you working on?" Charlotte asked.

"Oh, hi," said Marsha with a wide smile, tipping back her baseball cap to wipe the sweat from her brow. "A metatarsal," she replied. "One of the foot bones." She pointed to her own sandal-clad foot to demonstrate. The cracks between her perfectly painted toenails were brown with dirt. "This guy had three toes. We've got almost all of the bones." She pointed to a sharp, curved bone of glistening white. "Even the claws, which I still have to dig out. It's kind of like being a dental hygienist."

"What happens to it once you get it all dug out?"

"The pieces are wrapped in burlap that's been dipped in plaster of Paris. Then they're packed in straw, and shipped back to the museum in Beijing, where they'll be reassembled. Bert says it will take about three months to reassemble the entire skeleton. If we find the skull, it will be the most complete *T. bataar* that's ever been found."

"T. bataar?"

"*Tyrannosaurus bataar*. The Central Asian cousin of the *T. rex*. Apparently, they're very similar, but it isn't strictly correct to call this guy a *T. rex*."

"What are the chances that you'll find the skull?"

"I don't know." She shrugged. "I'm still a novice at this." She looked over at Bert, who was working on the tail with Dogie. "Bert, what are the chances we'll find the skull? Charlotte wants to know."

Seeing Charlotte, Bert stood up and ambled over. Despite his tall, heavy frame, his movements had the fluid grace of a dancer. He was a man who was at home with his body and himself. "I see that you've been talking with my newest field assistant," he said, reaching down to grasp Marsha's hand.

She looked up at him, her wide blue eyes smiling.

"It looks like she's coming along pretty fast," said Charlotte.

"I think we'll keep her on." He squeezed her hand. "What are the chances that we'll find the skull? Well, usually I'd say they're pretty slim. But in this case, I have a hunch we might find it."

"Why's that?" asked Marsha.

"Because of the position of the neck." Bert stepped over to the neck, where Peng was working with the other members of his team. "See how the neck is arched backward?" he said, pointing downward.

The upper back and neck of the skeleton were arched backward, almost as if the dinosaur had died in the middle of doing a backbend.

"That's from the shrinking of the tendons and the ligaments after death. We think the skull might have detached from the lower jaw and rolled up against the backbone, inside the hill here."

Peng translated what he was saying for the other Chinese, who nodded enthusiastically in agreement.

"Want to help us look for it?" Bert asked. "I'd be happy to give you a trowel and dental pick."

"No thanks," said Charlotte. She eyed the skeleton. Actually it looked as if it might be fun, if it wasn't a hundred and ten in the shade. "Actually, I just came out to talk to Marsha for a few minutes. Do you allow members of your work gang to take breaks?"

"Sure." He smiled down at Marsha. "Time off for good behavior. I need a break too. The cooler's over there." He pointed to a picnic table under the tent. "We've got orange soda and beer. Sorry there's no Coke or Pepsi, but we're a little far from the supply line out here."

Charlotte was parched. "Am I entitled to a beer even if I haven't earned it by discovering any fossils?"

"Sure. We'll give you a credit against a future discovery."

A few minutes later, they were sitting under the tent with Bert and Dogie drinking beer and watching the activity on the other side of the ravine: the five Chinese and Lisa working on the skeleton, and a lone figure in a porkpie hat on the boundary of the dinosaur quarry, measuring, writing, and shoveling.

"What's Orecchio doing?" asked Charlotte as she watched him digging up clumps of dirt from various levels of the strata. He carefully put each clump into a plastic bag and labeled it.

"Taking soil samples for potassium-argon dating," Bert replied. "He's going to try to show that this is reworked sediment, but any undergraduate geology student could tell you it isn't. It's very simple: in undisturbed sediment, what's on the bottom is oldest, and what's on the top is youngest."

"The poor sonofabitch is just goin' to have to face up to the fact that we've come up with one helluva postage stamp," said Dogie. "The stamp albums are goin' to have to be redesigned to accommodate this guy."

"I'm amazed at its size," said Charlotte. "I've seen the skeleton of the *T. rex* at the American Museum of Natural History, but somehow it looks a lot bigger when it's lying on the ground."

"Frankly, we're amazed at the size, too," said Bert. "If it is a *T. bataar*, and it may not be—it may be something entirely new—it will be the biggest one that's ever been found, above or below the K/T boundary layer. The *T. bataars* that have been found before were smaller than *T. rex*, probably due to their more limited diet—even back then, the Central Asian plateau was more arid than North America—but from the size of this guy's femur, we estimate that he weighed in at about eight tons, or the size of three average elephants, and as big as any *T. rex* that's ever been found."

"Each hind foot covered over seven feet," said Marsha, between swallows of the local beer. "He could cross a room with one step."

"She's learnin'," said Dogie.

"How did he die?" asked Charlotte.

"We don't know for sure," Bert said, "but we can piece together a little bit about the circumstances." He smiled at Charlotte. "Paleontology is a lot like detection, in more ways than one."

Marsha must have told him about Reynolds' asking her to look into the murders, thought Charlotte. So much for her being discreet.

"In addition to fitting together all the pieces to form a skeleton, you have to fit together what you know about the environment to get an idea of how the dinosaurs lived." He waved his beer bottle at the tortured terrain. "Sixty-three million years ago this was a dry interior plain, kind of like an African savannah. There were palms, reeds, and cypresses, but it was open, not jungly, like it was in *King Kong*. This area was the edge of an ancient lake."

Charlotte waited for him to go on, but he didn't. It was one of those wide-open spaces that she had come to expect in his conversation. "It looks kind of like that right now, doesn't it?" she said finally.

The landscape that lay spread out before them seemed to swim in the midday heat. The sand of the desert floor shimmered like the surface of a lake that was stippled with tiny wavelets, and the clumps of camel-thorn took on the appearance of reeds and cypresses. The terns skittering across the desert floor seemed to be skimming along the glittering surface of the water. Even the atmosphere seemed as if it were from another epoch: the glaring sun rimmed every boulder with a yellow aura, which gave the landscape the harsh appearance of a land in which the giant carnivores had roamed.

Pulling his pipe out of his pocket, Bert filled the cherrywood bowl with tobacco from his tobacco pouch and lit it. The still air was perfumed with its scent. Then he continued: "I would guess that our *Tyrannosaur* was drawn into a struggle with a duckbill at the water's edge, and drowned. After he died, the body drifted into a backwater and came to rest. The flesh decomposed, and the skeleton sank into the sand. Over the eons, the sand turned to stone. Minerals were deposited in the bone, turning them to stone, too. As the earth shifted, what had been the bottom of the swamp was raised up into a hill. Finally, ancient rivers washed away the rock, exposing the layers of sediment, and erosion weathered out the bones."

"Then Larry came along," said Marsha.

"Then Larry came along," Bert repeated.

He had made the pile of old bones come alive. Charlotte thought of Marsha's description of what the interior of Cave 323 had been like during the Tang Dynasty. Yes, they were two peas in a pod.

Dogie had stood up, and was studying the butte that overhung the neck of the ravine through his binoculars. "Look at that sonofabitch," he said angrily, as he passed the binoculars to Bert.

Charlotte could just make out the black-bearded figure perched on the edge of the butte. The way he was outlined against the sky reminded her of the vultures hovering over Larry's camp on that fateful morning.

It was Bouchard, lurking at the edge of the DMZ.

• II •

HALF AN HOUR later, Marsha and Charlotte were dousing their heads under the spigot in the courtyard. A shower would have been better, but . . .

Marsha had actually been glad for an excuse to leave the dig. "It's fun, but I can only take the heat for so long," she had said. And once Charlotte had explained her mission, Marsha was as curious as Charlotte to get another look at Cave 323. Neither of them remembered a painting of a jug of wine and a bowl of rice, but they could easily have missed it in the dim light.

But first came lunch. The dinner gong, which was actually a rusty old tire rim that the cook banged with a rock, rang promptly at one.

With the paleontologists working out at the dig, the dining room was less crowded than usual. Their dining companions were Ned and Emily, who appeared to be inseparable, and a group of the German conservation consultants, who were carrying on their own animated conversation in German.

Their talk was about Peter's death.

"I have a theory," said Ned who was dressed as usual in a tie-dyed T-shirt. "Not about who did it, but about why it was done the way it was."

"What's that?" asked Marsha as they were served their first two courses: a rice pilau with apricots, onions, and carrots, and a plate of thin-skinned dumplings stuffed with mutton and seasonings.

"I was reading an account written by a Swedish explorer who visited the caves in the early part of this century. At that time, none of the staircases and balconies had been built. The caves on the upper levels were inaccessible. Originally they had been reached by ladders, of course, but the ladders had long since disappeared."

"And?" prompted Marsha.

"And"—he smiled—"being a curious man, this explorer decided to check out some of the caves on the very uppermost level. He had his men lower him down over the edge of the cliff on a rope. And what do you suppose he found?"

Marsha shrugged.

"Human skeletons! Anyway, I figure that whoever killed Hamilton may have read the same account or a similar one, and gotten the idea of killing him in one of the caves on the upper level from there. If you think about it, a cave that's not open to the public is the logical place to kill someone."

He was right, thought Charlotte as she helped herself to some of the pilau. The murderer wouldn't have killed Peter in the desert. As they had learned from Larry's death, the vultures would be a certain tip-off. Nor would he have killed him in one of the rooms: he might have been seen or heard.

"How often do staff members get around to visiting the caves that aren't open to the public?" she asked. With only forty out of four hundred and ninety-two caves open to the public, it was doubtful that they got around to the closed caves very often.

"Only when a visiting scholar such as Ms. Lundstrom wants to look at the paintings or the sculptures," Ned replied. "I would bet that some of them haven't been visited for years. It was the murderer's bad luck that Ms. Lundstrom wanted to include Cave 323 in her lecture that day."

And that the insatiably curious Vivian Gormley had wanted to look at the paintings on the wall of the rear chamber, thought Charlotte.

"In fact, if Ms. Lundstrom hadn't come along, Hamilton's corpse might not have been found until nothing was left of it but the skeleton. Everyone would have thought he had mysteriously disappeared on his trip to Bezeklik, and the murderer would have gotten off scot-free."

"That's not to say he isn't going to get off scot-free anyway," said Charlotte, whose confidence in either the police's or her own ability to solve the crimes was wanting.

"I think we ought to change the subject," said Emily. "Poor Mr. Hamilton." She looked as if she was about to cry.

"Yes," Charlotte agreed. "I have something for you, Emily." Reaching into her bag, she pulled out a small oblong package that she had done up in the paper that her souvenir rubbing had been wrapped in. She handed it to Emily. "I would be very pleased if you would accept this as a gift," she said.

Emily looked puzzled as she opened it with her delicate fingers.

It was Charlotte's volume of Emily Dickinson. She had bought it years ago at a used bookstore for a few dollars; it was a facsimile edition of Dickinson's poems complete with the original steel engravings of trees and roses and the like.

This time, the tears did well in Emily's eyes. "Thank you very much," she said quietly as she ran her hand over the leather cover, which was embossed with a rose. "I don't have her poems in English," she said. "Only in Chinese. I will always treasure this," she added, clasping the book to her breast.

"I'm glad we ran into you," said Charlotte. "I've been carrying it around in my travel bag for two days."

"You beat me to the punch," said Ned with a smile. "A copy of Emily Dickinson in English was one of the first presents I was going to get for Emily when I got back," he said. "Her Chinese translations are full of mistakes." He looked at her fondly. "But I'm sure I can find something else she'd like."

Emily smiled lovingly back at him.

"I'm glad we ran into you too, Miss Graham," Ned continued. "I have something I wanted to tell you. I thought you might be interested to learn that one of the other stolen artworks has been returned."

"Really!" she said.

"Yes. An embroidery on silk—a temple banner—of an eleven-headed Kuan-yin. Emily discovered it in the secret library this morning when she was giving a tour. Somebody apparently put it there during the night. It was stolen from the Cleveland Museum of Art in May—one of their prizes, I understand."

"*After* the disappearance of the Oglethorpe sculpture."

"Yes. And since the Oglethorpe sculpture hasn't reappeared yet, I think the return of the temple banner probably means that the Oglethorpe sculpture wasn't part of the overall pattern of thefts of artworks that originally came from Dunhuang. Though I could be wrong, of course."

"Which also means that Bunny Oglethorpe isn't likely to get it back."

"To be quite frank, I don't think she would have gotten it back even if it had reappeared here. The Bureau of Cultural Properties considers the Dunhuang artworks stolen property, and has no intention of returning them. Chu has already asked Emily to mount the temple banner for display in the museum."

At least she had the problem of the Oglethorpe sculpture off her mind, thought Charlotte as the soup arrived, a steaming mutton soup in a big porcelain bowl. Not that she had been giving it much thought, anyway. But it was one less silk strand in the knotted tangle that she had been charged with unraveling.

After a dessert of apricots and tea, Charlotte and Marsha set out for the caves. Life in the little oasis came to a dead halt during the hour following lunch. The souvenir kiosk was shut up, as were the museum and the library. Even the birds were napping. The only sounds were the trickle of the irrigation stream that ran along the base of the cliff, and the tinkle of wind chimes.

As they mounted the first rock-cut staircase, Charlotte wondered if anyone was observing them, and then dismissed her concern. First, the place was as quiet as a cemetery (an unintentionally apt analogy), and second, if anyone had the right to be looking at the caves, it was Marsha. If anyone did challenge them, she could always claim she was doing research for her lectures.

"I just remembered something odd about the way Peter was dressed," Charlotte said as they reached the second level. The sight of the cave in which Peter was murdered looming overhead had brought back the memory of their excursion to the lake the evening before.

"What's that?" asked Marsha.

"He was wearing brown wool slacks and a navy-blue sweatshirt. First, why would he wear slacks in the desert? I've only seen him in Bermuda shorts. Second, why would he wear *wool* slacks?"

"Not exactly the clothes for the desert," Marsha agreed.

"And third, why would he wear brown wool slacks with a navy-blue sweatshirt? He was always impeccably dressed, and the combination of brown and navy-blue isn't one that's usually considered sartorially *de rigueur*. Unless he wanted to wear his darkest clothes so that he couldn't be seen at night."

"In other words, he was planning to visit the cave," said Marsha. She supported Charlotte's hypothesis about Peter being an art thief. There was a lively market in illicit Asian artworks, and Peter's background and connections made him ideally suited to that trade, she agreed.

"I figure he was killed either by a competitor or by someone who was in league with him," Charlotte said. "Maybe his partner killed him in an argument, or maybe his partner wanted the whole pie for himself." When she put it into words, it sounded corny. "Or maybe I've seen too many Westerns over the years."

Marsha smiled.

"It's something to go on, anyway," Charlotte continued. "The only other idea I've come up with is that Chu killed him because he didn't like the slant of his book, but that's pretty farfetched." She looked up at the cliff face. "Anyway, we'll soon see. Or at least I hope we'll soon see."

After ten minutes, they had reached the top level. At the porch, they paused while Marsha picked out the right key from the bunch on the heavy iron ring. Once inside, they took out their flashlights, and shined them at the frescoed walls of the antechamber.

The processions of elegant Bodhisattvas on the side walls still beckoned them toward the inner chamber. Now that Charlotte knew what had been waiting for them there, their beckoning glances took on an eerie quality.

"I don't see any jug of wine," said Charlotte as the beam of her flashlight played over the walls and ceiling of the antechamber. "Do you?"

Marsha shook her head.

They then proceeded into the inner chamber. On the south wall was the big mural of the Western Paradise that had been the subject of Marsha's lecture. On the north wall was a hunting scene in which gaily clad hunters rode on elegant Tang horses. Stepping around the broken pieces of the toppled statues, they slowly made their way around the central pillar in a clockwise direction, just as the pilgrims had a thousand years before, their flashlights scanning the lively flower-bordered paintings of scenes from everyday life.

"If there's going to be a painting of a jug of wine and a bowl of rice," said Marsha, "it's going to be here."

It was Charlotte who spotted the painting first, on the right-hand wall, just past the blood-stained spot on the lotus-patterned floor where Peter's body had rested: a small painting, close to the floor, of a woman passing a jug and a bowl through a window. "Here it is!" she cried. As she crouched down to get a better look, she was struck by its crudeness. Even to her untutored eye, it was clear that it hadn't been painted by the same artist, or even during the same period, as the other paintings. She turned to Marsha. "Is it my imagination, or is this painting from a different period than the others?"

"It's not your imagination at all," said Marsha, who had crouched down beside her. "It's a different period all right. By about a thousand years. I'd say this is late nineteenth century. Or even early twentieth. The paint looks practically fresh, and the colors are more crude."

Charlotte now noticed that the paint wasn't flaking off as it was in the other paintings, but was bright and clear. And instead of the subtle hues that characterized the Tang paintings, these colors were vibrant, if not garish.

"The execution reminds me of the statues that Wang commissioned in Cave 16," Marsha said. "Maybe he commissioned this painting as well. But why commission such an insignificant painting in such an obscure location? Who's going to see it behind the central pillar?"

As Marsha spoke, the beam of Charlotte's flashlight picked out something else unusual about the painting, or rather about the wall just below the layer of brown paint that represented the ground. It was a horizontal crack in the plastered wall. With the beam of her flashlight, Charlotte followed the crack across the bottom of the painting, down nearly to the floor, back across, and up again. It outlined an eighteen-inch-square cavity that had been blocked up and plastered over to look like the cave wall.

"It's a hiding place of some sort!" said Marsha.

"An old hiding place that's been recently opened," Charlotte added. On the floor of the cave beneath the hiding place was a line of fresh plaster dust that had clearly fallen out of the recently opened cracks.

Charlotte felt in her pockets for something they could use to pry open the cavity. She usually carried a small Swiss Army knife in her purse, but her purse was back in her room. Besides her flashlight, the only thing she had taken along with her was the list of hexagrams.

"What are you looking for?" asked Marsha.

"Something to pry this open with."

"How about a corkscrew? I think I've still got the one that we used to open the bottle of wine on the train." Shining her flashlight into her purse, she rummaged around for a second and then pulled out the corkscrew. "Voila!" she said, holding it up with a flourish.

"You *are* your father's daughter," said Charlotte. One thing that you could always count on with Jack: he was prepared for any contingency. He was the kind of person who always carried emergency flares in the trunk of his car.

"Trained from the get, as Dogie would say," said Marsha. "And if that doesn't work, we can try this," she added, pulling out the awl she'd been using to chip the rock away from the dinosaur metatarsal.

"Very good show," said Charlotte.

"Being an amateur paleontologist can come in handy."

"Actually, I think we'll need both." Taking the corkscrew, Charlotte stuck the tip into the crack at her side of the opening and directed Marsha to do the same with the awl on the other. "When I say three, we'll both pry at the same time." Then she counted: "One, two, three."

The slab of sandstone sealing the opening came away more easily than she would have thought. She had expected it to be thick, like a concrete block, but it was only about two inches deep. After setting it gently down on the floor, they shined their flashlights in the cavity.

"Whatever was here is gone now," said Marsha.

It was only an empty hole, but it was a deep one—three feet or more. It reminded Charlotte of a safe-deposit box. What would one store in a hole the size of a safe-deposit box? Jewelry, but there was no jewelry at Dunhuang; cash and securities, ditto; and . . . documents! Documents, and, by extension, manuscripts.

"What is it?" asked Marsha.

"In Victor's lecture on Cave 17, he talked about how, when the Chinese authorities learned that Wang had sold the manuscripts to Stein, they demanded that he ship the remaining manuscripts to Beijing. But he distrusted them, and only handed over some of the remaining manuscripts."

"Rightfully so," said Marsha. "Few of those manuscripts ever made it to Beijing. They were pilfered by petty bureaucrats along the way."

"According to Victor, the monk sold some of the remaining manuscripts to Stein on his next expedition. But he intimated that some of the manuscripts in Wang's nest egg may still be hidden away in the caves."

"And you think they might have been hidden here!" said Marsha. Her glance shifted to the empty cavity.

"Wang might have drawn up the list of hexagrams as a guide to where he had hidden the manuscripts he'd held back. He might have been afraid of forgetting which caves he had hidden them in. With four hundred and ninety-two caves, that wouldn't be hard to do."

"Then he commissioned the paintings to go with the list of hiding places."

"The only trouble is, I can't figure out why a Buddhist monk would use hexagrams from the *I Ching* as the key to his list. It seems more likely that he would have used Buddhist scriptures."

"He wasn't a Buddhist monk; he was a Taoist monk, and he made his living telling fortunes from the *I Ching*."

Charlotte raised an eyebrow.

"Fortune-telling was traditionally a Taoist enterprise," Marsha explained. "Taoist fortune tellers were in big demand because the fortune-telling trade in this area had been in the hands of the Mongolians for centuries, and the Chinese had nowhere to go for native Chinese fortunes."

Charlotte sat down on the edge of the dais, and leaned her head back against the shin of one of the fierce-faced guardian-warrior statues. "Well, I'll be hot-damned, to use one of Dogie's expressions."

"Hot-damned and halfway to hell," Marsha extrapolated.

"The other question is, If there were manuscripts in this cubbyhole, where are they now? I would bet that whoever has them is Peter's murderer." It was the race for the plunder of Central Asia all over again.

"And maybe Larry's as well," added Marsha.

"What do you say to checking out the other caves on the list? I'd like to see if they all have cubbyholes. And if they do, if they're all empty. Maybe we can find one that hasn't been opened up yet. Did Emily give you the keys to all of the caves?"

"I think so," Marsha said. Removing the key ring from her pocket, she examined the numbers on the keys. "Each key opens a block of caves. Yes," she said finally, "it looks like they're all here."

After replacing the slab blocking the hole, they headed across the cliff face for the first cave on the list, which was Cave 114.

"Are these manuscripts very valuable?" Charlotte asked as they made their way along a narrow walkway five stories up to the next cave, which was located about fifty feet to the south and two levels down. "Like, are we talking thousands of dollars or hundreds of thousands of dollars, or what?"

"Depends on what it is. The majority of the Dunhuang manuscripts are copies of Buddhist sutras, which are pretty common. They're surprisingly inexpensive because there are so many of them. A handwritten Tang sutra might be worth, say, six or seven thousand dollars."

"But there must be some that are worth more."

"Of course. Look at the *Diamond Sutra*, the earliest printed book. It's unique. I couldn't even begin to say what it would be worth, but it must be in the hundreds of thousands, if not millions. It's not inconceivable that Wang's nest egg could contain something equally valuable."

"And how would someone dispose of them?"

"It wouldn't be hard. As I said, most of the manuscripts that Wang sent to Beijing were pilfered along the way, and others were given away to local officials. Then there are the manuscripts that Wang sold to the Russians and the Japanese. No one knows what happened to the manuscripts that Wang sold to the Japanese. They haven't been seen since World War Two."

"Then what you're saying is that Peter, or his confederate, could claim that the manuscripts had come from one of these mysterious sources."

"Yes. He could claim that he'd bought them from a small antiquities dealer who didn't recognize their true worth. As a matter of fact, Dunhuang manuscripts come up for sale pretty regularly in dealers' catalogues. Hong Kong dealers, usually. But they could turn up anywhere."

"Victor said one had turned up in a Finnish rare-book dealer's catalogue just last year," said Charlotte. "And who buys them, museums?"

"Sometimes, although museums are reluctant to buy manuscripts that don't have a verifiable provenance. The major market is private collectors. There's a big market for early Chinese manuscripts in Japan and Taiwan. I've even been told the Shah of Iran was a big collector of early Chinese manuscripts."

Charlotte suddenly remembered Larry's interest in Asian art, and wondered if it extended to early Chinese manuscripts. And if so, if he could have been involved in the manuscript theft. For some reason, she thought of his Oriental rugs: roll the manuscripts up in them, and ship them home.

But on closer examination, the idea of Larry as an art smuggler struck her as absurd. If he had wanted early Chinese manuscripts, he could simply have bought them, just as he bought everything else.

After crossing the cliff face on a series of verandas, and descending several levels, they came to the cave they were looking for, which was just north of the Cave of Unequaled Height. Pulling out her ring of keys, Marsha picked out the correct one, and unlocked the door.

"It feels good, doesn't it?" said Marsha as they entered.

The coolness of the cave was a welcome relief from the sweltering heat outside. Charlotte could now see why the caves were closed at midday.

The layout was identical to Cave 323: an antechamber with a narrow doorway leading to an inner chamber. Here they were looking for a picture of a fox crossing the ice, which the *I Ching* described as a symbol for caution.

This time it took only a minute to find the painting. Like the other one, it was located behind the central pillar, near the ground. Again there was the outline of a cubbyhole in the plaster, and again they used the corkscrew and awl to pry out the slab that sealed the opening.

"Dammit," said Marsha, as the slab came away, and her flashlight revealed the empty interior. Replacing the slab, they headed out for the second cave on the list. "Onward with our treasure hunt," said Marsha.

The second cave yielded the same result, as did the third, fourth, and sixth. But with the seventh cave, they got lucky. There was a cubbyhole in the wall under the painting—in this case, a painting of a goat butting against a hedge, the symbol for being stuck in a predicament—but it hadn't been opened.

Taking out her awl, Marsha prepared to start prying it open.

"No," said Charlotte, laying a restraining hand on her arm. "If the murderer was working in the fifth cave two nights ago, I would guess that he was working in the sixth cave last night, and that he'll be working in this cave tonight." It suddenly struck her that Peter's murderer had probably been removing manuscripts from the sixth cave on the list at about the same time that someone else had been returning the stolen temple banner to the secret library. How odd, she thought—two thieves passing in the night.

"Do you want to come back tonight?" asked Marsha.

"You bet I do," she replied.

Darkness came late in Dunhuang: the sun didn't set until after ten. Once it was completely dark, Charlotte and Marsha took up their observation posts. They had talked about stationing themselves on the cliff face, but finally decided that they would have a better view from the base of the cliff. Although the moon hadn't yet risen, they didn't want to risk being spotted, and whoever was removing the manuscripts from the caves would have to climb up the cliff to the cave and come back down, anyway. Working on the assumption that whoever they were looking for would be coming from the direction of the guest house, they picked a spot about twenty yards to the south of the cave, at the southern end of the cave complex. As their observation post they chose a ledge on the bank of the irrigation channel that ran along the base of the cliff. The spot was concealed from sight not only by the bank of the channel, but also by the twisted bases of a small clump of poplars. It was very still. The only sounds were the occasional croak of a frog and the hoot of an owl. Occasionally the wind would rise, setting the wind chimes tinkling and rustling the branches of the poplars and willows.

It was an ideal location, except for the comfort factor. After fifteen minutes of crouching in the mud, they were ready to start looking for another spot. They were also getting cold. Although the daytime temperature here was in the nineties or above, it dropped quickly when the sun set, and their wet feet made it seem colder than it was. They were discussing the possibility of moving when Charlotte heard a footfall on the plank bridge spanning the irrigation channel to the north. Turning to Marsha, she raised a finger to her lips and nodded in the direction of the sound. At first they couldn't see anything. But as their eyes adjusted, they could make out the silhouette of a man of medium height and build against the whitewashed surfaces of the stairways and verandas. He was carrying a dark-colored laundry bag. After stopping briefly at another cave—it looked like Cave 291, the third cave on Wang's list—he proceeded to Cave 294, a few caves away. He paused for a second to unlock the door—they could see the beam of his flashlight play fleetingly on the lock—and then slipped inside.

"Did you get to see who it was?" whispered Marsha.

Charlotte shook her head. Their decision to set up their observation post to the south of the cave had been a bad one. The face of their quarry had always been turned in the other direction.

"I didn't either. Maybe we'll be able to see him when he comes out."

Charlotte figured it would take him about half an hour to open up the cubbyhole and close it again. It had taken her and Marsha only ten or fifteen minutes in Cave 323, but there the seal had already been broken.

They waited patiently, no longer cold now that their vigil had yielded results. After a few more minutes, Charlotte checked her watch. Twenty-five minutes had elapsed. She was just changing her position to get more comfortable when she felt the nudge of Marsha's elbow in her ribs.

"Look," she whispered.

The figure had emerged from the cave, but instead of going back the way he had come, he headed down the cliff on the series of staircases and verandas to the north of the cave.

Turning to Charlotte, Marsha mouthed the words, *Where's he going?*

Charlotte shrugged.

Five minutes later, he reached the base of the cliff about twenty yards to their north. Now that he was closer, they could see that his laundry bag was heavy with the weight of its contents.

"The manuscripts," said Charlotte.

As they watched, he disappeared into the row of poplars lining the avenue at the base of the cliff. A few seconds later, they spotted him crossing another bridge over the irrigation channel to their north.

"Come on," said Charlotte.

Leading the way, Charlotte followed the footpath that ran along the bank of the irrigation channel. A few minutes later, they had reached the bridge, where they turned right onto a dusty dirt lane.

Though they couldn't see their quarry, they assumed that he must have taken this lane, which wound through a settlement of small peasant houses of sun-dried brick hidden away among the old orchards, each with a plot of cabbages, a farmyard with a chicken coop and a pigpen, and a grape trellis covering a courtyard. At the edge of the oasis, the lane ran into a bridge that crossed the stream bed, and then joined the highway that led into Dunhuang town. But the highway was empty. For a moment, they thought they had lost their man. Had he entered one of the peasant houses? they wondered.

But then they spotted him.

As they looked on from the cover of the trees, he clambered up the terraces on the other side of the road. Here, he paused for a moment to take out his flashlight before setting out past the series of reliquary stupas overlooking the road toward the base of the Mountain of the Three Dangers.

"He's going out into the desert!" whispered Marsha.

Charlotte was really baffled now. Who was this person—they still hadn't gotten a look at his face—what did he have in his laundry bag, and where the hell was he going? "Come on," she whispered, waving her arm. "We're going to see what this guy is up to."

Marsha looked at her with a skeptical expression, but she followed as Charlotte set out toward the open desert.

Once they got used to it, it wasn't difficult to find their way. Though there wasn't a moon, the starlight alone provided enough illumination. It seemed to infuse the air with a glowing transparency that turned the dull brown plain to shining silver and left little shadow puddles under every stone.

The flashlight was easy to follow, a pinprick of light in the clear desert air. After a few minutes, their quarry's destination became clear. "He's heading toward Larry's camp!" said Charlotte, as he came to the track that led out to the camp, and then turned left.

"Either there or the dinosaur quarry," said Marsha.

But they were both wrong. Leaving the track at the spot where the pilgrims' path broke off, he wound his way up the mountain trail toward the stupa that marked the spot where Lo-tsun had seen his vision of a thousand Buddhas in a cloud of glory. At the stupa, the light disappeared.

"What do you think he's doing?" asked Marsha. They had paused to wait where they were. They didn't want to get too close.

"The stupas are memorials to important monks, right?" asked Charlotte.

Marsha nodded.

"Question: Are they just giant memorial stones, or are they burial chambers for the monks? What I'm asking is, is there a chamber inside the stupa where the monk was buried?"

"Of course!" said Marsha. "That's where he went. Not a burial chamber, but a reliquary chamber. For objects associated with the monk and related to his teachings, and so on. Usually there's a statue of the monk, too."

"How big is the chamber?"

"Small. But big enough to stand up in. About like the secret library. In fact, some scholars think the secret library was a reliquary chamber that was later turned into a storage room for manuscripts."

"I think we've found where the murderer is storing the manuscripts or art objects or whatever it is that he's been removing from the cubbyholes."

"I think that's a very good bet."

The stupa's proximity to Larry's camp gave Charlotte a thought. It may have been absurd to think of Larry as an art smuggler, but it wasn't at all absurd to think of him as an innocent bystander. Seeing a light in the middle of the night, he wanders over to investigate. The murderer concocts some explanation, and then sneaks back to his camp later on to kill him. It was a theory, anyway—the only one so far that explained both deaths.

Spreading out their sweaters on the gravel, they sat down and waited. They said little. They didn't want to risk being overheard, but it was more than that: it was as if the big empty spaces demanded silence. Suddenly Charlotte understood those gaping holes in Bert's conversation.

Lying back, she was amazed at how close the stars looked. They didn't twinkle in the sky like distant lights, as the stars at home did, but hung low like glowing orbs that you could almost reach out and touch. Instead of a murky gray blotch, the Milky Way was a shower of phosphorescent pinpricks of light that lit up the heavens like a swath of daisies in a field of green.

It seemed like hours before the figure emerged from the stupa, though it was only forty-five minutes. As they watched, he made his way by flashlight back down the winding path, and then headed back along the track to the guest house. When he came to the pair of stupas framing the Cave of Unequaled Height, about halfway back to the oasis, he switched off his flashlight.

They waited until he had reached the guest house, and then continued their trek up to the stupa—sans flashlights, to avoid being seen. Ten minutes later, they had reached their destination.

In shape, Lo-tsun's stupa was similar to the ones lining the stream bed. It reminded Charlotte of a miniature Palomar Observatory—a rounded dome resting on a square base about eight feet high. The door was on the east wall. It was about three feet square, and stood about three feet off the ground. It was made of rough wood planks, and had a round iron door pull, like the door pull on the moon gate at the Oglethorpe Gardens.

"It reminds me of the door in *Alice in Wonderland*," said Marsha as they stood there, wondering what lay on the other side.

"I hope we don't end up falling into a rabbit hole," said Charlotte.

Reaching out, she tugged gently at the pull. Much to her surprise, it opened right up. Pulling out her flashlight—there was no risk of being seen from this side of the stupa—she shined it into the chamber.

• 12 •

THE INTERIOR OF the stupa was similar to that of the secret library—a small chamber about ten feet square with a domed ceiling. As Marsha had said, it was a reliquary chamber: against the wall facing the door was a sculpture of a cross-legged Lo-tsun, meditating. As in the secret library, the walls were painted with a procession of Bodhisattvas carrying offerings. The paintings, sutras, and other documents that must have once been stored here were gone, probably carried away by looters centuries ago. But in their place was a new cache of treasure—a stack of manuscripts three feet high and equally as long piled up like logs against the north wall.

"There it is," said Charlotte, shining her flashlight on the cache. "Wang's nest egg." The manuscripts were stored in wrappers made of coarse canvas, which were open at the ends. Each held a dozen or more manuscripts.

The beam of Charlotte's flashlight continued its swing around the chamber, revealing a makeshift desk that had been set up against the opposite wall, using a slab of plywood and a couple of sawhorses. A large, battery-operated torch at one corner served as a desk lamp. On the other corner were a couple of smoothly rounded rocks and a magnifying glass.

"It looks as if the stupa has been doubling as a photographic studio," she said, as she shined her flashlight on a battery-operated photographic lamp that was mounted on a metal stand at one side of the desk.

"Why would he need to take photographs?" asked Marsha.

"I don't know. Maybe he wasn't going to be able to get the manuscripts out of the country right away. In which case, he could store them here, and try to sell them on the basis of photographs."

She nodded at the manuscripts. "Will you be able to tell what he's got here?"

"If they're in classical Chinese. A lot of the manuscripts from Dunhuang were written in obscure Central Asian languages that it would take a linguist to decipher, but I would imagine that the manuscripts Wang held back for himself were in Chinese, since that's what he read."

Walking over to the desk, Charlotte switched on the torch, and then gestured to the old cane chair that was pulled up to it. "Have a seat, my dear." As Marsha sat down, Charlotte chose two of the most antique-looking bundles from the top of the pile, and set them at the left side of the desk.

"This is a sutra," said Marsha as she removed a manuscript from the first bundle and untied the purple silk cord. "The title is here." She pointed to the outer fold, which bore an inscription in Chinese. Placing the rounded rocks on the right-hand side of the manuscript, she proceeded to unroll it.

"I wondered what the rocks were for," said Charlotte.

"These manuscript rolls are awkward to handle. That's why the book form was such an important innovation," Marsha explained as she scrutinized the text with the magnifying glass. As she read, she unrolled the manuscript with her left hand and rolled it up with her right, moving the rocks as she went along.

The manuscript was about a foot wide, and neatly wound on a wood roller whose end knobs were inlaid with ivory. It consisted of a series of sheets of paper—each about a foot and a half long—which had been glued together. The sheets were lined with columns of tightly packed Chinese writing.

"The trouble is that the colophon, if there is one, is always at the end," said Marsha as she continued to unwind the long roll.

"Colophon?"

"It's a tailpiece that's appended to the manuscript that gives the name of the person who's acquired merit by paying for the manuscript to be copied, and the name of the person he wants to receive the merit, usually a dead relative. It also gives the date, usually by hour, day, and year. The Chinese saw the importance of dates early on."

As Marsha unrolled the manuscript, Charlotte marveled at the paper. She had expected it to be coarse brown, like the early European manuscripts she had seen in museums, but this was fine and smooth and crisp. Nor was it brown, but a deep golden yellow. "Did they dye the paper?" she asked.

"Yes. Usually it's yellow, but it can also be other colors. I've seen blue, green, pink, orange. I once worked on a manuscript that was made up of a bunch of variously colored sheets all glued together."

"It's beautiful," said Charlotte.

"Yes. The quality is amazing, especially when you consider that paper was still unknown in Europe during the entire period covered by the Dunhuang manuscripts. The Chinese invented paper in 105 A.D.; the Europeans didn't get around to it until more than a thousand years later."

"If they're all this long, we'll be here all night," said Charlotte as Marsha continued to unroll the manuscript. So far, she had unrolled about fifteen feet and there was no end in sight.

"I'd guess this one measures about twenty-five feet, which is about average. Some are much longer. But I won't unroll all of them. I'll just unroll a few to get an idea of what kind of goodies Wang decided to keep for himself." She continued unrolling. "At last," she said, as she came to the end.

"Is there a colophon?" asked Charlotte.

"Yes," Marsha replied. Leaning over the manuscript, she translated the text: "Recently caused to be made for universal free distribution by so and so on behalf of his parents. Copying made at the shen hour on the fifteenth day of the fourth moon, etc. It's Tang," she said. "Nine hundred and four."

For the next half-hour, Charlotte brought manuscripts to Marsha, and Marsha scanned them. As she worked, the pile of finished manuscripts at her right grew bigger and bigger. At last, she leaned back in the cane chair.

"Finished?" asked Charlotte, who had taken a seat on the platform that supported the sculpture of Lo-tsun.

"I guess so," she said.

"And?"

"Except for the first manuscript we looked at and one or two others, there isn't a Buddhist sutra in the lot."

"What are they, then?"

"The British Museum catalogue describes these kinds of manuscripts as Taoist, but they're really not religious texts. They're treatises on medicine, divination, dream interpretation, and calendar-making, all of which the Chinese traditionally considered Taoist activities."

"If Wang was a Taoist monk, it would make sense that those would be the kinds of manuscripts with which he would be least willing to part."

Marsha nodded. "They're also valuable because they're so unusual." She beckoned Charlotte over. "Come here. There's one that I want to show you."

Charlotte came over and stood by Marsha's shoulder.

From the pile on her right Marsha extracted a worn-looking manuscript whose protective outer fold with the silk tape used for tying it up had been torn off. Placing the rocks on the right-hand side to hold it down, she slowly unfolded a section of the manuscript.

Like the Buddhist sutra, the paper was covered with vertical columns of Chinese writing. But interspersed among the blocks of text were several large individual Chinese ideographs.

"What is it?" asked Charlotte.

"It's a copy of the *I Ching*. The selfsame book of wisdom that you've been consulting, but of course"—she smiled—"a much earlier edition. It would make sense that Wang would hold this one back, being a soothsayer."

"Really!" Charlotte exclaimed. "Are these the hexagrams, then?" she asked, pointing to the large ideographs.

"Yes. And this is the commentary." She pointed to the blocks of text. "This is the 'The Wanderer,' the hexagram you had Kitty cast for you. If you look closely, you'll see that it wasn't handwritten, it was block-printed."

"Like the *Diamond Sutra?*" asked Charlotte.

Marsha nodded. "Which makes it very unusual indeed. The Stein Collection contains only twenty specimens of block printing."

Studying the document, Charlotte saw that the letters were more uniform than those of the handwritten manuscript. "I see what you mean. The paper's not like the other manuscripts either." Instead of a deep golden yellow, it was stained a light lemon color.

"That deep yellow is characteristic of the Tang," said Marsha. "This may be later. I didn't look to see if there was a colophon on the first go-round." Unrolling the manuscript with one hand and rolling it up with the other, she moved ahead to the end of the roll, which wasn't as long as the first, but was still well over ten feet. "It's here," she said, studying the tailpiece. Suddenly she spun around and looked up at Charlotte. "It's Sui," she said quietly, her thick dark brows creased together in bewilderment.

"What does that mean?" Charlotte had yet to master the dates of the Chinese dynasties. As a mental exercise, it was matched for tedium only with memorizing the dates of the British kings and queens. She knew the dates of the Tang and a couple of the other most important dynasties, but beyond those she referred to her trusty wallet card.

"Let me take another look," Marsha said. "I can't believe what I'm seeing." With the magnifying glass, she slowly went over the colophon again. Then she looked back up at Charlotte. "It means"—she laid a hand on the manuscript—"that this is the oldest printed book known. The date is 592 A.D."

"Older than the *Diamond Sutra*!" said Charlotte. Even she knew the date of the *Diamond Sutra* off the top of her head: 868 A.D. It was one of those dates, like the Norman Invasion or the defeat of the Spanish Armada, that every schoolchild in her day was made to memorize.

Marsha nodded. "By almost three hundred years." Her low voice trembled with excitement. "And older than the Gutenberg Bible by close to a millennium."

They decided to put the manuscripts back on the pile to avoid tipping off the manuscript thief that they had been there. As they worked, Marsha talked about the *I Ching* manuscript. Chinese historical documents claimed that block printing had been invented in the Sui dynasty, and it made sense. The *Diamond Sutra*—which had been the earliest known example of block printing until their manuscript thief found the *I Ching* manuscript in a cubbyhole—was a very sophisticated work. By its very excellence, it supported the idea that it must have had predecessors. But until now, no earlier examples of Chinese printing had turned up, which Sinologists attributed to the destruction wrought during the civil wars at the close of the Tang dynasty. As Charlotte was now learning, the Cultural Revolution was only the most recent of many paroxysms of anti-intellectual ferment that had convulsed China over the centuries, each with its attendant book-burnings and library sackings. Her new perspective on Chinese history had given her renewed confidence in the ability of this great culture to rise again from the ashes of its most recent destruction.

The discovery of the *I Ching* manuscript was bound to cause a sensation. Charlotte imagined how Chu would gloat: the world's oldest known book would now be the property of the Dunhuang Academy instead of the British Museum.

It took them only a few minutes to put the manuscripts away. Though they were probably under some sort of obligation to notify the authorities of their find, they decided to wait until they could identify the manuscript thief. The memory of Ho's convoy tearing out to Larry's camp was still fresh in Charlotte's mind. If they did notify him, she was afraid that his careless handling of the case would tip off the thief in some way, and that they would lose their chance of finding out who it was who had murdered Peter, and probably Larry as well. Besides, it was only a matter of another twenty-four hours. If the thief held true to pattern, he would be working on the eighth cave on the list tonight.

They said little on the way back. For one thing, they were both still awe-stricken at having stumbled across the world's oldest printed book; for another, voices carried dangerously well in the desert silence. They were also fighting a piercing west wind that had come up while they were in the stupa.

As they drew near the compound, the air suddenly began to vibrate with a weird, unearthly sound, like a ghostly chorus of thousands of lost souls from the depths of hell, sobbing and wailing.

"What's that?" asked Charlotte as the "voices" swelled to a haunting crescendo. She wasn't afraid. She knew the strange vibrations must have some physical explanation, but she was definitely spooked.

"One of the desert's weirdest phenomenons," said Marsha, as the eerie wailing faded away into a quavering moan. "They're sounds caused by the fracturing of rocks. During the day, the rocks expand in the heat. Then, when the cold night wind plays over them, they contract and crack. Marco Polo wrote about them: the locals attribute them to ghosts from the battle of Dunhuang, or to the *kwei*, the devil spirits who lure travelers to their deaths in the desert."

As if in response to Marsha's comments, two *kwei* suddenly appeared out of nowhere. They were slender spirals of sand about ten feet high, which seemed propelled by an invisible force. For a moment, Charlotte and Marsha watched them swirl and dip across the desert floor as if dancing to a soundless orchestra. From a distance they looked elegant, but Charlotte had the feeling that had they been closer, they would have been very frightening.

"Marco Polo wrote about the *kwei* too," Marsha continued. "They almost always come in pairs: yin and yang, each spinning in a different direction. The yin, or female, spirits are said to fold their dusty cloaks around them from left to right and the male, or yang, spirits from right to left."

"Ginger Rogers and Fred Astaire," said Charlotte.

"The desert people say they're spirits connected with darkness and death who want to be reclothed in the flesh. If they don't find a human body to possess, they'll settle for the dust of the desert to cover their nakedness."

"Reynolds told me that Larry's servants attributed his death to the *kwei*," Charlotte said. She wrapped her sweater more tightly around her against the wind. "I can see why."

Again, the desert began to give off its eerie wail, and then the *kwei* skipped blithely off into the darkness as mysteriously as they had come.

By the time she got back to her room, Charlotte felt as if she was about to collapse. It was nearly three o'clock in the morning. It had been a very long day: the meeting with Reynolds, her search of Peter's room, the traipse out to the dig, their search of the caves, and finally, their trip out to the stupa. No wonder she was tired. But it had also been a rewarding day. If she hadn't unraveled the knotted tangle, at least she had separated a few of the most important strands.

She wanted to go right to bed, but she couldn't resist the temptation to throw the coins again, to seek guidance from the world's oldest book of wisdom, a book that was already old when some Chinese printer set wood block to paper almost fifteen hundred years ago. The piercing desert wind was still blowing, and, when she crossed the rug to fetch the *I Ching* from her desk, the static electricity made the hairs on her arms rise and gave her fingertips a shock when she touched the desk's metal rim.

Kneeling on the carpet, she threw the coins on the dusty tile floor. The hexagram she cast was Hexagram 5: "Waiting." The image was of clouds massing in the sky, a sign that it would soon rain. The *I Ching*'s advice was to wait: there was little else she could do until the rain fell, it said. "It is the same in life when destiny is at work," it went on. "We shouldn't interfere before the time is ripe." Meanwhile, it said, she should quietly fortify her body with food and drink, and her mind with gladness and good cheer.

Further insight into her situation was provided by the changing line, which said that the waiting would soon be over, at which time she would face great danger. She would fall into a pit, and, "precisely in this extremity," her situation would take an unforeseen turn. Three "uninvited guests" would arrive. At first, she would think they were her enemies, but they would turn out to be her rescuers. She certainly couldn't complain about a cryptic reading, she thought.

She continued reading. The conclusion was, "Even happy turns of fortune often come in a form that seems strange to us."

"Amen," she said to herself as she closed the book.

After washing up in her washbowl, she fell asleep secure in the knowledge that, for the moment at any rate, she didn't have to do anything.

She decided to wait out her destiny at the dinosaur dig. The team needed all the help it could get, and she didn't have anything else in particular to do until their second vigil at the caves that night, anyway. Actually, she did have something to do. Victor and Marsha were going to visit the West Caves at South Lake, a small group of cave temples several miles to the west of Dunhuang, but she decided to skip it. For the moment, she needed a break from Buddhas and Bodhisattvas. She remembered having the same feeling in Italy, about paintings of the Madonna and child. After a while, the numbers became overwhelming. When Bert had asked her if she wanted to join the dig, she had decided that the *T. bataar* looked far more interesting.

She had been assigned to a section of the backbone just above the hips. Like the others, her job was to chip the rock away from under the bone until the bone was left standing on a rock pedestal. Then it would be wrapped in strips of burlap that had been soaked in plaster. Once the cast had hardened, the plaster-encased bone would be broken off and packed in crates for shipment. They had begun work early to avoid the midday heat. There were nine of them stretched out along the length of the skeleton—four Americans: Bert, Dogie, Lisa, and Charlotte; and Peng and the four members of his team. As before, the tape deck was blaring out rock and roll music—the Beach Boys, this time.

Charlotte worked next to a young member of the Chinese team who, ignoring the Beach Boys, hummed his own tune, which sounded suspiciously like "Ching, ching chow, chingee ringee roo, Chingeeroo was a Chineeman, Ring chingee choo." She liked the work, which, like weeding the garden or washing windows or any other repetitive task, induced a relaxing, Zen-like state of mindlessness. After only an hour of scraping, she had exposed most of her section of four vertebra, each of which was nearly the size of a manhole cover. As she went along, she patched in with household cement, any small chunks that had dropped out, and put the pieces she couldn't find a place for in a little pile.

There was little conversation. It was too hot to talk and work at the same time. The landscape that had been like a dream world last night now looked as if it had been cast out of scrap metal by some brutalist sculptor. The edges of the rocks were hard and sharp, and the sky was flat and yellow. Occasionally, one of the young Chinese paleontologists would fetch a bucket of water from the well at Larry's camp, and they would all douse their heads to keep cool.

Keeping everything organized was Dogie's job. He acted as informal site superintendent—deciding when to mix up the plaster, making sure that everyone had enough to drink, and keeping everybody happy and productive.

"How're ya doin'?" he asked, as he came around to check on Charlotte. Though the work required more elbow grease than skill, it was Dogie who had given her the limited amount of instruction she had required.

"Pretty well, I think," she replied. "I just have to clean out a little more from underneath here." She pointed to where she had dug the sandstone out from underneath her section of vertebrae.

He squatted down next to her. "Looks like this fella had a touch of arthritis," he said. He pronounced it arth*ur*itis. "See how these two vertebrae are fused. Back problems were common among the big dinosaurs."

"No kidding!" said Charlotte. In the course of her work, she had been developing an affection for this giant beast, who may have been among the last of the great *Tyrannosaurs* to walk the earth. Now that she knew he had a bad back, he became almost human to her.

"Supportin' eight tons or so of weight was one helluva job for the spinal column," Dogie continued. "These are the back ligaments here." He pointed to the ossified ropes that ran along the spinal column.

"I wondered what those were."

"They held the backbone in place, like hawsers. The big dinosaurs suffered from fallen arches too; their arches collapsed from their weight." He stood back up, and held out a plastic bag. "I'm takin' up a collection—any bone fragments you can't find a place for."

Charlotte handed him the pieces from her pile, which he numbered and put into the plastic bag. Then he moved on to her young Chinese companion, and Charlotte sat back to rest.

The landscape that lay spread out below her was dry today. There was no lake—only dust devils, dozens of them, swirling and dipping. Beyond the dust devils rose a fortress, complete with battlements and turrets that seemed to rise and sink, as if they were floating. It was another mirage: the shimmering heat had transformed the cliff face into a picture out of a storybook.

She had known many people who loved the desert of the American Southwest. "There's something about the desert," they said, "that makes you feel more alive." But she wasn't among them. In her mind, there was something about it that gave her the creeps. Sand, wind, mirages, sharp rocks, thorny plants, eerie dust devils. To her, it was a hostile, spooky environment.

Turning back to her work, she began digging out the next vertebra. She was removing a big chunk of rock when a clunking sound told her that her trowel had struck bone. Unlike the vertebrae, which were covered with spiny projections that she now realized were the attachment sites for the dinosaur's powerful ligaments and muscles, this bone was straight and smooth.

When she had exposed a fair amount of it, she signaled to the young Chinese man next to her, whose name was Yeh, to pass over the empty whiskey bottle filled with hardener that they shared. The hardener was liberally poured on the fragile bones at regular intervals to keep them from disintegrating. As he was passing the bottle to her, Yeh suddenly stopped in mid-action to stare at the bone she was working on. Then he pointed excitedly at his teeth. Like those of many Chinese, they were stained brown from drinking tea. She was thinking about how having your teeth cleaned was still a luxury in China when she realized what he was saying: she had discovered the dinosaur's tooth!

Yeh had stood up, and was signaling to the rest of the crew to come over and take a look. Dogie arrived first. "Whadda we have here?" he asked. Stepping up to the hole in which Charlotte had been working, he peered into it to see what the fuss was all about. Then he dropped to his knees, grabbed Charlotte's trowel, and started scraping away like an energetic fox terrier going after buried backyard treasure. After a few seconds of this, he leaned back and let out a holler: "Whoopee, ti yi yo, git along little dogies," he cried to the heavens. Taking off his Stetson, he waved it in the air. Then he slapped Charlotte on the back, and yelled to Lisa: "Lisa, git this lady a beer!"

"What have I found?" asked Charlotte, as Bert squatted down next to Dogie. Next to him was Peng, who jabbered excitedly with the other Chinese.

"You've uncovered a tooth of our reptile friend here," said Bert, who was as quiet as Dogie was loud. "And it's attached to a great big, beautiful skull, which is back in the hill here." He indicated where the rest of the skull was buried. "It was just as I suspected: the skull detached from the lower jaw and came to rest with the snout up against the spinal column."

Charlotte looked up at Dogie as Lisa handed her the beer that she had fetched from a nearby cooler. "Have I paid back my credit?"

"I'll say you've paid it back," Dogie said. "In spades. I'd estimate that we owe you another case, at least." He turned to the crew. "Okay, troops. Get your picks, get your trowels. We're gonna uncover some *dirt*."

Charlotte felt lightheaded, and it wasn't just from the heat: it was the thrill of discovery. Now she knew what Bert had been talking about. She had been the first person to see this bone in sixty-three million years.

Instead of breaking during the midday heat, they kept on working, eager to see what lay buried in the hillside. They divided into two shifts. While one worked, the other rested and drank. Heat stroke was an ever present risk.

After an hour and a half, they decided to quit. They had partially exposed a near-perfect skull, one of only a handful of skulls of the giant carnivore ever found. It was about five feet long, as long as a standard desk. The huge serrated teeth were the size of bananas.

With its giant empty eye sockets, it reminded Charlotte even more of Ozymandias. "He reminds me of a poem," she said as they were standing around taking a last look at their find.

"What poem?" asked Bert.

"*Ozymandias of Egypt*," she said. "It's by Shelley.

"I never heard of it, but that doesn't mean anything," Bert said. "I never got around to studying English literature."

"I didn't either, but I had to recite it in a movie once." Her finishing-school education had taught her how to balance a book on her head and choose the right frock, but there were embarrassing gaps in the scope of her knowledge that regularly cropped up to annoy her, like English literature.

"Let's hear it," said Dogie.

Her stage comprising a slab of rock above the quarry, Charlotte proceeded to recite the poem, stopping after every couple of lines for Peng to translate:

> *I met a traveller from an antique land*
> *Who said: Two vast and trunkless legs of stone*
> *Stand in the desert. Near them, on the sand,*
> *Half sunk, a shatter'd visage lies, whose frown*
> *And wrinkled lip and sneer of cold command,*
> *Tell that its sculptor well those passions read.*
> *Which yet survive, stamp'd on these lifeless things,*
> *The hand that mock'd them and the heart that fed;*
> *And on the pedestal these words appear:*
> *'My name is Ozymandias, king of kings:*
> *Look on my works, ye Mighty, and despair!'*
> *Nothing beside remains. Round the decay*
> *Of that colossal wreck, boundless and bare,*
> *The lone and level sands stretch far away.*

Her recital at an end, Charlotte stepped down and joined the others at the edge of the quarry. She was met with hearty applause.

"That's a good name for him," said Lisa. "Our *T. bataar* is hereby christened Ozymandias: Ozzie for short."

"*Gan bei*, Ozzie," said Dogie, and everybody drank. They were all a little punchy from the heat and the excitement of finding the skull.

"You know," said Bert quietly, as he squatted down next to Ozzie's skull with a beer bottle in his hand, studying his shatter'd visage, "I don't think our friend Ozzie is a *Tyrannosaurus bataar*."

"Not a *T. bataar!* What do you think he is, then?" asked Dogie. He crouched down next to Bert to get a better look.

"Look at this row of ridged irregularities on top of the nasal bones," said Bert, pointing to the prominent ridges that ran down the front of the skull. "They're much more pronounced than those of a *T. bataar*."

"What is it, a horn boss?" asked the pith-helmeted Peng, who had joined Bert and Dogie next to the massive skull.

"I think so," said Bert. "A horn boss that I suspect supported a row of hornlets. Probably something like the horns of a *Ceratosaurus*, only smaller."

"What's a *Ceratosaurus?*" Charlotte asked Lisa.

"A horned dinosaur," she replied. "Something like a rhino."

"Judging from the horn morphology, I suspect we've got a brand new species of *Tyrannosaurus* on our hands," said Bert. "A knobby-nosed *Tyrannosaurus*."

Charlotte and Marsha decided not to go to the caves that night. They hadn't slept much the night before, which, combined with a full day's activities, had left them worn out. Besides, their man wasn't going anywhere until he had finished emptying out the cubbyholes in all twelve of the caves on the list, and he was only up to the eighth. But they ended up not going to bed early after all. Dinner turned out to be a celebration. In addition to wine and beer, there were many toasts of *mao tai*, the potent Chinese vodka-like liquor that Dogie called tarantula juice. "This stuff would raise blood blisters on a rawhide boot," he said. They toasted Ozzie of the bad back and fallen arches. They toasted Larry, Bert, Peng, and Charlotte—in fact, they toasted anyone who offered the least excuse for a drink. After dinner, they retired to the terrace for a repeat performance of the show put on by the guest house staff, this time for the benefit of a group of new arrivals from Japan. After the performance, Emily again invited the guests to contribute. Buoyed by their discovery and emboldened by the alcohol, the Chinese paleontologists were the first to take the stage. To everyone's delight, they sang "Red River Valley" in English accompanied by Dogie on the harmonica. They were led by Peng, who had traded in his pith helmet for a cowboy hat, a gift from Bert and Dogie. After that, Charlotte was persuaded (not that she was ever reluctant to mount a stage) to repeat her rendition of *Ozymandias*.

But the most popular act was a song that Dogie composed on the spot about "a *Tyrannosaur* named Ozz with a bit of a schnozz with a yozz for a duckbill named June." Marsha translated for the Chinese, but without the puns and double entendres, it must have lost a lot, because they seemed baffled as to what the Americans found so hilarious.

They were still laughing when Ned took the stage. He announced that he would sing two classical songs from the Tang Dynasty, whose scores had been discovered among the manuscripts in the caves. The first was called "Golden Sands of Shachow." Shachow, he explained, was the ancient name for Dunhuang, and meant "Prefecture of the Sands." He was well into the song when Charlotte realized that he was accompanying himself on a pear-shaped stringed instrument that was made out of wood inlaid with figures of mother-of-pearl.

The Artful Dodger had said he'd seen a foreigner carrying a lute talking to Feng. Could that foreigner have been Ned? She had seen Ned disembarking from the shuttle bus later that afternoon—the afternoon of the day she had found Larry's body—but he hadn't been carrying a lute. If he had been carrying a lute earlier that day, what had he done with it? She nudged Marsha. "Look at Ned's instrument!" she whispered. "Is it a *pipa?*"

Marsha looked up at the instrument and then back at Charlotte, and nodded.

Charlotte leaned over again to whisper in Marsha's ear. "But the boy said it was a foreigner who was carrying the *pipa*, and Ned looks Chinese," she said as the haunting melody of the ancient song filled the air.

"He's fourth- or fifth-generation Chinese-American," Marsha whispered back. "There's a big difference. To a Chinese kid who only rarely sees foreigners, his clothes, his demeanor, and his accent would have made him seem as foreign as you or me."

As Charlotte looked at Ned, the eyes behind his round wire-rimmed glasses closed as he lovingly plucked the strings of his beautiful instrument, she tried to imagine him as the person who had killed Larry, planted the shortwave radio on Feng to make it look as if he had done it, and then killed Peter. He was credible as a suspect: he had access to the caves and he knew the value of the manuscripts. But somehow she couldn't imagine Emily's gentle Heathcliff as a murderer. If it was Ned who the Artful Dodger had seen with Feng, it was more likely that he had been giving him a handout.

It was after midnight by the time Charlotte got to bed. "Fortify the mind with gladness and good cheer," the *I Ching* had said. She had most certainly done that. But she would still have to wait until the clouds broke.

· 13 ·

ALTHOUGH THE *I Ching* had predicted she would be spending her time waiting, the next day was actually fairly eventful. After being awakened by the buzzing of flies at the crack of dawn (the crack of dawn actually wasn't so bad, coming as it did at close to eight), Charlotte was startled to hear a loud knock on her door. She opened it to find Chu's son standing there in his aviator glasses and Boston University T-shirt. He was there to tell her that she had a telephone call from the United States. After flinging on a robe, she followed him back through the guest house's maze of paths and courtyards to the lobby to take the call. To her surprise, the connection was as clear as a bell. Though conditions in China were generally backward by comparison with those of Western countries, she had often been pleasantly surprised by such efficiencies as telephone connections that were fast and clear, souvenir stands that accepted Western credit cards, and laundry that was returned the same day, neatly folded and stacked.

Its high-toned accent unmistakably identified the voice that had traveled halfway around the globe as that of Bunny Oglethorpe. "Charlotte Graham, is that you?" the voice asked.

Charlotte replied that it was.

"I didn't think I'd be able to reach you so easily. This is Bunny Oglethorpe. I just got a call from Chief Tracey. He told me that he'd just heard from the New York police. They have a special fraud squad that investigates art thefts. They found our sculpture."

"Where?"

"At the country house of a professor at the Oriental Institute who was murdered last April during a robbery attempt. The house is somewhere up on the Hudson, near Catskill. The heirs found it when they were cleaning out. When they took it to be appraised, the dealer informed them that it had been stolen."

"What was the professor's name?" asked Charlotte.

"Boardmann," she said. "Adrian or Avery or something like that."

"Averill," said Charlotte. So much for getting the problem of the Oglethorpe sculpture off her mind, she thought. Instead of having one less thread in the tangled skein, she now had more than ever.

"Do you know him?"

"I know of him. He was scheduled to lead the study tour that I'm on. When he died, the Institute was looking for someone to take his place, and my stepdaughter, Marsha Lundstrom, asked me. She's also a professor there. I'm on this trip as his replacement."

"What a coincidence!" said Bunny.

"Maybe," said Charlotte, for whom there had recently been a lot of coincidences. "Do the police think he stole the sculpture?"

"Yes, but out of what motive, they don't know. Maybe he was planning to sell it after some time had passed. Or maybe he just wanted to live with it, like that man who stole the Rodin bronze from the Victoria and Albert."

"But why that sculpture?"

"That's what I asked. I'm very fond of our monk, but it isn't a Rodin. Unless he just stole it because it was easy to steal, and, being a professor at the Institute, he knew about the series of thefts of artworks that had come from Dunhuang and thought he could pass it off as part of that."

"Maybe," said Charlotte.

Bunny sighed. "Anyway, I thought I ought to let you know. I didn't want you going to a lot of trouble trying to find it. It's on its way back to its place of honor in the garden. With a hole in its back, but otherwise okay."

"A hole in its back?"

"Yes. The dear professor smashed a hole in its back. Which is one reason why the stealing-it-because-you-want-to-live-with-it theory doesn't make sense to me. Why would someone deliberately vandalize a piece of sculpture that they stole because they wanted to live with it?"

"The damage couldn't have been accidental?"

"I haven't seen the sculpture yet myself. It's due back here on Friday. But the New York police told Chief Tracey that it looked deliberate. They thought he had used a hammer. But they also said it looked as if it could be easily repaired."

They chatted for a minute more, with Charlotte promising to drop by when she got back, to say hello and to look at the statue.

She was sure of it, she thought as she walked back to her room. Boardmann's theft was linked to everything that was going on in Dunhuang. She was reminded of what Bert had said about piecing together a dinosaur skeleton. The skeleton of the *T. bataar* was unusual: except for the skull, it had been as neatly laid out in its sandstone bed as a body in a casket, but this case was like most of the dinosaurs that Bert and his team spent their winters assembling—a jumble of unrelated bits and pieces. Before you could start putting it together, you had to develop a feel for the individual parts; how one fit into another, where each fit in relation to the whole, where the big pieces went and the small pieces went. Bunny's news about Boardmann was like finding a crucial missing piece. She was now reasonably certain she had all the important pieces. Now she had to get to know them—to turn them over in her hands, to run her fingers over their bumps and hollows and ridges.

The first piece she wanted to take a look at was the newest one—the hole in the back of the statue. Something about it rang a bell. And then it struck her what it was. Item one: a cache of manuscripts had recently turned up inside a statue, and it was to translate these manuscripts that Marsha and Victor had been invited to Dunhuang. Item two: the statues that had been toppled from the dais in Cave 323 had had holes in their backs which had been made by looters looking for concealed treasure. Item three: Marsha had said that manuscripts and other valuables were traditionally hidden inside the bellies of the statues at Dunhuang to give them spiritual power. Charlotte had examined the piece. Now she put it into place. They had figured out that Wang had hidden the manuscripts in the cubbyholes, and then drawn up a list of his hiding places, a copy of which Charlotte had found in Peter's room. But they had never thought to wonder where Wang had hidden his original list.

It made very good sense to her that he had hidden it inside a sculpture, namely that of the Oglethorpe's monk.

* * *

Later that morning they scouted out the ninth cave on the list, under the guise of doing research for Marsha's lectures. If Ned, who was now her chief suspect—the Boardmann connection had only strengthened the case against him—had taken the manuscripts from the eighth cave last night, he could be expected to visit the ninth cave tonight, and they intended to be there. The cave, which was Cave 328, was located in the southern group of caves near the Cave of Unequaled Height.

As they climbed the cliff, Charlotte filled Marsha in on Bunny Oglethorpe's call. "One more thing," she added, after telling her about Boardmann's theft of the statue. "It had a hole in its back."

"A hole in its back?" asked Marsha, puzzled.

"Like the Tang statues in Cave 323. I think the Oglethorpe sculpture was also used as a hiding place—by Wang."

"For more manuscripts?" asked Marsha.

"No. For the list describing where the manuscripts were hidden. As accustomed as he was to hiding things away, Wang wouldn't have left the list just lying around. It was a valuable document, and, as you pointed out, there was a long tradition of hiding treasure inside of statues."

"Do you know who the Oglethorpe sculpture was supposed to represent?" asked Marsha. "I know it was a Buddhist monk, but do you know which one?"

"I don't remember his name," Charlotte replied between breaths. Thank God for all those hikes up the mountain to her cottage in Maine; without them, she wouldn't have been up to this trip. "He was the famous pilgrim who carried the Buddhist scriptures across the Himalayas from India."

"Hsuan-tsang," said Marsha. "He was Wang's patron saint. If Wang was going to choose a particular sculpture in which to hide his most valuable document, it would have been a sculpture of Hsuan-tsang."

"That's right!" said Charlotte. "Victor talked about Hsuan-tsang being Wang's patron saint in his lecture."

"That's how Stein won Wang over: he also claimed Hsuan-tsang as his patron saint," said Marsha. "Okay," she continued. "Wang hid his list in the statue of Hsuan-tsang. After Wang died, the sculpture was sold to an art dealer, who sold it to the

Oglethorpes. But after that, I'm lost."

They had paused to catch their breath on the porch of one of the caves, about halfway up. In the distance, the jagged ridge of the Mountain of the Three Dangers was sharply outlined against a deep blue sky.

"You mean, how did Boardmann know that Wang's list was hidden inside that particular statue when there are twenty-four hundred statues at Dunhuang?"

Marsha nodded. "For that matter, how did he know the list existed?"

"That's where I'm stuck too."

For a moment, they studied the view. Charlotte could no longer see Larry's white Toyota Land Cruiser in the shadows of the foothills, nor could she see the tents. Reynolds must have given orders for the camp to be dismantled.

After a few minutes, Charlotte spoke. "The only explanation I can think of is that Boardmann, in the course of his research, came across a document in which Wang mentioned that he'd drawn up a list of the manuscript hiding places and where he had hidden it."

"His daybook!" exclaimed Marsha. "Wang was a meticulous record-keeper. That's how the Chinese know which foreigners took away what from the caves. There's a photocopy of it in the library. But"—a frown crossed her face—"Averill wouldn't have had any reason to study Wang's daybook."

"Why not?"

"His specialty was sculpture. The entries in Wang's daybook all have to do with the manuscripts and artworks that he sold to Stein and the other foreigners. The only sculpture that was removed from the caves during the period of Wang's stewardship was the Bodhisattva that Langdon Warner carried off to the Fogg."

"What about Peter?" asked Charlotte as they continued their upward climb. "Would he have had occasion to study Wang's daybook?"

"Yes," said Marsha thoughtfully. "Very much so."

"Okay, let's say it was Peter who comes across the entry in Wang's daybook. The entry says that he's drawn up a list describing where he's hidden the remaining manuscripts, and that he's hidden the list in a statue of Hsuan-tsang in Cave X. Peter goes to Cave X, and finds that the statue is missing."

"Of course! If Peter had wanted to trace the missing statue, the first person he would have consulted was Averill. He is—or rather, was—the reigning authority on Dunhuang sculpture. It's because of his work that the Academy has been able to track down so much of the missing sculpture."

"How well did they know one another?"

"Pretty well, I think," said Marsha. "They were both here together for three months last year. Peter was working on his book, and Averill was studying the sculptures. People can become quite close very quickly in such a small place." She smiled at her statement, which applied as well to her and Bert.

"So I've noticed," said Charlotte with a raised eyebrow.

Marsha grinned.

"To continue," said Charlotte. "Peter goes to Boardmann and says, 'Look what I've found.' Maybe he even showed Boardmann the reference in Wang's daybook. He asks Boardmann if he knows where the statue is, and Boardmann tells him. Then they plot together to steal the statue."

"They both would have known about the thefts of the Dunhuang artworks," added Marsha, "and they probably thought it would be easy to make the theft of the Oglethorpe sculpture fit in with the others."

"Did Boardmann need the money?" asked Charlotte.

"Academics always need money. But Wang's daybook still doesn't answer the question of who killed Peter. Whoever it was must also have had access to the list of hiding places, or wanted access to the list."

They had paused at the foot of a staircase.

Charlotte turned to Marsha. "How did Averill Boardmann die?" she asked. "I want all the details."

"Do you think . . . ?"

Charlotte nodded. Though she might be wrong, her intuition told her that Boardmann's death was linked to the other murders, and experience had taught her that more often than not, her intuition was right.

"He was murdered on the street in New York during a robbery attempt. He was out walking his dogs, a pair of Pekingese. It happened early in the morning, just as the sun was coming up."

"And the guy they arrested?"

"A vagrant, an ex-con who hung out on the upper West Side."

"How was he killed? With a gun, a knife?"

"A knife," Marsha replied. "Stabbed through the heart. They never did find the murder weapon. The police said he had struggled with his attacker. He had slash marks on the undersides of his forearms."

"Just like Peter," said Charlotte.

"He died several hours later on the operating table at St. Luke's. The vagrant they arrested had been seen picking garbage out of the garbage cans in the vicinity, but he denied committing the murder."

"Then what evidence did they have?"

"Averill's watch. He was wearing Averill's watch."

They had reached their destination, which was the same cave from which Langdon Warner had taken the Bodhisattva. The Buddha in the center of the group of sculptures was flanked by three figures on the right, and two on the left. Where the third figure should have been on the left was only an empty dais with a post in the center that had once supported the missing sculpture.

Marsha pointed to a sign on the wall behind the empty dais. "It says, 'Stolen by American so-called archaeologist Langdon Warner in 1924. Now in the Fogg Museum at Harvard University in Cambridge, Massachusetts.' "

"Looks like Chu's work," said Charlotte.

Marsha nodded. "He's put up signs like this in all of the caves from which artworks were removed by Western explorers."

"The statues are exquisite," said Charlotte. "Especially this one," she added, nodding at the small Bodhisattva that was the twin of the one in the Fogg. Its erect posture was stately, its long limbs graceful and elegant, the expression on its broad, smooth face serene. Its necklaces, armlets, and bracelets were sumptuous and the colors of its long, pleated skirt—vermilion, malachite, and gold—were rich and vibrant.

"It's early Tang," said Marsha as they both gazed at the statue, "before the figures became more massive and opulent. I think it's one of the most beautiful statues at Dunhuang. I'm not surprised that Langdon Warner chose its twin to carry off to the Fogg."

"And I'm not surprised that Chu wants it back."

It didn't take long to find the cubbyhole: it was located at the rear of the inner chamber, near the floor. The painting above it depicted a man treading on the tail of a tiger, the symbol for the caution demanded by a dangerous enterprise. After a bit of discussion, they chose the adjacent cave as their observation post.

This time they didn't want to risk not getting a good look at their man. The two caves were connected by a doorway that had been cut through the wall between the antechambers.

The shape of the skeleton was beginning to take form, Charlotte thought as they descended the cliff. As she read the pieces, they fit together something like this: Peter finds the reference to the list of hiding places in Wang's daybook. He solicits Boardmann's help in tracking down the statue, and they plot together to steal it from the Oglethorpe Gardens. Somehow Ned Chee finds out about the plot. He might also have come across the reference to the list in Wang's daybook during the course of his research, and figured out that it was Boardmann who stole the statue. He had worked closely with Boardmann, he said. Maybe Boardmann had said something or done something that tipped him off. In any case, Ned decides that he wants the manuscripts for himself. After stealing the list, most likely without Boardmann's knowledge, he stabs him on the street—thus eliminating the competition—and camouflages the murder as a robbery attempt. Pretending to be a vagrant on a cold April morning in New York wouldn't have been hard. All he would have needed was a stumbling gait, a plastic garbage bag full of aluminum cans, and a hooded parka to conceal his face. Then he arranges a return trip to Dunhuang, romances Emily to get her to hand over the keys (poor Emily), and starts assembling the manuscripts in the stupa. Then comes the second killing: Larry innocently wanders over to the stupa to check out what's going on, and Ned sneaks back to his camp later to murder him in his sleep. Having succeeded in pinning the murder on a vagrant in Boardmann's case by planting Boardmann's watch on him, Ned repeats this ploy by planting Larry's portable shortwave radio on Feng. He then continues with his nighttime work of removing the manuscripts from the cubbyholes with the intent of selling them later on. All is going well until Peter shows up. Using his copy of the list, Peter locates the cubbyholes, only to find that somebody has already cleaned some of them out. By keeping a close watch on the caves, he figures out which cave his adversary will visit next, and goes there to confront him. Not knowing that Ned has already killed Boardmann and Larry, he demands a piece of the action, and ends up as Ned's third victim.

It wasn't a complete skeleton yet; there were still some missing pieces. For instance: if Ned had been in Dunhuang for eight weeks, why had he only recently gotten around to removing the manuscripts from the cubbyholes? One reason might have been that he wasn't able to figure out Wang's code right away. The *I Ching* might have been in fashion with New Agers like Kitty, but it was off the beaten track for an art historian, Chinese-American or not. Another might be that it had taken him that long to convince Emily to part with the keys. In any case, the basic structure of the skeleton was there, and it seemed to fit together pretty well.

They would find out how accurate it was soon enough.

At nine that night, Charlotte disembarked from the minibus with Marsha, Bert, and Dogie at the traffic circle at the center of Dunhuang town. With nightspots in short supply, they had eagerly taken the bus driver up on his offer to drive them into town for the evening. They had nothing to do until they took up their watch at the caves later that evening. So they had decided to do what all sensible people did when they needed a little recreation and had some extra time on their hands (in Charlotte's mind, anyway), which was to go to the movies. They had noticed on Sunday that the local movie theatre was showing a Charlie Chaplin movie, and, since language wasn't going to pose a problem—most of Chaplin's movies had been silents—they had figured "why not?"

The movie theatre had been designed in the fifties during the period of political alliance with the Russians, and was typical of Russian-style architecture—a featureless block of stucco with a colonnade here and there. Chu's son may have considered Charlotte's movies spiritual pollution, but they were in the finest taste compared to the pollution of the Chinese landscape by this hideous Russian architecture, which was ubiquitous. On the balcony above the doors a hand-painted sign advertised the picture, which was Chaplin's masterpiece, *The Great Dictator*. In it, Chaplin played both the evil dictator and the common man who is crushed by the dictator's policies. Charlotte remembered when it was released. It was 1940, the year after Hitler's invasion of Poland provoked a declaration of war from Britain and France, and the year after the release of her own first picture. She hadn't seen it since.

After buying their tickets, which cost the equivalent of twenty cents, they went in. Inside, the theatre was a big, barnlike structure with a cement floor, hard wooden seats, and dim lighting. As the film unwound, Charlotte found herself profoundly moved, not only by Chaplin's brilliant performance, but also by the reaction of the audience. The theatre was charged with emotion. There were those who were no doubt remembering their own humiliations during the Cultural Revolution, but there were also those who were no doubt remembering their own misdeeds. For Chaplin's dictator was a man who does evil because he is a man to whom evil has been done, and the wounds inflicted by son turning in father, student turning in teacher, and friend turning in friend must still have been raw in the minds of the audience. Many were probably intellectuals from Beijing and Shanghai who had been shipped out to the western regions, the People's Republic's equivalent of Siberia, and never had the chance to return.

When the lights came on at the end of the movie, Charlotte could see tearstains on the cheeks of many in the audience. She thought again of Reynolds' proposal, and ached for it to come through.

Afterwards they wandered around the town. At ten o'clock the dusty streets were still crowded. It seemed as if everyone was out for the evening: peddlers hawked shish kebab and melons, young men played pool at tables that were set up on the sidewalk, lovers strolled languidly, arm in arm—a big change from a few years before when public displays of affection were prohibited. Townspeople eager to practice their English approached them with the question: "Are you very happy?" This concern with their state of happiness puzzled them until they figured out that the phrase was from a popular English phrasebook.

They were trying to decide where to go next when Dogie let out one of his hoots of glee. He was staring at a moon-faced woman wearing a white cap who was turning a tin drum on a nearby street corner. "If that woman ain't sellin' ice cream, my name ain't Percival V. O'Dea."

"Percival!" said Charlotte.

"Yep. It means knight in Old French. My mama was a schoolteacher. Taught history. My father was a no-account scalawag who never finished seventh grade, but we don't talk about him."

"What the V. for?" asked Marsha.

"Virgil. After the Roman poet."

"With a name like that, it's no wonder he's called Dogie," said Bert.

"It's not much worse than Albert," countered Dogie.

Stopping the drum, the woman scooped out a white substance with a wooden paddle, and deposited it in a paper cup for a customer.

"I think you're seeing correctly, Percival," said Marsha.

"My mama called me Percy," said Dogie.

A few minutes later they had all bought paper cups of the cold ice cream. Everyone had vanilla—it was the only flavor. It was rich and creamy and much better than they ever would have expected, they agreed as they ambled on down the dusty street, trailed by the usual crowd of curious Chinese.

They were turning a corner when Marsha suddenly grabbed Bert's arm. "Come," she said. "There's something I want to show you. We still have time to kill before the bus comes back, don't we?"

Charlotte checked her watch. "Forty minutes."

A few minutes later they were examining the dragon bones at the herbalist's kiosk. A lot of them turned out to be the bones of donkeys and sheep, but there were also a fair number of dinosaur bones, which Bert identified as those of common dinosaurs, mostly duckbills. They each bought at least one as a souvenir. Charlotte bought two—one for herself and one for Kitty. Hers was incised with the ideograph for "The Wanderer," which looked like a jaunty figure in a big hat with an upraised leg frozen in mid-step.

"Speaking of dragon bones," said Bert as they wandered back toward the bus stop with their bags of bones, "I have some news for you lady detectives. Regarding the circumstances surrounding Larry's death."

"What?" asked Marsha eagerly.

"Lisa went over to Bouchard's camp this morning. Crossed the DMZ, as we say. He invited her over to look at a scorpion. She gets along well with him, as she does with everybody. He's an expert on arachnids—the spider family—and scorpions in particular. He was pretty excited about it—some new kind of giant scorpion that lives in colonies rather than by itself."

"And?" prompted Marsha.

"He was showing her a picture of a scorpion in a book—pointing out how his new scorpion differed from its nearest relative, or something—when she spotted a piece of paper among his things."

"The missing page from Larry's field diary?" said Charlotte.

Bert nodded. "It was just as you suspected, Charlotte. He went over to Larry's camp to investigate after we left. Finding Larry dead, he took advantage of the fact that no one was around to take the page from Larry's field diary. He was planning to steal Larry's claim."

Charlotte remembered her confusion at his open-mouthed reaction to her news that she and Lisa had found the *T. rex* skeleton: so he had been reacting that way because he had intended to claim Larry's find as his own. Instead, all he had found was a new kind of scorpion.

Bert dug around in the pockets of his jeans, and eventually produced a crumpled sheet of paper. "Here it is," he said, handing it to Charlotte. "I thought you might want to take a look at it."

They stopped for a minute for Charlotte and Marsha to read the page from the diary. A lump rose at the back of Charlotte's throat as she read the first lines. They said: "To north slope of ravine in A.M. Feel lucky—as if it's going to be one of those days when something terrific might happen."

"The hundred-pound nugget of solid gold," said Marsha.

Bert nodded.

The rest of the entry, made after Larry had found the *Tyrannosaur*, went on to describe the locality in great detail: the exact position, the type of soil, the lay of the land, and so on.

"Lisa didn't say anything then," Bert continued after Marsha handed back the page. "But when she got back, she told Peng about it. He was incensed. He'd always been cool on Bouchard anyway, but he was under political pressure to include him. He confronted Bouchard, and he confessed. He's been barred from the expedition. He's packing up his things now."

Charlotte felt a bit sorry for him—the scorpion lover who couldn't find a dinosaur fossil if he tripped over it. "What's going to happen to him? Is his career as a paleontologist finished?"

"I imagine so," said Bert.

"In my book, it's no great loss," said Dogie.

"But he'll still have his scorpions," Bert added. "He's been working on a book about scorpions for a decade. He says it will be the first book to encompass everything that's known about them."

They had almost reached the bus stop when they were accosted by a pretty young woman who was selling paste jewels. Her wares glowed in the golden evening light: topazes, amethysts, and rose quartz in all shapes and sizes. Some were loose, others had been set into rings, bracelets, and earrings.

"They remind me of the jewelry on the Bodhisattvas we saw this afternoon," said Charlotte. Like the statues themselves, their richness was all the more striking by comparison with the dry, dusty, impoverished surroundings.

"Yes," said Marsha as she examined the trayful of stones. "The Prefecture of the Sands was known in ancient times for its high-quality paste jewelry. These must be the same kind of jewels that were sold to travelers on the Silk Road a thousand years ago. I love the pink ones," she added.

"Okay, ladies," said Dogie, who stood by impatiently tapping the toe of his boot. "Time's up. We've got to get back to the bus."

They left reluctantly, and promised the girl they would return.

The minibus picked them up at the traffic circle a few minutes later. After passing the fields on the outskirts of town, and beyond the fields, the wavelike Southern Dunes, the minibus entered the narrow valley in which the caves were located. It was an eerie sight. The rays of the setting sun bathed the jagged ridge of the Mountain of the Three Dangers in a blood-red light. Below the mountain yellow dust devils swirled across the desert floor as they had the previous afternoon, but this time there were many more of them, and they were spinning much faster—hundreds of miniature cyclones, sucking sand into the air and then speeding off. The day before, they had reminded Charlotte of a few graceful couples waltzing expertly at a Roseland tea dance; today, they made her think of a dense pack of alienated youths gyrating wildly on a crowded dance floor.

"*Buran*," said the driver, gesturing at the menacing mass of yellow clouds that hung low on the horizon to the southwest, blocking out the setting sun.

"What's a *buran*?" asked Charlotte.

"A black hurricane," said Marsha. "One of the Gobi's infamous sandstorms. The Chinese call them 'flying sand and running stones.' " She leaned forward to ask the driver a question.

The driver gestured at the cloud bank as he answered.

"He says he doesn't know when it's going to hit," Marsha told them. "Only that it's very close."

Knowing that their manuscript thief had started work at about two the other night, and figuring that after a week or more he must have worked out a routine, Charlotte and Marsha waited until one-thirty before taking up their positions in the adjacent cave.

If the caves were spooky by day, they were even more so by night. The gilding on the fierce faces of the warriors guarding the Buddha gleamed in the light of their flashlights. Charlotte had fears about being attacked by bats, as she had once been in one of her early, and eminently forgettable, if not to say downright embarrassing films (in those days she couldn't be choosy): *I Married a Vampire*. But Marsha reassured her that there were no bats in the desert. The harsh climate couldn't support a large enough insect population for bats to feed on. The atmosphere was spooky too. Though the air was deathly still—the hot, dry wind that had blown all day had died down at nightfall—it seemed to vibrate, like a guitar string that has been stretched too tight and is about to snap. Even the animals were restive, alert as barometers to the change in the weather. The dogs of the small settlement yelped plaintively, and from the distant mountains came the menacing howl of wolves.

"By the way," said Marsha, once they were settled in the cave. "I checked Wang's daybook this afternoon at the library."

"Was there a reference to the list of hiding places?" asked Charlotte.

"Yes. It said, 'On this day I have made a record of the hiding places for the manuscripts. I will hide my record in a statue of Hsuan-tsang in Cave 206.' I forget. Is that the cave the Oglethorpe monk came from?"

"Yes," said Charlotte. *Click*. Another piece had snapped into place.

They had been waiting only about ten minutes when they heard a light footfall on the floorboards of the gallery outside. They had expected their quarry to come from the direction of the guest house, but instead he came from the direction of the staircase to the north.

"He's coming this way!" whispered Marsha.

In a minute, they heard the jangle of a ring of iron keys, followed by the click of a key in the lock. But it wasn't the door of the adjacent cave that he was unlocking, it was the door of their own! Why would he be opening the door of their cave, unless he was searching them out?

Charlotte felt Marsha's icy fingers clutching her wrist.

Placing her other hand over Marsha's, Charlotte led her back to the inner chamber, where they hid behind the central pillar, with its awesome array of gilded deities. Without the flashlight, it was totally dark, except for a faint outline of light seeping in around the edges of the door. Charlotte could feel her heart pounding in her chest. What would they do if he tried to kill them? They weren't armed except for . . . Reaching out for Marsha, she felt for her shoulder bag. She was sure she had been carrying it. There it was—a leather bulge at her side. She tugged gently on the shoulder strap.

At Charlotte's prompting, Marsha removed her hand from Charlotte's wrist, and quickly rummaged around inside the bag. Seconds later, she pressed the awl into Charlotte's hand, and then reached back into her bag for the corkscrew. Thank God she was her father's daughter, Charlotte thought.

They were just in time. As the heavy wooden door opened, the moonlight fell clearly on their pursuer's face, revealing the high, sharp cheekbones, the round wire-rimmed glasses, and the long black hair drawn back into a ponytail. As Charlotte had suspected, it was Ned—Ned of the theory of why Peter had been murdered in a cave, she thought ironically. No tie-dyed T-shirt tonight—he was dressed entirely in black. They waited in near-panic for him to come after them, but instead he crossed the antechamber to the door leading to the adjacent cave. Charlotte expected him to go in, but he stopped just inside the door. Maybe he was just waiting to see if the coast was clear, she thought. But as the seconds ticked by, it dawned on her that he was there on the same mission they were. He had also come to spy on Cave 328! What in the name of Sam Hill—to use one of Howard Tracey's favorite expressions—was going on?

They didn't have to wait long to find out. Although it seemed much longer, it was probably only five minutes before they again heard footsteps on the veranda. This time it sounded like more than one person. A few seconds later they again heard the jangle of a ring of iron keys, followed by the click of a key in the lock. Then they heard the squeak of the hinges as the door of the adjacent cave opened. First one person entered—slow, heavy steps and a lot of labored breathing, like an old steam engine—and then the other. After the two intruders had closed the door behind them, they switched on their flashlights. Charlotte could see the light from their beams sweeping across the floor of their own antechamber. She strained her ears to hear. One spoke a few words in Chinese, which were followed by a vague rustling, and finally by a grating noise accompanied by some more words in Chinese, these uttered in a commanding tone, as if the one were giving orders to the other. She waited for the ring of a hammer on a chisel, but it didn't come. Whatever they were doing, it wasn't removing the stone slab that blocked the opening of the cubbyhole.

The labored breathing reminded her of someone. She was trying to think of who it was when one of the men coughed—a deep, phlegmy cough, followed by a hawking noise, and the hiss of spitting. She had heard that cough before—once while sitting on the bench at the foot of the cliff, the other time while drinking tea with Ho in the guest house reception room. It was Chu's cough, the emphysematous cough of the heavy smoker. But who was the other man? And then she knew the answer to that question as well. The cough was followed by a few more steps, and then a dull thud, as if something was being set down on the floor of the cave. "Shit," said the other man. It was a young voice—an American voice, but with a Chinese accent. The image rose in her mind of a young Chinese man in a red and white Boston University T-shirt; a slender, round-shouldered man with protruding front teeth and aviator glasses.

Then it struck her what they were doing there. They were returning the sculpture of the Bodhisattva that Langdon Warner had taken sixty years before. It was Chu's son, in collaboration with his father, who had been stealing the Dunhuang artworks from Western museums and returning them to China!

A few minutes later they were gone.

Charlotte was dying of curiosity. She wanted to rush in to take a look, but Ned beat her to the punch. They could see the light from his flashlight through the doorway. They could also hear him talking to himself. "Son of a bitch," he muttered. If he wasn't an accomplice, and it seemed clear that he wasn't, then he must have been there to confirm his own suspicion that it was Chu's son who had been stealing the artworks from Western museums. In which case, there was no risk in revealing themselves to him. Charlotte was trying to decide whether or not to do so when another sound caught her attention.

It was a low, throbbing hum, like the faint sound of an engine heard through the wall of an adjacent building.

Ned heard it too. "Jesus," he said.

A second later, the hum became a roar, and a blast of cold, sand-laden wind blew in through the door of the adjoining cave, which Ned had opened to leave. The force of the wind was so great that it took him several seconds to close the door behind him. The *buran* was finally upon them.

Once Ned had closed the door, Charlotte switched on her flashlight and turned to Marsha, who was crouched behind her. "Are you okay?"

"I'm fine. But I wouldn't mind knowing what's going on. If it wasn't Ned who's been removing the manuscripts from the cubbyholes, who was it? And why was Ned spying on them?"

"Whoa. One question at a time. It was Chu and his son, and they weren't removing anything. They were putting something back. Ned was here because he suspected what they were up to, and wanted to confirm his suspicion."

"If I could raise an eyebrow, I would," said Marsha as she stood up.

Gesturing for Marsha to follow her, Charlotte led the way into the adjacent cave, and then directed her flashlight into the inner chapel. "Look," she said, aiming her beam at the third figure on the left, which knelt on a lotus blossom with its offerings to the Buddha.

"The Fogg's Bodhisattva!" said Marsha.

"Yes," said Charlotte. "Restored to its original home."

·14·

As the winds raged outside, Charlotte reiterated what Chu had told her about his family, and particularly about its being his father who was responsible for the Nationalists' looting of the art treasures from the Palace Museum. "My guess is that he hatched this scheme to steal the Dunhuang treasures from Western museums to atone for the sins of his family. He's very grateful to the Communists."

"For incarcerating him in a prison camp for eleven years?"

"He's glad they didn't kill him, as they did many other class traitors. He could have lost his life." Her tone was ironic. "Instead he only lost an arm. He's been rehabilitated, you see. He was blinded before by his bad class background. But after ten years of reeducation, he's able to see the virtues of a system that allows someone with a class background such as his to rise to a position of such great responsibility."

Marsha sighed. "China is such a tragedy."

Charlotte continued. "The son was just the cog in the wheel of his scheme. Chu dictated what objects to steal, and the son stole them. Stealing the Bodhisattva from the Fogg must have been a difficult trick, but stealing the Dunhuang manuscripts from the British Museum and other Western libraries was probably pretty easy; it's hard to keep track of so many, and libraries are notorious for their bad security."

"Even the Fogg's Bodhisattva wasn't that difficult," Marsha said. "I read about it at the time. The thief just deactivated the burglar alarm while the security guard was sleeping and walked off with the sculpture during the night. And Ned? What was he doing here?"

"He's the one who's been tracking down the missing artworks for Chu, with Boardmann's help. Once Ned had located an artwork, Chu would send a letter asking for it back. Bunny Oglethorpe got one. In many cases, the theft came immediately on the heels of the letter. Ned must have put two and two together, and concluded that Chu was connected with the thefts."

The dull, throbbing hum outside the wall of the cave had been growing steadily louder, and was now accompanied by the rattle of sand and gravel lashing against the wooden door.

"We'd better get out of here," Marsha said. "I've heard these sandstorms can be like blizzards—the atmosphere can get so thick with sand that you can't see your hand in front of your face."

As they were heading toward the door, Charlotte felt a blast of sand-laden air. The door had suddenly opened. She found herself facing the beam of an intruder's torch—the roar of the wind must have obscured the noise of his key in the lock. She turned to flee to the adjacent cave, but it was too late.

"Not so fast," he growled, moving between her and the door.

Charlotte couldn't see who it was, at first. Like a deer caught in an automobile's headlights, she was stunned by the brightness of his torch. As her eyes adjusted, she could make out the short, wiry build, and the white face with its neat black Vandyke beard. It was Victor Danowski. Of course! He had come for the manuscripts. If not Ned, therefore Victor.

"I saw the light under the door," he said as he inched closer. "If you ladies are going to play at being detectives, you ought to be more careful. But then, you won't have to worry about that much longer."

It was then that Charlotte noticed that he was brandishing a knife—the same knife that had killed Larry Fiske, Peter Hamilton, and Averill Boardmann. "I wish Averill were here," she remembered him telling her when they had talked outside the library. She had believed him.

"Are you going to kill us?" asked Marsha, terrified.

All Charlotte could think of was the crude painting on the cave wall that illustrated the changing line from the *I Ching*. Without even realizing it, they had stepped on the tiger's tail.

"I don't think so," he said. "You're going to be a missing persons case. Two American ladies who got caught in the middle of a sandstorm. They won't know where to begin to look—you'll be buried under a mountain of sand somewhere between here and Kashgar."

As he spoke, Charlotte surveyed the escape routes. Victor blocked the doorway to the cave they had just come from, but the doorway on the opposite wall led to a passageway, which in turn led to another cave. If she remembered right, the Cave of Unequaled Height was about three caves away.

"I've read about these sandstorms," Victor went on. "The *burans*. They bury whole camel caravans, armies, even cities. Hsuan-tsang wrote about a sandstorm that once buried three hundred cities in twenty-four hours. Next to that, two missing American ladies will be nothing."

"The security police are going to catch you, you know," said Marsha. "You can't kill five people and get away with it."

Good. Keep him talking, Marsha.

The only way out of the Cave of Unequaled Height was a staircase that led down through the various levels of the giant cave. Or rather, staircases—there was one on either side. Either that, or parachute off of one of the nine balconies. But here they didn't stand a Chinaman's chance, as the saying went.

Victor was ignoring her.

Marsha continued bravely. "They'll know it was you who did it," she said. "Charlotte already told them you were our chief suspect."

"Maybe some day hundreds of years from now a desert wind will expose your bones, just as it did those of the *Tyrannosaurus*," Victor continued. "I can just see a paleontologist of the future coming along and saying, 'Here are the bones of two women who died in the desert.' " He laughed, a high-pitched, crazy laugh, and lunged toward them with the knife, whose sharp edge gleamed.

Charlotte thought of the twisted corpse of the mummified donkey at the side of the asphalt, and shuddered. Then she grabbed Marsha's arm and fled.

The passageway led to another cave, which in turn was linked to another. Running at full speed, they passed from one cave to another. They had no idea how close Victor was behind them—the deafening roar of the storm drowned out any sound. At the third cave, they ran up against a blank wall.

"We'll have to go outside," said Charlotte.

Turning the bolt in the lock, Charlotte opened the door. Fortunately, the storm had momentarily abated, allowing them to see their immediate surroundings. As a waterfall of sand and pebbles from the top of the cliff rained down on their heads, Charlotte took stock of their situation. They had emerged onto a veranda that was linked to a series of balconies and stairways that led across the cliff face to the Cave of Unequaled Height, about forty feet away. From here, there was no route down. They would have to take one of the staircases in the big cave.

Suddenly they heard the sound of running footsteps on the other side of the wall. Victor was right behind them.

Where was Jack now with his flares? thought Charlotte as she looked around for something that would help them. Then she spotted an old rafter next to Marsha that must have blown down from up above. "There!" she said, pointing the beam of her flashlight at it. "We'll use it to bar the door."

Marsha quickly passed the rafter over to Charlotte.

"This won't stop him, but it should slow him down," said Charlotte as she propped one end of the rafter under the knob of the cave door and the other against the cement base of the balcony railing. Instead of chasing them along the cliff face, Victor would have to backtrack to the previous cave and exit from there, which would mean taking a stairway down to another route that also led across the cliff face to the Cave of Unqualed Height, but a couple of levels below. By then, they would be well ahead of him.

With Charlotte in the lead, they headed up a stairway toward the big cave. Behind them, they could hear the thudding of Victor's shoulder being pounded against the door as he tried to force it. They were barely midway across the cliff face when the storm burst upon them with renewed vengeance. Sharp particles of gravel blasted their faces, and the wind sounded like a thousand shrieking voices. Charlotte could now see why this was called the Mountain of the Howling Sands. Slowly they groped their way across the cliff face through the blinding murk. They couldn't see—not even the floor beneath them—and it was difficult to breathe. At last, they reached the door on the other side.

The door opened onto the eighth story of the nine-story cave, at about the height of the colossal Buddha's neck. Unlike the other caves, which were pitch-black, this cave was faintly lit by the votive candles on the altar at the Buddha's feet more than a hundred feet below. From above, the face of the Buddha gazed down through half-closed eyes like an apparition. A swirling haze of sand that had blown in through the openings in the front wall of the pagoda-like building hung in the air, and the wind chimes jangled wildly.

"Buddha be praised," said Marsha, looking up at the colossal figure.

"And pass the ammunition," added Charlotte.

The stairwell was pitch-dark. With her flashlight, Charlotte led the way down the mud brick steps. If Victor had already reached the cave, he would be waiting for them at the foot of this set of stairs. But the chances of that were practically nil. If he'd had to backtrack, he should have been far behind them.

When they came to the bottom, she breathed a sigh of relief—not that she had really expected him to be waiting for them there.

She had just turned to descend the next flight of stairs when an arm reached out and grabbed her, and pulled her back behind the wall that separated the cave from the stairwell. A hand was slapped over her mouth to keep her from screaming. *Damn!* The only noise she succeeded in making was a piglike grunt, which was hardly enough to warn Marsha over the roar of the storm. Nor could she move, as much as she struggled. Her assailant was frighteningly strong, and held her right arm in a hammerlock. She was pondering her predicament when it dawned on her that the man who was holding her wasn't Victor. Victor was her height—five feet eight, or even less—this man was at least six four. She could feel the back of her head pressing against the button on his shirt front—a hard metal button, the button of a Western shirt. She could also feel the bristle of a beard against the back of her head, and she could smell the sweet smell of pipe tobacco on the hand that was cupped over her mouth.

The man who was holding her was Bert!

A wave of suffocating paranoia swept over her. It was Bert whom she had always meant to question, Bert who had been absent from his room on the morning Larry was killed. She suddenly remembered Bert pulling a knife out of the holster on his belt to scrape the sandstone from the jawbone of the *Protoceratops* skull. Why hadn't she thought of that knife before? she asked herself. Then she wondered if he had it now. A spate of other questions coursed through her mind. Could it really have been Bert who murdered Larry? Was he somehow in league with Victor? If so, what was their joint interest? But none of the answers made any sense. Poetic, courteous, dedicated Bert. The Bert who loved Marsha, the Bert who might even have been her stepson-in-law one day. But if he wasn't in league with Victor, what was he doing in this cave at three o'clock in the morning trying to squeeze her to death? The hammerlock on her right arm was so tight that she thought her shoulder was going to be wrenched out of its socket.

These thoughts took just a few seconds to race through her mind, the same few seconds it took Marsha to reach the foot of the stairs. Though she couldn't hear Marsha's footsteps over the roar of the storm, she could see the beam of Marsha's flashlight as she approached the foot of the stairs. If Bert let go of her to grab Marsha, she would be able to make a run for it, she thought. But she didn't get her chance. A second later, Bert backed slowly away from the edge of the wall, with Charlotte still in tow, to make room at the head of the stairs for Dogie, who was just behind them. So loud was the storm that Charlotte hadn't realized he'd been standing only a couple of feet away. As Marsha turned to descend the next flight of stairs, Dogie lunged out and grabbed her, and then quickly slapped a hand across her mouth.

What was going to happen now? thought Charlotte, who as a consequence of over forty years in front of the cameras had a tendency to view the more dramatic events of her life—and there had been more than her share of them—as if they were elements of a plot that was unfolding on the screen. Critics of her personal character, who included two of her ex-husbands, considered this attitude a symptom of her lack of grasp on reality; but she preferred to think of them as being overreactive. The fact was that there was little that she took in life—including the prospect of her own death (especially at this age, when she had already lived a far more rich and exciting life then she ever could have hoped for)—as sufficently serious to warrant getting upset about. Which wasn't to deny that she was scared.

As a victim of too many screen assaults to count, she knew her options: she could kick Bert in the shins, she could jab him in the ribs, or, if she could pull his hand down far enough, she could bite his thumb. If she could get at her pocket, she could also stab him with Marsha's awl, but for now her pocket was out of reach. None of the first three options were likely to get her anywhere—even if she did get away, he would probably catch her. They might even get her in worse trouble: he might decide to hit back. But doing something was better than doing nothing.

She decided on all three, at once. After counting slowly to ten to muster her courage, she seized Bert's wrist and pulled down on it, hard. That maneuver didn't work: his hand didn't budge. But her others did. "Jesus," he muttered as she simultaneously kicked him in the shins and elbowed him in the ribs. Still holding his hand over her mouth, he spun her around to face him. Raising a finger to his lips, he pointed at the staircase leading down to the next level. Then he mouthed the word, "Danowski," and let her go.

Turning around, he repeated this for Marsha.

Of course! Bert and Dogie were their rescuers, just as the *I Ching* had predicted. "Precisely in this extremity," three rescuers would come to her aid, it had said. There were only two, but she wasn't complaining. How could she have been stupid enough to think that Bert was in league with Victor? But how had Bert and Dogie known they were here? she wondered. Then she realized what must have happened. Bert must have been in Marsha's room when she left for their midnight mission. Either she told him what she was up to or he figured it out for himself. In any case, when the *buran* hit, he had gotten worried and had solicited Dogie's aid in looking for her. They must have seen Charlotte and Marsha blockading the door to the cave, and concluded that something was amiss when they saw Victor taking off after them a few minutes later.

Bert and Dogie had moved up in front of Charlotte and Marsha, and were lying in wait for Victor at the head of the stairwell. Charlotte still hadn't figured out how he had reached the big cave so quickly. Seconds later, she saw Bert's body stiffen. Then he lunged again, but this time he was jumping an armed man who was ready to kill, not an unarmed woman. After a brief struggle, Bert managed to get the knife away from Victor, but even with Dogie's help, he wasn't able to pin him down. The three men struggled on the floor of the cave for what seemed like an eternity but was actually only a few minutes. Finally Victor broke away, and went running past Charlotte and Marsha toward the nearest exit, which was the door to the balcony. His plan was clearly to cross the balcony, reenter the cave on the other side, and descend the other stairway.

Bert took off after him. Dogie was about to follow when he was stopped by Charlotte.

"Go that way," she said, directing him to the catwalk spanning the front of the cave and linking the platforms on either side of the enormous statue. If Dogie could get to the platform on the other side before Victor, he could block his access to the stairs. And if the ferocity of its roar was any indication, the storm was bound to slow Victor down.

A second later, Victor had opened the door to the balcony, letting in a cold rush of sand.

"Come on," said Charlotte, shouting in Marsha's ear to be heard above the howl of the storm. "We can watch from there." She pointed at the windowlike aperture that opened off of the catwalk.

"I don't know if I want to watch," Marsha shouted back.

Following in Dogie's footsteps, they made their way across the catwalk to the opening, which by day let light into the dark chamber. Now all it let in was a dark, swirling cloud of sand and gravel. At first, they couldn't see anything. Then they saw a slight, wind-whipped figure slowly making its way across the balcony. And behind it another figure—taller, and burly.

"Where's Dogie?" asked Marsha.

"There," said Charlotte. A bandy-legged figure with a beer belly had just materialized out of the sand cloud at the other end of the balcony.

"All right, Percival," Charlotte shouted through cupped hands.

Though he hadn't yet realized it, Victor was fenced in. Bert was closing in from the rear, and Dogie from the front.

As they watched, Victor turned around to see if Bert was gaining on him, and then, as he turned back, caught sight of Dogie. For a second, he froze. Then he started looking around him—down over the edge of the railing, and up at the opening at which they were standing. Then he tucked his knife into his belt, and crouched down in preparation for a jump.

"He's going to try and climb up here!" said Marsha.

The opening, which was only a few feet above the level of the catwalk, was protected by a wrought-iron grate that reached about halfway up. In order to get back into the cave, Victor would have to catch hold of the iron grate, and pull himself up. What they needed was a baseball bat to hit him over the head with, but there wasn't even a loose brick lying around.

"We'll have to push him over," said Charlotte, speaking into Marsha's ear to be heard above the storm. "You get on that side, and I'll get on this side. When I give the signal"—she raised her forefinger—"put your foot up against his shoulder, and push."

Seconds later, Victor leaped up onto the grate as agilely as a monkey leaping onto a bough. As he leaned forward to get enough purchase to pull himself over, Charlotte gave the signal. Bracing themselves against the window jamb, she and Marsha simultaneously put their feet on his shoulders and pushed.

"Shit," he muttered into the wind.

For a few seconds, they pushed and he resisted. It was like pushing against a weight machine at a gym, except that Victor was stronger. Charlotte could see his knuckles turning white with the exertion of hanging on. But finally he had to let go, and he dropped back down onto the balcony.

"Good work!" shouted Dogie, who by now was only a few feet away.

But Victor's attempt to climb up had given him another idea: to climb down instead. With Bert and Dogie closing in, he quickly climbed over the balcony railing and inched himself down on his hands and knees toward the edge of the red-tiled roof that overhung the balcony on the preceding level. If he was lucky, he would be able to get to the stairwell on the level below before Bert and Dogie could get to him. But it was a big if: it was at least a ten-foot drop, and the fierce winds could easily pick him up and fling him into the void. And even if he did get away, what would he do then? It wouldn't be easy for a murderer to escape from an oasis in the Gobi without going through the desert itself. And the perils of traveling in the desert in a sandstorm were notorious, as he had pointed out himself.

At the edge, he carefully lowered himself over. Charlotte could only see his hands, but she could guess what he intended to do. Recessed below each of the roofs that gave the structure its pagoda-like appearance was an ornate latticework cornice of red-painted wood. If he could fling his feet forward far enough to get a foothold in the openings in the latticework, he could then work himself over like a monkey on the wall of a cage to one of the supporting columns, and shimmy down.

He missed the first time. From above, they could see his legs fly backward in reaction to his forward motion. A second later, they saw his legs fly backward again, but this time a huge dust devil, like a miniature cyclone, came whirling across the top of the Mountain of the Howling Sands with a wild shriek and caught his body in its grip. It was as if it were trying to suck him up into the heavens. He managed to hang on for a few seconds, his body outstretched as if he were flying, and then the wind pried him loose.

For a second, the wind spout held him suspended in the air as if he were a plaything that it was amusing itself with, and then it dropped him as unceremoniously as a child drops a toy when another of greater interest comes along. They didn't see him land. They couldn't see the base of the cliff. But they saw his white face disappear with a scream of terror into the darkness, like a bad memory fading into time.

It took a few seconds for the shock of his fall to sink in, it had happened so quickly. As Charlotte and Marsha looked on, Bert and Dogie peered over the railing, but there was nothing to be seen except a dark, swirling mass of sand that choked their lungs and stung their eyes.

"Come on," said Charlotte. "Let's get out of here."

Turning their backs on the opening, they made their way back across the catwalk to the platform on the north side of the cave. Above them, the gilded face of the Buddha glowed through the haze, serenely unperturbed by the drama that had been unfolding before him.

A few minutes later, Bert and Dogie appeared at the door, their hair and eyebrows coated with sand. They looked like the figurines of Santa Claus playing the electric guitar which were on sale at the souvenir stand.

As they entered, Marsha rushed into Bert's arms. "I'm so glad you're okay," she said, as he enveloped her in a bear hug.

"Same here," he replied.

Charlotte couldn't help thinking how frightened she had felt in his embrace only a few minutes before.

• 15 •

THEY FOUND VICTOR'S body spread-eagled on the paved avenue at the foot of the cliff. The force of the wind spout had carried it about twenty feet out and an equal distance to the south of the spot where he had lost his grip. Though there was little blood, it was clear that he had landed on his head: the left side of his skull was caved in like a jack-o'-lantern that has begun to rot. The only other evidence of injury was to his hands: his fingertips were bloody from the strain of hanging on, and there were bits of red-painted wood embedded in the flesh; and to his skin: the wind had torn away his shirt, exposing his chest and back to the lashing of the storm. His skin was stippled with red where it had been pelted with flying stones. He was also missing a shoe. They found it a couple of dozen feet away, near his knife. It was the same kind of dagger they had seen for sale in the bazaar, with a hand-worked silver haft inlaid with polished stones.

The wind that had raged so furiously had spent itself, for the moment. The sudden calm was uncanny after the roar and howl of the storm. The sand suspended in the motionless air sifted down, like a gentle snowfall.

As they stood there over Victor's body, Bert explained how he and Dogie had come to be at the caves.

"That's what I thought," said Charlotte when he had finished. "But what I don't understand is, how did Victor reach the big cave so fast? We thought we would be past the seventh level before he got there."

"He didn't go back and down and around," Bert explained. "He climbed over the railing and down to the next level. It was the same stunt he tried to pull here, only this time it didn't work. What was he doing here, anyway?"

"It's a long story," said Charlotte. "It'll take a while to explain. Why don't we head on back to the guest house?"

As they turned to walk back, Charlotte noticed that Bert was limping. "Were you injured in the fight with Victor?" she asked.

"I was injured in a fight, but not the fight with Victor. I was injured in the fight with you. That's a pretty mean kick you have there," he added with a smile.

"Worse than a riled-up mule's," added Dogie.

"Sorry about that. I mistook you for the enemy. I should have known better." She proceeded to tell them about the *I Ching*'s prediction that she would fall into a pit and be rescued by "uninvited guests" whom she at first would mistake for enemies.

"I know that line," said Marsha. "It's from 'Waiting.' "

Charlotte nodded.

"But I've always thought the word 'pit' was translated incorrectly," she continued. "The edition you've been using was translated into English from the German, which in turn was translated from the Chinese. In my opinion, a lot of the text got garbled in the process."

"What word would you have used?" asked Charlotte.

"Cave," she said.

They were up until dawn explaining their interpretation of events, not only to Bert and Dogie, but to Ho of the tadpole mustache, and to a bunch of other Chinese officials who arrived about forty-five minutes after their call. They hadn't expected their call to go through, but the phone lines had somehow survived the storm. Though Ho had a good grasp of English—or Chinglish, as Marsha called it—none of the other security police did, and Marsha was called upon to translate and to clarify the points that Ho didn't understand. They sat in the reception room, sipping tea and answering questions: how Victor had found the entry in Wang's daybook disclosing that the key to the manuscripts' location was hidden in the Oglethorpe sculpture; how he had consulted Boardmann on the statue's whereabouts; how they had plotted together to steal the statue; how Victor had killed Boardmann, making it look like a street homicide; how he had hidden the manuscripts in the stupa with the aim of smuggling them out of the country at some future time and selling them; how he had killed Larry, again making it look like a vagrant had done it; and finally, how he had killed Peter because Peter, who had come across the reference in Wang's daybook independently, had wanted a piece of the action. Chu presided over the proceedings with an air of self-righteous indignation. Occasionally he made pointed remarks about the rapacity of the bourgeois capitalists or Dunhuang's long history of plunder at the hands of the Western "so-called" archaeologists. Even the revelation that the world's oldest printed book was among the manuscripts in Victor's haul didn't crack his suit of red armor.

But it was a different story when it came to the earlier events of that evening. Having already explained how she and Marsha had come to be in Cave 328 at one-thirty in the morning and their subsequent encounter with Victor, Charlotte now backtracked to explain what had happened before Victor appeared on the scene, starting with the arrival of Ned.

"Aha," said Ho, his mustache quivering with the thrill of deduction. "Mr. Chee had also figured out that Mr. Danowski was stealing the manuscripts, and had come to spy on him."

"No. Not exactly." Charlotte's gaze shifted to Chu, whose Mao jacket was buttoned to the throat even though he had just been roused out of bed. "He had figured out that Mr. Chu was the thief, and had come to spy on him."

For a moment, Chu's reserve dropped, and she could see the scars on the soft yellow spot of flesh revealed by the chink in the armor—the scars left by the torture, the starvation, the hard labor.

"Comrade Chu was the thief!"

"He wasn't in league with Danowski. But he was also stealing manuscripts and sculptures. Or rather, his son was." She proceeded to explain how, under Chu's direction, his son had stolen the artworks from Western institutions.

"My son wasn't stealing the artworks from Western institutions, he was *recovering* them," said Chu, explaining in his defense how the artworks had been looted from Dunhuang by the foreign imperialists.

"We thought at first that Mr. Chu was Mr. Danowski," Charlotte went on, ignoring the interruption. "But then we realized that there were two people, and that they were Mr. Chu and his son. They were returning the Bodhisattva that was taken from the Fogg Museum."

For a few minutes there was a rapid exchange in Chinese between Ho and Chu. It was clear that Chu was painting himself to the police officer as the savior of China's cultural heritage.

Afterward, Ho turned back to Charlotte. "Comrade Chu tells me that this sculpture was stolen by the American so-called archaeologist Langdon Warner in 1924. In which case, it would be incorrect to label Comrade Chu a thief."

"Whether or not he is a thief is up to international authorities to determine," said Charlotte. But she doubted that the Fogg would ever get its lovely Bodhisattva back.

Chu leaned his head back against the crocheted antimacassar on the back of his chair and took a self-satisfied puff from his cigarette with his manacled-scarred hand, holding it as usual between thumb and forefinger. The chink in the armor had been plugged up.

It was after five when their little party broke up. By the time the convoy of security police vehicles took off for Dunhuang town with Victor's body, it was clear that the storm was abating. Though the wind still rattled the shutters, it had lost its fearful roar.

Charlotte did her best to wash up before going to bed, but it was a losing battle. She had sand in her ears, her eyes, and her nose. Sand crunched between her teeth. The sight of herself in her mirror was frightening: her eyes were red and bleary, her face and hair were coated with grit, and any skin that had been exposed was flecked with blood where she had been hit by "running stones." Her "China catarrh," which had been on the wane, was back in full force: her sinuses were so stuffed that her head felt like a medicine ball. As she fantasized about the pleasures of a long, hot, steamy soak in her own bathtub back at her townhouse in a city halfway around the globe, it dawned on her that right about now the population of America would be setting off fireworks, watching parades, and eating hot dogs.

It might have been going on six A.M. of July the fifth here, but at home it was going on five P.M. of the day before. Her realization that it was the Fourth of July at home brought with it the realization that she was a wanderer who was getting a little bit homesick. At least for a hot bath.

Like the wind, she had retired with the dawn, only to get up again two hours later to accompany Ho to the stupa to retrieve the manuscripts. She rode out into the desert with him at the head of the convoy of security police vehicles. The menacing black clouds of the previous evening were gone. In their place, the sun shone in a serene, cloudless sky. The air was crystal clear; it was as if the storm had scoured it of any vestiges of haze and dust. But if the sky bore no sign of the ferocity of the storm, the landscape did. The band of asphalt that comprised the highway was covered with drifts of sand, like a snow-blanketed New England country road after a nor'easter. Crews of road maintenance workers were already out, clearing the sand away with hand shovels. No backhoes here. Familiar markers had been swept away. The twisted corpse of the mummified donkey that had served as a signpost for the turnoff was gone. Nor was there any track to follow out to the mountain—it had been obliterated by the storm. Not that they had any trouble finding their way. After parking at the foot of the mountain, they followed the winding path of pilgrims' track up to the stupa. The effects of the storm were in evidence here as well. The door had been nearly buried by a six-foot drift of sand. After sending some of his men back to the trucks for shovels, Ho set them to work digging it out.

After twenty minutes, the door was exposed. With Ho at her shoulder, Charlotte grasped the iron ring and pulled. Stepping over the four-foot foundation, they entered the cell. Once inside, Charlotte shined her flashlight at the north wall. To her amazement, it was bare. There were no stacks of manuscripts neatly piled like logs against the feet of the Bodhisattvas. The desk was there, as were the lamp and chair, but no manuscripts.

"There's nothing here," said Ho as he turned to her, mustache quivering. "I thought you said there were manuscripts hidden here."

"There were," she said. "They were here two nights ago."

"Then where did they go?" he asked, waving a white-gloved hand at the empty cubicle. "Did they just get up and walk away?"

"I don't know," she replied, mystified. "Maybe someone smuggled them out of the country for Mr. Danowski in the interim."

"In the middle of a *buran*?" he said contemptuously.

Charlotte shrugged.

"Or maybe you took the manuscripts and hid them somewhere else," he said. "Maybe Mr. Danowski's death wasn't an accident. Maybe you"—he pointed a gloved finger at Charlotte's chest—"killed him."

* * *

"He took me into custody then and there," said Charlotte. "We were on our way to the Public Security Bureau in his jeep when I figured out what had happened to the manuscripts."

She was talking to Reynolds, who was back for the third time to make arrangements in connection with the death of an American national. They were sitting in one of the guest house courtyards, taking a melon break.

"Believe me, I was scared. I hadn't been that frightened when Victor was chasing us, but I was frightened then. Ho can be a scary guy, just by virtue of his incompetence, and it didn't help that I was on my way to a Chinese jail with all of these Chinese police, none of whom spoke English except for Ho."

"And he far from fluently," said Reynolds, as he leaned over to take a bite of the succulent orange melon.

"Fortunately I never did find out what the Dunhuang jail was like—"

He corrected her: "The Dunhuang Municipal Detention Center."

"The Dunhuang Municipal Detention Center," she repeated. "But I had a clear image of what it was like in my mind: a single dim light bulb hanging from the center of the ceiling, a small window with rust-pitted iron rungs, a narrow cot with a filthy mattress."

"What an imagination! Forget the cot," he said with a dismissive wave of his hand. "It would have been a wooden plank. This is China after all."

"How could I have forgotten!"

"Actually, it's not bad," Reynolds continued. "I went there to talk to Feng. Every inmate has his—or her"—he looked over at Charlotte with a twinkle in his eye—"own private accommodations. The cells are a little on the small side, like about four by six, but at least you wouldn't have had to share—"

"Thanks for the reassurance, Bill. I imagine I would have had my own private john too. In the form of a hole in the ground."

Reynolds looked at her over the tops of his reading glasses. "That's only for the first-class offenders. As a foreign devil, you would only have rated an enamel pot under your bed."

Charlotte rolled her eyes. "I once played the mother of a college student who was arrested in Turkey for smuggling drugs—

actually only a single marijuana joint," she went on. "He ended up being jailed for nine years."

"I remember that one. As usual, you were excellent in it."

"Thank you," she said. "Anyway, I had visions of being jailed for years before the United States Government could prove my innocence. As so many people were during the Cultural Revolution."

Reynolds leaned over and patted her hand. "Don't worry. We would have gotten you out in jig time."

Charlotte believed him. In his checked shirt—red-and-white this time—Bermuda shorts, and knee socks, his presence in this desert oasis was as coolly reassuring as a cold compress on a feverish brow. "I was dumb to worry, but there it is. What's the penalty for murder in the People's Republic anyway?"

"According to Chinese law, a convicted murderer should suffer immediate execution following sentencing."

"Oh," she said with a sigh. "Anyway—there I was, thinking about assembling radios at Mao Zedong Thought Study School—that's what Chu told me he did in prison—when I thought of 'Waiting,' the hexagram I got when I consulted the *I Ching* after we found the manuscripts in the stupa."

Reynolds nodded. She had told him before about the *I Ching's* prediction that she was destined to establish a more permanent connection with an exotic foreign country as a result of her encounter with a circle of friends.

"The interpretion talked about going resolutely to your fate—the importance of calm, courage, inner fortitude. The minute I thought of the hexagram, my panic subsided and I was able to think clearly. We had been operating all along on the assumption that money was the motivator."

"As it was for Boardmann and Hamilton," said Reynolds.

"But the earlier events of that evening—namely Chu and his son returning the Fogg's Bodhisattva—pointed up the fact to me that it wasn't the *value* of the Bodhisattva that was at issue—neither party was interested in selling it—but rather, which party had the right to claim it as their own."

"It was the right of ownership that was at stake."

"Exactly. That got me to thinking that the same might be true for Victor. If he had made one of the century's greatest archaeological discoveries, and I think the *I Ching* manuscript would qualify, his name would have gone down in archaeological history. Students of the future would read about Carter, who discovered King Tut's tomb; Schliemann, who discovered Troy; and Danowski, who discovered the world's oldest printed book. But not if he reported the find to the Academy. Which, as a visiting scholar, he was required to do."

"It was just as you thought when you were speculating about who had murdered Larry: the motive was professional jealousy."

"That's right. Except that we were in the wrong field; it should have been archaeology, not paleontology. In fact, Peng was happy to credit his American colleague with the discovery of the *Tyrannosaurus*, but Chu was another story. He wanted everything for China. He wouldn't even let Victor freely examine the manuscripts that he had come halfway around the globe to study. He parceled them out one by one, like candy to a child. He would have claimed the discovery as his own, and Victor would have remained an anonymous laborer in the fields of academe. Faced with this prospect, he decided to temporarily remove the manuscripts from their hiding places, and take them out to the stupa to photograph them. We had seen him returning some manuscripts to the caves on that first night we spied on him, but we didn't know then who he was or what he was doing. His intent of course was to publish his findings, with the photographs, in an academic journal before notifying the Chinese."

"Thereby making sure that it would be he and not the Chinese who was awarded academic recognition for the discovery," said Reynolds. "I think I would have done the same in his case."

"Any ambitious capitalist would have," said Charlotte with a smile. "Thank goodness that for a few moments there, I was thinking like any ambitious capitalist. If I hadn't been, I'd now be acquiring an intimate acquaintance with the luxurious accommodations at the Dunhuang Municipal Detention Center."

"Of course, someone at the Academy would eventually have discovered that Victor had returned the manuscripts to the cubbyholes. But it might have taken a while, and in the meantime you would have been dining on rice gruel and mutton fat."

"I thought you would have gotten me out right away."

Reynolds smiled. "Well," he said. "Sometimes it takes a little longer than one would hope for."

Charlotte raised her signature eyebrow.

"By the way, Feng identified Danowski as the foreigner who gave him Fiske's shortwave radio," he said. "Ho showed him the photograph of Danowski that the Academy had in its files. I think we can safely assume that it was he who planted the shortwave radio on Feng."

Charlotte was perplexed.

"What is it?" asked Reynolds.

"When Marsha and I went to the bazaar on Sunday, we questioned Feng's cronies. The crippled boy that hangs around with Feng told us that the foreigner he had seen talking to him had been carrying a lute. When I saw Ned Chee playing a lute, I assumed the foreigner had been he."

"Danowski was carrying a lute," Reynolds explained. "But it was Chee's lute. Chee had bought it at the bazaar that morning. Danowski and Chee had ridden into town together on the minibus. Chee was going to stay behind with his girlfriend, the young Chinese guide."

"Emily Lin?"

Reynolds nodded. "She had the morning off. After Chee bought the lute, they were going to go to the District Revolutionary Committee office to apply for a marriage license. Chee asked Victor to take the lute back for him."

Charlotte nodded. That's why Ned wasn't carrying the lute when he got off the minibus, she thought. *Click.* Another piece had fallen into place. "Emily confided in Marsha about her troubles getting Chu's approval."

"He was finally forced to give it. Chee wrote directly to the Central Committee of the Party, and requested permission to marry from Deng Xiaoping himself. Deng sent down instructions that their request should be approved."

"That's wonderful!" Ned and Emily made an odd pair—he in his tie-dyed T-shirt, she in her white anklets. She was reminded of a line from Emily's favorite poem: "Then there's a pair of us—don't tell! They'd banish us, you know."

"Emily is going to make an application to study English literature at Berkeley," Reynolds continued. "Chee told me about it yesterday. He was talking with me about how to go about getting a visa for her."

The mother goose and her goslings had appeared from under the zinnias again. Charlotte and Reynolds watched them for a moment as they finished eating their slices of the delicious melon.

"What about the other stuff that was missing—the calculator and the wristwatch?" asked Charlotte after a while.

"Stolen by a servant. One of his neighbors turned him in."

Click. Another piece in place. It was a little one, but Charlotte was a fanatic when it came to details. Maybe she should spend her retirement working with Lisa in Bert's paleontology lab, piecing dinosaur bones together.

"He's in jail now. Speaking of jails, I have some good news for you. I spoke yesterday with Kong. The Chinese Academy of Dramatic Arts has approved your participation in the production of *The Crucible*."

"That's great news!" said Charlotte.

"Of course, it's all very iffy. The Ministry of Culture still has to give the project its stamp of approval. But it's a good start."

She was surprised at how relieved she felt. It was as if a great weight had been lifted off her chest. She hadn't realized until now how much she had wanted to do this; or conversely, how little she had wanted to do any of the other projects that had recently come her way. "Goodbye to the glamorous grandmother, goodbye to the wife of the man with Alzheimer's disease, goodbye to the dowager who founds a shelter for bag ladies."

"And let a hundred flowers bloom," added Reynolds.

Flinging her arms around him, she gave him a big hug. "May I?" she asked, drawing back and looking him in the eye.

"It would be the fulfillment of a lifelong fantasy," he replied.

Then she gave him a big kiss on the cheek.

Two days later, Charlotte and Marsha left for the Dunhuang airport, half an hour from Dunhuang town. They would be taking the four-hour flight back to Lanzhou, the capital of Gansu Province. From there, they would fly to Beijing, and then home. Despite the early hour—the plane left at seven-thirty in the morning—Bert and Dogie came to see them off. They would be staying behind to work on the dig. The sandstorm had set their work back several weeks. The part of the dinosaur skeleton that hadn't already been removed, which was most of it, had been buried by the sandstorm under six feet of sand, all of which would have to be carefully removed, trowelful by trowelful.

As they waited in the terminal, Bert was talking about the element of luck involved in fossil hunting. A skeleton like that of the *Tyrannosaurus* had probably been exposed for only a short time before being buried again by the same desert gales that had brought it to the light of day. "If Larry hadn't gone to that particular spot during that brief moment in time when it was exposed, it might never have been found," he said. He paused, and they waited for the clouds of thought to roll across the big sky. "In fact," he continued after a while, "when you think about it, it's a wonder any dinosaur fossils are found, she thought at all."

"Not here, it ain't," said Dogie, whose thoughts only took a fraction of a second to find expression. "This here is fossil wonderland." He explained: "It looks like our friend Larry has discovered the world's richest lode of post-Cretaceous dinosaur fossils."

"Too bad he didn't realize it," said Marsha.

Charlotte remembered Larry's shining eyes on the evening she had met him, and the tableau she had come across the following morning: the cigar, the espresso, the decanter of brandy. He was well aware of the significance of what he had found, she thought; he had been celebrating just that.

Bert agreed. "How could he not have realized it? His discovery of the Dragon's Tomb Site is going to change the face of paleontology. Even Orecchio is changing his tune: he's still singing the impact song, but not as loudly. He's talking now about the impact being an *element* in the great dying."

"You mean you're not right-wing warmongers anymore for thinking the dinosaurs could survive a nuclear winter?" asked Marsha.

"I guess we've been rehabilitated," said Bert.

"Tell them about the name," prompted Dogie.

Bert adjusted his big, heavy frame in his plastic chair. "We're not sure yet—we have to talk some more with Peng about it—but we'd like to name the new *Tyrannosaurus* after Larry. If Peng approves, our knobby-nosed *Tyrannosaurus* will be *Tyrannosaurus fiski*. Like Andrews' *Protoceratops andrewsi*."

"*Tyrannosaurus fiski,*" said Charlotte. "He would have liked that."

"I talked with his family to see if they approved, and they were delighted. They're also talking about donating a new wing to our museum that would be named after him. It would be dedicated to the late dinosaurs."

"Very, very late," added Dogie with a wide grin.

The plane had arrived.

"Before we leave, I have a question to ask you, Bert," Charlotte said as they rose to head out to the tarmac. "The last little piece in the skeleton that I've been piecing together," she added. "Where were you early in the morning on the day that Larry was murdered?"

Bert looked at her quizzically.

"Dogie said you weren't with him; Marsha said you weren't with her. It's not important now, but I've been wondering."

"You mean I was a suspect?"

"Only for a brief moment in time," she said with a smile. "Before the desert gales exposed the identity of the real villain."

Bert smiled. "I was out in the desert."

"Doing what?"

"Oh, looking at the stars, sniffing the air, feeling the wind on my cheek." He looked away with a little smile. He obviously didn't want to tell her what he had really been up to.

"Nature called you into her embrace for three hours?" She raised a skeptical eyebrow and waited again for the clouds of thoughts to roll past.

"I was writing a poem," he admitted at last. "I guess I'm what you'd call a closet poet." He looked over at Marsha, who grinned. Then he smiled sheepishly. "I was inspired, you see."

"Did you tell Ho that's what you were doing?" she asked, remembering Reynolds telling her that everyone except Dogie had claimed to be asleep.

"No," said Bert. "He didn't ask."

So much for Ho's thoroughness.

As the access ramp was maneuvered into place, they all said goodbye. Then Bert and Marsha embraced, and that was that. Bert and Dogie left, and Charlotte and Marsha headed out to the plane.

"There's Bouchard," said Marsha, pointing at a broad khaki-clad torso mounted on skinny legs in the throng of passengers ahead. Under his arm, he clutched a wooden box with shiny brass fittings. "Do you suppose that box is full of dried spiders and scorpions?"

"I'd say it's a pretty good bet."

"Ugh," Marsha said with a shiver.

Just then, Bouchard turned around to look back. At what, Charlotte didn't know. But she was struck by his expression. The frown was gone from his forehead and his lips no longer curved downward at the corners. He was a happy man; his face glowed with fulfillment.

She'd been thinking of it as something of a tragedy that he had been barred from the expedition, but instead it was probably the happiest day of his life. Now he could devote himself entirely to his scorpions.

On the plane, a People's Aviation stewardess showed them to their seats, which weren't built to accommodate American physiques. Charlotte's knees were crammed up against the seat in front of her.

Once they were seated, Marsha started rummaging around in her carry-on bag, which she had stashed underneath the seat in front of her. As she did so, Charlotte noticed a new ring on her finger, a beautiful paste jewel.

"You have a new ring!" she said.

Marsha held out her hand to display the stone, a large imitation rose quartz in a simple setting. "Bert gave it to me last night. He bought it from that pretty girl in town who was selling the paste jewelry. He went back yesterday to track her down."

How thoughtful of him to buy a ring that symbolized the Tang era that Marsha loved, Charlotte thought. Not only that, but their first night together had inspired him to poetry. No wonder Marsha had to travel halfway around the world to find him. He was the kind of man who was a rare commodity.

"It's an engagement ring," Marsha added. "We're planning on getting married sometime around Christmas."

"That's what I really wanted to ask, but I didn't want to pry," Charlotte said. Turning in her seat, she gave Marsha a big hug. "Congratulations! I think you'll be very happy together. But I'll miss my faithful and trustworthy friend," she added plaintively. "Who will I go to museums with?"

"I'm not moving to Bozeman."

"You're not! Is Bert moving to New York, then?"

"He's not moving to New York either. We're going to have a long-distance marriage—go back and forth."

Charlotte raised an inquiring eyebrow.

"We've both been married twice before," Marsha explained. "Maybe we've learned a little something. I certainly hope we have. His marriages didn't work because he didn't want to be a traditional husband. Mine didn't work because I didn't want to be a traditional wife. Besides, he doesn't want to live in New York and I don't want to live in Bozeman."

"That's the difference between the women of your generation and those of mine," Charlotte said. "Even the most liberated women of my generation, me among them—at least in my youth—would have dropped everything to live with their husbands. Maybe I should have come to a similar agreement with your father." One reason for the failure of their marriage had been his insistence that she move to Minneapolis.

"I know," said Marsha. "Minneapolis is a nice city, but . . ."

"But, is right." If ever there was a fish out of water, it was Charlotte Graham among the skiers and snowmobilers of that northern city. In effect, she and Jack had a similar arrangement now. Although she avoided Minneapolis if at all possible, he often visited her in New York, and she sometimes accompanied him on his business trips.

"Maybe it's not too late. Daddy is educable, you know. It's just that after forty years of being married to Mother, it's hard being married to Charlotte Graham. By the way, did he ever call you back about that trip to the Virgin Islands?"

"Yes. Yesterday morning. Sorry, I forgot to tell you."

"And?"

"And . . . I'm going."

Marsha leaned back with a happy smile.

Marsha was right. Instead of thinking of their marriage as a failure, maybe she and Jack should simply redefine it. They were both satisfied with the arrangement; it was only their peers who said there was something wrong with it. Maybe they should look to the younger generation for their models. She turned to Marsha. "So how *are* you going to arrange it?" she asked.

"Well, Bert's on the East Coast a lot for conferences and so on, and I can get out to Bozeman several times a year. Then we'll spend our summers here."

"Here?"

"In Dunhuang. The fossil grounds are so rich that Bert figures he'll be spending his summers here for years to come. Which is fine with me. I can do my work here as easily as I could do it in London. If Chu will let me, that is. In addition to the manuscripts I came to look at this time, the library here has microfilm copies of all the manuscripts in the Stein Collection."

"Plus there's Wang's nest egg to look at now," said Charlotte.

"That's right! Hundreds of new manuscripts. Including the world's oldest printed book. In fact, I've been thinking about an entirely new project."

"What's that?"

"A new translation of the *I Ching*. Based on the oldest extant text."

As the pilot taxied the plane into position, Marsha started rummaging around again in her carry-on bag. "Found it," she said, pulling out a bottle of wine and the same two wineglasses she had produced on the train ride out. "I brought one bottle for the trip out, and one for the trip back. And," she said, reaching back into her bag, "our indispensable corkscrew."

Actually, Charlotte thought, someone like Marsha would be an invaluable addition to a paleontological expedition. If ever there was someone who could plan an expedition down to the last teabag, it was Marsha. Bert and his crew would never be stranded without a corkscrew or any other vital necessity.

As the engines roared in preparation for takeoff, Marsha poured the wine. "To our safe return from our journey to the west," she said, referring to the Tang poem about the willow tokens. "Which came very close to not being a safe return."

Charlotte thought of the meaning of the name Taklimakan: "Once you get in, you can never get out." They had gotten out, but barely. "And to our return to the Celestial Kingdom," she said.

"*Our* return?" said Marsha, "Did you hear from Bill Reynolds?"

"This morning. It looks like this deal with the Ministry of Culture is going to go through. Which would mean that I'd be here from May to July—roughly the same time as you. Of course, I'd be in Beijing, and you'd be in Dunhuang, but . . ."

Marsha laid a hand on Charlotte's arm. "But you could visit us in Dunhuang. And Daddy could come along too. He would love it." She gazed eagerly into Charlotte's eyes. "Why not?" she asked.

"Why not?" Charlotte agreed.

The plane was finally taking off. As it rose into the air, Charlotte saw below her an ocean of sand waves edged by a wilderness of badlands—deep ravines and towering buttes, canyons and ridges, chasms and cliffs—all tinged flamingo-pink by the light of the rising sun.

She thought of the sandstorm that Victor said had once buried three hundred cities in twenty-four hours, and wondered how many ancient sculptures and manuscripts lay buried beneath the sands, how many not-as-ancient-as-you-might-think dinosaur skeletons were still entombed in the eroding hillsides.

Reaching down for the bottle, Charlotte refilled their glasses. "To the sand-buried ruins of ancient Cathay," she said, raising her glass to the desert-scape below.

"*Gan bei*," said Marsha.

·16·

"IT ARRIVED LAST week, all patched up and as good as new," Bunny Oglethorpe was saying. She and Charlotte were walking down the pine-needle-carpeted path that led through the forest to the moon gate in the section of old Chinese wall that enclosed the Oglethorpe Gardens.

Charlotte wrapped her sweater more tightly around her. It was blessedly cool: a damp fog was rolling in off the ocean, wreathing the garden in the tendrils of mist that gave it its mysterious aura. At the end of the path, they came to the moon gate. As they entered, Charlotte noticed the round iron door pull—exactly like the one on the door of the stupa. She would never be able to enter the garden again without thinking of that distant monument on the Mountain of the Three Dangers.

The sculpture of Hsuan-tsang was the centerpiece of the north end of the garden. He sat cross-legged under his shelter as he always had, looking out over the fish pond to the brightness of the flower garden beyond. Charlotte had come here to see him dozens of times before. But where he had once been merely a pleasant *objet d'art*, he now carried a multitude of associations, some of which she would just as soon put behind her.

"It must look very different to you now," said Bunny.

In fact, it did. The mysterious little smile that had seemed only vaguely archaic before now seemed to look past her gaze with an ineffable compassion for the human weaknesses that prompted men to covet, to steal, and to kill.

Leaning to one side, Bunny pointed to the back of the statue, which faced the rear wall of the shelter. "We had a conservator from the Asian Department at the Met fix the hole in the back for us."

Charlotte stepped over to look. She could just make out the edge of the patched spot on the sculpture's lower back.

"If the sculpture were free-standing, the patch would be noticeable, but in this position, you have to crane your neck to see it," Bunny said. "I'm just glad to have it back, patch or no. With Chief Tracey's help, we're installing a new alarm system to prevent this from happening again."

"Speak of the devil," said Charlotte, who had caught sight of Tracey approaching out of the corner of her eye.

Joining them at the end of the garden, he tipped his Red Sox cap in greeting, and extended his hand to Charlotte. Though she had talked with him at great length on the telephone, this was the first time she had seen him in person since her return.

"Nice to see you again, Miss Graham," he said, the boyish round face under the visor of his baseball cap gleaming.

"Charlotte, please," she reminded him, once again.

"Charlotte was just telling me about how the thefts of Dunhuang manuscripts and artworks from museums around the world were planned by the director of the Academy and his son," Bunny said. "I wonder what, if anything, is going to happen to him now."

"I happen to have the answer to that question," said Tracey.

As usual, he was one step ahead of the game. For someone so reluctant to leave his little corner of Maine—he had once told Charlotte that he'd only been out of state twice in his life, and then only to Boston—he managed quite nicely to keep tabs on his interests around the world.

"I thought Miss Graham would be interested in following up, so I called my contact at Interpol headquarters outside of Paris. As you know, Miss Graham and I worked on a rare-book theft case together a couple of years ago. As a result, I know some people in the art thefts department there."

"I remember," said Bunny. "The Saunders' neighbor. A terrible thing."

"The countries from which the artworks were stolen have petitioned the Chinese government for the return of the artworks through the United Nations. But my Interpol contact tells me that he doesn't expect the Chinese to return them. In cases like this, their policy is, 'what we have, we hold.' "

Kind of like the British Museum's policy, thought Charlotte.

"But," Tracey continued, "this is very interesting: they are going to remove Chu as director of the Academy."

"I thought he would be a cultural hero," said Charlotte.

"I did too. But apparently tourist dollars are more important to the Chinese than cultural relics. They've done a lot to promote tourism in Dunhuang. They've built a guest house, an airport, a museum. Chu was already in hot water because of his attitude, which was putting off tourists."

Charlotte thought of his obnoxious interruptions of Victor's lecture, and of the signs he'd posted telling which Western countries had "stolen" the missing artworks.

"The thefts were the final straw," Tracey said.

"What will happen to him?" asked Charlotte.

"Nothing serious. He'll just be transferred to another museum. He'll probably like it better. It's bound to be in a less remote location."

"And his son?"

"His son is going to have a lot of trouble finding a country that will accept him as a foreign student," he said. "Boston University certainly isn't going to take him back."

"My stepdaughter is going to be very pleased to hear this news."

"Why's that?" asked Tracey.

"She's planning to go back to Dunhuang next summer with Bert Rogers—he's a paleontologist she met there. They're getting married. She wants to do some work translating manuscripts in the library while Bert digs up dinosaur fossils, and she was afraid that Chu would make it tough for her."

"I don't think she'll have anything to worry about," said Tracey. "The new director will probably be glad to have an American scholar of her caliber there to study for the summer."

Charlotte wondered if the same would be true of an American movie star and her businessman husband.

An hour later she had repeated the whole story for the third time—to Kitty Saunders. Once again, they sat at Kitty's kitchen table. Outside, the gulls wheeled and dived in the cerulean-blue sky, and the sun glittered on the little cove. The fog had retreated as quickly as it had come.

"Would you like some more tea?" asked Kitty, after Charlotte had answered all her questions. Insatiable curiosity was one of Kitty's chief characteristics, one that had prompted her husband to nickname her Walt, short for Walter Winchell, the gossip columnist.

"No thank you," said Charlotte. She had already had three cups of good old Lipton orange pekoe, Kitty's enthusiasm for odd-tasting herb teas having waned after her book-collecting neighbor was poisoned with an herbal concoction two years ago.

"I have a present for you," said Charlotte.

"Oh, how nice!" said Kitty, clapping her hands together dramatically. Though Kitty hadn't trod the boards since their days in summer stock, she still liked to think of herself as a dramatic type and had cultivated the mannerisms to go with the image.

Reaching into her pocketbook, Charlotte pulled out the present, which was wrapped in lavender tissue paper, and handed it to Kitty.

"What is it?" Kitty asked, after she had unwrapped it.

"It's called a dragon bone, but it's really a dinosaur bone. The ancient Chinese used them for divination. These are ideographs representing the hexagrams from the *I Ching*," she said, pointing out the characters that were incised in black on the bone's surface.

Kitty slowly turned the bone over in her perfectly manicured fingers.

"I bought it from an herbalist at the Dunhuang bazaar." Charlotte smiled. "Ground-up dragon bone powder is sold for its aphrodisiac properties."

"How fascinating!" said Kitty, with a salacious little grin.

"I have one, too. Mine's incised with the ideograph for 'The Wanderer.' Marsha didn't say what the ideographs on your bone stand for, but we can ask her next time she comes up to visit. She estimates from the style of the calligraphy that the writing dates from the tenth century."

"I'm very touched," said Kitty, getting up to give Charlotte a kiss and a hug. "This is one of the nicest gifts I've ever received."

"The bone itself dates from about sixty-four million years ago," Charlotte continued. Or maybe, sixty-three million years ago, she thought. Like those of the *T. fiski*, this bone could have come from a post-Cretaceous dinosaur.

Holding the bone in her hand, Kitty studied it for a minute, and then looked up at Charlotte over her reading glasses. "Shall we?" she said, her blue eyes, which were still her best asset, gleaming.

"Shall we what?"

"Consult the *I Ching?*" Without waiting for an answer, she got up and fetched her antique Chinese coins and a pad of paper and pencil from the counter. "Here, you throw," she said as she returned to the table. She handed Charlotte the coins. "I'll go get the books."

Charlotte threw the coins six times. After each throw, she wrote the line down on the pad of paper. The first line, a yang, or solid, line, was followed by five yin, or broken, lines.

Kitty was back in a minute, her gray-jacketed volume of the *I Ching* clutched in her hands along with several books of interpretation. "What have we got here?" she asked, leaning over to look at the hexagram. "It's number twenty-four: 'Return,' " she announced after looking it up in the index.

For a moment, she consulted the *I Ching* and the books of interpretation. "Here's my reading," she said finally. She looked up at Charlotte again over the tops of her glasses. "Are you r-e-a-d-y?"

"Shoot."

"You are beginning a new stage in your life after a long period of stagnation. The powerful light that was on the wane is coming back, as when winter changes into spring, or nighttime into day. With it, it will bring new forces, refreshingly different and more powerful than before. This applies both to your professional life and your personal life." Kitty looked up. "I'll read you what this book says about relationships."

Charlotte nodded.

She read the relevant passage. " 'Return' also refers to the new forces that are forming in an old relationship. As a result of the new light that has been shed on this relationship, the problems inherent in it should now be more apparent. The new light should also help you become aware of how the basic structure of the relationship relates to your own needs." Kitty looked up again. "Is this making any sense?"

"Perfect sense."

"As a result of this new light, you will see the changes that must be made. But you can't forcibly seek these changes," Kitty continued. "You have to let them come of themselves at their own natural and deliberate pace."

"Yes."

"Another aspect of this hexagram applies to your relationship with a group of people with similar interests to yours. 'This is the time for you to work harmoniously together toward a common, and high-minded, destination,' " she read. She continued. "If you ask me what I think—"

"You'll tell me whether I ask or not."

"That's right," said Kitty, with a pert nod. "I think this means that you are going to return to China to work with the Chinese Academy of Dramatic Arts, and that it's going to be a very exciting experience for you." Raising her head, she looked Charlotte straight in the eye. "I also think it means that you're going to work things out with Jack."

"Kitty," protested Charlotte. "I don't think you're an objective soothsayer. You and Stan have a *stake* in this." As her oldest friends, Kitty and Stan had often met Jack, and they liked him enormously.

"That's absolutely right," Kitty said. "But that doesn't deny what the *I Ching* says, does it?"

Charlotte had to agree. "No, it doesn't."

"Actually," Kitty went on, "I haven't been consulting the *I Ching* as much lately as I used to. I've moved on to something else now."

"Tea leaves?" teased Charlotte.

Kitty ignored her. "Numerology. Numbers are very powerful. I can tell you what kind of year it's going to be for you just from your birth date and the letters in your name." She paused for a moment to think. "I'll bet it's going to be a 'one' year for you: new beginnings."

When it came to change, Kitty was the expert. She had a new enthusiasm for every day of the week.

Picking up the pencil, Kitty started writing out Charlotte's name and assigning a number to each letter. Looking up at Charlotte, she suddenly stopped. "Maybe I should save this," she said. "I think the *I Ching* has given you enough to think about for today."

Charlotte leaned back in her Windsor chair and stared out the window at the sun sparkling on the cove. "Enough for a long time to come," she said.